1960

This book may be kept

FOURTEEN DAYS

A fine will be charged for each day the book is kept overtime.

AP 1 71			
GAYLORD 142			PRINTED IN U.S.A.

CHARLES A. BRADY

STAGE OF FOOLS

STAGE OF FOOLS

BY

CHARLES A. BRADY

EST·1852

New York   E P DUTTON AND COMPANY   *Mdccccliii*
INCORPORATED

FOR MY THREE MOTHERS:

Belinda, Kathryn, Ellen

When we are born, we cry that we are come
To this great stage of fools. . . .

— KING LEAR

TABLE OF CONTENTS

Table of Contents

STAGE OF FOOLS

CHAPTER I

PORTENT ON EARTH:

After Midnight, February 7, 1478

THE night was clear and cold and pure as the heart of a diamond. Some fine powdery snow had fallen just before midnight, and now, as the wind sprang up, whisks of diamond dust blew round the corner of Milk Street, where stood the little parish church of St. Mary Magdalen, and against the long gabled front of the only house still lighted on that sleeping Cheapside lane. The wind was northeasterly and blew in gusts from the open country outside Bishopsgate down Bucklersbury and St. Pancras Lane to lose itself at last somewhere in Watling Street on its cold way to London River. As it lulled, the church bells of Bow Street and St. Giles began pealing out the hour of three. The silver notes hung in the diamond air under the pendant moonstone of the winter moon. Even as they died away, the heavy wooden door of the lighted house swung open and a man came out into the moon-bright street.

He was of middle height—no longer young, but twenty-seven years are not so very old, either—wearing a mantle with a fur tippet and carrying an astrolabe in his right hand. Before sighting the instrument, he looked at the long range of stained-glass windows that stretched along the front of his building and burned armorially, thanks to the moon fire without and the wood fire within, in perfect shields of purple and crimson and green and blue on the white snow. Satisfied with what he saw, he took, then, his measurements with the astrolabe and went inside again.

Portent On Earth:

The firelit room was spacious, with carved moldings crowning the four walls, and frescoes ornamenting two of them. On both sides of the blazing hearth stood tall armoires filled with crackling rolls of vellum. Other parchments covered a massive oaken table upon which two candles burned low now in their sockets. Altogether a comfortable and solid room, as befitted so considerable a personage as Master John More, lawyer and butler of Lincoln's Inn, now rising fast in what was no longer his so very little world. It had been a long vigil; but it was over now. And, like any barrister worth his salt, he was prepared to exorcise any unsettling bugs and goblins attendant upon the birth of his second child, and first son, by jotting down all the circumstances in a common book; in this case the back leaves of his favorite chronicler, Geoffrey of Monmouth. First he wrote in English:

"Mars and Venus stand in Taurus, the night house of the Cyprian goddess."

Then, after a pause, the scratching quill continued:

"We come out of the Mores of Ireland, where mór means great. Perhaps this child is destined to match the high challenge of his name."

Last of all he set down in very workmanlike law Latin:

"M^d quod die Veneris proximo post Festum purificacionis beate Marie virginis videlicet septimo die Februarii inter horam secundam et horam tertiam in mane natus fuit Thomas More filius Joannis More Gent. anno regni Edwardi quarti post conquestum Angliae decimo septimo."

Which, rendered into plain English, reads:

"Memorandum. On the Friday next after the Feast of the Purification of the Blessed Virgin Mary, namely, the seventh day of February, between the second and third hour of the morning, was born Thomas More, son of John More, Gentleman, in the seventeenth year of the reign of King Edward the fourth of that name after the Conquest of England."

Then, for John More, Gentleman, was a very human man and a most average father in the face of the mingled splendor and terror that is birth, he put down his lawyer's quill, a great thirst suddenly come upon him. Mother Maude waddled grumbling in to satisfy it, a silver bowl and two tankards carefully cradled in her arms. Her wadmal gown and starched coif were more than a little rumpled, for Mother Maude, too, had stood a long vigil, with neither astronomy nor philosophy to stay her, but only a goodly store of country saws and proverbs; fables of talking animals and other fond foolish tales. A whiskered upper lip curled a little as she looked at her master busy over one of his eternal books. No man, not even John More, her kindly master and, on occasion, her most intimate gossip, was popular with Mother Maude on occasions such as this.

"Always reading!" she grunted disdainfully. "Even tonight! Cannot the birth of a first son change your habits even for an hour? Come, man, drink your posset."

John More downed the steaming cup of spiced hippocras in one long grateful gulp.

"Thank you, thank you, gossip," he said affectionately. "And you shall drink, too."

He raised his cup.

"To Thomas!"

But if John More had raised his mug, not so Mother Maude.

"Thomas, is it?" she asked suspiciously. "Why not John? John is a good name, and your own to boot."

"So is Thomas a good name, Mother," he said tolerantly.

Mother Maude persisted.

"Aye, but not your own," she pointed out.

John More poured himself another aromatic cupful.

"No," he said. "Not my own, it is true. But a saint's. Great à Becket's of Canterbury."

"So is John a saint," said Mother Maude, undaunted. "And a better one, too. Thomas is an ill name. He of Canterbury was killed by his King."

"What odds then?" asked John More, touching together the finger tips of both hands in a gesture of judicial tolerance. "Did not John,

13

too, lose his head long before, and all because a foolish king lusted after a light wench? But I grant you, Mother Maude, there is a king in it somewhere, and a queen as well. A King of Arms and a Queen of Love. I've just cast the lad's horoscope and found that he entered the world while Mars and Venus stood in Taurus. As they stand at this moment and will stand till morning."

"What is Taurus?" asked Mother Maude, more suspicious than ever.

"A bull," explained John More expansively. "A royal bull prefigured in the stars. Add my bull to those animals you are forever telling tales of."

Mother Maude cackled all of a sudden; it was a shrill eldritch sound and John More found himself looking at her almost with distaste.

"A bull," she screeched, mocking. "A bull! Aye, Master More, you do well to see bulls in the stars. All men are bulls. But I'll thank you to keep your royal bull and your stars to yourself. I tell you it is no Christian act to meddle with those same unchancy stars."

She went to the window, opened it, and looked out.

"I see no bull, no king, and no queen, either." she said over her shoulder, grumbling the while. "Only the blessed star way, white as morning milk, that leads to our Lady of Walsingham."

"Very well, very well, Mother," John More soothed her, closing the casement against the winter chill. "If it will make you happy, I yield you Walsingham Star Way, and surrender my King and Queen. There! *Absit omen, absit omen.* Now let us seek another sort of portent. Let us try the *Sortes* and see what our man child may come to be in later years. I open a page at random—so!—and do you prick down your finger on the place."

Mother Maude drew back a step.

"Is it a Bible?" she asked, pointing to the hasped volume in the back of which the lawyer had earlier entered the newborn's name. "I play no such heathenish tricks with the Holy Book."

John More clapped her affectionately on the back.

"No, Mother," he said. "It is not the Holy Book. Nor is it altogether an unholy book, either, but the *History of the Kings of Britain* as set

14

down by a monk of Monmouth, Geoffrey. See, I open again—here.
There is nothing to fear, Mother. Do you plunge down your finger
now."

Mother Maude did as she was bid; only very apprehensively. Then,
craning over her master's shoulder:

"What does it read, Master?"

"It is writ in Latin, Mother," said John More. "In our tongue it goes
something like this."

Very slowly he began to translate the Latin sentences into the
strong English of old Layamon:

> *"The time came that was appointed for Arthur to be born.*
> *Fays took him as soon as he entered on earth.*
> *The child they enchanted with magic right strong.*
> *They gave him the might to be best of all knights.*
> *To that king's child they gave virtues right good*
> *That he was most free-handed of all living wights.*
> *This the fays gave him, and thus the child throve."*

Mother Maude nodded her old head at every sentence.

"I like not that part about the fays, Master," she said sagely. "We
want no changeling bantlings in our cradles."

John More seemed a little awed by what he had just read aloud.
Or, if not precisely awed, at least sobered.

"I do not think, Mother," he said slowly, "that it has anything to do
with changelings. Nor yet with fays. And to think I laughed at wife
Agnes' dream of the face of the child on her marriage ring, the one
that shone so bright it blinded her!"

Mother Maude felt herself on home ground at last. Dreams were
something that belonged to her rural province. There she could
speak authoritatively.

"Aye, Master," she said. "It was the king-light good Mistress Agnes
saw in her dream. And she was the one to see it—all the Grangers
have second sight. It was the king-light like the light that poured
from Dane Havelok's mouth, he who was Birkebeyn's son and slew
the traitor Godard, and after became King of England. Fisher Grim's

15

wife saw the magic flame first, as Havelok lay sleeping; and after her Princess Goldborough who became Havelok's Queen."

The rationalist and the mystic, who dance their bickering dance in every good man's soul, shook hands that diamond night of snow and birth and moon fire in the humorous heart of John More.

"No tale so foolish but that it will serve a purpose, eh, Mother Maude?" he rallied her. "Yet who knows? So let us try again. This time do you choose the page, and let me prick down my finger."

Very solemnly the old woman and the lawyer nearing thirty played the *Sortes* again. While Mother Maude looked on in silence, John More plunged down his index finger. Then, removing it, he read aloud—this second time even more slowly than before:

> *"Then was it come to pass, as Merlin said in yore-days,*
> *That there was great sorrow at Arthur's forth-faring.*
> *The Britons believe yet that he is alive,*
> *And dwells now in Avalon with fairest of fays.*
> *And the Britons yet look for Arthur to come.*
> *In time past was a prophet, Merlin his name.*
> *In words he foretold—his sayings were true—*
> *That an Arthur would come the English to aid."*

Mother Maude shook her old head till the starched coif nodded.

"The fays again. I like it not, Master More. Nor all this talk about departure, either, when our blessed babe has scarce made his entry this hour past. Does your book say nothing of marriage?"

John More roared with masculine laughter as Mother Maude finally gave him the opening he had been waiting for: her never-ending preoccupation and his no less endless joke.

"Always marriage—eh, Mother Maude? But why speak of marriage so early in the game for the poor lad? Time enough, I should think, when the boy comes to man's estate. Then let him fend for himself in the matter. As the best of us must—as I did, and my father, and my father's father before me—when we dip our hands in the blind bag full of snakes and eels together, seven snakes to one eel—and an eel not the pleasantest of mortal creatures, either."

But this time John More had gone a good deal too far in his goading of the gammer. Vanished the nurse, vanished the white witch who, in her day, had vended more than one love philter; and in their stead appeared the midwife angry with a righteous female anger.

"Blind bag, indeed!" she spat in fury. "You've managed to have fine sport of your own poor eel, and she, dear innocent, has had to groan a-plenty for your precious fun. You are like all men, Master More. You would fain make out that all women are shrews."

"Not so, Mother Maude," said John More, chaffing her. "Not so. A wise man has said—and I believe him—there is but one shrewd wife in all the world. Only—and here, Mother, is the rub—only, every husband thinks he owns her himself and will not have it otherwise."

Mother Maude had been bested as usual; and, as usual, her invariable gesture of defeat was to fling her apron over her head and sink back moodily onto her settle in the inglenook.

"Go to, go to!" she muttered angrily. "You have a naughty tongue. But, even so, I know a trick worth ten of your silly *Sortes*. We played it in the servants' hall in the old King's day. By your leave, I'll play it now. It needs only a bit paper and a live coal."

John More began to sip his posset once again.

"As you will, Mother," he said, negligently throwing one leg over the carved arm of his chair. "But take this foul copy, not a fair one."

He handed the old woman a spoiled sheet of parchment and leaned back in his armchair as she went about her preparations. Mother Maude set the parchment on a fire shovel and touched a glowing ember to it. A great light flared up and fell. Then she held the shovel close to the wall and fell to pondering the shadows it cast thereon. John More watched her, vastly amused.

"What make you, Mother Maude?" he asked. "A marriage?"

The old woman gave a tiny squeak of excited satisfaction.

"Aye!" she squealed. "And more than one. Two. I see two women's heads."

"A fair reckoning," he indulged her. "Anything more?"

Mother Maude squinted at the humped shadows.

"I think," she announced, perplexed, "I think I see a monkey."

For once John More was startled.

17

"A monkey, faith!" he jerked out. "But why not? Is not your addled old head stuffed with tales of Reynard and Chantecleer and Isegrim Wolf? Come, hold the shovel up again, before the ashes fall together. Let me have a peep."

Mother Maude did as she was bidden. He looked close for one long moment; then struck up the shovel with a curse. It clattered loud on the tiles. Mother Maude stared at him as he turned back to the table, visibly shaken, to pour out what was left of the posset and drain it at a gulp.

"Master More, Master More!" she called to him. "What ails your worship?"

"Your old wives' tales, Mother," said John More gruffly, but not unkindly. "Hereafter I shall stick to my own *Sortes*."

"But what saw you?" asked Mother Maude.

"What saw I?" John More echoed her. "Nothing. A shadow. No more. No more but a shadow."

"But a shadow of what, Master?" she insisted.

He looked at the old woman strangely.

"God forgive me," he said halting. "I thought I saw a gibbet and a headsman's block."

Upstairs the baby gave a thin cry. John More saw to the fire before he snuffed the low-burning candles. Outside in the winter dawning St. Giles called back the hour of four o'clock to the bell tower of St. Mary Magdalen. It was turning very cold.

Many, many years later, dying in his Flanders' exile, the old dramatist, John Heywood, whilom actor, director of the singing boys of St.Paul's, player of virginals, and husband of Sir Thomas More's niece, Joan Rastell, would remember his uncle's rosemary at Chelsea: how the great Chancellor had planted it himself on his first taking possession; how he liked to see it spread over his garden walks and walls; "not onlie because his bees loved it, but because 'tis the herb sacred to remembrance."

There were so many things for the Chancellor to remember those last days in the Tower: winter mornings by the fire in that first Milk Street house in the old ward of Cripplegate Within; summer mornings in Sir John's pleasant Hertfordshire manor of Gobions; Sunday mornings without season amid the clangor of Bow bells; evenings in the inglenook with Mother Maude and her animal tales that linked a free English boy with the Greek slave Aesop. One evening in particular when there came a sudden rapping at his father's door with the news that King Edward was dead; whereupon up rose a neighbor who lived in Redcross Street without Cripplegate with the exclamation: "By my troth, then will my master, the Duke of Gloucester, be King!" Another evening, not much later, when there came the dreadful tidings of the murder of the Princes in the Tower. The lad, Thomas, was but five at the time. Thus early did he learn how far one may place trust in the word of kings.

Memories of the terror under Richard Crookback and its bloody end on Bosworth Field; of the coming to the throne, then, of that cold-blooded and provident victor, Henry Tudor, Earl of Richmond, and of the guns booming out the births of his sons, Arthur and Henry, the Prince who died and the Prince who lived to become Henry VIII. Memories of stern Master Nicholas Holt ruling with ferule of iron St. Anthony's School in Threadneedle Street near the Hall of the Merchant Taylors; of the disputations in Bartholomew Churchyard between the Anthony pigs and the pigeons of Paul's, as the rival schoolboys dubbed each other. He had been, he remembered now with a smile, very good indeed at those disputations.

Memories of life as page with the great Chancellor, Cardinal Morton, at his archiepiscopal palaces of Lambeth and Canterbury and

19

his manor house at Knowle near Sevenoaks where the Christmas revels were held and where, to the Cardinal's delectation, the lad used to step impromptu in among the players. The lad loved Lambeth best. It was embowered in green hills, looking, lordly, one way toward the Surrey fields, and, another, toward Westminster Palace and the silver reaches of the Thames. High talk went round the Cardinal's board: politics, literature, religion, manners, York and Lancaster and the Countess of Richmond, a pretender newly appeared in Ireland, the inequity of capital punishment for theft. The lad heard and remembered and waxed in years and wisdom. Never, afterward, did he forget the great Cardinal, so "fine, eloquent, and pithy" of speech, of profound knowledge in the law, incomparable of wit, in "memory wonderful excellent."

Memories of the nine painted pageants he designed for his father's London house, and the verses composed therefor: Childhood, Young Manhood, The Triumph of Cupid, Old Age, Death, Fame, Time, Eternity, The Poet. As it turned out, they were prophetic of his own life and death. Except, of course, Henry was seeing to it that he did not reach Old Age: nor, perhaps, had he ever been more than an indifferent Poet. There was one panel in the pageant life he painted that the Chancellor did not see. It came to pass long after the rosemary grew less thick in Chelsea. Silver trumpets blew at the Elevation in the great Basilica where Wolsey never sat as Pope; and throngs knelt at the name of a new saint.

Memories warmed the gray stones of the Tower. Of golden bees, which are achievement, and silver river, which is time, and fragrant rosemary, which is remembrance.

CHAPTER II

OH, BRAVE NEW WORLD:

Sunset and Evening, Late October, 1492

SUNSET burned blood-red over Guanahani. The utter silence was unbroken except for an occasional gull cry and, now and then, a slatting of canvas as the galleon or one of the caravels swung broadside to the green palms and white beach of the little Bahama island. A slow Spanish song drifted sleepily across the water; an anchor rope rasped; and there was silence again. Except that, now and again, a slight splash broke the evening stillness as a fish leaped in the motionless green water.

It grew darker. Some early stars pricked out. Soon, a starry baldric on the dark flank of conquistador night, gleamed the wheeling splendor of the Northern Cross. A full moon rose. All the gold of El Dorado and the Seven Cities of Cibola could not match the cloth of gold the New World moon flung prodigally over the dark table of the moving waters. So the Admiral's great shout sounded even louder for the gold-and-ebon hush.

"Holá! Bos'n!" he shouted. "Have the men stand by for orders. We lift anchor at dawn! The New World lies before us!"

Startled by the human noise, the gulls set up a keening. Like ripples in a pool the mewing cries spread out and out. Soon the crews of the *Santa María*, the *Pinta*, and the *Niña* could hear them no longer, but they continued to lengthen out over ocean, carried from bird to bird, reversing the wheel of the sun as the cold dark came flooding westward. Eastward flew the white-winged sea birds, flying over Iceland where Leif and Karlsefni had moored their dragon ships. Over the Orkneys where, by peat fires, Viking voyagers had first heard the Irish tales of Hy Brasail and Brendan's coracle and the islands in the west. Over Ireland itself whence came the Mores of

Oh, Brave New World:

England; where chieftains still lay out in the long grass even as their wild forbears had done four hundred years before; where even now, brooding sleepless beside a black bog, a Gaelic captain thought on the morrow's act of obeisance to Tudor Henry which would forever slay for Ireland the age of hero Finn and usher in the sinister new world of Renaissance intrigue. Over Land's End, a blacker mass in the black night. Over sleeping Wales and Cornwall. Over London where Sir John More worked late at his law, and inland to the dreaming moon-marbled spires of Oxford where his son Thomas worked later still with the Canterbury players who, on the morrow, were to play *Antigone* before King Henry VII on his triumphal Progress to the University.

The wind flapped a shutter to and fro on one of the windows of Canterbury College's Common Room. Leaving off for a moment his argument with Master William Grocyn, who had certain serious reservations about the Greek tragedy chosen expressly for his Majesty's hearing, Master John Colet walked clear across the room to close the troublous casement. As he was closing it the sleeve of his academic gown caught on a rough point of stone that jutted up from the ledge outside. Leaning out to free the cloth, Master Colet found himself face to face with a resting gull.

"Is there anything wrong?" called Master Grocyn to him, eager to suggest that their point of difference was intellectual merely, and not at all personal.

"No," said Colet, closing the shutter. "Nothing but a stubborn bird beating its wings on the ledge. I do not remember seeing sea birds so far inland before."

At twenty-six Master John Colet, son of Henry VII's wealthy merchant friend and twice Lord Mayor of London, Sir Henry Colet, was slim and finely made; his face sensitive, ascetic, with a firm set to the lips that warned one here was a man not lightly deflected from his purpose. He had been at Oxford since 1483, reading deep in Plato and the Fathers of the Church, excelling in mathematics, suspicious, contemptuous, even, of the fine-spun cobwebs that were tangling the brains of the latter-day Scholastics. His fellow professor, Master William Grocyn, knew Greek every bit as well as Colet; but he put it to a different use. Where Colet was basically scholar and teacher, Grocyn, soon to be named Rector of the Church of St. Lawrence in the Old Jewry, was essentially a preacher. He had studied sacred eloquence in Florence under the tutelage of Chalcondylas, the famous Greek rhetorician. Both men were what the world had begun to call Humanists; eager, somewhat severe acolytes of the New Learning, lovers of the *largior aether*, the "larger light" which had come surging into dark monastic cells after the fall of Constantinople to her Turkish besiegers. It was, as Colet was fond of pointing out, another case of the divine economy; of God's providence seeing to it that good came out of evil. In their different ways Colet and Grocyn loved the New Learning this side idolatry; but always well this side. For, unlike some of their successors, they saw no particular wisdom in becoming wise at the cost of denying the Divine Wisdom. They knew the *literae humaniores* they pursued were the studies that made men more human rather than less.

To the right of the tall oriel windows young Thomas More, now in his fifteenth year, went on with his own noncontroversial task of directing the college players in their rehearsal of *Antigone*. Colet and Grocyn watched him with both pride and affection.

"Cardinal Morton did right," said Master Colet, "to send Sir John More's son on to us here at Oxford. The lad is wonderfully apt. Never have I seen an apter. He will go far if he stays at Canterbury College. Just see him step in among the players and set them right with a word or gesture."

Then, with a sidelong glance, for he knew the next utterance would renew hostilities:

"The King should be well pleased tomorrow. These great words of Sophocles are two thousand years old now. Yet, till tomorrow, they shall never have been spoken in our island by men of English tongue."

Master Grocyn flushed, but managed to keep a tight rein on his temper.

"I wonder," was all he said.

"You wonder?" asked Colet with an affectation of indignation. "Did I not travel to Venice, to the great press of Aldus Manutius, for these old plays of Sophocles? The Tudor is no country boor. And, even if he were, he would preserve a sober face to keep himself in countenance. Come, friend Grocyn. You must think better than this of Kings on their royal Progresses."

Master Grocyn tucked back the purfled sleeves of his gown.

"It is not Sophocles I question," he said, "but his play. I marvel you give over the choosing of it to a beardless boy. *Electra* would be safer. Harry Monmouth could find nothing smacking of sedition in *Electra,* though Richard Crookback might have. Quite to the contrary. Harry Monmouth would approve such prudent sentiments as: *With Kings 'tis ill to strive.* But *Antigone,* friend Colet! A play that sets up subject against ruler! I fear me Harry will not like to think of himself as tyrant Creon, no matter how hard he swaggers the role in fact in counting house and council room."

"I had not thought of that," admitted Colet, a little dashed. "Perhaps you are right. Perhaps it is unwise."

He raised his voice.

"Thomas, lad!" he called.

Young More looked up from where he stood among the players. Then he walked over to Masters Colet and Grocyn.

"Yes, Master Colet," he said quietly.

Colet laid a paternal hand on the boy's shoulder.

"What know you of Kings, friend Thomas?" he asked him.

Young Thomas More reflected. In point of sober fact he knew quite a lot of Kings. He remembered the night when the knocking came at his father's door bearing the tidings of Edward's death, and how neighbor Pottier had sprung to his feet with the muttered exclamation that the Duke of Gloucester would now be King. He remembered the somber night of Bosworth Field and the gayer mornings when the bells pealed, the cannon boomed, and wine butts ran in the streets to herald the births of the Princes, Arthur and Henry. He remembered also the high tale of Arthur his father had read him out of Geoffrey's *History.* But Sir John More came of sturdy burgess stock and, whatever his fondness for romance, he had early taught his son something of the freedom of London citizens. Finally, the boy had seen the fleshless grinning King who lorded it on the walls of graveyards and charnel houses; and, with his own few pennies, he had bought a skeleton-headed signet ring bearing the Latin pun: *Memento Mori.* He returned Colet's stare with a level look from his own clear-sighted, hazel-flecked gray eyes.

"Why," he said, "I know that they are men like other men."

"Nothing more?" asked Colet, continuing his catechizing.

"That they rule," answered Thomas More. "Some well, some ill."

Master Colet laughed—not altogether at his ease.

"These are a philosopher's answers," he said. "And very true, of course. Answer now as a man of affairs. As your old master, Cardinal Morton, might have answered, had he been set the same question. As, indeed, he was—many times. Come, Thomas. What else know you of Kings?"

This time the boy did not stop to think.

"That," he said quickly, "they do not like to have their letters patent of reign inquired into too closely."

"Exactly," said Colet, pleased by the lad's swiftness of thought. "Exactly. Not even by a Greek poet dead these two thousand years and more. Now, Thomas, do you still think *Antigone* is a safe play to play before a King?"

"If the King have a good conscience," said Thomas More. "If not, it will help him to have one."

"But what of us, friend Thomas?" asked Grocyn, intervening. "What of you and me and Master Colet and the players and Masters Linacre and Lilly? And what of your father, Sir John? We read *Electra* together yestereve, you and I and Master Colet. Do you remember Chrysosthemes' reply to sister Electra. That: *There is a time when even right may harm?*"

"Aye," said the boy impetuously, capping Grocyn's quotation with another. "But do you remember the brave maiden's reply? *I do not choose to live by laws like that.* Nor do I, good Master Grocyn. Nor, I hope, does the King."

He called over to the players.

"Simon," he said, "do you read out Creon's lines where he tells the maid she must obey his man-made edict. And do you, Rafe, respond for the maid.'

Simon and Rafe studied their scrolls for a minute. Then both struck their respective postures.

"That man," intoned Simon who was playing Creon, *"who holds just sway over his household, will be accounted just in the City as well. But he who affronts or flaunts the laws, or thinks to over-rule his lawful rulers, will not fare well at my hands. For whomsover the City shall stablish in authority, he must be obeyed in all, in matters great or small, in matters just or unjust. I should find such an one a leal man whether fate called him to rule or to be ruled. Staunch would he stand in the storm of steel, dauntless, true, where he was set.*

"But not to accept the ruler's will is the very worst of evils. Through anarchy the City is undone, the home destroyed, the spear-shaft broken in the comrade ranks. It is obedience secures the lives of the loyal. Therefore must we defend authority, and not be worsted by a woman's will.

"Now tell me plain and short, Antigone—knew you not it had gone forth by edict that thy brother lie unburied?"

Rafe answered in falsetto for Antigone.

"I knew it. Clearly was it proclaimed."

Then Creon again:

"And yet you dared over-ride the laws?"

And Antigone in mounting exaltation:

"Yes, for it was not of Zeus these laws of which you speak were stablished; nor yet of holy Justice who dwells with the gods below. Nor did I think thy human writs so fixed that thou, a mortal man, though king, might over-rule the unwritten and unfailing statutes of high heaven. These laws I speak of now are born not of today nor yesterday, but from always; and no man knows the day of their promulgation."

Thomas More watched his two professors shrewdly. He saw Colet's calm eye kindle and Grocyn bite his lip.

26

"How like you that, Master Grocyn?" asked the boy. "Are they not brave words?"

Grocyn did not answer for a moment.

"Brave words, indeed, friend Thomas," he said at last, very slowly. Then, picking up and bending a scroll in his vehemence:

"By God, Colet, the lad is right. It is what the Barons told John Lackland at Runnymede when he yielded up to England the Great Charter that is the repository of our liberties. Where else is the King's conscience unless it be in the Church and the University? As yet the people has no tongue. We must be the people's tongue. And, after all, Harry Monmouth may not mind. Canterbury College is not the green field of Runnymede. Nor are John Colet, Thomas More, and William Grocyn great lords to fright the wearer of the crown. We have no claim upon his scepter. What are York and Lancaster to us?"

Colet had put his arm again around the boy's shoulder.

"Yes," he said, "they are brave words, Thomas. And there are more, many more of them, on the parchments that flood in daily from Florence and Venice and Constantinople. It is a new world we are discovering. A new world, lad, of beauty and truth."

The bell of St. Frideswide's Priory boomed one o'clock in the quadrangle outside.

"To bed, gentlemen," said Colet briskly, gathering up the scrolls and setting the room in order. "We must be clear-eyed and bell-voiced in the morning to greet our liege lord of England, Henry, the Seventh of that name."

After the players had gone out, conversing in friendly fashion, the room seemed very quiet. The wind began to flap the shutter once more; suddenly it rattled open again. As it did so, the gull, which had nested on the ledge all this time, took off with a rush of powerful wings. It flew steadily in the direction of Ireland and the morning; and toward that little island of San Salvador which, only a fortnight ago, had been called Guanahani. It was already growing light over the Golden Horn; and, in Vienna, eastward windows began to pale in the half-light of early dawn.

The rosemary had not yet begun to grow in the river garden at Chelsea; but the silver river flowed on, the golden bees hummed amid the flowers, the memories burgeoned.

Memories of the beginnings of love. At the outset the years had lagged like the faltering steps of Childhood in the first panel of the goodly painted cloth that hung in the house on Milk Street; Childhood whose mind was all on play, to "cast a quoit, a cocksteel and a ball. . . . Then might I lead my life always in play." The play was different now; and the coursing years galloped on like the swift horses of the King's equerries; and had so raced ahead ever since the headlong murmurous night among the musk roses in her father's Thameside orchard when he had first seen the laughing eyes of Elizabeth.

Then the duenna and the guarded door
Baffled the stars and bade us meet no more.

Ten years later he had affixed a better love poem to his life of Pico della Mirandola.

The first point is to love but one alone,
And for that one all other to forsake,
For whoso loveth many, loveth none:
The flood that is in many channels take,
In each of them shall feeble streamés make,
The love that is divided among many,
Unneth sufficeth that every part have any.
So thou that has thy love set unto God,
In thy remembrance this imprint and grave,
As he in sovereign dignity is odd,
So will he in love no parting fellows have:
Love him therefore with all that he thee gave,
For body, soul, wit, cunning, mind and thought
Part will he none, but either all or nought.

At present—there is but one tense in memory—there was a fresh young girl walking in the quiet lanes and green fields of Essex. There was also this troublous matter of a more tremendous nuptials within the thick walls of the Charterhouse. Meanwhile the memories came crowding thick and fast.

Memories of Sir John, grown suddenly overpractical, packing son Thomas posthaste off from Oxford to become a true Londoner for the first time behind the clean-scoured red and blue-black bricks and white stones of the Inns of Court and Chancery: New Inn first; then Lincoln's Inn; then Furnivall's. Then Parliament from within, with young barrister More sitting as burgess for the City of London.

Memories of London days. The morning of November 12, 1501, when Prince Arthur's child-bride, Catherine of Aragon, made her shyly triumphant entry into London. The Spanish dons attending her seemed black-a-vised devils enough, he had thought then with a grimace of honest London distaste—this from the boy barrister who would one day be the most representative European, perhaps, in history!—but Catherine herself looked radiant. He had quite lost his English heart to her, and he remembered, with a new pang, the sharp sword of compassion for her winsome person which had pierced that self-same heart of his when the passing bells tolled for Prince Arthur's early death.

Memories of smoky London nights, by the autumn fire, communing with Augustine's eagle soul. Memories of hundreds of upturned faces —lawyers and burghers from the City of Man—listening to him lecture in Master Grocyn's Church of St. Lawrence Jewry on that greatest of books, the City of God. Memories of country excursions stolen from the weary round of courts and law suits. Like the walk with Erasmus to the old palace of Eltham in the mellow autumn of 1499, with yellow leaves clogging the moat and ivy reddening along the mullioned windows that opened into the great council hall where, for the first time, he had met the bonny younger son of the King, Prince Henry. Dearest Erasmus! He could rhyme—for a ducat; it had to be for a ducat, though—on anything. On a feather; on a glove; on a lady's eye-lash. Yes, Desiderius was always a clever devil in more ways than one— he had seen to it that Master Colet lectured Erasmus many times. But, despite what his enemies said, in the long run he was on the side of the angels. Say he was neither hero nor martyr and you had said the worst that could be said about him. He was still the best of friends; and he had done his best to hold Christendom together in the days

29

when counsels of moderation might still have prevailed against the forces of rancor and disruption. There would be worse epitaphs than that.

Speaking of Master Colet, the Dean of St. Paul's rarely came to London in those years. Or even so close to London as his country parish of Stepney. Not that he ever blamed friend Colet for preferring the blessed country. Had he not written Colet, in the November of 1504, that London was naught but a hive of "butchers, confectioners, fishmongers, carriers, cooks, and poultrymen, all occupied in serving sensuality, the world, and the world's lord, the devil," whereas in the country one saw nothing "but the generous gifts of nature and the traces of our primeval innocence"? What did one see in city life, he had gone on to ask, and then given his own answer thus: "Pretended friends, and the honied poison of smooth flatterers, fierce hatreds, quarrels, rivalries and contentions."

Yes "pretended friends" were the worst, especially those who wore on their backs the cope of Christ. The "honied poison of smooth flatterers" he could handle easily: a native skepticism made checkmating such as them almost second nature. As for the "fierce hatreds" of Kings, had he not, in the Parliament of 1504, outfaced an angry Henry VII, balking him of his inordinate and unjust levy of monies on the body of England? Henry had struck back at the "beardless boy," as he contemptuously labeled him, by fining and imprisoning his father, Sir John, in the Tower. But the real danger he ran came from the smooth duplicity of the vulpine Dr. Foxe, Bishop of Winchester, who had tried to dupe him into a confession of treason. Only Master Richard Whitford, the Bishop's Chaplain but More's friend, had saved him. "Master More," he had said, "follow not his counsel in any way. For my master, to gratify the King and to serve his own turn, will not stick to compound the death of his own father."

It was his first thorough lesson in high politics and his first heavy disillusion. So the memories thronged thick and fast like rosemary on the walls at Chelsea. The year 1504 was well-nigh choked with their tenacious roots and heady blossoms. Yes, there would have to be a decision soon. There was still that slim girl down in Essex; and the Charterhouse also waited on his answer to its importunate call.

CHAPTER III

WRESTLING WITH THE ANGEL:

Morning, December, 1504

MASTER HENRY PATENSON, *joculator*, had three excellent reasons for choosing the profession of domestic fool: his face; his wit; and, for want of a more exact term, his conscience. His face was broad on top, narrow below, snub-nosed and earthy; brutal at first glimpse; at second sensitive. The kind of face, in fact, that punchinellos have worn from the beginning of time; from the Sarmatian boor Horace saw dance a-top a Roman banquet table to the latest circus joey. His wit was as broad as his brow, with flashes of eldritch poetry in it, and a certain homely daring that, by fits and starts, merited either a coin or a drubbing, depending on the hearers' frame of mind. Gaging his audience's current temper was one of the skills Patenson never mastered perfectly; the failure kept him from entering the first rank of drolls. As for his conscience, he was neither saint nor utter rogue. Too lazy for swinking under a hot sun; too honest for thieving; too carnal for the quiet life of lay brother; at once too bitter and too graceless to play the role of courtier, he solved the economic riddle by letting his face and his mother wit go to work for him. He had tried the life of a strolling player in England and, as a member of an English troupe, in Germany as well. But it had earned him little more than dry crusts and the smallest of small beer. Service in a burgher's household—never, to the end of his life, did Patenson manage to qualify as a nobleman's Fool—proved a better living. So he bonded himself over to the profession of household Jester and was, at present, accredited *famulus* in the employment of Sir John More, Justice of the King's Bench. Old Sir John was a provident householder, and Master Patenson not at all averse to doubling in brass—

as now, for example, when he had been deputed to carry a message from Sir John to his son, Thomas, at the Carthusian monastery known to all good Londoners as the Charterhouse, and to the monks who lived within as the House of the Salutation of the Mother of God.

Henry Patenson liked to walk abroad whenever he could. Rubbing elbows with the people in tavern, market place, and monastery alike, was grist to his Jester's mill. It gave him a chance to listen and observe; to catch, with the battledore of his wit, the latest shuttlecock of catchword and rumor which, afterward, he would send flying round the festal board. He liked to try out impromptus which later on could be worked up into routines. In addition, he was a species of artist in the ribald, and Sir John did not care overmuch for the ribald. So these little outings also provided him with a kind of esthetic catharsis. They allowed him to sluice the ribaldry out of his system; and—since, outside the somewhat austere precincts of the Justice's house, ribaldry seemed to pay very well indeed—they helped him turn an extra penny here and there. Just at the moment, wrapped in a warm cloak against the early chill of a December morning, he was sitting on a stone marked 1371, the date of the Charterhouse's founding, before the vaulted cornice and great oak doors of the Entrance Gate. Partly to warm his half-frozen fingers, partly to keep his hand in, but mostly to seize the infrequent chance of singing the kind of song he loved so well and Sir John More not at all, he unstrapped the lute from his back and began to strum it. As he did so, the Father Porter who kept the door peered inquisitively out of his little warder's wicket. At first Patenson paid him no attention. He knew he would get no silver florins from that particular direction; but, at the same time, he always needed an audience, no matter how meager or unremunerative, before he could perform at all. So he sang pensively to himself but loud enough for the monk to hear:

> *"Western wind, when wilt thou blow,*
> *The small rain down can rain?*
> *Christ, if my love were in my arms,*
> *And I in my bed again."*

32

Then he put down his instrument and stared impudently into the monk's face.

"Like you my song, reverend Father? I like it. But not everybody likes it."

The Carthusian was inwardly amused. Patenson did not know it, but he was the son of a nobleman, and had, moreover, flown a falcon with the best of them in the days of his youth and, besides, fought with much credit in the French wars.

"It is a secular sentiment," he said, pretending to ponder the matter, "but theologically unobjectionable."

Patenson watched him warily. A prophetic pricking in his thumbs warned him that he was in the presence of a kindred spirit; of one who, but for his cowl, might well have been a Jester. So he placed himself *en garde* at once.

"You are a liberal sort of priest, friend monk," he began tentatively. "Not everyone with a shaven pate, however, shares your liberal sentiments. A monk of Erfurt, for example, didn't like my song nearly so well as you seem to like it. It was one day last autumn that my singing of it in the town square of Erfurt cost me dear. To be exact, two bakers' dozens of hot stripes and a long stay in the stocks to cool them off. But what, Master Monk, is a body to sing of, if not of love? Not that it's unmixed bliss, either—a fact you monks are always pointing out to hot young lovers. Sometimes it's no more than a carnal itching; sometimes a pox. But it's a thing to reckon with at all times. Money makes the mare go; love makes the world last. So here's another chanty, mate. Same subject; different tune."

The monk smiled indulgently as Patenson began to pluck the strings again.

> *"Who shall have my faire lady?*
> *Who shall have my faire lady?*
> *Who but I, who but I, who but I?*
> *Under the leavés grene!*

Wrestling with the Angel:

*"The fairest man
That best can,
Dandirly, dandirly, dandirly dan,
Under the leavés grene!"*

The monk applauded sardonically.

"Well sung, Sir Troubador," he said. "And, again, theologically valid."

"Thank you," said Patenson, louting low before the wicket. "I, too, have always considered it an unimpeachable and moral sentiment. But the monk of Erfurt I was telling you of would not agree with us. He was about your size and habit; mild-looking, too, until he started haring down the garden path after sinners like myself. Funny thing, now I recall it. He'd a great lubber fellow with him. Built like an ox. Arm like a blacksmith's. Belly on him like a maltworm. Bull-necked. The pair of them talked on more freely than they would have if they knew I had the High Dutch. Learned it on the London docks, loading and unloading wine kegs for a Rhineland merchant."

Patenson grinned reminiscently.

"The lubber fellow was going for a monk," he continued, still grinning. "For all he had a lickerous eye rolling in his round German head. I still mind me the droll reasons he gave for choosing the cowl."

The Jester tossed his lute high in the air and deftly caught it on its way down.

"Heigh ho!" he crowed. "Dandirly, dandirly, dandirly dan! Show me a monk, and I'll show you a man! I can hear the lubber fellow yet, when I cock up my mind's ear, prating on there in his snorting High Dutch!"

It was true enough. Like many other Jesters Henry Patenson had a marvelously retentive memory; and his Erfurt stocking had taken place no earlier than the autumn before. Without very much effort he recalled the feel of the cold bench on which, queasily, he had awaited sentence; and the colloquy between Brother Anselm, Augustinian master of novices, and Patenson's temporary jailer, and

34

one Herr Martin Luther, young esquire of Saxony and candidate for the degree, Master of Arts, at next Epiphany's granting of degrees, who had, apparently, just reached a most momentous decision concerning his earthly and heavenly destinies. Brother Anselm had briefly dismissed Patenson's own wretched presence with a few contemptuous words.

"The English varlet will not trouble us long," Brother Anselm had said to young Martin Luther, jerking an indifferent thumb over the shoulder of his brown monk's habit. "Taken up for ribaldry he was by the watch, though his fellow players got clean away. Now he is sentenced and waits for the Elector's men to fetch him off to the stocks. He will neither discommode us by his presence nor eavesdrop while he waits. For, like most stupid Englishmen, he knows no language but his own."

"Ho!" Patenson had thought to himself, eager in his misery to snap up any crumb of comfort. "Then this time a stupid Englishman may be a match for two clever Germans."

And he had promptly looked up from the uncomfortable monkish form on which he sat with a great deal more interest than he would otherwise have shown.

"So, Master Luther," Brother Anselm had then gone on while Patenson listened. "So, to our business. *Alea jacta est.* The die is cast then, I take it—once your degree is secured, of course. You are set, now, on serving God? No more temptations or incitements of a fleshly nature?"

At that point the young esquire had crossed himself.

"Nay!" he had said hoarsely. "More! A thousandfold more! *Despero de me ipso!* I fare worse than blessed Anthony tormented by visions of *voluptas* in the desert. I have no peace night or day. My carnal eye strays always to the wenches' plackets. Yet I will it not, which often leads me to wonder if man's will is truly free. Why must God try a man thus? The reproduction of mankind is a great scandal and mystery. I marvel me God did not make generation on man's part after the way Father Adam was fashioned, the simple cleanly way of clay. His second thought was a filthy substitution."

35

The Augustinian had begun to look more than a little distressed.

"Take care, Master Luther!" he had interrupted. "Ware heresy! The awkward necessity of human generation is but to test our mortal clay. Let those that can take the better way to bridal—those elect ones who would be brides and bridegrooms of the Lamb."

The veins had stood out like whipcord then on Martin Luther's powerful neck.

"The breed of woman," he had gone on huskily, heeding Brother Anselm hardly at all, "is the breed of the *succuba,* the loathsome night-lier who drains man's strength from his limbs and loins. I have read the Fourth Book of Esdras, where the old prophet truly says: *The wine is strong, the King is stronger, woman strongest of all.* Then he goes on to add: *But the truth is even stronger than woman.* I would follow holy truth, Brother Anselm."

Just then the Elector's archers had come for Henry Patenson to hale him off to the stocks; so he never really got to know the upshot of the conversation. But, so far as it had gone, he had pondered it, sitting philosophically, leg-locked in a wooden embrace, till sunset; and he told it now to the Carthusian who kept on nodding his shaven head at almost every sentence.

The Jester was no prophet. He cared not a jackstraw for the young Saxon's torment of spirit. He saw neither the devils nor the angels Master Luther contended with as mightily as any saint or prophet. He heard no premonitory echo of the words of power that would soon shake his world.

"Was not that a pretty credential for monkhood?" Patenson wound up his tale. "Faith! A lust for a soft piece and a fear of the breed! At that happy rate, I should be Father Abbot somewhere at this very moment."

The Carthusian broke into an open laugh.

"So you should," he agreed, "if that were the only credential. But you are better off out in the world, Sir Fool, even as I am in my proper place behind this wicket."

"Yes," sighed Patenson with mock seriousness. "I fear me the fat fellow made but an indifferent monk after all."

He placed his arms a-kimbo, and strutted about, mimicking the high-pitched German tongue.

"*I marvel me,*" he pranced and postured, "*I marvel me God did not make generation on man's part after the way Father Adam was fashioned, the simple cleanly way of clay.* The way of clay, indeed! Faith, if that were the fashion of generation, the world would be full of monks and to spare, savoring their roasted chicken and their Rhenish, and their lawful doxies, too. That would be making the best of all possible worlds, and with a vengeance. How do you like the lubber's new fashion of conjugation? *Orthodoxy, heterodoxy,* plain two-legged plump little young *she-doxy!* The way of clay, indeed! There is a time for making mudpies, and a time for other things. Sure, cannot we men allow God a second thought, especially when it be a better thought? My present master, old Sir John More, is a godly man. He has also had two wives in his day so far, and never have I heard him utter such nonsense as this. His son, Thomas, too—he who lodges in this very Charterhouse—young Thomas has monkish inclinations enough in all conscience. Yet is he ever for a merry jest. And, this side of sin, he holds a man's way with a maid no evil thing. The Charterhouse will get a good monk in him, mayhap. Or, if not, some maid will have a better man for his monking it a space."

And, after his long disquisition, Patenson began another song:

> "*My love in her attire doth show her wit,*
> *It doth so well become her:*
> *For every season she hath dressing fit,*
> *For winter, spring, and summer.*
> *No beauty she doth miss*
> *When all her robes are on:*
> *But Beauty's self she is*
> *When all her robes are gone.*"

This time the Carthusian paid no attention to Patenson's amorous descant. Something the Jester had said just before he began to sing seemed to have caught the monk's interest.

"So you are Sir John More's Fool," he observed. "A good man, Sir John."

"And a good man his Fool," retorted the Jester, springing to attention. "Henry Patenson, *joculator et famulus familiae Mori.* At your service, friend monk."

"I am glad to make your acquaintance, friend Fool," said the monk politely. "And, in return for your courtesy in entertaining me this past hour, perhaps I can do you some slight favor of my own. To the small extent, at least, of informing you a few minutes beforehand that your master's son is returning to the world after four years spent among us. We monks sang a mass for him this morning. I stood in the Brothers' Choir throughout the service and listened to them chant the responses in the Fathers' Choir beyond the rood screen where the great lamp always burns. I prayed a good prayer this morning for your master's goodly son. He has been fast friend to all of us here. In his honor Prior William ordered a special repast to be served to all just as if it were a Holy Day—to Brothers and Fathers alike—in the Refectory next to the Guests' Hall. It is just over now, and the leave taking will take place in the Little Cloister to which lay people like yourself may be admitted. If you wish to, you may step in through the Entrance Gate here and see lawyer Thomas More bid farewell to his brothers in Christ."

Henry Patenson was more than willing to accept the invitation. Anything that concerned the house of More concerned him as well. He buckled on his lute again and followed the monk through the Entrance Gate, past the oak-balked staircase leading to the Lay Brothers' cells, past their Obediences, as they chose to call the workshops which stood in Wash House Court, and into the grassy quadrangle known as the Little Cloister. The knot of monks clustered about their favorite friend and servitor, Thomas More, was headed by their Prior, the great priest, William Tynbygh. All were smiling, except for one old Friar with whom More had broken more than one not altogether friendly lance in argument during the four years of his stay as pensioner in the Charterhouse.

Prior Tynbygh extended his right hand in affectionate farewell.

"So, friend Thomas," he said, "in the end it is to be the Law and not the Lord."

Thomas More shook his head a trifle sadly.

"Yes, Master Prior," he acknowledged. "You say right. Henceforth it is to be the Law I follow and not the Lord—though, in strict construction, the Law must always be admitted an aspect of the Lord. But, not to quibble, I have tested myself in many fastings and vigils; and have concluded that I shall live more holily as a chaste husband than as an impure priest. The desire of the married state is too strong upon me. I cannot shake it off."

"Nor should you try, friend Thomas," said Prior William at once. "Marriage, too, is a holy state. What does the Office of Our Lady say? *As arrows are in the hand of a mighty man, so are the children of them that have been shaken.* It is a blessed thing so to be shaken— always within the bonds of holy wedlock, mind—by the ecstacy that was in the beginning. We spiritual Fathers help Christ in His great work of Redemption. You fleshly fathers help God the Father in His great work of Creation. And always remember, Thomas: in this matter you and you alone are the best judge of what you do, of what you must do here. The world needs good men, too, as well as the cloister. God go with you in His world."

As Prior William raised his right hand in final benediction, the other Friars nodded to one another in friendly agreement. All but one: Thomas More's old adversary in dialectical dispute. He stepped forward all of a sudden and took the Prior by the sleeve, vehemently.

"By your leave, Master Prior," he said harshly. "I have a word to say to Master More before he goes from these gates forever."

Frowning, William Tynbygh narrowed his fine eyes. His delicate sense of spiritual discrimination recognized fervor when he saw it; it also recognized fanaticism. He knew and was apprehensive of the gossamer's difference in flame that separated the bonfire of *Caritas* from the *auto-da-fé* of intolerance.

"Say your word, Friar John," he said after a pause. "But take care it be in friendship. You have had your contentions out before, and ever courteously has he answered you."

Friar John shook his head in bitter denial.

"Not so, Father Prior," he dissented. "Did he answer me so courteously, think you, when we two clashed over the holy matter of the Rosary?"

"I think so, Friar John," said Thomas More.

"I think not, Thomas More," said the Friar. "I say again what I said before: that if a man say his beads daily he will not suffer damnation."

Another fire burned in the breast of Thomas More; a passion for truth and reason; an almost physical hunger for the precision of legal definition.

"I say nothing against the bead saying, Friar John," he said, growing hot in argument. "It is a holy and desirable practice. But some men there are, both in and out of the world, who say their beads thrice daily as if bead saying were dancing around a fairy thorn. Put it this way, friend Friar; I grant you a King is more ready to pardon offense against himself at the prayer of his mother. Yet is there nowhere, to my knowledge, a King so great a fool as to promulgate a law to encourage the audacity of his subjects against himself by a promise of impunity to traitors on condition of their paying a certain homage to his mother."

"It is well reasoned, friend Thomas," commented Prior William who had followed the closely mortised parallel with attention.

"Rather is it a secular figure," shouted the Friar, "and one not to be countenanced. And, Thomas More, if you are so far astray on a simple question of devotion, why may you not be equally far astray in your present much more difficult decision? Have you thought on what your fair lady must look like in forty years' time, if, indeed, she have the misfortune still to live so long a space? Her light bones rattling with a fair fervent fever, her wanton flesh wasted clean away, her fair soft skin leathered to the goodly color of a kite's claw?"

This time it was Thomas More who flushed brick-red with anger.

"As yet I have no lady, Friar John," he reminded the monk. "But let me, in my turn, tell you two things a pair of wiser men than either you or I once said. Clerk Langland warns us that Chastity without Charity is fit only to be chained in hell. And did not the great Augustine tell us that they who hate the goodly gifts of God are naught but

40

Manichees and the very worst of heretics? Did not Christ sanctify our flesh and blood by entering it? Did he not sacramentalize the twice-blessed things of earth by using them holily in His Seven Sacraments—bread and wine and oil and water and the sweet clay of married lovers? I tell you to your teeth, Friar John, you are not much above a Manichee, and your vaunted chastity without charity no better than Maid Malkin's sluttish maidenhead."

The old Friar gave him an ugly look.

"Preach away, if you must, Thomas More," he spat out venomously. "Oh, you are eloquent enough, I know. They tell me thousands flocked to hear you mouth about Augustine in the Church of St. Lawrence Jewry. Things are come to a pretty pass indeed when mind-proud laymen are hailed Doctors of the Universal Church; and yet can still lie late abed of mornings with their warm wedded lemans, so that they enjoy the best of both worlds. I tell you it was not so intended."

The argument had gone too far already. Prior Tynbygh stopped the Friar with a decisive gesture.

"Go in peace, friend Thomas," he said. "I shall be glad to sing a *Te Deum* at your wedding."

On their way back to Sir John More's house in Milk Street, Henry Patenson found occasion for a trenchant observation.

"I like not your grim and grave old Friar," he commented. "I dare hazard the guess that the crackling of Smithfield fagots about some poor heretic's feet sounds sweeter in his ears than the chime of the sacring bell. Are there many like him in the Charterhouse?"

"None other that I know of," said Thomas More. "But even in his case take care, friend Patenson, that you do no man an injustice. He is a good man after his stern lights, and his Prior is very careful to check him in excess."

"I like not priests much anyway," continued Patenson, "though the Father Porter at the wicket had a pleasant enough tongue in his head."

"There, friend Fool," said More, turning squarely to him, "there you are wrong. It may be there are too many priests ordained nowadays. I think myself the Bishops should be more scrupulous in their sifting of candidates for ordination. But we in the world are too foolish hard on our clergy. Nothing they do—good or bad—passes unreproved. If they are serious we call them solemn. If they are merry we call them mad. If they are holy we call them hypocrites. If they keep few servants we call them niggards. If they keep many we call them purse-proud and pompous. No, friend Patenson, we do great wrong to do nothing but criticize. For, as I once heard Master Colet preach in Paul's, if the clergy be evil we, the laity, must needs be worse. For our Savior called them the salt of the earth and the light of the world. And, said He, if the light be darked, how dark will then the darkness be?"

They were just passing St. Paul's. Patenson began to unstrap the lute at his back.

"You know more than I do of the matter, Master More," he answered indifferently. "Nonetheless, I am glad that you, for one, have decided to remain in darkness with us other weaker vessels. You will needs be going wooing next. I have a song for that."

He sang his first song of the morning through again.

> *"Western wind, when wilt thou blow,*
> *The small rain down can rain?*
> *Christ, if my love were in my arms,*
> *And I in my bed again!"*

As the Jester finished his aubade a few snow flakes spiraled lazily down over Paul's roof.

"It will not blow this Christmas month, at least," said Thomas More, laughing. "And Lady Spring is five months off."

"To Spring, then," said the Jester, drinking a mimic toast from his upturned lute. "To the soft season of love and west wind's rain! We go a-wooing then. Will it be in Essex, Master Thomas?"

CHAPTER IV

THE TRIUMPH OF CUPID:

Afternoon, Spring, 1505

BEFORE the new Under Sheriff of the City of London, his recent honors and responsibilities still lying heavy on his young shoulders, paid his formal visit to Netherhall, he saw fit to visit Roydon Church and there receive the sacrament at the hands of Rector William Daud, after first being duly shriven kneeling on a *prie-dieu* beside the small quatrefoil opening in the paneling of the old church's beautiful rood screen. After mass, Rector Daud, who knew somewhat of his London visitor's intentions, took him back into the Sanctuary to view the Colt brasses. Thomas More looked with vast interest upon these mortuary memorials of the Essex country family into which he had made up his mind to marry. Sir Thomas and Lady Colt, the grandparents of his intended bride, seemed very cool and quiet lying there lapped in funereal brass, although it was hot enough outside in the churchyard under the persistent sun of early May. Old Sir Thomas, as befitted a leal knight of Edward IV, wore in death his armor and spurs, his *misericorde* and baldric, and the embroidered tabard that made chain-mail shirts more seemly at the council table. Lady Colt was dressed in her matron's lappets and in her prized girdle clasped with its ornate Tudor rose. At their feet sported a little metal bevy of grandchildren, boys and girls; and Thomas More wondered humorously which of the little brass maidens, all alike in their dog-kennel headdresses, was the one to whom, if all went well, he would be ritually betrothed before nightfall. He noticed, too, and with approval, the emblem of the Trinity and the medallions of the four Evangelists which surrounded the memorial brass. He liked it well that the Colts were so pious a family.

After a sparse collation taken with Rector Daud the new Under Sheriff ambled, at a gentle jogtrot, down to Netherhall. Thomas More was no horseman. He was a burgess and a son of London, not a squire and a son of the shires. But on occasion—and this, distinctly, was one of them—he could enjoy a leisurely saunter on horseback. The sun shone hot on the Essex countryside. A fragrant surf of apple blossoms still broke rose-and-silver in the orchards. The wild flowers smelt delicately sweet and fragrant in that fringe of Epping Forest through which he rode. The Manor of Netherhall itself was some three miles from Broxbourne: a magnificent Tudor mansion girt by a little river, with a moat, with great ivy-mantled towers, with a fine brick gatehouse where the porter lived, and, off to one side, with a tithe barn silvering its old boards under the suns and rains of many years.

Thomas More, who had been to Netherhall many times before—but never on so ambassadorial a mission as this—chose not to enter by the gatehouse entrance. Instead, handing his horse over to a groom, he walked halfway round the moat to a small postern door of weathered wood which had been cunningly let into a wall of dark red and dark blue bricks faced with gray stone. It admitted one into John Colt's pleasant orchard close where, More knew, the three daughters of the household liked to spend their well-ordered morning hours, sewing, chatting, and enjoying the cool of the trees. A traveler had forestalled him, it appeared. Habited in a dark and dust-stained traveling mantle, he stood by the postern and chaffered with hedger Diccon. More's suitor's heart slipped a beat out of jealousy. Then, quickly recognizing its mistake, it jumped an additional three counts from love and pride.

"Erasmus!" he cried out. "Oh most Erasmic Erasmus! *Erasme erasmiotate!*"

44

Erasmus turned. The great Dutch Humanist, now in his fortieth year, looked prematurely old. His quizzical blue eyes crinkled with crows' feet at the corners; the once yellow hair had turned almost silver. His shoulders still bore their familiar scholar's stoop, and his step halted a little more than usual, for he was saddle sore after his long ride from Dover, even if the nag he had managed to beg from Rector Ursewick, the sporting Vicar of Hackney, was as gentle-paced a palfrey as England could provide. But the famous mobile mouth was still unlined. It quivered now—not with a shrewd satiric impulse, or a jest on the point of being born—but with honest masculine affection.

"Thomas More!" he said. "*Ave, amicissime!*"

Old Diccon looked on, a trifle perplexed. Erasmus of Rotterdam spoke no English. So the two old friends conversed in Latin; and Diccon of Netherhall had no more Latin than *Ite, missa est.*

"Come in, come in, my Masters," he invited them. "Good morrow, Master More. You would see Master Colt? He is from home."

"No, friend Diccon," said Thomas More, helping him lock the postern after them. "I would see Mistress Colt—the second Mistress Colt of your master's three Mistresses Colt, that is."

"She is on the river, Master More," said Diccon. "She will be back a little after noon. You will wait?"

"Yes, friend Diccon," said Thomas More. "We shall wait here in the orchard, Master Erasmus and I, till Mistress Colt returns. It is cool and pleasant here in the shade. The busy commonwealth of bees gives forth a pleasant hum. Let us not keep you from your proper doings, Diccon. We shall sit here and tell time by the dandelions and watch your pears grow."

"I shall fetch two stoups of wine for your worships," said Diccon, standing first on one foot, then on the other.

"Do not trouble, friend Diccon," said More, anxious now to get rid of the old hedger.

"It is no trouble, Master More," insisted the old man. "It is for the honor of Netherhall."

"As you will then, friend Diccon," said More with a sigh, trying another tack. "Then we shall drink it for the honor of Netherhall."

As the old hedger went off, satisfied at last, Thomas More turned to Erasmus, measured the scholar's slight frame affectionately with his eye, then embraced him.

"*Desiderie desiderate tam diu!*" he exclaimed. "Desiderius! *Dimidium animae meae!* Best of friends! So! It is close on ten years now since we last met. You look much the same, I must admit. Let me see, though."

Thomas More stood off some paces and pretended to consider his friend more closely.

"H'm," he said judiciously. "A trifle wiser, perhaps—if that is possible. A trifle wickeder, certainly—if that, also, is possible. But indubitably Desiderius Erasmus. And you have ridden posthaste to visit me so soon as your vessel docked! But, come. Explanations are in order. How did you know that I would be at Netherhall?"

Erasmus gave a cornery, Puck-like look at the Under Sheriff's holiday attire.

"A little bird whispered in my ear," he said mysteriously, "what your present gay gear proclaims is no lie. Tell me, Thomas, is your chosen one *semper silens* as you wrote to Candidus every good wife should be?"

Impishly Erasmus began to recite a Latin squib from Thomas More's salad days.

> "*Proculque stulta sit*
> *Parvis labellulis*
> *Semper loquacitas;*
> *Proculque rusticum*
> *Semper silentium.*
> *Sit illa vel modo*
> *Instructa literis*
> *Vel talis ut modo*
> *Sit apta literis—*"

> *Let no prattle,*
> *Tittle-tattle*
>   *Riot*
> *On her lips !*
> *Nor yet doltish,*
> *Country-coltish,*
>   *Quiet—*
> *Worse than quips!*
> *If she's no learning,*
> *Well, a yearning,*
>   *For letters*
> *Will do at first—*

A doggerel English translation, punning on Mistress Colt's name, had begun to form in Thomas More's mind. But he would let Erasmus go no further.

"A little bird named John Colet, I'll be bound," he said, ignoring the recitation. "But enough of these dark inferences for the moment. Tell me something of yourself. What make you from Italy, anyway? You said, on your last leaving England, that you would never return until Englishmen learned to toss a salad properly; and that would be Doomsday."

Erasmus laughed.

"So I did," he admitted. "But that particular obstacle no longer exists now that Stephen Gardiner has returned from France where our Stephen lived long enough to find out that lettuce does best when seasoned with butter and sour wine."

"I talked with our young Stephen just the other day," said Thomas More. "He is going far. Rumor has it that he will be preferred to the See of Winchester. But in sober truth, Desiderius, what make you from Italy?"

"The Bishop of Rochester has invited me to Cambridge," said Erasmus, "there to finish my *Novum Instrumentum.*"

Thomas More looked grave enough as Diccon brought up the two stoups of wine. Erasmus drank his off with a connoisseur's smack of appreciation. More, as was his fashion in company—when alone he never touched wine at all—barely put his lips to the vessel before setting it down on an arbor table.

"You and I are old enough friends, Desiderius," he said very seriously, "for me to speak in utter frankness on this matter. You will encounter much and weighty opposition to your project at Cambridge. The conservatives there find the Vulgate version enough and more than enough. They fear a new critical text will be but a steppingstone to a vernacular version."

Erasmus' lip lifted a little in disdain.

"Of course," he said contemptuously, "the Vulgate is enough for them. Of course they fear my *Instrumentum* will be but a steppingstone to a vernacular translation. Well, let me tell you, Thomas, their fear is my most passionate hope and desire. What of the people who do not read Latin and who do not have a sermon preached to them, as things are going nowadays—and they are going very badly—above once in twenty Sundays? No, Thomas, I totally dissent from those learned pedants who are unwilling that the sacred scriptures should be read by the unlearned, and who oppose translation of them into the people's tongue, be it French or Flemish or English—as if, indeed, Christ had taught such subtleties that they can scarcely be understood but by a few theologians, or as if the strength of the Christian religion lay in men's ignorance of it! The Lord Christ thought not such at Pentecost when the Holy Spirit descended in tongues of flame and each man understood his fellow's speech: Cappadocian, Greek, Persian, Latin. As for me, I would with all my heart that the sacred writings were translated into every language in the world. I would have the weakest woman read the Gospels and the Epistles of St. Paul—in the name of Christ, had these scholastic logic-choppers we are speaking of no mothers that they thus scorn one half of Creation? Or were they, like the frogs of the Nile, spawned of river mud as thick as their intellects? I would that not only Scots and Irish, but Turks and Saracens, too, might read the holy words. I long for the plow boy to sing them to himself as he follows the plow, the weaver to hum them to the tune of his shuttle, the traveler to beguile with them the dullness of his journey. For these sacred words give you the very image of Christ speaking, healing, dying, rising again, and make Him so present to us that, were He before our very eyes once more, we should not more truly see Him."

It was a long speech and an impassioned one for the ironist who was Erasmus of Rotterdam. He paused for breath, shaking a little for his unaccustomed vehemence.

"You are right, Desiderius," said Thomas More, "but I would have you know the strength of the forces ranged against you. The Universities are very powerful and they oppose. So are the Bishops of—"

"So," broke in Erasmus, setting down his second stoup of wine, "so is my patron, John Fisher, Bishop of Rochester, my friend, William Warham, Archbishop of Canterbury and Chancellor of England, and my most august examplar, Cardinal Ximenes, Primate of all Spain. Cardinal Guiliano Medici, Bishop Foxe of Winchester, Robert Aldrich of Carlyle--they, too, all back me. So much for the great ones of earth. I regard the small ones even more. You and I, Thomas, are proud to rank ourselves in the high fellowship of Humanists. Shall we not remember that man is of the company of angels, the son of God, the heir of immortality, a member of Christ, a member of the Church? That our bodies are temples of the Holy Ghost, our minds the images and also the secret habitations of the Deity?"

"*Bravo, bravissime*, Desiderius mine," said Thomas More very softly. "So you have taken friend Colet's good words to heart and turned away a little from your first darlings, the old pagan writers you and I used to study together in the City—the City of Man, Desiderius, no matter how fair we thought, is not Augustine's abiding City."

"Do you know how friend Colet ended his last letter to me?" asked Erasmus with a laugh. "He was acknowledging my gift to him of Reuchlin's *Cabalistica*, and he closed thus—or at least so closely as I can remember it now at some months' distance: *Oh, Erasmus, of books and knowledge there is no end, but there is nothing better than that we should live a pure and holy life, which in my judgment will never be attained but by the ardent love and imitation of Jesus.*

Sometimes, Thomas, I fear friend Colet preaches too much. I have only preached one sermon in my life, and you had the good fortune just now to hear it. How do you suppose I closed my last letter to Master Colet?"

Thomas More smiled, but said nothing.

"It was a letter," continued Erasmus, "in defense of that same secular wisdom you called my 'first darlings' but a short space back. Again as closely as I can remember at this far remove, I ended with this gay flourish of figure, prefiguring my old pagan books as Solomon's Queens: *It should be no rebuke to me if, after the example of Solomon, I nourish up at home in my house sixty Queens, eighty sovereign ladies, and damsels innumerable of secular wisdom, provided only that the wisdom of God be above all other my best beloved, my love, my dove, my beautiful one, my sweetheart in the cleft of the rock who alone seems beautiful.*"

Thomas More laughed aloud.

"Aha!" he said. "This sounds a little more like my old wicked Erasmus with the unregenerate Adam still smoking fresh and hot in his liver."

"And do you know, Thomas," pursued Erasmus eagerly, "who is the Sabaean Balkis among my sixty Queens? Why, none other than your own *Life of Mirandola*. There she sits in my house, queening it on my library shelves, throned higher in my heart than all but the Divine Wisdom of my *Novum Instrumentum*."

"Thank you, Desiderius," said Thomas More, touched to the quick by his friend's sincere compliment. "But it is just this sort of jesting as your present jape about the sixty Queens which is sure to be misunderstood among the Scotists of Cambridge. No, Desiderius, you were safer far in Italy."

"Ah!" said Erasmus. "But I have still another reason for coming to England at this moment."

He drew a paper out of the pouch at his girdle and flourished it in More's face.

"The King is dead," he intoned. "Long live the King! Henry VII, royal curmudgeon, yields to Henry VIII, imperial patron of Muses, and all is well. England is become a Paradise of Scholars now. Listen to what our old friend Mountjoy writes me from abroad."

And Erasmus held the parchment out in front of him with all the ostentation of a herald in the lists.

"Heaven laughs and the earth rejoices; everything is full of milk and honey and nectar. Avarice has fled the country. Our King is not after gold, or gems, or precious metals, but virtue, glory, immortality. I will give you a taste of it. Just lately, he was saying that he wished he were more learned. 'That is not what we want from you,' I said, 'but that you should foster and encourage learned men.' 'Why, of course,' he said, 'for without them life would hardly be life.' "

He looked over the parchment top at his friend.

"So you see, Thomas, in a way my coming is a royal command. There is much more of the same here which I will not take the pains to read you. Mountjoy winds up at last with this Cloud Cuckoo flourish:

"You will come to a Prince who will say, 'Accept our wealth and live at ease our greatest sage.' "

"Well—what think you of my coming to England now?"

"Give me your letter a moment, Desiderius," said Thomas More. He conned it, pondering.

"*Our King is not after gold, or gems, or precious metals,*" he repeated from Mountjoy's letter after a space. "True enough, Desiderius. Such categories suit his father better than himself. But what, exactly, is he after?"

Erasmus looked into his face, shrewdly.

"You have reservations, then, Thomas?" he asked. "What is he like, your golden young monarch, your newly minted Henry?"

"He is accomplished," said Thomas More slowly. "The best tennis player and wrestler in the realm. He is well trained in theology, too. Had Prince Arthur lived, Henry was intended for the Archbishopric of Canterbury. He might well have graced that first of English Sees."

"I am told," said Erasmus, "that he also writes music—Masses."

"Yes," said Thomas More. "Masses, yes; and love songs. Better love songs than Masses, perhaps. Patenson, my father's Fool, likes to sing a song of his that goes:

> *"Green groweth the holly, so doth the ivy,*
> *Though winter blasts blow never so high,*
> *Green groweth the holly.*
>
> *"As the holly groweth green*
> *And never changeth hue,*
> *So I am, and ever hath been,*
> *Unto my lady true."*

"Henry Patenson does it nicely. It has a quaint lilt."

"You were not," remarked Erasmus, "a bad hand at a love song yourself, once. Remember?"

And he hummed:

> *"Then the duenna and the guarded door*
> *Baffled the stars and bade us meet no more."*

He smiled slily at Thomas More.

"One Elizabeth, was it not, Thomas?" he asked. "How does she nowadays?"

"Very well, I believe," said Thomas More, laughing. "Married long since—though not to me—despite the dragonish duenna who baffled those old stars. But, tell me now, what think you of the maidens of this shire?"

Erasmus blew a kiss in the direction of Diccon's espaliered pears.

"I think them very well, indeed," he said. "I like well, too, your English habit of kissing, though it does not suit my own priestly habit overmuch. But it is a custom that cannot be sufficiently praised. Wherever I go, I am received with kisses from everybody. When I leave, I am dismissed with kisses. I return, my kisses are returned to me. People come: kisses. People go: kisses. Wherever people foregather: kisses. Whatever way one turns, the bussing air is warm with kisses. If ever I am exiled, may it be to England where soft kisses burgeon on every bush."

Thomas More took Erasmus by the sleeve.

"O most reluctant celibate, perpend," he said. "I have kissing news for you. You and Master Colet are right in your several surmises. I am to be married."

Erasmus bowed low, genuine respect and love commingled with his mockery.

"*Felicitationes!*" he said. "I must surely meet her that we may exchange a friendly kiss."

"So you shall, so you shall, Desiderius," said Thomas More expansively. "We await her now. She is the Mistress Colt Diccon spoke of as being on the river till sometime after noon. Master Colt has three daughters. The youngest scarcely more than a child. The younger gay and well favored. The eldest well favored enough, but graver than her younger sister; and somewhat dwarfish in stature."

"You court the dwarfish elder, I am to take it then?" Erasmus probed him.

"Not at all," said Thomas More. "The younger and fairer favored."

"The better for kissing then," said Erasmus merrily. "But, *amicissime*, I trust you will not think me over sententious if I plagiarize from your own lines on a lover and his lass:

> *Of his love, lo! the sight and company*
> *To the lover so glad and pleasant is*
> *That whoso hath the grace to come thereby*
> *He judgeth him in perfect joy and bliss;*
> *And whoso of that company doth miss,*
> *Live he in never so prosperous estate,*
> *He thinketh him wretched—unfortunate.*

"Except for a plaguy bad quantity in the last line, you are a troubador, Thomas—as good a one as ever was Guillaume de Machaut or Guido Cavalcanti or Petrarch himself."

"Thank you," said Thomas More shyly. "Thank you, Desiderius.

The Triumph of Cupid:

There was much poisonous nonsense spoken and written by those same old troubadours; and much that made good sense as well. Do you remember Pico della Mirandola's twelve properties of a proper lover?"

"Of course not," said Erasmus, jesting tenderly. "You know I read Jerome, not the jongleurs. I plead my suit nowadays to the divine maid, theology. She is a most jealous mistress, Thomas mine."

"It is all the same, Desiderius," said Thomas More in utter earnestness. "You are a lover, too, and a greater one than I. Love is the law of life and the conquest of death. The only sin is not to love; the only misfortune never to have loved. And, so far as your mistress, theology, goes, there is much sound theology in Pico's twelve conditions of the true lover."

He ticked them off, one by one, on his fingers.

> " I.   *To love one alone.*
> II.   *To think him unhappy that is not with his love.*
> III.   *To adorn himself for the pleasure of his love.*
> IV.   *To suffer all things even death, to be with his love.*
> V.   *To desire to suffer shame and harm for his love.*
> VI.   *To be ever with his love, at least in thought.*
> VII.   *To love all things that pertain to his love.*
> VIII.   *To covet the praise of his love.*
> IX.   *To believe of his love all things excellent.*
> X.   *To weep often with his love for joy or sorrow.*
> XI.   *To languish and burn in the desire of his love.*
> XII.   *To serve his love, nothing thinking of reward.*"

Erasmus listened to his friend's amorous catechism, saying nothing.

"Yes," he said at last in a changed voice, "you are a true lover, Thomas, in a world where, despite the troubadours, there are not so many true lovers as men think. May you enjoy the measure of happiness a true lover merits."

Then, in the old sprightly tone:

"But, Thomas, all unwitting I make you violate the second article

of your covenant: *To think him unhappy that is not with his love.*
Either I should leave you alone to be unhappy or else altogether free
to hunt her down. As for my own small affairs, it behooves me to take
time by the forelock a little. I've promised Mountjoy a melting Latin
epigram by high noon tomorrow. It is to be for his wife's birthday.
He has done me many a good turn. So I shall do my best to turn a
pretty compliment for his lady. Maybe, if I stroll by the river, I shall
gain inspiration from a sight of your betrothed."

As Erasmus went out by the postern, Thomas More began to pace
about the garden, humming King Henry's little song about the holly.
Striking a pose before one of Diccon's carefully mulched rose beds,
he declaimed aloud Pico's third article:

"To adorn himself for the pleasure of his love."

Then, suiting action to the word, he snipped a yellow bud and
twisted its stem about his embroidered lappet; then fell again to
humming. But he was no longer alone. A basket on her arm and keys
jingling at her slim girdle, Mistress Jane Colt, the eldest sister of the
household and diligent chatelaine of Netherhall, walked through
the arbor leading to the house. She wore a seemly dress he had not
seen before, of russet brown cambric, low cut and square in front,
with belling sleeves and a green petticoat that showed, rustling, as
she walked. Her costly girdle, an old-fashioned one of the last reign,
was silver-gilt, richly enameled. Her crisp brown hair was parted in
the center and bound with a gold fillet. It set off her pointed face in
such a cunning fashion that, with a start, Thomas More noticed that
her expression could not improperly be described as elfin. Decidedly, this was not the "graver" girl he had spoken of to Desiderius.
As their glances crossed, Jane Colt flushed to the roots of her curling
hair—and very prettily, too, he thought.

"Greetings, Mistress Jane," said Thomas More.

"Your servant, Master More," she said, curtseying. "You await my
sister?"

It was a statement more than a query. Nevertheless, Thomas More
looked at her long and searchingly before replying.

"And if I did, what odds?" he asked at long last.

"None, surely," she said, biting off a thread. "It was but a question."

She had sat down upon a bench, arranging some mending in her lap the while. After another long pause, during which he continued to gaze steadily down upon her, Thomas More seated himself beside the girl. With his riding gauntlets he busily set to flicking imaginary flecks of dust off his knees.

"Tell me, Mistress Jane," he said, after a second awkward interlude. "What if I were to say that I came to see you?"

"And if you did," asked Jane Colt, indifferently, aping his own earlier question, but the flush continued to mount her clear skin, "and if you did, what odds?"

"I do not jest, Jane," said Thomas More, embarrassed but persistent. "Tell me one thing. Why are you not married? You are a comely maiden and an industrious one. You would make a good wife."

Jane Colt gave a short laugh. The flush looked angry now. Any man who knew women even a little, as Thomas More, for all his poetry and quoting from Mirandola, patently as yet did not, would have recognized storm signals.

"You are known to be a man of the world, Master More," she articulated precisely, snipping off each syllable as if with the scissors she had by now taken from the box at her belt. "What reason can you have to shame me by such a question? I have ever wished you well."

"I do not mean to shame you, Jane," he said quickly.

"But you do shame me, Master More," she said as quickly, and now her clear voice was close to tears. "You shame me, you and the world you serve. We make fine targets, I have no doubt, for your blunt shafts of wit that wound but do not kill—we elder maidens whose younger sisters marry before them."

Thomas More's eyes—never without merriment for long—began to twinkle now.

"That is easily mended, Jane," he said slily. "What if you were to marry first?"

Jane Colt sprang to her feet, her scissors clenched like a dagger. Her lips had turned white and her delicate nostrils drew in.

"Your jest is an unseemly one, Master More," she said fiercely, yet in so low-pitched a voice that Thomas More was hard put to hear her.

He rose in his own turn.

"I tell you a second time," he protested, the merriment gone from his eyes, "that I do not jest."

Then, very suddenly, as if it were a surprise even to himself, as, in a very real sense, it was:

"Jane Colt, will you be my wife?"

She stared at him in disbelief. Before she could answer, the postern opened in the sunny brick wall and Erasmus came hurrying into the garden. Not seeing the white-faced girl, he cried out at once.

"Your eye is good, friend Thomas," he called gaily, "and mine own too dazzled to dwell longer on Latin epigrams in compliment of Mountjoy's wife. Just now, down by the river—"

Thomas More interrupted him in the nick of time. Jane Colt, he knew, did not understand Latin, but the Dutch savant's pantomine was all too vivid as it was.

"Desiderius," he said, placing the girl's unprotesting hand in his own, "may I present my betrothed, Mistress Jane Colt of Netherhall Manor?"

Before the startled Erasmus had time to collect his wits, the young woman curtsied distractedly and ran off toward the house.

"But," said Erasmus, almost sputtering in perplexity, "Mistress Colt is on the river. I saw her. This is her elder sister, the dwarfish one! The younger and fairer favored is just coming off the river now!"

Thomas More clapped him merrily on the back.

"Younger, yes, but not fairer favored," he corrected him. "I libeled Mistress Jane a little back. Today I looked upon her a little longer than my wont, and I find her a good deal comelier than I thought. Besides, I choose the lesser of two evils, you see."

"Oh, she is comely enough," said Erasmus impatiently. "But Thomas! Thomas! What was your reason? You have always a reason. What was your reason this time? Take care you do not betray Love. The Cyprian, too, is a jealous goddess. Come, what was your reason?"

"What is Love, Desiderius?" said Thomas More slowly. "There is the kind old Ovid writes of. Every man feels that sort burning delicately and luxuriously in his members. There is Plato's kind. You and I have read and written about that. There is the Pauline path of *Agape*. You and every ordained priest in Christendom lead the good way down that road. And there is pity, Desiderius. Just now pity took me by the throat. I could not see these leaves for pity."

Almost in a distraction fit Thomas More began to pluck down green leaves from an apple bough.

"Pity is all very well," Erasmus insisted. "But what of the sister? What of pity for the sister?"

Thomas More seemed to recover himself in part.

"She is younger and more beautiful," he said. "She has followers a-plenty, and I have never declared myself. There is no question of pity in her case."

Erasmus was still staring mutely at him when Diccon came out of the house.

"It is afternoon, my Masters," he said. "And Master Colt is come back by the Entrance Gate. He will receive you in his study."

"Well, Thomas," said Erasmus finally, as they entered the house together at Diccon's rheumatic heels. "Here is something even Guido Cavalcanti did not know of. But then he never visited this fair paradise of fools, my *Morus'* England!"

Bees hummed at Netherhall and rosemary clambered across the walks of Thameside. But they had not met as yet at Chelsea. First came those other homes he loved so well: Bucklersbury and Crosby Hall. In the beginning the fragrant rosemary memories had knotted and clustered and climbed and twined about his father's comely residences. Now they no longer did so, except that, once, just after he became Chancellor, Henry had visited him at old Sir John's More Hall of Gobions down in Hertfordshire where, in memory of the occasion, he had reared the arch later known as Folly Arch. He smiled now at the thought. Erasmus would have liked the touch of folly in Folly Arch. But that was a memory of rue and fennel, not of rosemary and columbine.

Now it was time to think of the homes he had had and the hearths he had built; hearths guarded by the good golden dragon that is named fire—he used to tell John and Cecily that Bevis of Hampton's great gold firedrake dwelt in their own fireplace. First, then, came the house at Bucklersbury in the street of the grocers and herbalists where, in simple time, the lanes smelt sweet with the smell of drying herbs, with lavender and rosemary. There he had brought his bride, Jane Colt. There Jane had borne him their four children: Margaret, Elizabeth, Cecily, and John. And there Jane had died—dear Jane, the little wife of Thomas More, for whom he wrote but one line in epitaph: Chara Thomae iacet hic, Joanna uxorcula Mori. *It had been enough. It summed up in its caressing Latin diminutives all that he could tell the world of his large love for little Jane.*

It was at Bucklersbury, too, that he had married Dame Alice Middleton, widow of John Middleton, citizen and mercer of London, and merchant of the Staple of Calais. "Nec bella nec puella," that is "neither a pearl nor a girl," Erasmus had unkindly said of her; and it was true. He could not expect to find another Jane Colt, nor had he tried. Nor would it have been right to try. The springtide of life came but once — to attempt to prolong it was a harlot's false promise and evil ambition. Dame Alice had made a good wife. A better wife, it was possible, than he a husband. But he had tried. Tenderly had she nurtured his four young children, and tenderly, in his turn, had

59

he cared for her child Alice, and little Margaret Giggs, the adopted daughter of both of them.

It was to Bucklersbury, too, Erasmus brought his Latin translation of Euripides' Hecuba. And there the two of them translated Lucian— it had been a daring stroke to send Henry his Declamation on the Tyrannicida; but in those days Henry had not yet lost the power of laughter. Moreover, not only was Erasmus' Praise of Folly composed under his rooftree, it was even dedicated to him. As Erasmus said in a prefatory letter, what first put the whole thing into his head "was your name of More, which is as near to the name of Folly, Moria, as you are far from the thing."

The prisoner in the Tower could still smile reminiscently at the compliment. Erasmus had been all too kind, of course. Thomas More had been as big a fool as the rest of them on a round globe of fools. What small wisdom he had followed had been Aristotle's unchivalric counsel: "The wise man does not expose himself needlessly to danger, since there are few things for which he cares sufficiently; but he is willing, in great crises, to give even his life—knowing that under certain conditions it is not worth while to live." Well, he had encountered one of those crises; and this was how he was meeting it. Desiderius' German contemporary, Sebastian Brant, had seen the world as a Ship of Fools. Desiderius himself had written, tongue in cheek, in Praise of Fools. Henry Patenson, both less of a fool and a better Fool than most, had cracked jokes to amuse fools. Perhaps, when all was said and done, there were worse things than being a fool; and there were fools and fools. There was not much left now for a fool in the Tower to do but pray for all fools, including himself.

The rosemary of remembrance grew thick over other homes than his. Homes that he had visited many times. Homes like Whitehall, Wolsey's glorious York House with its beautiful gateway built after Holbein's designs. Homes like Richmond and Greenwich and Hampton Court. Like the Jerusalem Chamber in the great Benedictine house where Henry IV had died. Above all, like the old Palace of Westminster, before Henry deserted it for Whitehall, where were situate the Law Courts and the House where the Commons sat.

Those were the places associated with his steady rise to fame and *office. From them, in 1515, he had set out with Cuthbert Tunstall on the King's Embassy into Flanders. . . . Next 1516, the golden lustrum of Erasmus' Greek* New Testament *and his own lighthearted jape, Utopia. . . . Then 1517, the dark year of the eagles' gathering; of London's Evil May Day; of the Sweating Sickness; of Luther defying the Pope at Wittenberg. It had lightened for a moment while Leo launched his great Bull for Peace, and, in response to the Pope's demand, Henry, Francis, and Maximilian laid down their arms for a space. But only for a space, and a short breathing space, at that, as it proved; and, when they next took them up again, the Pope had girded on his sword as well. Thomas More sighed in the Tower. His rise had grown swifter and swifter that same dark year of 1517. . . . Counsel for Leo at Southampton. . . . On embassage again, this time to Calais for Wolsey who had succeeded old Archbishop Warham as Chancellor. Details blurred and merged in his mind. . . . It had all taken place so long ago now. . . .*

But he could still hear, as if it were yesterday, the masculine thunder of cleansing laughter that had volleyed and crashed like culverins of Momus under the roof beams of Bucklersbury and Crosby Hall. Shriving, sacramental laughter that purged the mind and heart as the Sacrament of Penance purged the heart and soul. Surely those fabled giants of London, old Gog and Magog, had peered in through the leaded panes as the peerless jests went round. There was the Latin joke he had made in Bruges where a certain vainglorious Doctor Utriusque Juris in Charles' glittering retinue had challenged all comers to public dispute on any question in Civil or Canon Law, in science or literature. For the honor of English laughter he had confronted the imperial pundit with this question from Common Law: An averia capta in withernamia sunt irreplegiabilia? *Which is to say: Whether cattle taken in withernam be irrepleviable? The learned champion had retired in precipitate confusion with, as Erasmus later said, his withers wrung and More's withernams unwrung. So the rollicking laughter rolled round the board at Bucklersbury.*

Then there was that very English jest, Utopia. No one, unless it be Erasmus, had seen to the bottom of that as yet: not Busleiden, not Gilles, not Budé; not Ammonio, not Bonvisi. No, Utopia was a joke for the centuries. They would be arguing over it for a good long time to come.

Faster, ever faster, flowed the sands out of the hour glass. Thicker, ever thicker, grew the rosemary over the walks of Chelsea those last July nights in the Tower.

CHAPTER V

MASTER COLET PREACHES A SERMON:

Morning, Good Friday, 1518

THE muffled clappers had been sounded for the Elevation; the altar had been stripped of its gleaming white linen and gold sacrificial vessels; the statues stood swathed in purple cloths awaiting Resurrection morning; and the expectant audience settled back in their pews as Master Colet, Dean of St. Paul's, entered the high pulpit of the Chapel Royal to preach his good Friday sermon before King Henry, Queen Catherine, the Court, and the assembled Bishops of England. It was not only that Master Colet was, bar none, the best preacher in Britain. The Court knew him for a resolute and honest man who hated war and who had, moreover, often spoken out in private against what he considered the devious diplomacy of the new Cardinal Chancellor. It also knew his uncompromising views on corruption in the Church; and there were many rumors abroad that his Lordship, Richard Fitzjames, Bishop of London, was in for a surprise when Master Colet reached that part of his address which had to do with the coming Convocation for the Extirpation of Heresy which Archbishop Warham had ordered to open in St. Paul's Cathedral on Easter Monday. Bishop Fitzjames was so hot a zealot on the trail of heretics that Signor Andrea Ammonio of Lucca, Henry's Latin Secretary, could jestingly blame the current dearness of wood on the Bishop's excessive purchases of fagots for the bonfires of Smithfield. Archbishop Warham did not care for Fitzjames' extreme tactics. He appreciated Colet's strict probity and rational moderation, and he had selected him as Convocation speaker in order that his humane prudence should serve as a makeweight to balance

Fitzjames' thin-lipped rigor. But not even Archbishop Warham had bargained for what he was to hear in the course of the next half hour.

Master Colet looked out over the assembled heads in the Chapel Royal to the two halberdiers who stood stiffly, pikes extended, on either side the great doors that led into the antechamber. His glance paused a moment on Henry and Catherine; passed on to the heavy blond features of the Ipswich butcher's son who had become, in a few short years, both Cardinal of the Church and Chancellor of the Kingdom; lingered a little on the benches which contained his enemies, those episcopal pluralists, the most reverend Bishops of Bath, Wells, Lincoln, Hereford, Winchester, Salisbury and London; recognized two likely allies in the mournfully ugly yet powerful face of Archbishop Warham, his and Erasmus' patron, and the long, comely, serious one of Bishop Fisher of Rochester; and came to rest at last on the bowed head of the one man in the assembly who, the speaker knew, would approve to the hilt of what he was going to say: Thomas More, the new Speaker of the House of Commons. Master Colet settled the band about his neck; adjusted his lawn sleeves nervously; and began to speak in a strong voice:

"My Lord the King; Queen Catherine; my Lords Bishops; priests; and nobles of the Court:

"Ye are come together this morning to honor the Passion of our Lord and Savior, Jesus Christ, on the anniversary of His suffering death and torture for us on the tree of shame which, watered by His sacred blood, has sprung up everywhere a green and holy rood of our salvation. A Lenten subject befits a Lenten season. What I have to say today may not, perchance, please the ears of everyone here. Nevertheless, it cries aloud to heaven to be heard. My discourse, then, will have two sackcloth heads. I would fain speak first to the Church. Then would I address the State.

"My Lords Bishops, ye are come together to London from the length and breadth of our land to hold the great council known as the Convocation for the Extirpation of Heresy. What ye will do in this council, and what grave matters ye will handle, I do not yet know. But I wish that today, for some little space, before the Convocation is opened, mindful of your name and profession, ye would first consider of the reformation of ecclesiastical affairs. For never was it more necessary; never did the state of the Church more need your earnest endeavors. For the Church, our Church, the spouse of Christ, which He wished to be without spot or wrinkle, is become foul and deformed. As said Isaias: *The faithful city is become a harlot.* Hearken unto Jeremias speak: *She hath committed fornication with many lovers,* whereby she hath conceived many seeds of iniquity, and daily bringeth forth the foulest offspring. Wherefore I have come here today, my Lords Bishops, to admonish you to deliberate with all your minds and souls, in this your coming council, concerning the salutary reformation of the Church.

"But, in truth, I come here not of my own will and pleasure, for I am very conscious of my unworthiness, and I understand all too well how hard it will be to satisfy the critical judgment of such great and learned men as you. But I could not but obey the righteous mandate of our most gracious sovereign, King Henry, the protector of the Church in England, and the command of my most reverend Father and Lord Archbishop, the President of this Council and the Primate of our island, who have jointly imposed this heavy task upon me. Therefore, my brothers in Christ, Fathers and most reverend listeners, I pray and beseech you this day that you will bear with my weakness and ignorance through your most liberal forbearance and patience. And, before all other things, let us pour out our prayers for help to God the Father Almighty. First, then, let us pray for his Holiness the Pope, for all spiritual pastors, with all Christian people. Next, let us pray for our most reverend Father, the Lord Archbishop, President of this Council, and for all the Lords Bishops, the whole clergy, and the whole people of England. Then for our most gracious King and Queen, in whose Chapel Royal we are all of us favored guests this day. And lastly, for this assembly and Convocation, praying God that He may inspire our minds for the good and benefit of the Church and the Kingdom to the profitable end that, when this Council is concluded, we may not seem to have been called together in vain and without cause. Let us then, my Lords all, kneel down together and recite the *Pater Noster.*"

The murmured cadences of the Lord's Prayer rustled under the gold-fretted roof of the Chapel Royal. The Duke of Suffolk, Henry's brother-in-law, he who had once been simple Charles Brandon, comrade of the King's jousts, stifled an elegant yawn. There were those who wondered how the beefy roisterer had come so far; but, whatever the reason, good, bad, or indifferent, there he was, firmly ensconced as first favorite of the realm. His wining and dining comrade, Sir William Compton, leaned over and tapped him lightly on one burly shoulder.

"*Courage, mon ami, Charlot,*" he whispered. "Master Colet brings up his heavy siege guns in a moment."

"He'd better," grumbled back Suffolk. "Else, Will, you've lured me here on false pretenses and I owe you a grudge."

Compton laughed. He knew that Brandon grumbled by the book. If there was one thing constant in the King's mercurial character, under all the wayward whims and brutal caprices, it was a strong-grained, eccentric, but genuine piety. His favorites, like himself, might wench, drink, and curse as hard as they pleased; but one thing he would have from them, and no nonsense about it, either. They must be regular in their attendance at divine services.

The Dean of St. Paul's fingered the gold cross that hung round his neck.

"Perhaps, my Lords Bishops," he began again, "perhaps you are thinking reproachfully: 'What has all this to do with heretics? In heresy lies our danger. In the extirpation of heresy lies our remedy. To that end and to no other are we convoked.' True, my Lords. To that end and to no other are ye convoked. But I say to you: *Ye are the heretics!* Worldliness—your worldliness—is your foe. We have conformed ourselves to the world, and by this action of ours the face of the Church is marred. By worldliness is the Church's influence plainly destroyed far more than it was marred and destroyed either, at the beginning, under the Caesars, by the persecution of tyrants, or after that by the invasion of heresies which followed. For by the persecution of tyrants the persecuted Church was made stronger and more glorious. By the invasion of heretics the Church, being shaken, was made wiser and more skilled in Holy Scriptures. But after the intro-

66

duction of this most sinful worldliness, now, when worldliness has crept in amongst the clergy, the root of all spiritual life—Charity itself—is extinguished. And I say to you that without holy Charity the Church of Christ can neither be wise nor strong in God.

"It is true that in these days we are once again troubled by heretics —men mad with strange folly—but this heresy of theirs is not so pestilential and pernicious to us and to all Christian people as the vicious and depraved lives of the clergy which, if we may believe St. Bernard, is a species of heresy and the greatest and most pernicious of all. For that same holy Father, preaching in a certain convocation to the priests of his time, in his sermon spoke these words: *"There are many who are Catholic in their speaking and preaching who are very heretics in their actions, for what heretics do by their false doctrines these men do by their evil examples. They seduce the people and lead them into error of life; and they are by so much worse than heretics as actions are stronger than words.'* These things said Bernard, that holy Father of so great and ardent spirit. And by these words he plainly shows that there are two kinds of heretical pravity —one of perverse doctrine, the other of perverse living—and of these two the latter is the greater and more pernicious; and this condition now reigns in the Church, to the miserable destruction of the Church, her priests living after a worldly and not after a priestly fashion. Therefore, do you Bishops, you Fathers, you priests, and all of you of the clergy, awake at length, and rise up at last from this your sleep in this forgetful world. And, being awake, listen at length to Paul calling unto you: *Be not conformed to this world.*

"To speak of pride of life—what eagerness and hunger after honor and dignity are found in these days amongst ecclesiastical persons! What a breathless race from benefice to benefice, from a less to a greater one, from a lower to a higher! Who has not seen such things? Who, seeing them, does not feel sorrow? Priests give themselves to feasts and banquetings, they spend themselves in vain babbling, they give themselves to sports and plays, they apply themselves to hunting and hawking, they drown themselves in the delights of this world. What other thing seek we nowadays in the Church but fat benefices and high promotions? We care not how many, how various, how great benefices we take, so that they be of great value. All corruption, all the decay of the Church, all the offenses of the world, almost, proceed from the covetousness of priests! We no longer acknowledge and perceive what the master of humility, our dear Lord, Christ Himself, said to His disciples whom He called to the priesthood: *'The Princes of the Nations,'* said He, *'have lordship over them, and those who are amongst the great have power. But it shall not be so with you. He who is great among you, let him be your minister. He who is chief, let him be the servant of all. For the Son of Man came not to be ministered unto, but to minister.'*

"Let us better remember, then, the holy rules handed down from our ancestors concerning the life and character of the clergy, which prohibit any churchman from being a merchant, usurer, hunter, or common player, or from bearing arms. Let us better remember the laws which prohibit the clergy from frequenting taverns, from having unlawful association with women; those laws, also, which command sobriety and modesty in vestment, and temperance in dress.

"Above all let those laws be recited once again which concern and pertain to you, most reverend Fathers and Lords Bishops, regarding your just and canonical elections, in the chapters of your churches, with the invocation of the Holy Spirit. For, because this is no longer done in these our days, and because prelates are often chosen more by the favor of men than by the grace of God, so, in consequence, we sometimes have Bishops too little spiritual, men more worldly than heavenly, wiser in the spirit of this world than in the spirit of Christ, possessing thus that awful thing, power without semblance of grace.

"The clerical and priestly part of the Church being thus reformed, we can then with better grace proceed to the reformation of the lay part, which indeed it will be very easy to do, if we ourselves have been reformed first. For the body follows the soul, and, as are the rulers in a State, such will the people be. If priests themselves, the rulers of souls, are good, the people in their turn will become good also. For our own goodness will teach others how they may be good more clearly than all other kinds of teaching and preaching. Our goodness will urge them on in the right way far more efficaciously than all your suspensions and excommunications. So, Lordings of the realm spiritual, if you wish the lay people to live according to your will and pleasure, you yourselves must first live according to the will of God, and thus—believe me, my Lords Bishops—you will easily attain what you wish in them.

"These, reverend Fathers and most distinguished brothers in Christ, are the things that I thought should be spoken concerning the reformation of the clergy. I trust that, in your clemency, you will take them in good part. If, by any chance, I should seem to have gone too far in this sermon—if, for example, I have said anything with too much warmth—forgive it me, and pardon a man speaking out of honest zeal, a man sorrowing for the ruin of the Church; and, passing by any incidental foolishness of mine own, consider the thing itself. Consider the miserable state and condition of the Church, and bend your whole mind and will to its reformation."

Dean Colet paused, gazing out over the heads of the congregation. The clerical benches sat still as stones, not a white rochet moving. Bishop Fitzjames' pale face had grown paler. The Franciscan secretary beside him wore a purple flush above the furled-back cowl of his brown robe. There was a shifting of limbs and a stir of conversation from the lay benches. The Duke of Suffolk looked back at Will Compton with a ribald wink.

"I *trust that, in your clemency, you will take my words in good part,*" he minced, in parody, from Colet's sermon. "Look at Bishop Fitzjames bending his whole mind to the Church's reformation, said reformation to begin with the reformation of Deans of St. Paul's who speak out of turn. But someone likes what Colet has to say—so far, at any rate. Just see how Henry grins."

It was true. The King grinned from ear to ear at the discomfort of his Lords spiritual. He said something to Cardinal Wolsey which made that crimson-robed prelate smile a little, too. It mattered less than nothing to the King's first minister, who already possessed the sees of Tournai, Bath, Lincoln and York, and the Deanship of Lincoln, not to count the revenues from the several small monasteries he had suppressed and the gold crowns he received as annual bribes from Maximilian and François—it mattered less than nothing to the Cardinal what Dean Colet thought or said. Accusations of simony and pluralism might catch in their coarse meshes the little fishes who were not strong enough to swim out of the net. A king-sized carp like himself could always break the heaviest cords at will, and even, if he chose, snap up such small crusading fins as Dean Colet. And some-day, if all went well—and so far all went very well indeed—the bland cleric on the King's left intended to add to his other benefices the greatest of them all: the see of Peter.

Only the Queen remained immobile amid the shifting kaleido-scope of color that moved restlessly from ham to ham in the royal pew. She sat there as stiff and silent in her severe Lenten black as an effigy of one of her queenly ancestors in the somber Escorial. Lent or no Lent, Henry's flamboyant taste for sartorial splendor was not to be denied. His auburn hair was bare in deference to the sacred edifice in which he sat. That single note was, however, sufficient condescension to the deity. Otherwise he blazed more splendid than a Spanish monstrance in his purple mantle lined with white satin, his doublet of slashed white and crimson silk, and his jeweled dag-ger that swung alongside a pouch of cloth of gold, both ornaments dangling from a brocaded belt.

A stillness fell over the benches, lay and clerical alike, as John Colet finally finished his long meditation, gave back the silver sal-ver and cup of water to the ministrant altar boy, wiped clean his lips with a linen strip, touched his rochet, and raised an eloquent right hand for silence.

"Now, my Lord King and Queen, and my Lord Cardinal," he began the second part of his sermon, "it is you, and no longer my Lords Bishops, from whom I must beg clemency for what I have to say next. But, whether ye yield indulgence to me or not, say it I must. Today hangs the Prince of Peace upon a cross; and today hangs by a thread the peace of England and of all Europe. And why? Because it fits well with the policies of ambitious Princes that the dogs of war be once again let slip after the bleeding hart of the world.

"But, my King and Lordings all, such dread decisions do not rightly lie with us. I tell you it is plainly laid down in the Gospels what we are to think in this matter. Remember what the Lord Christ said of the coin the subtle lawyer showed him. He pointed to the effigy of Caesar stamped upon the minted round and said: *Reddite Caesaris Caesari, et Dei Deo. Render unto Caesar the things that are Caesar's, and to God the things that are God's.* Mark well. The Lord Christ did not say to us: *Render unto Caesar the things that are God's.* Let Caesar stay on his throne, not squat on the impious altar of Moloch, the brazen devourer of bodies. Since Constantine's faroff day Caesars have been Christian. It is lawful, then, for Christian subjects to yield up to Caesar tribute when he asks it. But only tribute that is lawful; tribute of shekels and denarii; tribute of pounds and pence. Never tribute that wastes the patrimony of sons and squanders the livings of widows. Above all, not the unlawful tribute, the awful Moloch tribute of human lives which belong to God alone.

"Caesar is Caesar and will needs act like Caesar. But, my Lord King, is it not passing utterance monstrous when Christ falls to playing Caesar? When the Vicar of our heavenly Lord puts on the gold mask of a pagan emperor? It was no Holy League Pope Julius spawned but yesterday against the kingdom of France. It was, rather, an unholy league spawned of the devil. And so is its successor today an unholy league spawned of the devil. I tell you this new papal bull invoking war is as blasphemous a thing as any issued by the great Spanish bull who lately sat upon the chair of Peter. What has Christ's Vicar on earth to do with wars or rumors of wars? Let him bind up the wounds of the smitten and staunch the blood of the dying. His are the keys of the Kingdom of Heaven, not the keys of the armories of earth; not the keys of powder magazines and donjons.

"So much for the Pope who is our Holy Father and the Vicar of our Lord Christ. What of us men of England? What of you, my Lord King? And you, my Lady Queen? And you, my Lord Cardinal, who are both a priest and a statesman, and so have a dual reason for wishing peace? And you, Knights of the Council? And you, Lords

71

and Gentles all? Send not men out to die in an unjust quarrel. Dying is a fearful thing at any time. It is most fearful of all in war. When we die, it is well we die well. But few there are that die well in a battle. For how can men charitably dispose of anything when blood is their argument? The great conqueror, Julius, was great in war; but he died like any dog. That greater hero, Alexander, was even greater in war. But life left him empty, and in death this greatest of conquerors was pitiful. Our Lord Christ had nothing to do with war. He died, it is true—we are here today to bear witness to the manner of His passing. He died, but not as Julius and Alexander, those impious conquerors, died. He died our Lamb, not a ravening Lion who goes about seeking whom to devour. Do you, my Lords and Ladies all, follow the Lamb Christ to life; not the Lions, Julius and Alexander, to death and destruction!"

Master Colet's resonant voice rang like a trumpet over the hushed throng. He finished and knelt down there in the pulpit, covering his face with his hands. A confused babble rose from the audience. The Queen continued to stare straight ahead. King Henry had long since ceased to smile. He bit his lip; the royal gauntlets clutched the jewel at the end of his golden chain till the fine links snapped asunder. The grizzled old Duke of Norfolk barked out a grim laugh.

"Dean Colet is right," the old warrior said to his eldest son. "We need no war with France."

"He is also a brave man," said young Surrey in reply; "and a fair one. He distributes his buffets impartially."

Suddenly the brouhaha lulled as Henry, recovering, got to his six feet four of arrogant stature amid the hubbub. Flanked by Cardinal Wolsey and Queen Catherine, he swept out of the Chapel Royal. Two heralds blew a flourish on their silver trumpets and the ceremony was over. Suffolk nudged his friend, Will Compton.

"Well," he said, insinuatingly, "we got riccochets instead of broadsides. But, judging by his face, Henry was well able to gauge their range, if no one else could. What do you suppose Dean Colet meant by Julius and Alexander? Surely not a long-dead Roman, and an old Greek dead for even longer."

Old Norfolk, who looked on both Suffolk and Compton as idle popinjays, happened to jostle against them in the crush of people. He was not at all averse to growling out his own bluff soldier's answer to Brandon's languid question.

"He meant the Borgia pontiff, of course," he said gruffly, "and Julius his successor. I thought it shrewdly thrust."

Compton and Brandon accepted the exegesis but coolly disregarded the old moss trooper exegete who gave them this forthright gloss on the margin of courtly innuendo.

"It may be so," said Suffolk insolently, ignoring his fellow of Norfolk. "But how will Henry take it? Both he and Wolsey are the Pope's men; and *Defender of the Faith* is a pretty title for herald and pursuivant to bray forth on their trumpets when Harry meets François on the Field of the Cloth of Gold. *Anglorum Rex Henricus Fidei Defensor.* It has a fetching ring to it."

"So it has," said Compton patronizingly in the tone of one who is above all others privy to the monarch's secrets. "Assuredly it is a pretty enough title. But of Leo's making, remember. Popes Alexander and Julius are long since dead now. They say the Borgia had even burst and was rotten before they buried him."

Old Norfolk had not done with them yet. He tapped Suffolk familiarly with a battered leather gauntlet that was fitter far for the saddle than the court.

"Dean Colet meant Leo, too, my friends," he said evenly, through his teeth. "Make no mistake about that. Did you not catch his reference to the ravening Lion? Henry will be a wise man if he accepts Master Colet's sage and virtuous counsel."

"We shall see," said Charles Brandon coldly, addressing him directly for the first time.

Once outside the Chapel Royal Henry had gone straight to the garden of the Franciscan monastery that adjoined the Palace of Greenwich, and had there summoned to his side his Speaker of the House of Commons. Thomas More found the King sniffing a nosegay of fresh violets and gold-chaliced daffodils he had plucked from the border of one of the neatly sanded paths. Henry handed the flowers to him.

"For Mistress More to wear at Easter Mass," the King said gaily. "A pity there is but one Mass today. Yesterday I heard three Masses. Easter I shall hear five."

Thomas More, who understood the curious compulsions of his monarch's conscience and who knew, besides, that Henry often had the ceremonies curtailed in order to maintain his numerical quota, bowed.

"It is a seemly practice, my Lord King," he said politely.

"How many Masses do you hear, Sir Speaker?" asked Henry with interest.

"Usually, your Grace," said Thomas More, "one is all I have time for, except on Christmas Day."

"The Holy Mass," said Henry in an exalted tone, "is a sovereign remedy against the mortal sickness of heresy."

More's eyes twinkled. It was his most lovable weakness. He could never find it in his heart to resist a joke.

"Not in Dom Luther's case, Sire," he said with suspicious gravity.

"A bad monk," Henry pontificated with the utmost unction. "Doubtless he gabbled his Mass."

"Not so, Your Grace," More was audacious enough to correct the King. "His piety on the altar used to slow him to a snail's pace. The Roman canons liked to mock him for the time he took over saying Holy Mass. But then, Sire, is not Rome ever a stumbling block? It tries and sometimes corrupts the staunchest faith."

"Eh?"

Henry looked sideways at his Speaker. He loved Thomas More as well as he could love any man—more, much more, when one got down to it, than he loved those official favorites, Charles Brandon, Will Compton, and Frank Bryan, two of whom he had knighted and one dowered with an earldom—but he sometimes found it disconcertingly hard to tell if the fellow weren't laughing at him. Come to think of it, though, if those useless waterflies, Compton and Brandon merited knighthoods, why not this most faithful and least demanding of the King's good servants? Henry made a mental note to speak to his Master of Heraldry as soon as possible about the matter.

"And now," said Henry sententiously, hooking two fat thumbs into the lace loops of his doublet and rocking back and forth on the balls of his feet, "and now it is Dom Luther's turn to mock me. What did he call me for my *Defense of the Seven Sacraments?* You took care of the interminable correspondence."

"Among other things," said Thomas More smiling, as he ticked off the scurrilous epithets on his fingers, *"rex infelix, stolidissimus, delirus, sacrilegus; latro, asinus, porcus, truncus, antichristus; rex mendacii; damnabilis putredo, faeces latrinae; scurra levissimus; porcus Thomistica, et caetera, et caetera.* To translate a few of the choicer items— for the man is a master of invective, and artistry must needs be acknowledged, no matter how unseemly the manner of its manifestation: *a pig of a Schoolman; dung from a privy; a light-minded buffoon; a King of lies; robber, ass, swine, and half-wit.* My Fool, Henry Patenson, says the low names he calls you really sound even lower in Master Luther's High Dutch. Is my tally long enough? I could go on for some space. Dom Luther is very fertile of invention."

Henry threw back his handsome head and volleyed out peal upon peal of loud laughter till the monastery garden rang again.

"Faith, Sir Speaker," he choked, while the tears ran down his florid cheeks, "your count is quite long enough already. And you make it marvelous well. You must be an admirable tutor for Master Patenson. But, seriously, tell me something. Did you not think Master Colet's discourse just now smacked of Lutheranism a little?"

More shrugged his shoulders humorously. He had known the King would get around to Master Colet sooner or later, and he had done his witty best to make sure it should be later—after the Majesty of England had given vent to a hearty laugh or two.

"Master Colet did not call you lunatic, robber, or anti-Christ," he pointed out. "That in itself should be sufficient to clear him of any imputation of Lutheranism. I think Master Colet's fashion of utterance is still too classical to show any trace of Dom Luther's taint."

But the King was not to be satisfied with another witticism.

"Just the same," he said, no longer laughing, "I liked not what he said about the Pope and the French wars."

At once Thomas More showed himself every bit as serious as his royal master.

"Your Grace," he said respectfully but firmly, "on that especial point I think Master Colet is right."

The King appeared distressed.

"Master More!" he exclaimed. "Leo is the Vicar of Christ on earth!"

Thomas More was adamant.

"Let him stay so then," he stated, unyielding. "May I remind Your Grace that he is also an Italian Prince? He is an Italian Prince of great possessions, even as you are an English Prince of great possessions; and he is in league with other Christian Princes. It may hereafter so fall out that Your Grace and his Holiness may vary upon some points of your league together. Therefrom may grow breach of amity and war between you both, even as, in the recent past, within a single Pontificate the same Pope has been, at different times, first at war and then allied with both France and the Empire. As a member of Your Grace's Council I think it best to suggest that you commit yourself in public a bit more slenderly on this vexing question of the Pope's authority."

Henry beat his hands together and paced up and down the pleached alleys in evident agitation.

"Master More," he said, turning abruptly, "you surprise and sadden me. We are so much bound unto the See of Rome that we cannot do too much honor unto it."

"Not nearly so bound as your fathers were, Your Grace," persisted More. "The Statute of Praemunire has pared away the better part of the Pope's pastoral care in this Kingdom. It is a goodly statute."

"It is an abominable statute," fairly shouted the King, narrowing his little eyes in anger. "Let me, friend Thomas, whisper a word in your obstinate ear: whatsoever impediment there be to the contrary, we intend to set forth and publish Leo's authority to the uttermost. For we received from the See of Rome our crown imperial."

It was not the first time More had heard from Henry's own lips

76

this cryptic intimation anent the papal certification of the Tudor claim to the throne. Since the beginning of the Wars of the Roses royal authority had rested on shifting sands in England. At best it was a difficult matter to legitimize power, to sacramentalize possession. Far be it from the quizzical philosopher of history who had written *The History of Richard III* to stir up the treacherous bog water that sucked and gurgled about the squelchy tussock of the Tudor claim. No later than the previous reign Perkin Warbeck had drowned chasing that particular will o' the wisp over the Welsh marshes that the Tudors knew better than anyone else. No, it was enough for More as a mystic that the Archbishop of Canterbury had insured continuity by pouring the holy oils of kingship over Henry's broad brow. It was enough for him as a lawyer and constitutionalist that Henry derived succession from his father, Henry VII.

"Of that, Your Grace," he said skeptically, "I know nothing. But, Sire, we were speaking of peace and war. What has England to gain from an alliance with either France or the Empire? Or from playing the Pope's devious dynastic game? Chancellor Warham was a wise Chancellor and a great Churchman. He prized peace above all other worldly goods."

"So is my Lord Cardinal Wolsey, my new Chancellor, a shrewd man," said Henry, puffing out both his cheeks. "And it is his thought that the Pope is in the right in this matter."

"Even so, Your Grace," said More. "But shrewdness in itself is a somewhat lower quality than wisdom. And my Lord Cardinal happens to have a battle-ax of his own to grind which disqualifies him from judging impartially on these issues. The fief of Milan would be a sizable addition to the papal estates. I have heard it said in certain quarters that my Lord Cardinal would one day like to sit in Peter's chair."

Henry laughed aloud.

"You are a sharp observer, Sir Speaker," he said. "But is that a sinful ambition? Who would not like to sit in Peter's chair? I should like to sit there myself."

"So should I not, Your Grace," answered More equably. "But I do not presume to judge my Lord Cardinal. Judgment is a matter that lies between his Maker and himself. I merely observe that he is ambitious of the Papacy."

"You insinuate, nevertheless," said Henry, "that my Lord Cardinal is more concerned with his own possible future perquisites than with the safety and the comfort of the realm. Well, Thomas, I would have you know it is also my Lord Cardinal's opinion—and mine as well, mark you—that Tournai and Thérouanne have rich castles and fair demesnes."

"I am sure of it, Your Grace," said More. "They have also rich episcopal palaces and fair bishoprics with even richer revenues attached. However, besides the moral issue that they belong to the throne of France, your own great realm of England is already full of rich castles and fair demesnes—none richer or fairer in all Christendom. Your father built one at Westminster and another at Richmond. You were once pleased to compliment me, Sire, on some verses written on the death of the Queen, your sweet mother, Elizabeth of York."

The King had loved his mother dearly. More counted on that fact.

"I remember, I remember," said Henry, softened. "I mind me they were pleasantly mournful. Do you keep them still in memory? I should like to hear them once again."

Not many politiques have been able to carry on the art of diplomacy through quoting poetry written by their own hand. While the King pensively plucked another daffodil his Speaker recited:

> *"Where are our castles? Now where are our towers?*
> *Goodly Richmond, soon art thou gone from me;*
> *At Westminister, that costly work of yours,*
> *Mine own dear Lord, now shall I never see.*
> *Almighty God vouchsafe to grant that ye*
> *For you and your children well may edify.*
> *My palace builded is; and lo! now here I die."*

Tears stood in Henry's eyes—both from nostalgic sadness and from affectionate mirth. He put his arm familiarly around the Speaker's neck as they walked there in the monastery garden.

"Thomas, Thomas" he said. "I see your artful, honest drift. Thou art a good and honorable man. I respect thee for it. But there are better ways to build a fortune than the forthright way you take. Well, again you prevail. And, as usual, you have spoken more eloquently for others than for yourself. Master Colet's head is still secure. Let everyone have his own doctor, and let everyone favor his own. As for me, Masters Colet and More are the doctors for me!"

As Thomas More went straight from Greenwich to his Speaker's rooms in Westminster he reflected that, however rough going he had had with the King, he was likely to make even heavier weather out of the Bishops' delegation which was presently to wait upon him. He knew roughly what they wanted. It had something to do with the forthcoming Convocation for the Extirpation of Heresy which Master Colet had so auspiciously or—depending on the point of view—so inauspiciously inaugurated. He had heard that the Bishops intended to ask him to engage in formal controversy with the German heretic monk, Martin Luther; and he was more than willing to comply with this request. Already the Lutheran revolt had made the foundations of the Church quake. The fabric of society itself would be rent next. Thomas More, clear-sighted realist that he was, had no illusions about the Renaissance Papacy. He knew that, ever since the great schism of Avignon, things had not been altogether as they should be within the Roman Curia. The administrative arteries of the Church had hardened. They needed freeing at the hands of some such skillful leech as Hildebrand, the mighty ecclesiastical reformer of yesteryear. But he realized the danger of identifying man and office in one's strictures against evil and corruption. That was why Luther was wrong and Colet was right. If, after Luther's fashion of indictment, the vices of men should be imputed to the offices they held, not only the Papacy would fall. *Omne coelum ruat.* Kingship would go as well; and Parliament, and consulship, and every kind of magistracy. The people would find itself shorn of rulers, law, order itself.

If, however, at the bitter instigation of Bishop Fitzjames, the prelates had decided to include John Colet in their denunciations, then he intended to balk. The larger part of them would listen to him, too.

Of that he was sure. After all, he had done them yeoman service in the Hunne case three winters back, at a time when popular feeling ran high in the London hierarchy's regard, and when a Coroner's jury had brought in a verdict of murder against the Bishop's Chancellor of the London diocese. Richard Hunne had been a prosperous Merchant Taylor, a freeman of London, and an enemy of Bishop Fitzjames. Embittered by the death of a beloved child—and understandably so, taking into account the lovable weaknesses of human nature, the compassionate More had always thought—Hunne had refused to pay the priest the customary mortuary fee for the burial of his child. He was sued for this in an ecclesiastical court and lost the case. By then Hunne was almost choked with grief and resentment. He promptly brought an action in the King's Bench, under the statute of *Praemunire*, the grounds being that the legatine court, which had rendered the verdict against him, was a foreign tribunal and hence illegal. Bishop Fitzjames countered this new thrust with a charge of heresy. Hunne was then imprisoned by order of the Bishop of London in the Lollard's Tower where, early one bleak morning, he was found hanging from a timber balk in his cold cell. The Londoners raised a hue and cry against the detested prelate. The Coroner's Jury brought a verdict of murder against the Bishop's Chancellor— Fitzjames snarled that the City was so bent on heresy it would convict a clerk, "were he as innocent as Abel"—and, in desperation, Archbishop Warham asked Thomas More to pull the chestnuts out of the fire. More was able to do so, after he had carefully sifted the evidence and was convinced that, crazed by his troubles, the unfortunate Hunne had actually committed suicide. Had he reached the opposite conclusion, Bishops or no Bishops, he would have washed his hands of the matter. The devil himself always got a fair hearing in Thomas More's court. But not even Thomas More could dampen the anticlerical fury that now began to blaze in all its crackling fury against the unpopular Fitzjames. As a matter of fact, he thought that Fitzjames and his men were largely to blame for the serious plight they found themselves in. Legally, of course, they were in the clear—to More's lucid mind there was no doubt whatsoever about the mercer's having made away with himself. But, in cases involving the emotions, legality was hardly enough. He felt that there had been defects in Christian charity in the original instance of the priest's demanding the burial stipend, and later in the decision to thrash the ticklish issue out in the ecclesiastical court. So he had told the London Chancery a few stiff home truths about human nature. It had not gone down too well with Bishop Fitzjames, More had been informed. Frankly, he was a little surprised that the Bishop's Council had renewed their overtures to him.

His secretary had a pleasant fire burning in the Speaker's iron grate. There was still a good quarter of an hour left before the deputation was to wait upon him, so Thomas More, who did not have so very much time nowadays for the humanistic pursuits of his dearest delectation, picked up a copy of Lucian's *Necyomantia*. He was hard at work on it when his secretary opened the heavy door to announce their Excellencies, the Bishops of London, Lincoln, Chichester, Salisbury, and Winchester. More heaved a sigh as his practiced eye made out the exact complexion of the delegation that acknowledged his formal greeting. It was probably too much to have hoped for Warham—the old Archbishop was overburdened with official duties even as things stood. Fitzjames he was stoically prepared to endure. The Convocation, after all, was taking place within the confines of his diocese. But Richard Foxe of Winchester who, if he could have managed it on a certain memorable occasion, would have delivered over a boy burgess to the lethal wrath of Henry VII—surely, thought the Speaker with a wry quirk of his mouth that did not go unnoticed by men skilled in reading expression, surely he might have been spared this final cross.

Bishop Fitzjames began badly by picking up the *Necyomantia* with a sour smile.

"Another of your pagan philosophers, Sir Speaker?" he asked. "What is this one's claim upon your learned attention?"

"It is Lucian," said Thomas More shortly, with a flush of resentment.

"Then we have more important work in hand for you than Lucian, Master More," observed Fitzjames, flipping over the manuscript in disdain.

From any point of view it was a poor beginning.

"I assure you, my Lord Bishop," said More doggedly, "my old Lucian is well enough in his own way. He is a paragon of human reason. His *Necyomantia,* which you so lightly spurn, attacks in wittiest fashion the impositions of conjurors, the empty fictions of bad poets, the uncertain sparrings of pseudo-philosophers on every possible subject. No, my Lord Bishop, whether you know it or not, my old Lucian has much of profit in him. He defends our sovereign palisade of reason against the strong onslaughts of those who would fain take it by storm."

"Reason?" sniffed Bishop Fitzjames. "Reason is a pagan goddess. We of the new dispensation have long preferred to speak of faith. There lies our pearl and prize."

Thomas More's flush grew deeper still.

"I am afraid, my Lord Bishop," he said, "that Martin Luther would be in agreement with you on this point. What is it Master Luther says? *You must wring the neck of the beast, reason.'*"

The blow told. It was Bishop Fitzjames' turn to flush with anger. But he found an ally in More's old vulpine foe, Foxe of Winchester.

"What is Master Lucian's opinion as to the survival of the soul, Sir Speaker?" Foxe asked, innocently enough; or so it seemed at first glimpse.

Thomas More was too wary a campaigner not to spy out the trap.

"He is not sure of his own immortality, my Lord of Winchester," he said blandly. "But would you indict him of heresy for not knowing in advance what was not yet revealed—for not hearing the good tidings Abraham himself did not hear? Nor does it much disturb me, my Lord Bishop, to find Lucian unsure of his immortality. It does not shake my faith—why should I be disturbed by the opinion or lack of opinion of a pagan on matters which are among the chief mysteries of the Christian faith? Moreover, his uncertainty at least certifies his own humility. No, my Lord, we must esteem a man for what he is—if, of course, he is anything at all—not reprove him for what he is not because he never had a chance to be the thing in question. And old Lucian is a great champion of that god-given faculty, sweet reason. We could do, I think, with a little more reason

82

and a little less pious fabling in the seminaries which train our priests. If faith is the Mary, reason is the Martha of the human personality. They must dwell together as sisters, in amity and in the same household. Like man and maid betrothed they must tread a married lover's dance, quarreling sometimes but never severing from one another."

Their Lordships of Lincoln, Chichester, and Salisbury stayed uncomfortably silent. They knew from of old Thomas More's powers as a controversialist. They also respected him as a man; and, if the truth were known, they did not care overmuch for the extremism of their two outspoken colleagues of London and Winchester. They had come, finally, to ask the Speaker a favor, not to harangue him on mythical shortcomings in orthodoxy.

"Is it your veneration for reason, Master More," asked Bishop Foxe cunningly, "that leads you to contemn the professors of Cambridge?"

There is a famous proverb about a man's falling into the pit he digged for his enemy. Master More knew what his episcopal adversary was leading up to, and he rejoiced in a golden chance for a thrust in tierce. Old Sir John More had been unwilling to spend a single groat on suppling his son's wrist for the new sport of *escrime*, imported from France. But he had helped perfect young Thomas in the far tougher touch-and-go of dialectical fence. Bishop Foxe's "professors of Cambridge" were Erasmus' old opponents, the conservative enemies of his *Novum Instrumentum*, and of any vernacular translation of the New Testament. Thomas More metaphorically flexed his blade before he lunged.

"There, my Lordship, I confess you have me," he began guileless as a child, but a child who, like the Child in the Temple, possessed the mingled wisdom of the serpent and the dove. "I yield up my secular goddess, reason, to holy Revelation. Before the Sacred Scriptures those learned men you speak of are but tumblers and mountebanks of reason. The busy bees who buzz about the *Summa* make a pleasant summer humming in our ears. But their wings are sluggish next to the winged words of the living truth. To dance or to bend double like an acrobat is more difficult, I must confess, than to walk; and it is likewise easier to chew good bread than to grind potsherds between the teeth. But who would not prefer this honest toil of the evening table to the empty feats of fair day? And where is one to find better and more nourishing spiritual bread than that ground for us in the holy mills of God's own blessed words? No, the Cambridge students of Scotus and Aquinas are but kitchen scullions in the presence of the Queen of all books, the Holy Bible. My Lord of Winchester, you have prevailed. I give over my professors of Cambridge in favor of the book they prefer others not to read and will not read themselves."

There was a whiplash in the last remark; it cut Foxe and Fitzjames to the quick. His Grace of Chichester had the grace to smile; his Grace of Salisbury the even greater grace to laugh aloud. Fitzjames gave them both a black look.

"Your arguments are devilish cunning, Master More," said the Bishop of London viciously, "but specious. I turned them aside only yesterday after Maundy Service. A young cleric from the country up for the Convocation—William Tyndale was his name—you know him, I suppose?"

"I have not the pleasure," said Thomas More, bowing.

"Faith," said Fitzjames bitterly, "you do not know him. Yet you might have made him, Erasmus and yourself, between you, so infected is he with your ideas about vernacular translation. The young cub even had the audacity to propose that I stand his sponsor in an English translation of the Scriptures. I soon sent him packing, I can tell you, and with more than one flea in his provincial ear."

"That was a great pity, my Lord," said Thomas More coolly. "He might have served the Church well in his chosen project."

"Aye, so you say," continued Fitzjames even more bitterly than before. "Like Erasmus, perhaps. But it is my considered opinion that your runagate Dutch friend has not served the Church well in his chosen projects. And, barring Dean Colet and yourself, no one of influence supports him in these chimeras. No Cardinal—"

"Except," said More swiftly, recovering the old imp of laughter that became him so much better than the acrid gorgon of controversy, "except Cardinal Ximines, Primate of Spain. And, what would you say, my Lord Bishop, if I were to tell you that Desiderius Erasmus has twice refused the red hat—once from Adrian VI, and, just a few months ago, again from Leo X?"

"Refused a cardinalate?" said Fitzjames, caught off guard, literally gasping in disbelief. It was, to do him justice, a course of conduct he could not understand. But, whatever his antagonism to Thomas More, he knew that his old adversary never lied.

"Refused a cardinalate?" repeated Fitzjames. "On what grounds?"

"On the fantastic grounds," said More mischievously, "that it would be like putting a cat in petticoats."

For the second time in a row the joke was at the expense of Bishop Fitzjames. Taking pity on a choleric colleague, his more mellow Lordship of Salisbury had the tact to intervene.

"Our conversation is most pleasant and profitable, Sir Speaker," he said diplomatically. "But we come here on serious business. It is our mission's purpose to ask you to undertake a defense of Christendom in writing against the hurricane of heresy that is at present raging in Germany. Will you do it, Thomas More?"

The dancing laughter left More's eyes.

"I thank you for your trust, my Lords Bishops," he said gravely, giving his hand to Bishop Fitzjames who took it with good enough grace considering. "Yes, I will do it. The wind is rising indeed. It shall rise higher before it finally lulls."

The sea is never far from an Englishman's thoughts. More walked to the window and, with a spacious gesture, pointed to London River where the Thames was just nearing flood.

"Yes, my Lords," he said, and his eyes were far away. "Once again, as in the days of Noah, the tide is reaching flood. But the bow in the clouds will always shine forth in the end. As the sea shall never surround and overwhelm the land utterly, and yet, in its time, it has eaten many places in, and swallowed whole countries up, and made places all sea now that were one time fair and well-inhabited lands, and has, in return, surrendered dominion to the land in other parts still, even so, though the faith of our Lord Christ shall never be totally overwhelmed with heresies, nor the gates of hell altogether prevail against Christ's Church, still and all, while in some places it wins a new people, so in others may there by negligence be lost the old. We win, my Lords, and we lose. But in the end we win."

The great sea image swam before their eyes; the long surging periods boomed and rang in their ears.

"Fore God," exclaimed His Grace of Chichester, "well spoken, man! What a preacher the Charterhouse lost in you, Master More!"

"But what a champion the Church has gained!" said Bishop Foxe handsomely, taking the Speaker by the arm. "Sir Speaker, you are our man, and no one else!"

Thomas More's sea-gray eyes were still exalted.

"Now is the time of travail, the long years of toiling, like Jacob, for the promised bride. But when, in the fullness of time, the Church shall change her place and have heaven for her dwelling instead of earth, after the final judgment pronounced and given, when God shall with his spouse, this Church of Christ, enter into the pleasant wedding chamber to the bed of eternal rest and joy—then shall these scald and scabbed pieces scale clean off, and the whole body of Christ's holy Church remain pure, clean, and glorious, without wen, wrinkle, or spot."

There was silence for a long space. Then, with grudging admiration, the Bishop of London spoke:

"I have not known this side of you sufficiently, Sir Speaker. My right hand upon it. Archbishop Warham—though yesterday I did not think it—was right to designate you England's spokesman in this grievous matter. With God's good grace, now, the Lutheran tragedy shall not play itself out without let or hindrance."

The gray eyes began to sparkle again. Laughter, bubbling and pure, ever played like fountains in the sunny mind of More.

"Lutheran tragedy, my Lords Bishops?" he asked, as he saw them politely to the door. "If, *salve reverentia*, I may drag in by their dog ears my old secular classics again, I should say we had rather to do with a comedy fit for the Court's Yuletide revels. Luther and Melancthon married first—for the mortification, one supposes, of their pious flesh. Ulrich von Hutten has had a plurality of wives. Oecolampadius, with whom, I suppose, I must now cross swords in controversy, married only yesterday. Let others talk of the Lutheran tragedy. I think it is a comedy, my Lords. For it always ends in a marriage."

This time the Speaker's Attic sally was greeted by an answering ripple of laughter from the Bishops. It was the kind of joke they could understand and relish. When they had gone, Thomas More stood stock still for a long time. Then, with a sigh, he sat down at his desk again while the long gray day drew on. A fog was rising from the river now.

Late that night, when the last Good Friday devotions were over and done with, Thomas More sat down in his study in Crosby Hall. He lit two candles and, with a rueful smile, pushed aside the *Dialogues* of Lucian on which he had, by fits and starts, been working. Heaving a second long sigh, he headed a new parchment: *A Dialogue concerning Heresies and Matters of Religion.* But, once the title was set down, he stopped again. Master Luther could wait. Master Colet could not; and today's had been a mighty sermon. The Speaker's fluent quill began to race over the vellum:

"Carissime Decane Joanne: Today in the Chapel Royal. . . ."

It was as well. There would not be many more letters written to John Colet. Before the end of September of the following year Erasmus would thus mourn the first of the high Oxford company to go to his eternal home: *He now is safely enjoying Christ Whom he always had upon his lips and at his heart.* John Colet would be lying then, lapped in lead, by the side of the choir in the great cathedral of St. Paul's under a simple monumental stone, inscribed, and, for once, without exaggeration:

> *Joannes Coletus, Henrici Coleti iterum praetoris Londini filius, et hujus templi decanus, magno totius populi moerore, cui, ob vitae integritatem et divinum concionandi munus, omnum sui temporis fuit chariss. . . .*

Master Colet Preaches a Sermon

*Here lies John Colet,   son of Henry Colet,   once mayor
of London,   and Dean of this Church,   mourned greatly
by the people, by whom, for his great purity of life
and his godlike gift of preaching,   he was the most beloved of all his time. . . .*

So John Colet would have gone before. But the young Oxford
student who once played *Antigone* for Master Colet still had a long
race to run.

INTERIM: CHELSEA

The bees of Netherhall and the rosemary of Chelsea had finally been brought together. Chelsea was the last and loveliest of his comely houses. He had planted the rosemary with his own hand and watched it run riot over the garden walks that led down to the river stairs. His rosemary still grows in Chelsea. Carlyle sniffed up its fragrant snuff of spring. Gilbert Chesterton touched it with his walking stick. When the German bombers roared over London, spawning their swart eggs of death on the body of the bleeding City, they burned and blasted, among other fair closes, the green gardens of Chelsea. But the rosemary only sprang up the thicker in the bomb craters alongside the fernseed that begets invisibility and is sacred to those fays John More and Mother Maude once read of one winter night now far, far in the past. They are herbs of power, the rosemary of More, and the fernseed of Midsummer Night. With Henry's newborn daughter, the little maid Elizabeth, it would be farewell, rewards and fairies, one of these fine days; farewell, fragrant rosemaried remembrance of that which had been England. The fairies would go, for a time, as would the gracious maid and mother who was Mary, Lady of Walsingham's starlit way, Lady of St. Botolph's; Mary, gentle Rose of Sharon. But the rosemary would keep on growing; and the fernseed would steal back; and, in the end, the Lady of the Rose as well.

Chelsea was a noble site. Henry had a royal manor there. The Bishops of Winchester maintained a lordly house next to the Parish Church of All Saints. Then, on a rising ground, embowered in pleasant meadows and wooded hills, came the sweet land More had bought and built on. The Great House was reared in 1524. Behind it lay gardens and stables; and, at the end of the long garden, a chapel, a gallery, and a library. Holbein had walked in his gallery; Erasmus and the King in his library. In his chapel, however, he entertained none but heavenly guests, with the sole exception of quiet John Larke, Rector of All Saints. He had liked John Larke as well as he had liked any man; and he had helped him rebuild Chelsea Church. The More unicorns and Moor's head crest adorned the east window; the western capital bore, carved on it in effigy, his Chancellor's mace.

Each night before bed he had led the family in night prayers: three *psalms*, Miserere, Ad Te, Domine, Levavi, *and* Deus Misereatur Nostri, *together with the* Salve Regina *and* Collect, *and the* De Profundis *for the holy souls who, alas, now that the chantries were abolished, had no one to pray for them. Erasmus had twitted him once on having no voice; and he had replied, laughing, that if he had no ear for music, at least he had a great will to worship. On Good Friday the family would all gather in the New Building—as he called the edifices which comprised his library, his gallery, and his chapel— there to hear secretary John Harris read the Passion through aloud. At table, after the Carthusian fashion, one of his daughters always read a passage of Scripture. But that was before the meal was finished. Afterward came Henry Patenson's turn to bring forward his own uncanonical commentaries on quite un-Scriptural topics.*

For under the More rooftree people laughed as well as prayed; only dicing was forbidden, and profaneness. He wondered now, in the Tower, if, perhaps, there hadn't been almost too much laughter. But then, he reflected with a rueful smile, the Scots were right when they said in their rough northern tongue that a man maun dree his ane weird and his ane nature. God had seen to it that it was both his nature and his destiny to laugh. Old Vergil had written of the tears that lie at the heart of things. With his own eyes he had come to gaze on the darkness that also lies tight coiled about the heart of things. But, in his inmost soul, he was sure that, in addition, there was laughter somewhere in the heart of things. Sunt lacrimae, tenebrae, et nugae rerum; *and, for him, the greatest of this human trinity was laughter. The tears cried out for faith, the darkness for hope, the laughter—for what? He thought that the laughter must be closest to love, to grace itself.*

Even in the writing he had done at the Bishops' instigation laughter had bubbled forth. They had not bargained for it; he had done his best to restrain it. But there it was. Friar Tuck and Maid Marian had danced their antic greenwood hay throughout his long, dull controversy with Tyndale. The "limping goodwife of the bottle at Bottle's Wharf" had bobbed up from nowhere during his tedious confutation of Friar Barnes. But, then, he was ever at heart half a giglot— and more than half, too. His first and chief comfort was always in

God; his second in a jolly jape. Like the nodding parishioner in the anecdote he could not long endure to hold up his head and hear talking of heaven, unless now and then in between—as though heaven were heaviness, forsooth!—he could be refreshed with a merry foolish tale of earth. But, on second thought, if heaven were not heaviness, then it must needs be lightness. And is not lightness levity, and is not levity laughter? Gravity was heaviness; was being earthbound. The angels knew not gravity. The greatest saints had levitated. Perhaps—who knew, whether in the body or out of it? God knows—perhaps, when all was said and done, heaven was laughter. Which, as a necessary corollary, was why there was so precious little laughter down here on earth and why, what there was of it, lasted so short a time. Henry had been able to laugh once. Well, God be praised, he could still laugh, if Henry couldn't.

Thomas More began to chuckle there in the Tower. Idle whimsies like this made him realize in retrospect why he had insisted on setting the ménagerie next to the chapel. The aviary glinted with the plumage of exotic birds; the wire cages swarmed with every animal he had been able to buy or wheedle from the ship captains who were his great good friends, thanks to brother-in-law John Rastell. Among others he owned a fox and a beaver and a weasel. Oh, yes, and a monkey! It did not do to forget Brother Marmoset. Lord, no! He had stopped short only of the lions in the Tower. Well, he had had his fill of their roaring since.

He always thought there was a great mystery about the animal creation. It, too, was involved in the Fall. It, too, must undergo redemption in time. Perhaps it, too, had a chance of some kind of survival out of time. He was more than half serious when he had written, in the Second Book of Utopia, *about that considerable sect among the Utopians which believed that the souls of brute beasts were immortal and everlasting, but—he had made haste to add— which also believed that their souls were nothing to be compared with men's, neither were they ordained nor predestinate to like felicity. It was, he supposed now, a foolish belief for so wise a folk as the people of King Utopus. Or, on further consideration, was it? For, though they did not suffer fools gladly, the Utopians yet took "singular delight and pleasure in Fools." There was a difference after all. There was a kind of folly which was like the innocence of children, and had not He said that unless a man becomes as a little child he will find the gates of heaven locked against him?*

No, it was not so easy as the rationalists of Cambridge might think. Perhaps old Mother Maude, with her eternal talking beasts, was nearer the truth than they. The great Aquin whom they pretended to understand had said once that all things return unto mystery. Who could tell now how it had been in the beginning, when the animal creation had first stood suppliant about the Tree and Adam named the animals by the names they yet bore?

He had told Hans Holbein once, as the two of them strolled through the ménagerie, that God was both Maker and Makar; i.e., both Creator and, to use the good old Scots equivalent, Poet. If man had been made after the image and likeness of God, so, in another way, had the beasts. Man expressed the rationality of God, and the beasts His tameless beauty and power. The peacock's tail was the rainbow wheel of Apocalypse; the tiger's furred pelt revealed the same fierce pencil of lightning that barred both the tawny jungle tendon and the indigo jungle sky. Leviathan and Behemoth reflected omnipotence unleashed; the lamb—as the Lamb Himself had pointed out—the incredible gentleness of divinity. It followed, by reasonable analogy, that God the Artist would appreciate human acknowledgment of His efforts. For his own humble part, Thomas More was very ready to testify how cool the pool, how sweet the grape, how iridescent-fleet the humming bird, how striped the zebra, and how odd the aardvark.

So were his daughters ready to attest the same, and his son John, and his stepdaughter, Margaret Giggs, and his stepson, Thomas Colt, and young Alice Middleton, and their wives and husbands and tutors and friends, including the gay young wife of Sir Thomas Elyot whose treatise on education, the Book Named the Governor, *was one of the fairest seedlings he and Erasmus had ever brought to goodly birth. They all belonged to that household circle of his which Desiderius liked to call Plato's Academy on a Christian footing, where the students were enticed with sweetmeats and chastened* with peacock feathers. Dame Alice herself was not quite so ready to fall in with such whimsies—though she was immensely taken with one member of the ménagerie, the monkey which used to tug at her skirts as she prayed. Her membership in the Academy was limited to mastery of the harp, the lute, the monochord, and the flute. A considerable achievement in itself, no doubt, but she never scaled the Parnassian slopes whereon, in 1529, More's daughters, Margaret, Elizabeth, and Cecily, disported before the King's Grace in a kind of philosophical tournament of Henry's own contriving. Nor could she follow them in their excursions among the heavenly bodies, with Master Nicholas Kratzer, Licentiate and Astrologer of Munich, and Fellow of Corpus, Oxford, at hand to descant on the miraculous clockwork of the Eternal Workman. Henry himself came quite often to hear Herr Kratzer.

The Chancellor sighed as he remembered how he and the King would go up onto the palace leads at night, under the blazing stars, and there discuss Boethius, fate, foreknowledge, the music of the spheres, the grave world spirits of the neo-Platonists, the chain of being, and the great cosmic dance. That was before Mistress Nan's green emerald stars of eyes totally eclipsed the sun and moon and Primum Mobile for Henry. He thought now on the last evening the King and he had thus spent together, stargazing and conversing affectionately, with the Galaxy shining in pale winter radiance overhead. Before they descended again, in midnight's chain-mail chill, for what was to be—although More did not know it at the time—their last star-walk together, he had quoted to Henry two lines from elvish Chaucer's old Parlement of Foules:

> And rightful folk shul gon, after they dye,
> To hevene; and shewede hym the Galaxye.

He hoped now with his whole heart they might all be merry again together in heaven; looking down then, not up, on the Galaxy, he and Henry and Catherine and Queen Anne, too, poor creature, if only half were true of what he heard of late regarding matters between herself and the King. It had all been very pleasant, those long evenings at Chelsea and Westminster and York House. When he wanted to—and in those days he had wanted to quite often—Henry could be the boonest of boon comrades. More had written to John Fisher once: "He is so affable and courteous to all men that each one thinks himself his favorite, even as the Citizens' wives imagine that Our Lady's statue at the Tower smiles upon them as they pray before it."

He had ridden down from Dover once with Catherine and Henry to keep the feast of Pentecost at the shrine of Canterbury's holy blissful martyr, Archbishop à Becket, by rite of canonization, Thomas, Saint of the Universal Church. The Emperor Charles, who had landed at Hithe with the Queen of Aragon only the day before, cantered on his aunt Catherine's right, and Cardinal Wolsey, on a pillion of scarlet, in fine crimson satin lined with black velvet and a tippet of sables about his neck, sat his horse on the Queen's left. But Thomas More, at Henry's express request, rode next to the King all the long way. And together they had knelt before the shrine of Saint Thomas.

Thomas More shook his head sadly. Rosemary always mingled with rue at Westminster and York House. But naught but rosemary grew over the flagged and sanded walks of Chelsea. Its perfume wafted in through the curtained windows of the dining room in the Great House, touching with trailing fingers of memory the fireplace, the clock case, the tapestry-covered cupboard, Dame Alice's flower pots and elbow chair, kissing the spinning wheel and the books on the large center table round which the family used to gather in the evening. They had been reading Seneca, he remembered—both the Epistles and the Oedipus—when the dread summons came that last day of all the days he had spent in his comely house.

A vagrant whiff of honeysuckle sweetness floated in through the dank Tower grate that rusted over his head. The Tower bell tolled nine of the clock of a soft July evening. Mother Maude used to say it took nine tellers to mark a man. He wondered how many strokes of that same beating bell it would take to mark the passing of a Chancellor. It had been ten for Buckingham—the ax had fallen exactly at ten of the clock—and eight for Bishop Fisher; but only six for the eight monks of the Charterhouse who had gone to Tyburn so short a while before he, too, must go. Well, he would soon know.

But rosemary coiled its loving tendrils round the bell ropes of

94

*brighter bells than the Tower's bronze giant. The bells of Willesden
had rung merrily for Elizabeth More and William Dauncey, son of
Sir John Dauncey, Knight of the Body to Henry VIII; and, with a
second gay campanile clamor that fluttered the doves again that same
golden morning of September, 1525, for little Cecily More and Giles
Heron, son of Sir John Heron, Treasurer of the Chamber to the King.
Latest of all had he heard the bell tower of Barnborough rock for the
nuptials of young John More and pretty Anne Cresacre; and before
them, at Saint Stephen's Walbrook, for darling Margaret More and
son William Roper. Besides these of his own flesh and blood, Margaret Giggs had been married from the Great House to John Clement,
Reader in Greek at Oxford and Court Physician to Henry; from it
John Harris, his beloved secretary, had been espoused to Dorothy
Colly, Margaret Roper's maid. And ever the pealing bells had clashed
for joy in silver-chiming epithalamium.*

*They had shouted so twice for himself and four times for his father.
Soon he would keep a grimmer tryst than with small Jane or faithful Alice. The fleshless bridegroom grinned at his shrinking soul. He
remembered Emperor Hadrian's tender lines of twelve hundred
years before:*

> *Animula vagula blandula,*
> *hospes comesque corporis,*
> *quae nunc abibis in loca*
> *pallidula rigida nudula*
> *nec ut soles dabis iocos!*

*Poor, trembling, quaking little soulkin! Now shall you go into the
abodes of darkness where there will no longer be the jests you loved
in life! But a newer Roman than old Hadrian, Tuscan Dante, put it
better in his great Purgatorio: "From the hand of Him Who loves her
before she is, there issues like a little child that plays, with weeping
and laughter, the simple soul." There had been more laughter than
weeping in his life. God grant that at the end he make a good and
holy death. As the last resonant clapper-stroke quivered into a silence
broken only by the shrill chittering of the Tower bats, Thomas More
crossed himself there in his solitary cell.*

95

CHAPTER VI

MASTER CROMWELL READS A BOOK:

Evening, Spring, 1525

SOMETIME during the hard winter of 1469-1470 a turbulent knight by the name of Sir Thomas Malory, one time follower of the rebel Duke of Warwick, and recreant to His Majesty, Edward IV, wrote down in prison these last words upon the last page of his parchment manuscript:

> *Here is the end of the book of King Arthur and of his noble knights of the Round Table, that when they were whole together there was ever an hundred and forty. And here is the end of the death of Arthur. I pray you all, gentlemen and gentlewomen that heareth this book of Arthur and his knights, from the beginning to the ending, pray for me while I am alive, that God send me good deliverance, and when I am dead, I pray you all pray for my soul. For this book was ended the ninth year of the reign of King Edward the Fourth, by Sir Thomas Maleore, knight, as Jesu help him for His great might, as he is the servant of Jesu both day and night.*

The same chill season that saw the completion of "this noble and joyous book entitled *Le Morte Darthur*," also witnessed the birth of a long-nosed Italian boy who would one day deal a more dolorous stroke to the high company of chivalry than ever Mordred did. Unlike Mordred he was no bastard; no King of Faëry was his uncle-father. But he slew an idea and an ideal as surely as Mordred slew the haute King Arthur in that last mythical battle "westward towards Salisbury." And the great monarchs of his day—Henry, François, Charles—were glad to play the recreant roles of foresworn Lancelots.

In Machiavelli's day fairyland went back to Avalon with Arthur. Meanwhile, for the century of *Il Principe* was also the century of

Utopia, a cooler, more Platonic elfland took its place. And, as usual, Rome won the campaign. *Morte Darthur, Il Principe,* and *Utopia* would all survive among the master books of the world; but there would be a difference in the manner of their survival. *Utopia* would continue to be a stimulus, a snare, and a good joke forever, depending on who it was who read it. *The Death of Arthur* would help bring back life to the most regal of man's faculties, the sovereign imagination. The life of *The Prince* would bring death to many souls and bodies.

Many men were to read *Il Principe.* None would ponder it to greater profit to themselves and greater damage to others than Master Thomas Cromwell, son of a man who kept a petty beerhouse and blacksmith's forge on the south bank of the Thames, just above London. He first came on Machiavelli's book while serving as a mercenary soldier in Italy—a fact, incidentally, which would surprise most of Master Cromwell's friends and enemies alike; but not his servants. Friends and enemies rarely know a man for what he really is; servants invariably do. Though his intimates knew him for an adventurer extraordinary, they always supposed that his usual weapons of intrigue were pen and purse; and that both these powerful instruments were controlled by a coldly astute brain. They were right about the brain. Cromwell was one of the cleverest Machiavellians who ever drew breath. But he had been a soldier, too, and a good one in his day, even if, at first sight, his waddling gait and toadlike corpulence did not suggest such a role. A second glance at Master Cromwell was sufficient to correct this superficial impression. Set deep in his doughy face were little eyes that glinted cold and sharp as slivers of steel.

Cold and sharp as slivers of steel. Yes, cold and sharp were the operative words for a proper understanding of Master Cromwell. Under the floury paste of his face coiled a mind and will of tempered steel. Coldness lodged at the very heart of his being. He was that most dangerous of mortals: a completely passionless human. It was fatally easy to make a mistake in his regard. Henry did so. When the King, who early developed a strong dislike for this new creature of Wolsey's, drew a knave at cards, he used to say he held a Cromwell. It was a dual error to speak so. Thomas Cromwell was by no

means a mere knave, and as yet no man had held him. Rather did he
hold men.

Cardinal Wolsey's Treasurer of York House was simultaneously
of the past and of the future; which was the basic reason why, for so
long a time, he was able to dominate the present. The sources of his
strength lay rooted in the distant past; the tentacles of his influence
were to stretch far into the future. In physical appearance he was
curiously atavistic; an archetypal churl crouched over a charcoal
pit in some immemorial forest; a squat Saxon swineherd fattened
like his pigs on the mast of the Kentish fens. His new master, Cardinal Wolsey, for all his faults, stood for the Roman organization the
Normans had brought, along with their grim bartizans and strong
granite columns, into the body politic of England. Henry Tudor
embodied, in part at least, the extravagance of an earlier and less
stable tradition. The evil flutes of a Celtic fairyland blew seductively
across the most bizarre of his excesses; his Welsh pulse sometimes
beat to a more ancient music than either the Normans or the Romans
knew. His court was simultaneously out of the Renaissance and out
of the *Mabinogion*. There were times when Merlin seemed more
than an old wives' tale to Henry. But Thomas Cromwell was rooted
in the river mud of pre-Norman Anglia; and, for a time, the swineherd, in league with an Italian realist he knew only in the pages of
a book, would control the kingdom.

As for the future, Thomas Cromwell was as much the archetypal
New Man as he was the archetypal churl. The tight-fitting black
biretta, with the velvet ear lappets that came far down on his thick
neck, was not very high in the crown; but already it had begun to
cast in prophecy the shadow of a later century's tall top hat. The
capitalist of Birmingham was implicit in the moneylender of Henry's
court. For all his greasy backstairs beginnings and his hole-in-corner
upward clamber, Master Cromwell had a way of exuding solid
respectability and unimpeachable success. It was characteristic of
his dispassionate, phlegmatic temperament that he had even now
begun, in his own mind at least, to translate the Machiavellian dicta
into respectable copybook maxims. The Italian tiger had been neu-

tered that he might seem more presentable in the parlor. But his teeth and claws remained unimpaired; and he would, perhaps, guard the royal mouse hole all the more effectively for the very fact of his gelding.

Thomas Cromwell had come up the hard way; but always steadily, never faltering. So far as any one could tell for sure, he had no inordinate traffic with women. There may have been something of the sort once. One of the few things really known about him, for example, was that his leaving England for an Antwerp clerkship under the assumed name of Smith had had something to do with a youthful indiscretion. Then, again, it was quite as likely that same early scrape had more to do with a falsified account than with a ruined girl. After Antwerp he had gone into the great banking house of the Frescobaldi in Italy. Sometime in the neighborhood of the year 1513 he had slipped back into England where, in the dirty lanes and alleys of London, he had combined a shady law practice with moneylending, blackmail, speculation in wool, and bribe taking on a rather large scale. He became marvelously adept as pander and go-between. Somewhere in the shabby course of his worldly ascent and Avernine descent he managed to set himself squarely across the resplendent path of Cardinal Wolsey. The butcher's son knew a good agent when he saw one. So, roundabout 1514, Wolsey appointed the son of the publican collector of his swelling revenues and general agent without portfolio; for, in the beginning, it did not seem prudent for the great ecclesiastic to acknowledge his dealings with such as Cromwell had been and was. A little later Cromwell came out into the open as John Allen's first assistant in the ugly task of liquidating those small monasteries Wolsey had marked down for dissolution in order that their revenues might be put at the service of the splendid new Oxford colleges the Cardinal was then setting up. Cromwell rapidly became a past master in the gentle art of polite extortion, here wringing 2000 marks from the Abbot of Peterborough, there wresting 300 pounds from the cellarer of St. Bartholomew's. He liked this aspect of his new connection. The margin of profit was far greater than in his previous petty operations; the margin of safety equally so under the aegis of the Cardinal's broad-brimmed red hat.

In the early 1520's Wolsey found a way of insinuating his new agent into Parliament where, at Blackfriars in April of 1523, Thomas Cromwell delivered his famous speech against the interminable French war. The performance was one of the Cardinal's subtler coups. People had been speaking a bit too openly at the time about my Lord Cardinal as the Pope's man and the Emperor's man instead of what, as Chancellor, he should have been, the King's man. Moreover, at this precise twist in the serpentine convolutions of a devious course, it suited the Chancellor's book to ease the pressure on the French a little and, incidentally, to foul the otherwise too straight trail that led from the door of the archiepiscopal palace to the grimy portal of Cromwell. So Thomas Cromwell, tongue in cheek, uttered, at the instigation of Thomas Wolsey, an eloquent protest against war. It was full of fulsome phrases about not risking the King's life in battle.

It was full of quotable references to the English outposts on French soil as "ungracious foxholes." It battened on the popular English prejudice against the Scots. It pleased almost everybody. It furthered Wolsey's tortuous policy of tergiversation and double-cross. It literally made Cromwell's fortune by, among other things, calling the King's attention to his astuteness for the first time. That address was now two years in the past. The time had come, Thomas Cromwell thought, to call himself to the royal attention again. He believed he knew just how it could be done. Messire Niccolo Machiavelli would be his skeleton key this time to unlock the door of the King's private closet. And, for a welcome change, my Lord Cardinal could play the role of go-between for him. He had, Heaven knew, played that same graceless part many times for my Lord Cardinal.

So now the publican's son waited for the butcher's son in the butcher's son's regal palace of York House. Quite evidently the smell of beer clung longer to a man than the reek of suet. For in his crimson robes, his red biretta, his sumptuous silver pectoral cross and great bronze chain of office, the tall, bland Cardinal-Chancellor looked every portly inch the gentleman he most distinctly wasn't; and, standing respectfully before him, *Il Principe* in one pudgy hand and his lappeted cap in the other, the short, heavy-set Treasurer of York House looked, as a matter of sober record, much, much less than what he actually was. Looked, in fact, with his cropped bullet head and utter lack of civil presence, not even an under-steward but very like the head turnkey of a prison.

Before inviting Cromwell to sit down on a leather-gilt chair, stamped with his cardinalate arms, Wolsey opened one of the leaded windows of his water palace—a latticed casement that swung inward onto his great candlelit gallery and outward onto the murmuring Venetian darkness that was the Thames in spring. He inhaled the honeysuckle-freighted air with all the delicate gusto of an epicure of sensation. Then, remembering that the dread sweating sickness was abroad again, he hastily sniffed the jeweled and hollowed orange filled with aromatic comfits that always rode in the Cardinal's scarlet Cordovan pouch.

"Good even, Master Cromwell," he said, extending his turquoise ring for the Treasurer to kiss. "What make you from Italy?"

Cromwell crossed his black hose comfortably and leaned back in the chair.

"Well, my Lord Cardinal," he said. "I may say very well. Very well indeed. Our affairs in that country are all wound up. The Venetians carry your message to the Emperor. The Milanese your message to the French. And here is the book I spoke of. You have the necessary Italian to understand it, if the King has not."

Wolsey arched his blond brows in an unspoken question. It was not at all like Thomas Cromwell to break into his few hours of retirement with idle chatter about an Italian book.

"So," he said, tilting it in his large, well-tended hands. "You have turned Platonist on us, Master Cromwell? You should show this volume to the author of *Utopia*, your parliamentary fellow at Blackfriars. He has much more of a taste for such Italianate curiosities than I. What did you say it is called?"

Thomas Cromwell showed his teeth in a mirthless grin.

"I did not say what it is called, my Lord Cardinal," he said. "But I shall now. It is called *Il Principe*. By one Messire Niccolo Machiavelli, a most acute Florentine who has served Lord Cesare Borgia, and who is not a Platonist at all. Plato published his dreams. Messire Niccolo scorns dreaming. He allows more to experience than to speculation. Reason is his goddess as Venus is other men's. He here lays down maxims and observations whose truth is confirmed by everyday experience. He writes of things as they are, not as they should be. I do not think my Utopian colleague would find Messire Niccolo very edifying. He is not, as a matter of fact, edifying at all. But he is most instructive. You, my Lord Cardinal, would profit much from him."

Wolsey hefted the book appraisingly.

"*The Prince*," he said, musing. "An ambiguous title."

"But not, my Lord," said Cromwell swiftly, "an ambiguous book. I know of no other book quite so unambiguous as this one in both statement and effect. I recommend you dip into it, my Lord. It will serve your purpose as well as Henry's, and Henry's purpose as well as yours. Listen."

He took the book from Wolsey's hands and began to read from it aloud, punctuating the sentences with short jabs of his stubby fingers.

> "*It is honorable to seem mild and merciful and courteous and religious and sincere, and indeed to be so, provided your mind be so rectified and prepared that you can act quite contrary on occasion. And this, too, must be premised: that a Prince cannot observe all those things exactly which make men be esteemed virtuous, being oftentimes obliged for the preservation of his state to do things inhuman, uncharitable, and irreligious.*"

Cromwell paused a little in his reading to see how Wolsey took it. The Cardinal had laid aside all affectation of indifference now. He pursed his lips and drummed with long powerful fingers on the carven arm of his chair. The Treasurer of York House smiled to himself as he marked the effect *Il Principe* was having on the great master of York House.

"I think," Thomas Cromwell said significantly, "Henry will like that qualifying clause: *for the preservation of his state.* Like Charity it is broad enough to cover a multitude of sins. And Henry's estate is great and wide. It takes much covering."

The drumming fingers stopped.

"That is all very well for the King," said Wolsey. "But what of me, Master Cromwell? What is there in your book for the King's first minister?"

Cromwell's face creased in a smile. It was a sinister enough tableau, red-lit as it was inside by the flaming cardinal robes and outside by the crimson sunset.

"How like you this, my Lord Cardinal?" asked Thomas Cromwell. And he read aloud:

> " *Princes leave things of injustice and envy to the ministry and execution of others, but acts of favor and grace to be performed by themselves.*"

The Cardinal's fine baritone sounded petulant in reply.

"Why, I like it not over much," he expostulated. "How should I? Your book, Master Cromwell, leaves me the bad name and Henry all the good game. It is a book for a Prince, not for his minister."

Master Cromwell shrugged his shoulders.

"Say you so?" he asked insinuatingly. "It must then needs be so. It is a good book for a Prince. It is a bad book for his minister. For all his ministers, one might add. But, my Lord Cardinal, are you not a Prince already, and may you not one day be a greater Prince than even Henry? What is it you want most, my Lord Cardinal? First?"

"The French war," said Wolsey, ruminating, speaking automatically, almost as if under a mesmeric spell.

"My book shall help you to that end," said Cromwell softly, taking the Cardinal by his scarlet sleeve. "Listen now:

> 'A *Prince should have no other aim or thought, nor select anything else for his study, than war and its rules and discipline; for this is the sole art that belongs to the ruler.'*"

103

He tapped a podgy forefinger on the page.

"Will not that passage chime in with Henry's very thoughts on politics, even as you have molded them? But impress upon the King that he must always use English troops. It is a hard rule, but there is no other road open. Englishmen must die for his aims. It is too dangerous otherwise. Listen, my Lord Cardinal."

The diabolical prelection continued while, in horrified fascination, the prelate-student listened.

"In mercenaries cowardice is the danger, in auxiliaries, valor; and the wise Prince has always avoided these arms and turned to his own, choosing rather to lose with them than to conquer with others, for a victory won by the arms of others is never a real one."

Master Cromwell looked up from his reading, lidless eyes fixed coldly on the Cardinal's.

"So," he said bluntly. "You have your French war, and the way to wage it as well. And with the French war the gratitude of the Spanish Emperor. And with Charles' gratitude—who knows? Perhaps nomination to—but do you still take my meaning, my Lord Cardinal? Charles elected Adrian of Utrecht at the last electoral conclave. The old Pope is on his deathbed this very week. The Imperialists control nine votes out of thirty-nine, and can sway twelve others. It is more than enough. Perhaps the election may light on the head of Wolsey of England this time. But I anticipate. What else do you want, my Lord Cardinal? Want with all your heart and soul? Tell me your dearest heart's desire."

Somewhere, swathed in the duplex crimson folds of his suave statecraft, there lurked a strange and very attractive direct honesty in Thomas Wolsey.

"I keep no secrets from you, Master Cromwell," he said simply. "More than anything else on earth I crave with all my heart the throne of Peter."

There also dwelt somewhere within him the relics of a vestigial humility.

"Except that," he added, "I sometimes fear I am not spiritual enough for that heavy task."

The shy and unexpected disclaimer literally jerked a retort from Thomas Cromwell; and Thomas Cromwell was a man not easily surprised.

"Not spiritual enough for the throne of Peter?" he gasped.

Then, recovering himself:

"It is true, my Lord Cardinal, I have known men more spiritual in my day than you. But none of them Cardinals and great Princes of the Church. And few of them Bishops, though John Fisher of Rochester is as clean a priest as any who ever drew on surplice. But all things human are necessarily relative, my Lord. Comparatively speaking you are as pure a man as the Italian whoremasters who have sat upon that throne of late—and as shrewd as they, to boot. I tell you, my Lord Cardinal, this is the book for you. Since Fortune is a strumpet, not only can she be taken easily—she is better raped. Listen once more."

Wolsey watched him, fascinated, as he read.

> *"For my part, I think it better to be bold than calculating, because Fortune is a female, and to down her we must beat and bully her; and we see that she yields more often to the bold than to those who go to work coldly. He who acts in accordance with the Spirit of the Times will, I believe, succeed."*

He pressed *Il Principe* into the Cardinal's unresisting hand.

"These are piping Times, my Lord Cardinal," he said, "and they have a piping Spirit. It is sweet to call the tune for them. Think you not so? How goes the Latin motto? *Fortuna fortes adjuvat. Fortune favors the brave.* I might also add the good old English adjunct: *Take time by the forelock.* Take time by the forelock, my Lord Cardinal. Let Messire Niccolo stiffen your right arm."

Never the most fastidious of men, the Cardinal felt suddenly appalled, sickened even by the moral coarseness of this monstrous mentor. The scales momentarily fell from his eyes in a salutary shock of revelation. He looked within himself and saw the dizzying abysses

of his own ambition. He looked without and beheld this devil's sara-
band of rational temptation.

"You said a while back," he observed drily, "that reason is your
Machiavelli's goddess. Sometimes, Master Cromwell, I think there is
something to be said for Dom Luther's definition of reason as the
devil's harlot."

Thomas Cromwell stared at him, puzzled.

"But," added Wolsey hastily, noticing Cromwell's bewilderment,
"let that pass. What is more to the point is a certain oath I took once.
What of one's pledged word to God? What of one's priestly vow?"

Thomas Cromwell began to feel more than a trifle irritated. He
shrugged his shoulders angrily. Really, this little game of his and the
Cardinal's was going on too long, and to no conclusion. He knew
that Wolsey hadn't worried over much about his priestly vow in the
instance of one Mistress Larke who had borne him a sacrilegious son
and daughter. He had even compounded this unchaste felony by
cynically appointing his mistress' brother first his personal chaplain
and confessor—a pretty Machiavellian touch that!—and then head of
one of the Oxford colleges of his beneficent foundation. He had also
loaded his son with some of the ecclesiastical benefices that dropped
like rich crumbs from the groaning board of archiepiscopal prefer-
ment. No, decidedly it seemed a work of supererogation to carry out
the masquerade to such a tedious length as this. But Master Cromwell happened to be wrong, as he so often was in the realm of the
spirit. The great Cardinal was occasionally visited by twinges of
compunction; by a kind of moral gout that, now and then, made his
red-slippered soul throb in agony. It was his earthly tragedy; in the
end it may well have been his heavenly salvation. In the last analysis Cromwell was the Machiavellian. Wolsey, like so many others of
the Roman court, was an errant Ovidian, doomed to *meliora pro-
bare deteriora sequi.* To approve the better course, to follow the
worse one.

"What of your priestly vow?" said Cromwell finally, and contempt
edged his voice. "What of your pledged word? Why, keep them if
you so choose, my Lord Cardinal. Or more accurately put, perhaps,

keep them if you can. I would seem to keep them certainly, in your case. It is always good policy to preserve appearances as much as possible. But is it an over great fault, after all, not to keep faith with brutes? Men, most of them, are brutes. The Prince is a Man among brutes who, oftentimes for the sake of polity, is forced to become a Brute among men. What says Messire Niccolo?"

Wolsey was very quiet as he listened to Master Cromwell expound his last thesis of the evening from the pages of *Il Principe*.

> *"The Prince, therefore, must know how to use the brute and the man: which is what the ancients signified by the fable of Achilles reared by the Centaur. And among the brutes the Prince should adopt the Lion and the Fox, for the Lion cannot defend himself against snares nor the Fox against wolves. . . . Therefore, a wise Prince cannot, nor should not, keep faith to his disadvantage, when the reasons which caused him to pledge it no longer exist. But it is necessary to know how to color such conduct, and to be a great dissembler, and men are so simple and so subject to present necessities that they are easily deceived."*

Almost physical distaste was evident on Wolsey's face as he drew himself to his tall height in token that the audience was ended.

"What you say about the Lion and the Fox is very true," he stated, "But you know, Master Cromwell, there is one thing in especial about Messire Niccolo's image that I do not much like. The God I serve called Himself a Lamb."

Cromwell was already muffled in his cloak. He shrugged his shoulders again, this time in cynical indifference, not irritation.

"He could afford the luxury," was all he said. "After all He was God, though that fact did not prevent His being betrayed by wolves, judged by foxes, and crucified by lions. I wish your Grace a good even."

"I shall present your volume to the King," said Wolsey as they parted at the door.

Cromwell bowed. Things had gone off as well as could be expected, he decided, as he rowed downstream to his favorite tavern in the marshes where he kept his hunting things. Hunting was the one taste he shared in common with the fine gentlemen in whose company he mingled; for Master Cromwell liked killing things. Those same fine gentlemen did not, however, return the compliment by sharing his great taste for beer. Not only had the malty smell of beer not worn off the publican's son—neither had a raging thirst for it deserted his undemanding palate. As the lights of Putney hove in sight Cromwell began to laugh soundlessly and long. There was, he had come to the conclusion, good reason for mirth. His petard was now in train; the slow match had begun to burn. It was true the Cardinal had proved a shade more delicate of stomach than he had reckoned on. But things would work out. The toad face was suddenly slit with another convulsion of voiceless laughter. The boatman stared uneasily at his queer passenger. When Cromwell was not looking, he crossed himself quickly.

Ordinarily Thomas Cromwell was not in the habit of permitting himself emotional luxuries. Tonight, however, with no one within earshot but an anonymous riverman he was most unlikely ever to see again, he felt self-indulgent. While his ferryman tied up at the rotting wharf, Thomas Cromwell struck an attitude of grotesque triumph on the planking above the man's bowed head.

"I shall present your volume to the King," he intoned in harsh mimicry of Wolsey's winy baritone. "Faith, my Lord Cardinal, please do present my volume to His Grace. It will go handsomely on Henry's shelves next to the Defender of the Faith's pious *Septem Sacramentorum.*"

Back in York House the Cardinal, too, was thinking. He did not, as it happened, find quite so much scope for laughter in the events of the evening as Master Cromwell seemed to. In fact, looking back on it now, he made a grimace of revulsion and held the jeweled orange to his nose. There was a night mist rising from the river; and the sweating sickness had begun to stalk abroad again. But it was not really the sweating sickness' mephitic fumes my Lord Cardinal now cleansed his nostrils of; but a more tangible and more immediate presence. Taking up *Il Principe* from where he had set it down on a

Spanish credence table, Wolsey put on his long mantle and fur tippet and prepared to go out.

As Thomas Cromwell well knew he would, the Cardinal had decided to bring the book to Henry. The King lay that night in his palace of Bridewell where a suite of rooms was always kept ready and waiting for the lady of his latest fancy. This time, thought Wolsey, wincing with a prophetic twinge of apprehension, of an all too constant fancy. For long months now Henry had not slept with Catherine in the great carven bed of state. Aside from considerations of policy and morality, the Cardinal had no great love for Mistress Anne Boleyn; or for her family, either. They were careerists, all of them, from her cold-eyed, urbane father—who had sold one daughter to the King already and, apparently, was not even blinking at the spectacle of a second on the auction block, except, of course, to see to it that the buying price had been raised considerably—down to her brilliant scapegrace of a brother, the rakehell George Rochford. Careerists? He did an injustice to the word. He was a careerist himself. Rather were the Boleyns adventurers to a man—even worse, adventuresses to a woman—for all their grand connection with the Norfolks and the Howards, and the Irish Ormonds, and the great family of Buckingham. It was the cadets who were unspeakably the worst, the wild cousins who had careened hell-for-leather through France and Italy: Francis Bryan, Henry's one-eyed "vicar of Hell"; Thomas Wyatt, the cavalier poet who wenched as well and as often as he rhymed—which was very often and very well indeed; and the aforesaid mad George Rochford. They were dangerous people to deal with; not coldly, rationally dangerous, as Thomas Cromwell might one day turn out to be dangerous, but rashly dangerous after the fashion of all unbridled prodigals who allowed their every decision to depend on the chance fall of the dice, never on carefully calculated policy. All but one, that is. Mistress Anne was neither rash nor prodigal. But she was all the more dangerous for being so incalculable.

The Cardinal was more than a little worried over the direction this latest affair of the King's was taking. He was no Puritan, God knew, and Mistress Larke as well; and he realized that Kings must, in the nature of things, be allowed longer tethers than lesser mortals. He hadn't jibbed at the red-gold tresses of lovely Elizabeth Blount, not even when she had complicated the dynastic chess game by presenting Henry with a bastard son, Henry Fitzroy, while Queen Catherine continued childless. Nor had he objected to the more anonymous dryads with whom Henry disported in the greenwood after hunting. He had not even refused to set on foot preliminary negotiations for an annulment of the marriage with Catherine, so long as he thought the King's fancy was set on a French princess. But that dynastic bird had flown months ago.

No, what really troubled the Cardinal was that this new light of love was not light enough; that the new whim gave every sign of turning into a passion and, more distracting than a passion, a settled, respectable habit. Henry looked almost married nowadays, something he had never seemed to be in the palmiest days of his romance with the Queen. Nor was Henry's uxorious expression the only portent, either. Without compromising his vow of silence under the sacrosanct seal of confession, the worried Bishop of Lincoln, John Longland, Henry's private chaplain and confessor, had nevertheless given the Cardinal to understand that, ever since late winter of 1521, Henry had been suffering recurrent fits of conscience. He had, of all things, become apprehensive that he was transgressing against the old Scriptural injunction regarding incest; that he was sinning grievously by uncovering the nakedness of his long-dead brother Arthur. Incest! God save the mark! Wolsey grimaced at the very thought. He was morally sure that the marriage between Arthur and Catherine had never been consummated, taking into account the Prince's youth and the Queen's sworn word on that particular head. And, in the unlikely event that it had, Pope Julius II had formally legitimized the union between Henry and Catherine by his bull of dispensation of 1503. But now the royal bull no longer considered a twenty-year-old papal bull sufficient. The Cardinal knew these regal qualms of conscience as of old; he had not scrupled to take advantage of them in the past, while a French marriage seemed a probability. He was contemptuously sure that they proceeded from Henry's queasy stomach and susceptible reins, not from his tender soul. The brute fact of the matter was that the English King no longer could endure his Spanish Queen. The royal couch knew him no more. My Lord Cardinal blushed now as he remembered his mistake over the French princess. The King had had other game in mind all the time.

But, cynically experienced as he was in the ways of men, the Cardinal could not honestly say that he understood the why and wherefore of Henry's most recent predilection. *La petite Boullain,* as François used to call Anne and her sister before her; *la grande putain,* as Uncle Norfolk sometimes chose to label his niece, was not precisely to Wolsey's taste. His own nickname for Mistress Boleyn was the Crow of Night. His own personal preference ran to the somewhat obvious blonde opulences of Mistress Larke. But, for all his acumen, the Cardinal was overlooking two things in his disparaging estimate of the blue-black hair and strange green eyes Mistress Anne inherited from the Irish Earls of Ormond. First, power was Wolsey's true mistress; not woman. This latter imperious demand of the flesh was to him an awkward exigence, never a consuming flame or a song to lift the sluggish heart. Second, the proverbial expression that one man's meat is another man's poison held truest of all in matters of *amour.* There was something in the sinuous Boleyn type that excited Henry's amorous reflexes to the point of teeth-chattering spasm. Another Boleyn sister, the pliant Mary whom the King had later fobbed off on his complaisant court officer, William Carey, had been his mistress first—unless one was willing to credit the malicious gossip that their comely mother had preceded both girls in the lists of love. Even a royal bull, who can range at will over what dewy pastures he chooses, will crop by choice a certain clover patch.

There were, in addition, one or two other things the Cardinal failed to take into account in Mistress Anne's regard. He knew a little—a very little, be it hastily added—of the way of a man with a maid; but nothing at all about that quite different matter, the way of a maid with a man. This latter subtler department of sexual deportment did not come within the experience of either his Chancellorship or his

Cardinalate. He knew, it is true, that Nan Boleyn was noted for her dancing prowess among the ladies of the Court. He had even seen her dance on two occasions, and in his own lordly manor of York House at that. Once, during the Christmas revels, when she had played in a cunning pageant with young Mary Tudor and five other ladies, all seven of them habited in high hennins of Venetian gold and in silken dresses studded with Moorish-looking "raisins" of yellow satin. Once, quite lately, when, basking in the warm sun of Henry's royal approval, she had sat a masquer's throne as Venus, and later danced, to the sound of the trumpet, in that same Cytherean role. But he still could not appreciate what Anne Boleyn's dancing did to the kind of man that Henry was.

He had not, for example, plucked off at midnight her domino of blue satin and gold. He had never seen her riotous private repertoire of rustic English dances—they were usually for Henry's eyes alone, although, if one were willing to place a side bet that Thomas Wyatt had once tasted of them in his time, there would be few gamesters forthcoming to back the counter wager. Nor had he heard the hautboys play while Henry leaned back, tearing at a pear in great slobbering gulps, and Anne shimmered into the capriole, the pavane, the gay French gaillards she had learned to foot under the tutelage of Queen Claude and Princess Marguerite at François' court.

The Cardinal had a very strong personal reason for feeling apprehension in the case of Mistress Boleyn. Just three years before, when the girl was only fifteen years of age and fresh from François' court, Wolsey had acted as the King's agent in smashing her approaching marriage to old Northumberland's son. Young Harry Percy had been a far cry from his famous ancestor, the Hotspur of the North who fell at Shrewsbury. He was a Coldspur, if there ever was one, a piddling, spindling youth who had easily been warned off the King's preserve and safely away from the milk-white hind the royal hunter had marked down for his own at first seeing. But Anne's rage had been terrible. She had really loved Percy. Afterward, half crazed with thwarted love and frantically casting about for revenge, she remembered how little her sister Mary had secured out of her undemanding compliance with the royal desires. If this was the way of the world, if Kings must have their will and Cardinals play the graceless role of pimps, why, then, so be it. But she had no intention of becoming Henry's mistress except on terms of her own choosing; and what those terms should be, she had not had time to decide, beyond the fact that they would be high. Very high. So she nursed her hot anger against the Cardinal, contemptuously rejected the clumsy Irish cuckold Henry had so conveniently and conventionally provided as her husband, and, for the time being, solaced herself with the wit and poetry and physical bravura of her gallant married cousin, Thomas Wyatt.

The Cardinal felt an ominous premonitory pricking in his right thumb of prophecy; and he had reason. Another of those pestiferous human equations was shaping up to interfere with his mathematical arrangements for the England he served and the Papacy he coveted. A new pattern was becoming apparent on the chessboard of domestic event. The White Queen was growing restive in her empty bed chamber; and her White King nephew, the Emperor Charles, had already served notice through Ambassador Chapuys that he resented the slight put upon his aunt in Henry's neglect of Catherine. As for the Red King himself, Henry had been unwontedly still of late; but there were signs and portents that he was meditating a move. The Cardinal's own piece, the Red Bishop, was still in a comparatively strong position, though it had always been hard, even before the days of à Becket, for ecclesiastical counters to match strength with royal ones. Matching wits was another thing; and luckily diplomacy, like chess, was—up to a point, at least—a duel of wits. But, unfortunately for the Red Bishop, the White King had a White Bishop on his side; a very powerful one who wore the triple tiara and whose see was Rome. That complicated the game a great deal. So did the rampaging Knights on both sides, and that disturbing Pawn who was Mistress Boleyn. Wolsey sighed as the heraldic images paraded and caracoled in his anxious imagination. He would have sighed still more deeply if he had realized that a revolution was about to turn the chessboard topsy-turvy. The dancing Pawn with the lissome limbs and quick Irish blood was on the very point of deciding to alter her Pawn's status. If her incomparable will only held firm and Henry's importunate desire did not waver, she saw her way clear to becoming Red Queen and checkmating her White adversary. *La Reine est morte! Vive la Reine! Échec est mat! Al-shāh-mat!* The game is won!

The Cardinal was very fond of chess. For some reason he had never been able to fathom, Speaker More was not. He had even gone so far as to refer slightingly to the King's game in his amusing squib, *Utopia.* But Speaker More, who knew all sorts of interesting out of the way things, had once told Wolsey a curious detail about the mating Pawn which accomplished checkmate. He said that Geoffrey Chaucer had once called it a traveling Pawn, a "poun errant," and he had gone on to quote certain lines from the old poet's *Book of the Duchess* which had to do with Fortune's sweeping the board whenever and wherever it so pleased her heathen goddess-ship; and how no man could win against her. It had struck the Cardinal as very odd at the time that Speaker More should know so much about a game he did not like and, moreover, that he should place such emphasis on Fortune in the economy of event. But the quaint lines had stuck in his mind.

> *At the ches with me she gan to pleye.*
> *With her false draughtes dyvers*
> *She staal on me, and tok my fers.*
> *And whan I sawgh my fers awaye,*
> *Allas! I kouthe no lenger pleye,*
> *But seyde, "Farewel, swete, ywys,*
> *And farewel al that ever there ys!"*
>
> *Therwith Fortune seyde "Chek her!"*
> *And "Mat!" in myd poynt of the chekker,*
> *With a poun errant, allas!*
> *Ful craftier to pleye she was*
> *Than Athalus, that made the game*
> *First of the ches, so was hys name.*

Master More had then gone on to gloss the unfamiliar words that were no longer English. "Draughts," he had said, were moves on the board. "Poun errant," the "wandering pawn," was what later players called the "mating Pawn." The "fers" was an old Persian word for "Queen"—for "wise man," actually. The old Persians, who had invented the game, did not regard Queens as Christian Europe later came to regard them. But "fers" was the equivalent of "Queen." It all fitted; it all fitted only too well. Anne was a wandering Pawn, and with a vengeance. She was also, given the present frame of Henry's mind and, more significantly, the restless state of his loins, very much of a mating Pawn in every sense of that ambiguous term. And, the Cardinal was sure, she intended to send England's "fers awaye" from the board. Yes, it all fitted.

It all fitted better than the Cardinal knew or feared. But the "poun errant," with the will of steel, was going to encounter another will of even more finely tempered steel: the conquistador steel of Toledo blade that was the proud heart and soul of Catherine of Aragon. Catherine would never yield her place on the board without a fight; nor her little daughter Mary's place, either. Also, the White Bishop was destined to complicate the decision. The son of Julian de Medici, the nephew of Lorenzo il Magnifico, the cousin and right hand man of Leo X, Clement VII might well have borne the Latin title on his coat of arms of *Cunctator Maximus*. Supple-minded, intelligent, diligent, he yet lacked strength of mind and final courage. All of his victories and some of his defeats as well were due to his tortuous policy of temporizing delay. He was not heroic, but he was tenacious. Already he had balked Wolsey's and Henry's preliminary maneuvering for an annulment—skirmishings the Cardinal had undertaken in the interests of the supposed French marriage. Brought to bay in the hill town of Orvieto by the envoys of both Henry and Charles, the wretched old man would palter and bargain. He would wish Catherine dead; he would try to persuade her to resolve the ugly coil by yielding and retiring to a convent. But, strangely, tradition and an inexplicable something else would stiffen his malleable backbone. In the end, miserably, he would hold firm after all his procrastination and tergiversation.

Of all the pieces on the board, Wolsey thought, Henry was far and away the easiest to estimate. For almost a decade now the Cardinal had controlled the King, pandering to his appetites, winking at his moral lapses. He had known for long what were Henry's rainy day diversions when the archery range stood deserted under the dull British downpour and the bridleless horses champed their oats in the rain-dim stables. He had not cared that kisses were snatched in dark corners or on darker backstairs; that maidenheads were purchased almost without chaffering. Perhaps now, for the first time, he was beginning to pay the penalty for this callous policy or—if one preferred—this fundamental indifference of his to any moral consideration. He only knew now that this time things had gone much further than was safe; much, much further than they had ever gone before in the hottest of the King's many *affaires de coeur*. He had seen a certain Valentine in French written by the King's own hand: a crudely drawn heart, the initials A. B. inside it, and surrounding the emblem the plain statement that Henry Rex sought no other than Anne; or, as the blunt but still courtly Old French had it, *aultre ne cherche*. And the Cardinal was afraid. He knew Henry for a sensualist of unbridled inclination and illimitable opportunity. That was dangerous enough in itself. This time, to itching reins, had been added the powerful lure of imagination. Puffing stertorously, gasping for breath, the royal carp no longer even struggled at the end of Anne's silken line. Her sister had ended by fishing up poor William Carey. They ordered these matters better in France. There earldoms and dukedoms and marquisates came swimming uxoriously up to the little feet of the frail but beautiful ladies who stooped to conquer at the court of Marguerite of Angoulême, she whose jeweled missal was the *Heptameron*. But Mistress Boleyn would do even better than a Château on the Loire. Only the time was fast approaching when she must perforce disclose her price; the monstrous wage of a more monstrous chastity.

This night, for reasons of his own, the Cardinal chose to enter Bridewell from the back. As he went by the stables, he noticed the grooms busy about the white palfrey the King had given Anne. That meant they had been riding together, Henry and she, cantering through the soft spring woods late that very afternoon, and now, most likely, were relaxing by the fire, after an intimate dinner *tête-à-tête,* in Mistress Boleyn's private apartments. Two members of the Wardrobe were hard at work buffing and cleaning the sumptuous saddlery Henry had instructed Lord Windsor, Keeper of the Great Wardrobe, to issue to Mistress Boleyn. The saddles were of French make; on them rested pillows of down, fringed with gold and silk, their upper surfaces of velvet, lustrous black as the bodies of queen bees. The saddle hose and harness were also of velvet. The cruppers were tufted with puffs of silk-covered bombast. Even the reins were of black velvet barred with gold.

The Cardinal was right in his surmise. Henry, coat doffed and linen sleeves rolled back on his brawny forearms, sprawled by the fire in an easy chair, a goblet of mulled wine in his hand. The Lady Anne Rochford, as her official title went, sat demurely opposite him in a more elaborate undress. Gone was the green riding habit and feathered hat she liked to ride to hunting in. She wore now a low-cut evening dress of jet-black satin lined with ebon taffeta. A crimson cloak was flung back from her white shoulders and lay draped across her chair. She stared out of her strangely-slanted green eyes at the Cardinal as the equerries ushered him in. In a fit of amorous transport Wyatt had once likened Anne's green eyes to the eyes of Morgan le Fay in Malory's romance; and a red-haired Piers Butler, whose estates lay across the Irish sea, had gone his poet friend one better by declaring them more like those of the pale ladies of the *Sidhe,* those *belles dames sans merci* who carried off into their faëry *raths* the souls and bodies of mortal lovers. Those were two more allusions which, if the Cardinal had chanced to have heard them, he would not have understood. For Wolsey, whatever he was, was certainly no poet. Henry was in a way; and so his soul as well as his body was now in thrall to the cold eyes of the fay.

The Cardinal bowed very low.

"Your Grace," he said in greeting. "Mistress Anne. I give you both good even. I also bring your Grace a present. The latest book on statecraft from subtle Italy, my Lord King."

Henry accepted *Il Principe* with no further show of ceremony than lazily to transfer the ruby goblet from his right hand to his left. Then, with his now disengaged right hand, he tossed the volume onto a fireside table and, with studied indifference, replenished the glass.

"I thank you, my Lord Cardinal," he said yawning. "I shall show it to our good friend, Speaker More. He has a nice taste in these matters."

Wolsey smiled a little. He was used to royal insolence; that could never put him off his stride. And, amusingly enough, he had the King so well tutored on matters of state that the two of them now seemed to think alike. It was precisely the same thing he had said to Master Cromwell earlier that evening. Now he could close the circle by using Master Cromwell's identical demurral.

"It is quite possible," he said, "that Speaker More will not care over much for Your Grace's present."

Henry narrowed his eyes in sudden suspicion. He had, Wolsey had noted more than once, been growing very difficult of late.

"Why should he not?" he asked abruptly.

"I think it very likely," said the Cardinal, "Speaker More will not hold with the sentiments expressed within. *Il Principe* is a book for a King. So far as I have been able to observe, Speaker More is the Commons' man, not the King's."

Henry literally growled a refutation.

"There, my Lord Cardinal," he said in passionate remonstrance, "I know you are wrong. Speaker More is the honestest and loyalest man in all the realm of England."

Wolsey made a deprecating gesture.

"It may well be he is the most honest," he admitted. "I do not challenge his honesty, Your Grace. But, as for his loyalty, the Commons, of which he is Speaker, only today refused to grant the 800,000 pounds necessary for the successful prosecution of Your Grace's war against France."

The King selected a green-gold pear from on top a pyramid of fruit, and very leisurely bit into it.

"You know, my Lord Cardinal," he said, after a long interval, tossing the core into a gilded wicker basket, "they are crying in the streets that it is your war, not mine. What do you say to that?"

He fixed his eyes on Wolsey and waited. Anne began to plait one of the King's hands in her own.

"Surely," said the Cardinal after an uneasy pause, "surely Your Grace does not credit the vain babble of a rebel rabble mouthing nothings in the street."

"I am not so sure they are nothings, my Lord Cardinal," said Henry, still staring him down. "Nor that the rabble is always rebel, either. My father always took great care to have the rabble roaring on his side. It did not hurt the day of Bosworth Field. But one thing I do know, my Lord Cardinal. Of this I am as sure as that I wear the crown of England: Speaker More is as honest a leal subject as any in Christendom. I know. We walk together of a spring evening and talk of the stars. There is no guile in him. I am a judge of men. I know there is no guile in him."

"I have heard tell of your walks together," said Wolsey, choosing his words now with great care. "Speaker More is indeed fortunate in enjoying the favor of so gracious a sovereign. I remember when Your Grace used to walk so with me. It is a wise condescension for a monarch so to unbend to a faithful subject. It binds men's fealties with hoops of steel. Signor Machiavelli would approve mightily. But to return to the French war. Surely Your Grace is not forgetting your pledge of assistance to your brother of Spain, the Emperor Charles?"

The Cardinal paused. He was approaching the slippery nub of the matter. Success or failure rode on the next cast of the dice. But a different kind of thought altogether seemed, all at once, to have struck the King. He gave Mistress Anne a meaningful look and got up from his chair.

"No," he said, with an ugly barking laugh, "no, I do not forget the pledge I made to my dear wife's favorite nephew. But it may well be I repent it even more than I repent the continued presence of my dear wife. But I forget, my Lord Cardinal. You have Mistress Larke's attentions to contend with, not Queen Catherine's. And you can well afford to have Charles' interests at heart. His word will go a long way when a new Pontiff is nominated, eh, my Lord Cardinal? It is always wise to stay in the good graces of a Popemaker."

Wolsey was a past master of that difficult diplomatic art which consists in making a virtue out of necessity.

"Your Grace is most perspicacious," he said blandly, refusing the rosy-fleshed apple which Henry offered him on the point of a jeweled poniard, even as he softly turned aside the proffered apple of discord in debate. "I freely grant the Spaniard might be a great help in that department. But I think Your Grace's interest may also be involved in any such maneuver. I take the liberty of pointing out that it has been many a long year since the world last saw an English Pope."

"I'm not forgetting that, either," said Henry. "The first and last was a monk named Brakespear."

The King tossed up the apple Wolsey had rejected and, with a laugh, caught it again on his dagger's tip.

"The world, my Lord Cardinal," he observed, "is not likely to remember England for any such outlandish name. As well remember the Warwick squire of a similar name who served under my father at Bosworth Field. We sent Master Shakespeare a pedigree and patent down to his rural Stratford for that service. But, as you say, to return to the present war. We did not do too handsomely in the last one. The Frenchman, to give him his due, is tenacious. Thérouanne cost many a gilded penny and many a brave knave left to manure the rich soil of France."

The Cardinal noted, with a growing unease, that Mistress Anne was nodding in emphatic approval. She had cause to remember the French court with affection; and she had no cause at all to love my Lord of York. But Henry was still a lusty hater; and he had hated the French King ever since the gangling, sinewy Valois had thrown him in wrestling before one of the gay pavilions of the Field of the Cloth of Gold. So, holding his breath, Thomas Wolsey played the last trump left him.

"Yes, my Liege," he said with a sigh, "the Frenchman cost us a

pretty penny at Thérouanne and before. And, I believe, you have had
no good reason to embrace the Frenchman since. How liked you
François' hospitality at the Field of the Cloth of Gold?"

It was a risky play; but it worked. The King purpled from his
ruddy crown to where his bull's chest vanished from sight in a froth
of fine gathered linen.

"God damn the thin-shanked jackanapes," he said venomously.
"I did not like it at all. I swore then to pay the Frenchman back in his
own treacherous coin. And, by God, I shall—with interest! My Lord
Cardinal, you shall have my war, and I shall have your Papacy. A
fair exchange, eh, my Lord of York? Instruct the Commons to vote
the monies required."

It had been touch and go; but no one would have guessed that from
the Cardinal's imperturbable face.

"There should be no difficulty, Sire," he said in a calm voice. "If
Speaker More presses them, they will do it without question. Otherwise, we are apt to find it a hard task."

Henry preened.

"Have no fear of Speaker More," said the King. "He is my best
friend. I can easily talk him round this one more time."

"I thank Your Grace," said Wolsey, drawing on his long scarlet
gloves. "I shall address Parliament in the morning. Meantime, with
Your Grace's permission, I think it wise to instruct Lord Admiral
Surrey to stop all ships, English as well as foreign, sailing from our
coasts. Even now there are several vessels lying in the Channel, waiting for the wind to turn and bear them to the New Found Land."

The Cardinal did not think it necessary to add that he had those
same instructions for my Lord Admiral Surrey, already drawn up
and sealed with the great seal of the Chancery, lying snug in his
pocket.

"As you will," said Henry indifferently, while the Cardinal bowed
to Mistress Anne and left. He cared not a whit if English ships sailed
or did not sail to the New Found Land. Master Cabot and his voy-
ages had been a whim of his father's. He intended to spend the royal
revenues on more tangible satisfactions than the wheedling decep-

tions of meridians and maps. Like another English Henry, it might be said that he preferred the white arms of a *Rosa mundi* to the spouting monsters of a *mappa mundi*.

Outside, the Cardinal drew a breath of vast relief. The stars shone clear now in a cloudless spring sky. It was not the kind of night in which one feared the sweating sickness. Nevertheless, the Cardinal sniffed delicately at his jeweled orange to rid his nostrils of the perfumed musk of Mistress Boleyn even as, earlier, he had been quick to rinse them of the mephitic presence of Master Cromwell. On the whole, though he had ended by sweeping the board, the Cardinal was more than a little anxious in Mistress Boleyn's regard. She had witnessed his maneuver; and the Boleyns were always quick to learn. It had been almost too instructive an object lesson.

It had indeed. Neither the King nor the Cardinal knew it yet, but Mistress Anne had, during their colloquy together, seen fit to raise her sights. The wandering Pawn was not only ready now to take the Queen's place; she would wear her crown as well. It all seemed so breathtakingly simple; and so it actually was. The Cardinal might have put it that the Boleyns were good fencers. Anne fenced with the natural weapon of a desirable and desired woman: the white beauty of her body. It was time now to slip the buttons off the foils and fence with unbated points. But she would not let slip from its covering sheath the white sword of her beauty until Henry tossed the stakes on the table. There was a way to make him; and the time was now. Both the Cardinal of York and the lanky Valois, who sat on the throne of France, were wrong when they called Anne Boleyn wanton. She was not wanton at all. She was ambitious; and she was patient. Very ambitious; and very, very patient.

Back in my Lady's chamber Henry turned to Anne with gruff good humor. Rightly or wrongly, he felt he had not come off second best in the duel of wits with Wolsey, which, as Anne well knew, was precisely what the Cardinal wanted him to feel.

"Well, Anne," he said, rallying her, "the Cardinal has had his will of me. It is your turn to ask now. What will you have of the King? A diamond brooch? A royal order? One of those same castles in France we are forever winning and never holding?"

For answer Anne Boleyn took up a silver extinguisher and, very slowly, very, very deliberately, snuffed two of the candles burning on the massive candelabra that stood, glinting, next to the tawny crimson pyramid of pears and apples. The apartment dimmed. The rich colors of the wall tapestry darkened and retreated. The ceiling marquetry glimmered. The hearth burned all the redder for the curtailed light. Anne stretched sinuously, languorously, white neck and arms gleaming ivory in the perfumed duskiness of the chamber. Then, leaning over the still figure of the King, she kissed him lingeringly full on his bearded mouth. Once; twice; and then again.

Henry's voice sounded very hoarse.

"Anne?" he said, deep down in his throat. "Anne? Speak! What shall it be?"

She kissed him again.

"Henry! Henry!" she said low, insistently. "Make me Queen!"

The King half struggled to his feet; then sank back, panting, onto the couch.

"Eh, Nan girl?" he said dully.

She stooped over him again, long sleeves hanging like the pinions of a swan.

"Henry, Henry, Henry!" she whispered in his ear, stooping soft like some great cygnet; murmuring low, hypnotic. "Make me Queen! Make me Queen! Make me Queen!"

The circling blades had engaged at last. Henry wagged his great head at her heavily, heavy jowls waggling like the dewlaps of some mighty bull. The stakes were on the table now; and they were very high; high enough to buy the honor of a Boleyn. Slowly, ponderously, the King lumbered to his feet. Spurning the silver snuffer, he pressed out the remaining taper flames between thumb and forefinger. The hearth fire, between its wivern andirons, burned red as the heart of love; red as the shield of the Pendragon who slept buried in the Welsh hills; the Pendragon who had sired great Arthur on a woman not his wife.

CHAPTER VII

MASTER PATENSON DOES NOT

HAVE TO READ A BOOK:

Evening, Spring, 1525

MASTER HENRY PATENSON, *joculator,* of the household of Master Thomas More, Speaker of His Majesty's House of Commons, shared two things—and only two things—in common with my Lord Cardinal Wolsey. First, he had a strong affection for Wolsey's Fool, Will Patch, although he felt convinced that, when it came to their joint trade of jesting, Will wasn't a patch on himself. Second, he dreaded the sweating sickness more than he dreaded the devil. As it happened, he had never seen the devil; but he had seen, in his time, a mort of good men and women cut down in their prime by that obscene evil known as the sweating sickness. To use his own grim phrase, whenever he thought upon the matter he found himself in a cold sweat lest he be taken off in a hot sweat. Physicians were utterly unable to do anything to help once the fever began. Not even the famous Dr. Paracelsus who had visited Henry's court in the train of his imperial patron, the Emperor Charles; and who prescribed, but to no avail, the expensively unpleasant specific of ambergris, mixed with musk from a civet cat and human excrement. Even the mountebanks who drove a thriving trade in the powder called Mother Cornelius' Powder, a sovereign remedy for the French sickness that came of too much venery, were completely at sea here. Will Patch who, if possible, feared the disease even more than he did had given him one of the Cardinal's spiced oranges only that afternoon; and now, picking his away along the river bank with the curfew of Bow Bells

Master Patenson Does not Have to Read a Book

answering the chimes of Saint Lawrence Poulteny, Master Patenson held the Cardinal's aromatic fruit often to his nose.

Even as he did so, the silver chimes of All Hallows', of Saint Martin's, and Saint Giles', began ringing vespers over the sunset water. The echoes quivered above the silver spray of cherry blossoms that misted Fleet Street and the Strand. Bargemen set to lighting their night links along the river bank. The Towers of Westminster looked blacker against a scarlet sky. High-masted foreign ships, from the Low Countries, mostly, spun inky spider webs of tangled rigging over the crimson air. Daisies and buttercups were closing for the night in Stepney marsh; and Henry Patenson, too, felt sleepy now. But he also felt thirsty—overpoweringly so; and he had, besides, a private theory, one, however, that found no corroboration in the writings of Galen or Hippocrates, that ale was the most sovereign remedy of all against the sweating sickness. So he went out of his way to make one last stop at a little tavern in Wych Street near the Inn of Court known as the Inn of Our Lady—even more commonly known, as a matter of fact, as New Inn—where once, years back, his master, Speaker More, had read for the bar.

One does not often see the invisible chains that bind our human destinies; and Henry Patenson was no exception to the general rule. If he had not felt thirsty this spring evening in the year of our Lord, 1525, he would never have turned down the winding close of Lilipot Lane; and if he had not turned down Lilipot Lane, he would never have met the mariner with the spade beard. In time, at that very moment, my Lord Cardinal, his jeweled comfit to his nose, was threading his way, under a sickle moon, delicately thin and crescent as one of Mistress Boleyn's nail parings, back from his disturbing conversation with Henry and Anne to his own great manor of York House. But, for the only time in his life, Henry Patenson was fated to walk straight out of time. And the rich cream of the jest—a subtler jest than any he had ever cracked—was that he would never know it. No hourglass' soft sift could measure the duration of that conversation; no rubric mark it red on any terrestrial calendar. But it happened nonetheless; and all the effect it had on Henry Patenson was to maze a little more a head already humming with strong ale.

Patenson lingered a trifle longer than he meant to, telling mine host of the Leather Bottle what Will Patch had told him that afternoon of the Cardinal's new man, Master Cromwell: how he was base-born like themselves; how his uncle John had been cook to Archbishop Warham; how his father Walter had kept a tavern near Putney Common, and how this same father had been up before the magistrates more than fifty times for watering his beer; how, at the tag end of his life, the beadle had seized everything he owned in copyhold because of his thieving from his Lord at Wimbledon. Mine host had relished Master Patenson's small beer about the newly great to the point where he pressed upon him a huge leather wallet full of his best spiced ale which Patenson, lurching a little by now, made shift to carry under one arm, occupying the other with the real reason for his afternoon's junket: the Dutch translation of Master More's learned jape, *Utopia*, which, on the Speaker's instructions, he had picked up that day at the wharf below London Bridge where the Dutch luggers were in the habit of docking.

Once outside mine host's brass-studded door a somewhat fuddled Jester paused to get his bearings. He knew he had to cross back under an arch in order to make his way out of Wych Street and into Lilipot Lane which pointed the crooked road back to Thameside and Chelsea. He also knew just which archway he was looking for in the rabbit warren of arches that honeycombed the dark precincts of the Inns of Court. The arch he wanted was blazoned in stone with a pot of lilies, the emblem of Our Lady who lived and died a clean maiden as pure as any lily flower. And there it was—just in front of him—the gray stone of the masonry fading into utter blackness as soon as one had advanced three paces out of the pale starlight.

"By'r Lady!" said Patenson to himself. "At least my alepot has not yet blurred my eyes to the point where I can no longer make out your lilipot of stone."

He started to walk under the arch; then stopped, perplexed in a foggy kind of way. Somewhere, far off and tiny as the susurrant murmurings in a seashell, and yet at his very feet, too, there was what seemed to be a chirking of little voices and a scurrying of little feet. Patenson groped for the precise word to hit off the miniature quality

126

of the wee rustlings and squeakings. If it were not so dark under the arch, he would have opened Master More's book to see if, by some chance, the proper term weren't there. Then dimly, through a distant malty haze, he remembered that this particular *Utopia* was written in Netherlandish; and he smiled a silly smile. There was a good joke here somewhere, if only he could twist his addled brain about it. But the effort was too much for Henry Patenson. He gave it up; sat down at the entrance and unslung the leathern bottle for another draught. All around him the little noises continued. It was a tableau rich in suggestive possibility had there been anyone there to note it: a drunken Jester in Lilipot Lane; under his arm the book named *Nowhere*, and about his lolling feet Lilliputians knocking at the ivory gate of the imagination; knocking, knocking insistently. But the time had not yet come to let them swarm through into the furnace of fancy that would one day rage in an Irish brain.

Patenson put down his bottle and, in a quavering, tipsy voice, struck up one of the jolly catches Will Patch had taught him that afternoon.

> *"Bring us in good ale, bring us in good ale;*
> *For our blesséd Lady's sake, bring us in good ale!*
> *Bring us in no beef, for there is many bonés,*
> *Bring us in good ale, for that goth down at onés.*
>
> *"Bring us in no bacon, for that is passing fat,*
> *But bring us in good ale, and give us enough of that.*
> *But bring us in no mutton, for that is often lené,*
> *Nor bring us in no trypés, for they be seldom clené.*
>
> *"Bring us in no eggés, for there are many shellés,*
> *But bring us in good ale, and give us nothing ellés.*
> *Bring us in good ale, and bring us in good ale:*
> *For our blesséd Lady's sake, bring us in good ale!"*

Patenson held the bottle away from him, a good arm's length, and fell to quizzing it like a connoisseur.

"A repetitive sentiment," he observed thickly, "but a fitting one. For our blesséd Lady's sake I now fill my tosspot's belly from my alepot here in her blessed lane of Lilipot."

Master Patenson Does not Have to Read a Book:

He laughed drunkenly till the bottle gurgled, and all the while the tiny laughter of little voices rippled about his slack legs.

"Alone by my lee-lane in Lilipot Lane!" he sang, beating time with *Utopia.*

Then, in maudlin doggerel:

"Now a pannikin befits a mannikin—"

The little laughter grew shriller at the word *mannikin.* Patenson stared at his feet; then shrugged his shoulders and went on with the song:

"And a potkin a Watkin;
A bottle a Tottel;
A jug a Lugg;
But for a Patenson—"

He got aimlessly to his unsteady feet, nodding in a foolish fashion, as if the arch were full of listeners.

"My wit fails," he confessed, tugging at a forelock in humorous apology. "And it is years too late to change my name. So I'll e'en have another pull, and then fall to rhyming."

The Jester's head began to clear. In drink a little more than enough is by much too much; a little more again, and a temporary stabilization sets in for all too short a time. Patenson began to caracole astride a mimic horse, yodeling the while as he had heard mountaineers do when he played with the mummers' troupe in Germany. While he was curvetting upon his imagined steed, a man stepped quietly out of the shadows of Lilipot Arch: sun-bronzed, squarely built, hardily middle-aged, wrapped in a sea-cloak, and wearing a square beard, like mariners John and Sebastian Cabot in the prints cheapjacks used to hawk in the streets in the old King's reign. The newcomer stared quizzically at the capering Jester.

"Good even, Master Patenson," he said in a faintly foreign, mildly mocking tone. "I preferred your English song."

Henry Patenson fell back, thunderstruck. Once again the gates of ivory opened, and a wind from elsewhere blew on England there on that pleasant night of spring in Lilipot Lane. There was a thunder of surf and a crying of gulls in his ears. He saw, as in a lightning flash, the faces of other fabulous voyagers: a weather-beaten man in goatskin recoiling before a naked footprint on wet gleaming sands; an old Prometheus with blasted face, angry and splendid as a fallen angel, cupping his hands to cry, through storm and spindrift, on a whale; a boy and a one-legged sailor in a cave through whose mouth the sea's blue laughter glinted. The leathern bottle dropped from Patenson's inert hands. Gurgling a little, the good ale serpentined in dark coils over the moonlit dust.

"Holy Mary!" said the Jester hoarsely. "Who are you?"

The spade-bearded man in the dark mantle bowed from the waist.

"Raphael Hythlodaye," he said. "At your service, if you should so choose."

Patenson shrank back further against the crumbling masonry of Lilipot Arch.

"And, pray tell," he questioned, summoning up a poor ghost of his former impudence, "*what* are you?"

Hythlodaye laughed a little to himself.

"A master mariner," he began to enumerate. "One who sails far over seas not yet charted. A Portuguese philosopher. A good European. A citizen of the world that may be—some, perhaps, would say that shall be. One addicted to the study of Greek and to the quainter speculations. Cousin german to such odd fish of the future as Jonathan Swift and Edward Bellamy."

At the sound of the name, *Jonathan Swift,* the little voices clamored shriller. But the Jester paid no attention now to what was going on about his feet. The pins and needles gone from his no longer numbed legs, he sprang gracefully erect. Confidence was fast returning.

"Whoa, Sessa!" he said. "Go not so fast! *Where* art thou from?"

"Most recently of Antwerp, Master Patenson," said Hythlodaye. "Of Antwerp, a fair city and a goodly one. Before that of Amaurot on the river Anyder in the land of Utopia. It is all set down in yonder book you carry under your arm."

Patenson pondered the volume judicially.

"This is the new Dutch edition of my master's book," he said.

Master Patenson Does not Have to Read a Book:

"Fresh from the presses of Amsterdam. Or so the Dutchmen told me at the docks. For I cannot read Hollands. But how is it, friend Hythlodaye, that Utopia is your country? Master More told me once that Utopia was nowhere."

"Faith, did he?" said Raphael Hythlodaye ironically. "That leaves short shrift, then, for men begotten like myself by a chimera on a daydream. Still: *Dico—ergo sum*. Surely, Master Patenson, you have mother wit enough to know that Nowhere must be Somewhere."

Henry Patenson began to feel at ease more and more. He might not know whether or not Nowhere was Somewhere. But, as a born citizen of Cockaigne, if not of Utopia, he could smell a joke when there was one in the neighborhood.

"My father," he said sententiously, "was too poor to leave my poor mother aught but a pair of patched shoon. Faith, he had no father wit to speak of, and less money. Do you tell a poor Jester, who lacks both father and mother, both pence and sense, where your precious Somewhere may be."

There was a roll of miniature drums and a proud skirl of wee pipes from under the arch.

"In the future," said Hythlodaye, lingering on every word. "In the spirit of man. Between the covers of just such a book as you carry. Between the covers of certain other books—and not so few in number, either—still to come."

Very ostentatiously Henry Patenson set down the volume, first taking care to blow a pinch of dust from its cover.

"Henry Patenson, *joculator*," he catechized himself. "You have been tippling too much."

"Not so," said Hythlodaye. "Not so, Sir Fool. But just enough. *In vino veritas*. Except for Master More no mortal has ever seen me so clearly as yourself."

"Eh?" said Patenson suspiciously, squinting his eyes into focus, only to find that the man in the cloak began to ripple and waver like images in water riffled by a falling leaf. "Then is Master More sib to a fool, if not to a drunkard. But *in vino veritas*—what may your law term quillets mean translated into honest English?"

"That," intoned Hythlodaye magisterially, "in wine thou shalt find veracity. I, friend Patenson, am veracity, though some of Master More's friends think I am but a jest—and a poor one at that."

Patenson turned a cartwheel to clear his spinning head.

"Faith, then, I am of their company," he said, right side up again. "But, on second thought, friend Hythlodaye, I believe I finally have you. You are, more likely, a poorly digested crumb of pasty—friend Patch fed me this noon on rich cates from the Cardinal's buttery— or else a vinous vapor. As for *vino*, as you call it, I seek in *vino* not veracity, but sleep or song or a lick of lechery. If such bugs and goblins as yourself are to turn up in my cups, why, so much the worse for my cups. Veracity came to me unsummoned. Let me see if song will come summoned. Sleep and lechery can wait a while."

He slung the leathern bottle over his shoulder again and struck a posture as if about to strum upon a lute. But Raphael Hythlodaye was gone, of a sudden, in the darkness. Patenson shrugged a little and let drop his bottle-lute.

"So," he said quietly. "He is gone again. Well, song will keep me cheerful company to Chelsea." Patenson trolled out another drinking stave as he trudged along the river bank, lowering his voice once for a pair of pikestaffed watchmen, striking up again *fortissimo* when there was only the moon to spy upon his noisy doings.

> *"Back and side go bare, go bare,*
> *Both hand and foot go cold.*
> *But, belly, God send thee good ale enough*
> *Whether it be new or old!*

> *"But if that I may have true-ly*
> *Good ale my belly full,*
> *I shall look like one, by sweet Saint John,*
> *Were shorn against the wool.*

> *"Though I go bare, take you no care,*
> *I am nothing a-cold.*
> *I stuff my skin so full within*
> *With jolly good ale and old.*

Master Patenson Does not Have to Read a Book:

"I love no roast but a brown toast,
Or a crab in the fire;
A little bread shall do me stead;
Much bread I never desire.

"Nor frost, nor snow, nor wind, I trow,
Can hurt me if it wold.
I am so wrapp'd within and lapp'd
With jolly good ale and old."

The Jester was singing his song through the twentieth time when, leathern bottle, book, and all, he finally trudged into Master More's lovely dining room where Mistress More's daffodils bloomed in the blue dish on the oaken sideboard. Mistress More herself, Dame Alice Middleton as she was in her first marriage, was kneeling at a *prie-dieu*, her strong-featured, kindly, not uncomely face bent over her evening missal. The family monkey did not add much to her powers of concentration as, with its little black paw, it tugged, by fits and starts, first at her voluminous skirts, then at her white coif, then at the heavy crucifix lying pendant on her breast.

Without looking up from her devotions Dame Alice dealt the marmoset a light blow on the side of its head.

"Drat the beast!" was all she said.

The animal retreated, its tiny face wrinkled and piteous, squeaking and gibbering like one of the thin-voiced *lemures* of old Roman folk belief Dom Erasmus had once likened it to. Patenson stopped short and emitted a low-pitched whistle at the sight of the strangely assorted pair.

"A drop too much again, eh, Sir Fool?" asked Dame Alice grimly, again without bothering to look up.

The Jester performed an antic dance behind her gaunt back.

"That was not Master Hythlodaye's opinion, Mistress," he said, grimacing at the marmoset. "A drop too little, if anything. One can never get a drop too much these degenerate latter days."

Mistress More crossed herself, gathering her skirts together and sniffing audibly the while.

132

"I dare say," was her only observation as she got creakily to her feet. Then, noticing Patenson's parcel:

"What is it you have under your arm? And who, pray, is Master Hythlodaye?"

Henry Patenson put up one hand in mock serious expostulation.

"One question at a time, Mistress," he protested. "This, under my arm, is the master's book in its Dutch dress new come from the booksellers. He is to present it to Dom Erasmus tonight. As for Master Hythlodaye, it is my measured opinion we should both forget him as quickly as possible."

Mistress More had already forgotten Master Hythlodaye in her consternation over the unwelcome news that Dom Erasmus was still in England; and, worse even than that, coming to her house again that very evening. She was expecting son-in-law Roper and brother-in-law Rastell, but her husband had said nothing whatsoever about the Dutch priest's coming, too. Probably, she reflected with a pursing of her lips, Master More had stayed quiet on this point by design, not accident. He knew all too well how she felt about Dom Erasmus. And he would never argue with her, except jokingly; but he always got his way.

"I had thought," she said to Patenson, "that Dom Erasmus would have taken ship for Rotterdam by now."

Patenson shrugged his shoulders. He, too, disliked the Netherlander.

"So he intended, Mistress," he said indifferently. "So he intended. But the winds have been adverse all week. What odds, though, in the end? We can endure his long nose one more evening, you and I, and the more willingly if we remember that he is to sail tomorrow. That, at least, is sure, Mistress, if anything at all is sure in this plaguy vale of sorrows. The wind was shifting at last, even as I came along the river."

"And, Sir Fool," said Mistress Alice somberly, "none too soon for my taste, either. Why cannot Dom Erasmus priest it as a priest should, and not gad about the world doing naught else that I can see but distract my husband from his work with bad jokes in Latin that no Christian soul can understand, anyway?"

Master Patenson Does not Have to Read a Book:

On the instant Henry Patenson turned perverse. One could not be sure of him for long.

"How then, Mistress," he asked impudently, "can you tell that they are bad? As for understanding them, our master seems to, if, of course, you account him a Christian soul, a thing I sometimes doubt. At least he laughs hard enough at them. And, as for Latin, why, does not Master More have to read his law books in that same crabbed tongue?"

Mistress More set down a dust cloth, snorting.

"*When* he reads his law books, you mean," she amended angrily. "Which is not very often while such dry, bloodless flibbertigibbets as Dom Erasmus are in town."

As she so often did in the presence of her lighthearted confidant, Mistress Alice began to work herself into a passion of complaint.

"Do you know," she confided to him, "I could beat your precious master sometimes. Yesterday I came upon him at high noon, when, by rights, he should have been with the King or my Lord Cardinal. But no, not Master More. There he was, sitting and musing and moping by the fire. Says I: 'What will you do, that you list not to put forth yourself as other folk do? Will you sit always by the fire and make goslings in the ashes with a stick as children do?' "

As usual, Patenson found himself strangely touched by her burst of confidences; and professionally interested, too, in just how Master More would manage to wriggle out of this latest pickle. For, wriggle out he would; of that the Jester was sure. Almost shyly he put his hand on his mistress' sleeve.

"Yes, Mistress," he said. "And what said our master in return to that?"

"He spoke me mild as mother's milk," said Mistress Alice. "Said he so sweet and slow: 'What would you have me do, I pray you?' It is ever his way, you know, to madden me with his mildness. Oh, at such a time, good Guernsey butter would not melt in his blandishing mouth. 'By God,' I told him, 'I would have you go forward with the first, man! For, as my dead mother was in the habit of saying'—God ha' mercy on her soul, Sir Fool—'it is ever better to rule

134

than to be ruled.' And therefore, by God, I would not, I warrant you, be so foolish as to be ruled where I might rule."

Patenson smiled affectionately at his mistress and patted her arm. He could see now the way the wind would blow. She never won; and she never ceased to try to win.

"And I warrant you, good Mistress," he rallied her ever so gently, "that our master had an answer pat."

Dame Alice began to laugh so hard that, at last, she had to wipe her eyes with one camlet sleeve.

"That he did, the merry rogue," she said, choking in the sudden mirth that mastered her as quickly and completely as her previous anger. " 'By my troth, wife,' said he with a wink, 'in this I dare say you say truth, for I never found you willing to be ruled yet.' And it is true, Sir Fool, and the sly rascal knows it. Dearly do I love to rule, but never yet has he let me."

"You know, Mistress," said the Fool, half seriously, "you should allot me better commons than I get. It is a hard task to play the fool well in a house where the master plays it so much better—and *gratis* to boot."

"*Bone deus, bone deus,* Sir Fool," wept Dame Alice in a very ecstasy of laughter, the tears coursing down her lean cheeks. "If it is hard for you, his Fool, think how much harder it must be for me, his wife. He is more horn mad than the mad ape who plagues us all at our housekeeping—the useless animal I was so angry at his buying from the Spanish sailor, but now can no more do without than I could do without his master. Eh, Sir Marmoset?"

She scratched the monkey behind its little black ear. It repaid her for her kind attentions by deftly lifting the scissors from the embroidered housewife at her girdle and running about the room clicking them.

"See?" Dame Alice appealed to Patenson with a helpless but mutely eloquent gesture.

Then, all efficient chatelaine once again:

"But have you the candles I bade you buy for this night's gathering? Master Rastell will need clear light to show the company his maps by."

135

Master Patenson Does not Have to Read a Book:

"Master Roper brings them with him, Mistress," said Patenson. "He stopped me, just as I was going in the door of the chandler's where we trade, and said he knew a Lutheran chandler who gave fairer measure, and, moreover, made his candles out of purer bees-wax. He said the Catholic chandlers had been cheating the world for centuries now, but that the Lutheran chandlers were still more honest, inasmuch as they were newer at the game. There is a deal of truth in what he says. And he says it very well. In fact, one might almost say that Master Roper turns wit himself these days. I only hope he is not turning Lutheran as well."

Mistress Alice paid no attention to the Fool's remarks on her son-in-law's religious opinions. She had no interest whatsoever in matters of theology, which latter study seemed to her but another parcel of masculine nonsense. Men, even good men like her husband, had so much nonsense in their heads. Why couldn't people go on worshiping God, as they had always done, and not be forever disputing about it?

"Mistress Meg will have taken charge of them, I suppose," she said.

Patenson could not help but notice how the step-mother's voice altered when she spoke of her husband's eldest daughter. There were no two ways around it. Dame Alice Middleton was jealous of Margaret More; and the girl's marriage to William Roper had not much altered things.

"I am sorry, Mistress Alice," he said carefully, gingerly picking his way over this particular quagmire. "I forgot to mention that Master Roper bade me tell you that Mistress Margaret must stay at home this evening. She is feeling queasy and must keep her chamber, and so cannot make one of your pleasant company tonight."

Dame Alice grunted ill-naturedly. In this matter nothing could please her. Suspicion woke on every side.

"My husband," she said, affronted, "will be sorry not to see his favorite daughter. I believe he esteems her more than he does me."

Patenson wisely saw fit to change the conversation.

"When," he asked, in a matter-of-fact tone, "does Master Rastell sail for the New Found Land?"

It was not the best possible tactical diversion, inasmuch as Mistress

Evening, Spring, 1525

Alice considered this husband of her own husband's youngest sister, Elizabeth, but another—and by no means the least of them, either— of the impractical visionaries who seemed to bloom on every More bush. The law, to which Master Rastell devoted some portion of his vigorous time, she thoroughly approved of. Coroner of Coventry, when all was said and done, was a completely respectable title. But the Rastell printing house hard by Paul's Gate, the Pageant of Heaven built there for the visit of Emperor Charles, the open-air stage alongside his otherwise seemly and sober house in Finsbury Fields, all the foolish pother about trenches in France and the proper emplacement of serpents and culverins, and now this present harebrained journey to the icy rim of the known world—all these made up a quite different kettle of fish. Dame Alice pursed her lips.

"Tomorrow," she said drily, "if the weather holds, Master Rastell's craft, the *Barbara*, sails for the New Found Land, and Master Rastell's other craft, the *Elizabeth*, can cool her keel in Coventry. But come, Master Patenson, you woolgather! And it is wool will fetch no very high price at the Flemings' Staple. You and I have lived too long, it seems, among these other Mores. Do you see to the table, then, while I set about drawing the wine. Master Rastell will be a long time pressing grapes before he squeezes out, in his precious New Found Land, even so middling a wine as we keep here."

She took a candle with her on her complaining way to the clean-swept cellar. Patenson left off his deft work about the sideboard, and, arms akimbo, cocked an impudently affectionate snook in the direction of Dame Alice's grumbling wake.

"So," he said to himself, "I woolgather. Well, as the mounseers would say, there is an easy remedy for that. If we woolgather, then *revenons à nos moutons!*"

The fancy pleased him and set his shrewd flibbertigibbet's brain to cantering, astride its new French hobbyhorse, down its own fantastic corridors of judgment and misjudgment. Not as the world judges, judged Henry Patenson. But he did not judge badly for all that. He knew very well that Mistress Alice would never be well liked on first—or, for that matter, even on second—sight. But she wore well. Very well. Much better than some others he could mention. If Dom

Erasmus happened not to like her, why, that was no great loss to any one. So much the worse for Dom Erasmus.

The Jester spun two gleaming butter-knives into the air.

"High Cockalorum!" he cried out, catching them again. "It's a mad world, my Masters! I said it once and I say it again! My master doth corrupt our ancient custom and cheapens trade by playing the fool *gratis!*"

"Does he?" said Thomas More in a quiet voice. "Good even, friend Patenson."

Not put out in the slightest, the Jester whirled round to find Speaker More and William Roper, his eldest son-in-law, already in the room and hanging their cloaks on a hook.

"Good even, cousins both," he said, flittering his feet in a kind of staggering bow.

"Good even, friend Henry," said Roper, laughing.

Henry Patenson was on very good terms with the frank, open-minded generous young lawyer who had married Margaret More. Despite his comparative youth, William Roper was even thus early a man of some considerable substance: Protonotary of the Court of King's Bench and Member of Parliament for Bramber in Sussex. He already owned a house in Chelsea and enjoyed, besides, the comfortable revenues from his father's estates at Eltham and Canterbury. It did not sit quite so well within the family, however—not that Patenson cared a jackstraw, one way or another, for points of doctrine he could not begin to understand—that for some time Roper had been powerfully attracted toward Luther's doctrine of justification by faith alone. It was bad enough, in all conscience, to have a crypto-Lutheran in an orthodox household, one who merely whispered the dangerous new tenets into the bated ear of secrecy, in hugger-mugger, as it were. But stiff-necked Master Roper must need shout revolution aloud, even on the very steps of Paul's Cross itself. As Speaker More put it, wrily, to Cardinal Wolsey, his brash son-in-law "longed so sore to be pulpited that, to have satisfied his mind, he could have been contented to have foregone a good portion of his lands"—even the rich bottom lands he had inherited from his mother's father, old Sir John Fineux, Chief Justice of the King's Bench. But all that lay well in the past now. For form's sake Roper had been convented of heresy before my Lord Cardinal who, for the esteem he then still bore Henry's Speaker, but winked at the charge and dismissed the case with a friendly warning. Of late months the eager young Member for Bramber had turned his impetuous attention from the dangerous matter of religion to the no less dangerous matter of politics. At the moment he was a King's man to the hilt and beyond, and rejoiced in his father-in-law's great good fortune. Rejoiced aloud, as now:

"I rejoice, Sir Thomas," he said, beating out the Speaker's cloak till it hung straight on its peg, a service he always performed for his father-in-law who was as careless about the hang of garments as he was meticulous about the fit of words, "I rejoice, Sir Thomas, in your having found such favor with the King."

"How is that, son Roper?" asked More, yawning a little as he leaned back in a chair. It had been a long hot day in Parliament; and a worrisome one.

"Why, Sir Thomas," said the young man, "I think he marvelously affects you. After dinner today he walked in the garden with you a round hour by the clock, his arm about your neck. Not even with my Lord Cardinal Wolsey does Henry so much as walk arm in arm."

"Oh, that;" said More embarrassed, almost, it seemed, uneasy. "You saw us, then. Yes, son Roper, I thank our heavenly Lord I find His Grace my very good secular lord indeed, and I believe he does as singularly favor me as any subject within this realm. Nevertheless, son Roper, I may tell you I have no great cause to be proud thereof. If my head could gain him a castle in France, it should not fail to go. It is a good thing to keep an innocent heart; but an innocent heart does not mean that we must also be the dupes of life. Place no trust in Princes, nor in the promises of Princes. Why, only yesterday, in York House, the King drew his dagger on Reginald Pole, the Dean of Exeter and his own near kin, and all because my Lord Pole could neither find it in his heart nor conscience, much as he loves his cousin Henry, to declare for the King, as a churchman and a scholar, in the matter of the divorce he desires. No, son Roper, the favor of Kings is the ficklest of all fickle things. Do you know what I care for far more than the favor of Princes, even that of mine own liege Prince?"

Roper stared, wondering, at his father-in-law. Rarely had he heard him speak so passionately.

"What is that, Sir Thomas?" he asked.

"Three things, son Roper," said More, speaking low but no less vehemently. "And, on condition that those three things were well established in Christendom, would to our Lord I were put in a sack and here presently cast into the Thames. Would you care to know what these same three things are?"

Roper put out his hand and touched his father-in-law's arm lightly, once.

"Marry, if it please you, sir," he said softly.

"The first is this," said Thomas More. "That where the most part of Christian Princes are at mortal war, they were all at a universal peace. The second, that where the Church of Christ is at this present sore afflicted with many errors and heresies, it were settled in a perfect uniformity of religion. The third, that where the King's matter of his marriage is now come in question, it were, to the glory of God and the quietness of all parties, brought to a good conclusion."

It was the second time within a short compass his father-in-law who, in general, never so much as spoke of court affairs, had touched on the King's marriage. William Roper had a sudden sense of discomfort, as if a cloud had crossed the sunny heraldic landscape of his great expectations.

"The King's great matter is going, then, so badly?" he asked. "I heard in the City things were mending."

All at once Thomas More looked very old.

"No, son Roper," he said quietly, "things are not mending at all. They cannot grow much worse without there be great trouble to the kingdom."

It was true. The monstrous seed sown in Henry's mind by the woman who would be Queen, before she so much as slaked a King's hot thirst, had already pushed up out of the damp earth of male frustration and passion and resentment against an aging wife who was no longer beautiful, and who had failed, moreover, to bear to His Grace of England the man child he wanted almost above all other things on earth. First had come, in grave procession, Anne Boleyn's chaplains, sprinkling in ritual *Asperges* the fast-growing green shoot of the King's desire, intoning grim texts from Leviticus: *He that marrieth his brother's wife doth an unlawful thing. He hath uncovered his brother's nakedness.They shall be without children.* It all referred, of course, to Catherine of Aragon's prior marriage to the sickly boy, Arthur. Was it not incest for the King to have lain all these barren years with the bride of his dead stripling brother? And had not the Biblical curse worked out? Were they not without issue? It was true Arthur had died before he could have carnal knowledge of the Spanish maiden. It was also true that, speaking strictly, Henry could not be said to be absolutely without issue by his wife, Catherine. There was, of course, Mary, already nine years old. But girl children did not really count; or so, at least, the King chose to construe Leviticus after his own deeply-rooted desire. So the royal siege engines were drawn up before the walls of the Roman Curia wherein sat the temporizing Medici who knew so little of Canon Law and so little—when one came right down to it—of anything else, either; who said Mass fewer times a year than the lowliest curate in Christendom; who yet held in his nervous grasp the keys of Peter that could bind and loose. Clement had been, in his day, the unwilling prisoner of both Hapsburg and Valois policy. Could not, this time, the subtle politician who bore, as Henry's gift, the arms of York enmesh him even more effectually in Henry's interests than had the ministers of Charles and Francis?

That, at any rate, had been the first plan. My Lord of York, sitting as papal legate *a latere*, with the complaisant and aged legist, my Lord of Canterbury, Archbishop Warham, sitting at his crimson side, would decide the case in England and declare the King's marriage to Catherine null and void. But three unexpected occurrences intervened. The King, for the first and only time in his life, showed himself reluctant to appear as plaintiff. The Emperor Charles' German troops sacked Rome and held Clement close prisoner in the Castle of San Angelo. The great Cardinal, who had had visions of using this appetite of Henry's for a new marriage as a pawn in his own dynastic and papal game, suddenly discovered what had been, up to then, the well-guarded secret that the King had no intention whatsoever of marrying a French princess but instead—who could have foreseen such an eventuality?—was almost ready to wed the fetching little Howard minx whose brothers and cousins had sworn enmity against the Chancellor. Wolsey had no further stomach for a game which opened so inauspiciously for him; he had never had much luck, anyway, in countering Queen's gambit. Half-heartedly, he informed Henry—what, as a matter of fact, was true enough—that, if Queen Catherine should make formal protest, nothing could finally clear the matter but a papal sanction straight from Clement himself. Then he turned the tortuous and thankless task of negotiation over to Henry's secretary, Dr. William Knight; and the cat-and-mouse duel began. But it was too late for Wolsey to withdraw. In the inscrutable house of the weirds, where three skinny sisters also sit at eldritch chess with dead men's bones, Anne had long since been set up as a portent and a sign of the death of Princes and Cardinals alike. The great Cardinal had finally moved one piece too many on the chessboard of empire.

Listlessly but skillfully he continued to go through the motions, overreaching himself only once when he placed at the disposal of Henry's permanent agent in Rome, Sir Gregory Casale, a credit for 10,000 ducats on a Venetian bank—to be used if and when Casale was able to induce Clement to accept the massive bribe. It was too much even for the case-hardened Cardinal Pucci. Had these Englishmen no finesse at all? One bribes intermediaries, certainly; one does not bribe the Fisherman in his own august *propria persona*. Even then, through the good agencies of Edward Foxe and Stephen Gardiner, two young rising canonists from his own secretariat, Wolsey was able to retrieve much that seemingly had been lost. He managed to persuade Clement that the hearing should be held in England, after all, and that Lorenzo Campeggio, who not only knew

England as of old but held the bishopric of Salisbury, should sit with him in the legatine court. Crippled with gout, a bitter but honest diplomatist, Cardinal Campeggio did his best to induce Catherine, in the Pope's name, to enter a nunnery and let her case go by default. It was one way out for everyone concerned. For everyone concerned, that is, but the daughter of Isabella of Spain. The daughter of Isabella stood firm. What is more, she was able to convince Campeggio that, inasmuch as she had come virgin to the bed of Henry, the wrangling over the legality of Pope Julius' original dispensation would be exposed, once the court met in earnest, as the merest quibble.

Meanwhile Henry had dispatched fresh envoys to Rome. One of them—even for Henry the cynical bad taste seemed incredible—was Anne's own cousin, the King's dissolute "Vicar of Hell," Sir Francis Bryan; and it was through Bryan, quite without Wolsey's knowledge, that the King played his trump card. If Clement did not bring pressure on Campeggio to convoke the court at once and to render the verdict which the King demanded, then Henry was ready to renounce his allegiance to the Holy See. It was nothing so formal as an ultimatum. No more, as yet, than a sinister intimation; and so far a secret one. But there are many ears and many tongues in Rome. Clement, despairing, talked to the French Ambassador. The French Ambassador sent a dispatch posthaste to François. François spoke to his Duchess sisters. Only that morning the threat of schism had been openly bandied about the corridors of Parliament. Wolsey would know the worst no later than the morrow. So it was small wonder Speaker More sighed so heavily in his pleasant Chelsea dining room, while the wind freshened along Thameside, and a nightingale sang in his river garden.

While More was still speaking to his son-in-law, Dom Erasmus and John Rastell had come in through the street door. The Dutch priest was coughing a little—there was some fog in the river bottoms, and his lungs had never been over strong. His thin face was the color of an Easter taper. He wore his black velvet cap pulled down low on his head and his dark cape plucked up high about his throat.

Like Roper, but with better reason—for there wasn't much Erasmus of Rotterdam failed to be *au courant* with in the Court—he was troubled by More's concern over the news of the King's pettifogging chicanery. He was even more disturbed by his friend's manifest distress, and indicated this, in eloquent pantomine, to Rastell. Rastell replied in dumbshow by shrugging his broad shoulders. There is nothing, he seemed to say, we can do about this. The great will have their way; and the world must needs wag on, willy-nilly, however Kings and Popes may fall out. More's brother-in-law, master of the *Barbara,* was a sturdy man just on the edge of vigorous middle age. Like Chaucer's Shipman of an earlier day, *with many a tempest had his beard been shaken.* Again like Chaucer's Shipman, he *knew all the havens from Jutland to Finistere.* And, if the wind but held until the morning, his next landfall would be a further *finis terrae* than the Spanish port whence came the yellow wines for Henry's table. It would hold, if John Rastell knew anything at all about air currents. The leaves rustled in the rising breeze as a waterman's boat, flare lit in the prow, moved upstream against the current.

"Bravo, Sir Speaker," said Erasmus, rallying his friend with affectionate irony. "You are in excellent voice tonight. You outdo even the English nightingale I hear in your river garden for what may be my last time. But, touching this same point of war and peace, is not your realm of England now at amity with both France and the Spanish Emperor?"

Mistress More had begun to pour out wine for the guests. Her husband, usually so courteous, did not seem to notice her. He stared straight at his friend, Erasmus, but he did not appear to see him, either; but rather something or someone far in the distance. John Rastell looked at his brother-in-law in some perplexity. It was a mood new to him as well as to Erasmus; but not quite so new to Henry Patenson. The Fool had seen his master in his many night vigils and his long watches.

"At amity with France and Spain?" asked More, making a kind of hopeless gesture. "It is so tonight. Will it be so tomorrow? My Lord Cardinal Wolsey wants his war; and he is first Councillor of the

144

Kingdom. The realm will find itself poorer for the spending of many a fair penny and the wasting of many a far fairer life before we come to an end of the Cardinal's matter. The Cardinal will have a war; the King will have a woman. What the Kingdom will have, what God will have—but who among us thinks of either God or the Kingdom? And once it comes to the point of war, and once the world is ruffled and fallen into a wildness, how long will it be, do you think, and what heaps of heavy mischief will there fall, before the way is found to set the world in order and peace once again? And this holds only for our poor bit of world here in the West. What of elsewhere? In the East Selim the Grim builds up again the hordes the Hammer smashed at Tours. Rhodes has fallen. The green banner of the Great Turk already waves over Belgrade. The Christian blood of knightly Hungary drains white on the triste field of Mohacs. And what of peace within the realm? The rich cheat the poor. The King cheats the Commons. The Commons tax the serving knaves and the very wenches who draw water. The merchants cozen everyone from lord to scullion boy. When I consider all these commonwealths which nowadays do flourish—France, Spain, Portugal, the Germanies, aye, and our own green realm of England is no exception to the thieving rule—so, God help me, I can perceive nothing but a conspiracy of rich men, procuring their own commodities under the name and title of the commonwealth. The people are no better. One evil May Day only eight years past, instead of tying ribbons on their May poles and hearing Masses for our Lady, the 'prentices of London, like hounds on the track of a panting deer, baying their evil cry *Up clubs!,* rose to stone and hang the blameless stranger dwelling in our gates. Poor wretched Flemings were their victims, poorer far than the wretched artisans who stoned them. Poor men and women like their English selves. Before that evil May Day was over, the King's Archers had hanged twelve of the miserable boys, and would have hanged hundreds more if the King had not harkened to my plea and the plea of his good Queen for mercy. Peace? *Peace, peace, they say, and there is no peace.* There is no peace anywhere."

Master Patenson Does not Have to Read a Book:

Thomas More looked down at the table with a groan. Erasmus, almost in spite of himself, laughed a short laugh.

"Except," he said ironically, "except within the Church, Sir Speaker."

Erasmus was by no means insensitive to the callousness of lay society; to the brutal greed of Princes and rulers. His great friend, Ludovico Vives, who had once taught little Mary Tudor Latin at Oxford, had written him an eloquent letter from Louvain about the evils of military violence and political cynicism. But the Church was Erasmus' specialty and his home. Whether or not he should have entered it in the beginning may well have been a moot point; and Erasmus could have argued with equal cogency, perhaps, on either side. But it was now, God help and forgive him, his nest; and, to the best of his lights, he meant to be a loyal, if bitter, fledgling. So, more gently, but no less insistently this time, he repeated what he had said:

"Except, of course, within the Church, Sir Speaker."

Thomas More looked up again, unsmiling.

"There least of all," he said with measured bitterness. "A bad monk preaches heresy in Germany and all Europe stops to listen. His Eminence of Brandenburg is a scoundrel, so all Germany agrees Master Luther must be a saint; and, what is more, a prophet. It is the devil's own arithmetic. And we chalk the same sums here in England. My Lord of York settles rich benefices on his bastard: Archdeacon of York, Archdeacon of Richmond, Dean of Wells; two rectories; six prebends; a provostship. When his doxy's son is thus richly beneficed, then it is time to make her brother my Lord of York's confessor. For the idle words of a Carthusian, a monk of that order I honor above all others, and will to the day of my death—for the idle words of a Carthusian, I say, and to the slander and infamy of all religion, the great Duke of Buckingham goes blameless to the block. If the salt be bad, what of the loaf? As Master Chaucer says, we cannot have a shitten shepherd and a cleansed sheep. The very soul of Christendom is at war within itself. And here, at home in England, let us ware of a weak clergy lacking grace constantly to stand to their learning."

Erasmus, nodding, ticked off each separate bead of acrid truth on the quick rosary of his mind. Buckingham's judicial murder—there was no other term for the craven act—had shown Henry's savage cowardice at its earliest and worst. It was true that Albrecht of Brandenburg, Dom Luther's bishop, was a villain fit to parch in the hellish lower circle of Master Dante's doomed simoniacs. But, when it came to the ticklish task of accounting for Master Luther's outbreaks, was the learned Dom Erasmus any less to blame, weighed in the impartial scales of God and history, than the venal Lord of Brandenburg? Or than the incalculable Dom Luther himself? Who, after all, had laid the spotted wivern's egg of doubt the broad-rumped Augustinian had finally hatched? Well, whatever the odds, there was very little he could do about it now. Even his famous weapon of satire was silenced. Dom Luther was the kind of heavy-handed adversary whose rhinoceros skin repelled any witty shaft the Erasmian bow might launch. Yet he was curiously tender-skinned, too: a passionate artist; a powerful orator; a man gifted by nature with the most tremendous personal magnetism. Master Erasmus, Dutchman of Rotterdam, had never cared over much for Germans. They were too headstrong, too undependable, too dangerous—too hysterical as well, for all their exterior placidity. But he would never make the mistake of underrating their power; either for mischief or for good.

As for all Europe stopping to listen to a German monk preach heresy, Erasmus wondered if even Thomas More had registered how deeply the dangerous new ideas had fleshed themselves within the ordinarily nonmetaphysical English. There were, after all, the Buckinghamshire Lollards who now prayed to Luther "beyond the sea in Almany." There was the harper, Robert Lamb, who went about the country singing a ballad in praise of the recreant Augustinian. Erasmus drew a long face at the bare idea of Luther figuring in a ballad. His nostrils twitched in fastidious amusement as he considered what the Goliards would have made of such a plump lecher on conviction. He himself had faced, in friendly but angry debate, those Cambridge scholars who now followed Tyndale, meeting them in their White Horse Inn that already was beginning to be known in the University as *Germany*. Tyndale's eloquent pamphlets began to be quoted everywhere in University circles; and beyond them, too, wherever men esteemed themselves connoisseurs of issues and ideas. The Pope is a great idol. The Mass is ape's play. The holy sacrament of Confirmation is no more than a Bishop's buttering a child's forehead. The humanist in Erasmus almost retched in physical disgust; the religious man drew back. Here was the sort of brass-bound fool he could never find it in his heart to praise. There was neither fine point nor fair game in these blasphemous jibes. Foolish priests and bad Bishops were legitimate targets; never the sacraments established by God Himself when as a Man He walked the earth. Someday someone should well butter this great booby's Lutheran breech for him.

John Rastell had other thoughts. His interests did not yet run to theology as, to his sorrow and misfortune, they would one day do. But he knew somewhat both of war and sailing. He tapped his brother-in-law on the shoulder.

"I know little of churchmen, brother Thomas," he said roughly. "But somewhat of war. There I am one of your Utopians. Like them war do I detest and abhor. Like them I count nothing so much against real glory as false glory gotten in war. But like them I allow of one exception. I count it not war to colonize. And, when any people hold a piece of ground void and vacant, to no good or profitable use, keeping other hungry mouths from the possession of it, I count it not war to displace them from that unjust and unprofitable abuse. My sailors want no gold or pearls from the New Found Land to which we sail at dawn. We want timber for houses; fish for food; tar for goodly manufacture; life, air, sweet rest for Englishmen."

Thomas More began to smile at last; and, when Thomas More smiled, his face was singularly sweet. He raised his tankard in a toast. Of all that company only Henry Patenson knew his master's can had naught but water in it.

"I bid you good voyage, brother John," toasted Thomas More. "In my name and in the better name of my fellow guarantor, old Sir John More, who sends his blessing to his dear son, the master of the *Barbara*. I am a magistrate, and I tell you, if we open up this New Found Land of ours to peaceful settlement, there will be fewer beggars in our stocks and fewer bodies on our gallows and fewer clean maidens dragged off by the claws of harpy hunger to rot in our stews. Poor wretched souls! I tell you, in this fair island of ours the sheep are eating men. Daily another hamlet is enclosed by the royal bailiffs, and away men must needs trudge out of their known and accustomed houses; all their household stuff sold for barely naught, so quickly must they be about their forced remove. And when, all too soon, they have, in their witless wanderings, spent those last few poor groats, what can they do but beg and be whipped, or else steal and be hanged, unless they choose to be honest and be starved. And the end of it all is the gallows and the limed ditch. For no man will give them work these latter days, howsoever cheap they offer themselves. Unless, God forfend, they be fair and comely women; and that road lies disease and damnation. You do the King's and Christ's good work, Master Rastell. I am proud to call you brother. I bid you good and prosperous voyage to the New Found Land. Do you set out your maps now—here on this table. And let the rest of us look upon the brave course you intend. Then we shall drink a second time to your settlement. *Vale, comes Raphäele!*"

Mistress Alice had just lighted two additional silver candlesticks and was clearing a space in the middle of the table when, loud as a thunderclap from a clear sky in the silence of the soft spring night, burst the first knocking on the outer door. The company looked at one another without speaking. The clamor was repeated a second time. And a third.

"Open the door, friend Patenson," said Thomas More.

It was the *Barbara's* boatswain who entered, silver whistle dangling at the end of its loop about his tanned neck.

"I have grave news, Captain," he said to Rastell. "We sail not on the morrow for the New Found Land. The *Barbara* is already seized and impounded by Lord Admiral Surrey's men. The Channel is closed by King Henry's order, and we are for the French war."

Erasmus turned white. More's face was of stone. Rastell never moved.

"So," said Patenson gently to himself, "so my Lord Cardinal wins the throw."

Then, turning to the seaman:

"Here, friend, take this stoup of wine. Your throat will be dry enough, it is like, before the Frenchman is beaten to the ground."

When at long last the quiet little company broke up that night, Henry Patenson made his usual rounds, lantern in hand, methodically latching every gate and door. He paused for a long time at the oaken river postern, watching the moon gleam white on the swiftly running water, drawing a breath of apple blossom into his bitter lungs, listening, death in his heart, to the nightingale's descant. Then he turned on his heel, went back into the dining room, knocked off the heads of the unopened bottles—and they were not few—and proceeded to get drunk as rapidly and efficiently as he could. It was thus Dame Alice found him two hours before dawn, snoring on the threshold. She stared at the Jester without saying a word, for a minute or so, took out a coverlet from the wall chest, and wrapped him snug against the early morning cold. Then she went back to her bedroom. Thomas More had fallen into a restless sleep. He cried out as she snuffed the candle, but did not wake. Dame Alice, her gaunt face softening, more compassionate than even Patenson could guess at, laid a hand on her husband's shoulder till he was quiet again.

Outside the night breeze, now become the dawn breeze, continued to freshen. Very suddenly it turned and blew the other way. There was a devil's providence in things, it seemed. By morning fair stood the wind for France. It blew steadily against America and the New Found Land.

My Lord Admiral Surrey's gallant fleet got up sail: the *Dragon*, the *Lion*, the *George of Falmouth*, the *Peter Pomegranate*, the *Mary Rose*, the *Barbara*, and—bitterest irony of all—the little brig, *Erasmus*, christened in honor of a Dutch humanist who hated war. The gunners checked their priming and their oakum-punk. Seamen rubbed down the brazen cannon until they glinted bravely in the morning air. It was sure to be a fortunate war with the flagship's great guns cast, at Henry's instigation, in the shapes of the twelve apostles. Only the seagulls cried mournfully overhead in the blue spring air.

CHAPTER VIII

BELLS ON THE WIND:

After Midnight, October, 1529

IF there was one thing Desiderius Erasmus hated above all else, it was cold. Cold made his thin blood run blue. Cold made the salt rheum gall his scholar's red-rimmed eyes, and stand, in bitter drops, on the tip of his meager nose. And a single brazier, with coals already falling into white ash at the rusted bottom of the iron grid, was scant defense against the dank north Atlantic wind that was sweeping into autumn Rotterdam at one past midnight on a bleak October morning. But, if there was one thing that could make Desiderius Erasmus forget even the rigors of the weather, it was corresponding with a friend; and he had been owing Ulrich von Hutten a letter for several weeks now. So, with a little sigh, Erasmus set aside his prized new copy of Josephus' *Jewish Antiquities*—it was a welcome gift from a new French admirer, one Doctor François Rabelais, author of that amusing pasquinade, *Gargantua*, who, judging by the epistle appended to his learned present, also wrote very entertaining letters indeed—lightly sanded the latest page of the *Commentary* he was working on, and devoted himself to the much more congenial task of communing with his beloved Ulrich. Even as he did so, a hoarse bell clapper, tolling the hour of one, cut across the raw Rotterdam air. Erasmus shivered and plucked his fur tippet higher about a corded neck; then he smiled a bitter smile. Herr von Hutten was an amateur of campanology; he loved bells almost as well as he loved books. Well, he would start with a pretty little titbit about bells. The feathered pen moved quickly over the crackling paper, as a cooling ember shifted in its bed of ash.

Bells on the Wind:

"My dear Ulrich von Hutten," he began. "In your honor I commence with bells. Do you know what François of France has done with the bells of Paris? No, have no fear of ultimate disaster. He has not melted them down into cannon. Except for the great bells of Notre Dame which Master Rabelais' Gargantua stole for the neck of his mare—I earnestly enjoin you to lay hold on a copy of the misadventures of that most entertaining giant—your beloved Paris bells are safe. But the bell founders of Paris are not quite so safe. François' engineers have worked out a most effective new gun, cast as bells are cast. It has a further range, by several hundred yards, than the best English or German guns. So, for a time, his long-legged Majesty of France will be cock of the imperial walk. The peace of Cambrai will not stand much longer now. But I do not by any means predict that François' standards will very soon be pitched in London or Madrid. Already, I have no doubt, François is blown upon. Already, I would wager my Greek Testament, English agents have bribed French gunsmiths—and bellcasters—and even now, I suppose, the new gun is in production under the supervision of Henry's master armorers. What is such a bitter pill for me to swallow in this matter is the source of these terrible new cannon. Up to today our bell towers rang out requiem and mass and marriage; now their brazen throat will blare forth death as well. Everything returneth unto death, my Ulrich, in this poor Europe of ours.

"To pass to pleasanter things. I am heartily glad to hear of your going to England, though you might have picked a better season for your first visit. Spring is the proper time of year to live in Arthur's island. However, there are good points even about this season of mists and cold, especially if you manage to get invited to a few dinners at court. From all accounts, as he grows older, His Majesty of England is become a king of trenchermen. He was no bad hand at table when I was living there. As I remember it, his favorite dish was then roast swan.

"I am also pleased to hear that you intend to pay a call upon my great good friend, Sir Thomas More. It is a pity you did not meet him earlier, for I am told he is now in the way of becoming a courtier pure and simple, always with King Henry, on whose council he sits daily. I should regret the more his being drawn into court life, were it not that under such a King, and with so many learned colleagues, London seems rather a University than a court. Still and all, there is infinite loss to laughter in this new arrangement. Whatever the odds, we shall get no more news from nowhere to set us laughing, and I know, from personal experience, that More would much rather laugh than be chaired in official state. I suppose we shall, instead, get much reliable news from somewhere. But that is not the same at all.

"But no matter. At home or at Court, at law or laughter, my darling More is still my darling More. And what is that? What our good friend Colet called the one genius of Britain. And a very genial genius, I may add. For angelic wit and singular learning I know not his fellow. No, nor for gentleness, lowliness, and affability. You will always find him, unless these new cares of state press too heavily, a man of marvelous mirth and pleasant pastime; and sometimes, if you come on him un-awares—not many know this, so say nothing of it at any time—you will find him of as sad gravity. In short, my dear Ulrich, let us call him a man for all seasons, and for every weather, and so have done."

The bell tolled the half-hour. Again Erasmus shivered a little, while he sprinkled sand from the pounce box.

"And none too soon either," the quill scratched on to its impatient conclusion. "It is half after one, by the clock, of a cold and dismal Dutch morning."

He folded the letter twice, held a pencil of sealing wax to the candle flame, then paused as another and merrier thought seemed to strike him.

"I recommend you also," [he closed with a flourish,] "a droll rascal of Sir Thomas' household—one Henry Patenson, *joculator*. And, to close as we began, with bells: you will soon, if you are lucky, make the acquaintance of *la belle* Boleyn. They say she beareth the bell away—bell, rope, and all—from the other Court beauties. At least in Henry's eyes, and his is the *imprimatur* which counts at Court.

"Yours, by all the bells of Rotterdam—Erasmus."

He signed the missive, sealed it, and blew out the shivering candle at long last.

As it happened, across the sullen North Sea, in his London house, the French Ambassador to the Court of Henry of England was writing a letter at that selfsame moment to his own *dimidium animae*,

Bells on the Wind:

Master François Rabelais, Gray Friar of the Monastery of Puy-Saint-Martin, about to become Benedictine of Poitou's Saint-Pierre, Doctor of Medicine by the gracious decree of the medical Faculty of Montepellier, and, by grace of his own immortal comic genius, author of the *Great and Inestimable Chronicles of the Great and Enormous Giant Gargantua.* The Ambassador-scrivener, still booted and spurred, though it already drew on to morning, was that witty churchman and patron of wits, Bishop Jean du Bellay, soon to be Cardinal Jean du Bellay, holder of the episcopal see of Bayonne, brother of the great Seigneur de Langey, and His Majesty of France's appointee to champion the cause of Henry's divorce with the Pope. This latter fact, plus the Bishop's gay personal attainments, undoubtedly accounted for the gifts *la belle* Boleyn had that day lavished on him, after their morning's hunting: a new hat, with a quite unepiscopal feather in it; a bow and arrow; and a greyhound; also a score of orange pies, sundry rare cheeses of the shape of millstones which he would forthwith dispatch to France; capons, strawberries, quinces, and numerous crusted bottles of old wine. It was a goodly return for the twinges of sciatica these plaguy English fogs were bringing on him. Monseigneur du Bellay took care to set it all down in due order in this letter to his *aimable* François; and, for good measure, certain shrewd animadversions on the way things were going at Court.

"O Monsieur Domine, *bellidonnaminor nobis!*" [It began with a fan-faronade of jesting compliment.] "Yes, I freely confess it. I've reached the age when all I want from life is a good wine, a good bed, my back to a good fire, my front drawn up to a good table, and a good deep dish before me! But what do I do in this damp, accursed country? Nothing but gallop over a soggy countryside with *la belle* Boleyn who evidently considers me her angel's advocate at the court of Peter Fisherman. And so I am, in a sense, though my heart is not in the unlovely task. I do not care too much for our pot-walloping *gourmand* of a King Henry. Put him down in your *Pantagruel.* You have my episcopal permission for that act of *lèse majesté.* It raineth food and drink at his table, even as it raineth rain in the muddy lanes of his kingdom. It is a veritable *vie de Cockaigne* here at Court; but I like not the fat monarch's manners—at bed *or* board. Again I say it: inter him indecently in the rich

154

Gallic dung of your *Pantagruel*. I can think of no more fitting fate for the royal *glouton*.

"And, speaking of *Pantagruel*, how is the threatened health of Gargantua's giant-spouse, Princess Badebec, daughter of the King of the great city, Amaurot, in the famous land of Utopia? Sir Thomas More—Thaumast, as you call him in your ineffable Disputation by Signs—was asking after the giant maiden only the other day. Sir Thomas was hugely delighted, as he should have been, when I first told him that neither Master Hythlodaye's discoveries nor the line of Amaurot were destined to pass from the mirth of men so long as one Master Rabelais kept alive. It will please you to know that More is become the great man here at Court. They say he will soon be Chancellor. Whether that be sure or not, I cannot tell. But this thing I can tell: that the wolves get ready to despoil my Lord of York.

"I think my own time at Court, as well as Wolsey's, grows short. It is as well. For, as I said before, I find Henry a most antipathetic personality: a *faux bonhomme*, cold, brutal, sinuous, like a great royal python; obstinate, violent, and, I greatly fear, thoroughly bad. Erasmus—your father-mother, as you call him—has a maxim concerning nature: *Naturam appello docilitatem et propensionem ad res honestas.* Nature, he says, is docility and a propensity toward decent behavior. Well, if Dom Erasmus is right about nature, then Henry is unnatural to the core. I see no propensity whatsoever toward decent behavior in his chill intellect. Nevertheless, in England quite as much as in Thélème, it is an ill wind indeed which blows no one any good. If Henry, as he daily threatens to do, takes matters into his own gross hands, why, then, one Jean du Bellay will be at liberty to go home with a clean conscience and with clean hands, relieved that he, at least, has done no injury to that gracious lady of Aragon, Queen Catherine.

"It is bruited about the backstairs of the palace that yesterday Henry told Catherine, if the Pope would not declare their marriage null and void, then he intended to denounce the Pope as a heretic and marry whom he pleased. There is a new man newly come to Court here, a Cambridge theologian by the name of Thomas Cranmer, who has suggested to Foxe and Gardiner that the King enlist on his side the theologians and canonists of the whole university world. Wolsey has already pleaded guilty to violating *Praemunire* and thrown himself on the King's mercy; it is almost as if Thomas à Becket had never lived or—what is more to the point—had never died to uphold the immunity of the clerisy from lay courts. The new royal council, moreover, is headed by the Cardinal's bitterest enemy next to Mademoiselle Ann—*ma foi*, François, I would not care to have that woman for an enemy!—her uncle, Thomas Howard, Duke of Norfolk. Rumor hath it that the Cardinal is on the point of giving over his Great Seal of Office on the King's demand. If this is so, and I have no reason to doubt it, then I am afraid churchmen will never wield the Seal again in England, and that the Church in England is in for many unpleasant surprises before this new Parliament has run its course. Chapuys, Charles' ambassador here, who is well intentioned toward religion, if not toward France, told me this morning that, once Wolsey is dead or ruined—it does not matter which—the great lords, led by Norfolk, intend forthwith to impeach the status of the Church and to dispoil it of its goodly holdings. I sorely fear this may be so. Chapuys also said that, since the King's great matter has become so pressing, Henry loves not jesting, as he once did. He will no longer have about him the *mocqueurs* and *gaudisseurs* he once—I will not say 'loved'; Henry never loved—let us say esteemed. But I both love and esteem *mon plus cher mocqueur et gaudisseur*.

"Jean, *Episcopus jam diu—et nunc Venator!*

"*A bientôt*, François—

I shall see you soon."

His Eminence, the Bishop of Bayonne, yawned delicately, and picked up a chased goblet brimmed with wine. A clock chimed two in the darkness of his ornate room.

A sovereign *mocqueur* and *gaudisseur*, of English stock and gristle, Henry Patenson by name, sat up late this night, while he waited for his master in one of the antechambers of the old Chapter House at Westminster. When he needed to, Patenson knew how to sleep huddled against a wall in such a way that he husbanded both energy and animal warmth. Tonight, however late the hour, he had other fish to fry. Tonight was rehearsal night for the latest Patenson turn which was designed to take the form of a walking *Court Gazette*, one that would never get itself certified by any Stationers' Register in this or any other reign, but which, nonetheless, would be laden with excellent history, including some that would, otherwise, never get written down. Henry Patenson had become at last the kind of prudent artist who knew when it was expedient impudently to improvise, and when it was the very reverse. Care may have killed a cat; it had certainly spared many a wary Jester a sound drubbing. It was true servants were never beaten in the More household; it was equally true that same immunity did not extend to the quick tempered noblemen Patenson encountered, in the company of his master, in the purlieus of Westminster and Whitechapel. So, very carefully, striking one playing card attitude after another, he rehearsed the morrow's drolleries, while Westminster clock struck two hours after midnight and an appreciative audience—at least, at the outset—of two grinning men-at-arms touched up a dying fire into fitful life.

"*Item:* by the King's favor," intoned the Jester to the men-at-arms, "Speaker More to have a tun of good red wine, and his father, Judge More, a hogshead.

"*Item:* Speaker More resigns office of Under Sheriff. Becomes Chancellor of the Duchy of Lancaster; High Steward of the University of Cambridge, at which latter accession Cuthbert Tunstall, Bishop of London and Durham, sends him a fly most cunningly preserved in amber, and he, in his turn, bestows on Scholar Cranevelt a gold coin of Tiberius, a silver coin of Augustus, and, for Scholar Cranevelt's wife, a gold ring of England with a rhyming posy inset."

"And what for Jester Patenson?" catcalled the red-haired man-at-arms.

"What for Jester Patenson?" mocked back the self-appointed Gazettist. "Why, longer hours, such as I enjoy this very night. But look you, sirrah Audience, my master hath an access of new office and of flies in amber; of new duties and new responsibilities. But no new monies, nor new perquisites. He groweth poorer, not richer, as he waxeth in honor. It is a paradox such as always attends upon Master More who sets at naught the way of the world. Even his grants have strings attached to them. Perpend!"

Patenson put finger to lips in exaggerated request for silence; and continued:

"*Item:* The City of London grants More ten pounds sterling toward

the purchase of a velvet gown in which to receive, for them, Charles
of Hapsburg on his imperial Progress through England.

"*Item:* Mistress Alice Middleton, mine and Master More's most
gracious mistress, requests that her Speaker husband wear his gold
chain of office to church. After judicious deliberation Speaker More
replies that, for his part, he will not wear said chain, but that she
may, if she cares to."

Here Patenson broke off for a mulled flagon the shorter man-at-
arms was good enough to offer him, deftly scooping it up from its
snug point of vantage on the fender.

"I wonder," he said to himself as he drank, "if I should use this part.
Sir Thomas jests freely enough about his lady, but always at home.
And I would do neither of them any harm."

Regretfully the Jester decided to table this particular portion of
his *Gazette.*

"*Item,*" he began again, munching a roasted crabapple between
gulps of the spiced wine-cup. "*Item:* His puissant Majesty, Henricus,
the eighth of that name, appoints his beloved Speaker of the House of
Commons, Thomas More, Knight of Chelsea, of the rank of *armiger*
and *eques,* Master of Requests in the Court of Poor Men's Causes. So
justly does the new Master of Requests conduct himself toward the
poor, and so little does he regard the persons of the rich, that the
prentices of London have now a new cry: *This is Robin come again!*"

"Huzza!" shouted the red-haired man-at-arms. "Huzza for Robin
and Maid Marian!"

Patenson hurled his apple core at the guard's flaming thatch.

"Well may you shout *Huzza!*" he observed in a lordly way. "But do
not presume too far. Master More is as generous as Robin Hood to the
poor, it is true; but as stern as the Sheriff of Nottingham toward
thieves."

"But I am poor," protested the guard.

"And a thief," grinned Patenson into his face. "A poor thief, if you
insist. But incontrovertibly a thief. To resume:

"*Item:* Speaker More completes the final removal of his whole
household from the Street of the Herb Sellers at the Barge in Bucklersbury to Thameside, Chelsea. There the Great House's barns burn

down and he writes Dame Alice from Woodstock thus: *Pray you, compensate our neighbors. For, if I should not leave myself a spoon, there shall no poor neighbor of mine bear loss by any chance happened in my house. I pray you, be, with my children and your household, merry in God."*

"Aye," said the shorter man-at-arms, hiccoughing over his flagon, "aye, there's the rub. It is all very well to be merry. Who would not be merry? I like merriment as well as the next. But how is a body to be merry in God when his notion of merriment is to lie with Alisoun, his neighbor's wife?"

"An insoluble dilemma, sirrah," said Patenson after due reflection. "I have met with the same kind of difficulty myself. But I begin to lag in my catalogue of the life and times of Master More, Speaker of the House of Commons in his Majesty's high Parliament of England.

"*Item:* at the King's request Speaker More engages in debate with Master Luther and Master Tyndale over the knotty matters of Miracles and Justification by Faith.

"*Item:* Speaker More buys a fox, a beaver, and a weasel for his ménagerie. His monkey does not much approve the weasel."

"Marry," said the shorter man-at-arms, giggling a trifle drunkenly. "Nor would I. I find myself of the monkey's mind. What is a person to do with a weasel?"

"Marry yourself," said Patenson imperturbably. "I would not know. Hunt rats, perhaps. One could do with a weasel here at Court—or are there ferrets enough already in residence? You must ask Speaker More yourself. It is one of the odd humors of which he is ever full."

And the Jester continued with the *Gazette:*

"*Item:* Signor Giustinian, Ambassador from the Doge, returns Speaker More a private scrap of paper that had got in, somehow, among the Speaker's communications to the Venetian Republic. When translated from diplomatic cipher, it bore the enigmatic message:

"*Margret, Lizbeth, Cecily, John:*
These are the names my mind runs on.
They are my daughters; he is my son.
I thank the Lord God for their benison."

Red-hair sneezed. It was growing colder in the antechamber, as the fire waned, and the night drew on. Patenson ignored the interruption.

"A pretty fancy," he pronounced judicially. "If only poems about children were in vogue, my master might well make a name for himself in still another department. Never have I seen such a father as he. But the Court is all for a bawdy rigadoon or a love snatch to set the veins to jigging; and for nothing else. *Amour* is the only salable commodity nowadays."

Then another kind of thought altogether struck Patenson. He laughed a barking laugh.

"But sometimes even *amour* fetches a damned low price in the open market.

"*Item:* Sir Thomas Wyatt, poet, receives his *congé* from Mistress Anne Boleyn. The royal chase draws nearer. It is safer for the two of them this way. Nevertheless, Sir Thomas Wyatt, poet, resents the prudence of his *inamorata*.

"*Item:* Speaking of love, a new disease, the *love pestilence*, waxes in fashion. This new white death is as deadly as the old Black Death, and as international. But nations will fall out over this as over everything else. Our one-time Spanish allies call it the *French disease* on the good and sufficient grounds that it sprang from the sexual congress of a French leper and a French whore. Our one-time French enemies stigmatize it as *morbus Germanicus* on the equally good and sufficient grounds that it sprang from the sexual congress of a German whore and a German leper. Our English chirugeons remain discreetly silent on this matter."

It was a capital opening for the guards, had they not been too tipsy now to take it. Patenson looked in their direction for a moment, then went on:

"*Item:* England and France are at peace once again—perforce—after the Spanish Emperor and the French King conclude their separate peace. Speaker More salvages English honor at Cambrai. But even Speaker More is powerless to advantage the fallen in battle.

"*Item:* Speaker More subscribes himself my Lord Cardinal's *most bounden beadsman*. Faith, and why not? He prays for his enemies

160

nightly. If I were not Speaker More's great good friend, I should choose to be his dearest enemy. It is the next best thing.

"*Item:* The Duke of Suffolk declares at Blackfriars on the King's behalf: *It was never merry in England, whiles we had Cardinals among us.*"

Patenson laid down his imaginary herald's scroll. Both men-at-arms, their mouths hanging open drunkenly, had begun to snore.

"Now, sirrahs," he said, "as honest dolts replying to a rascal Fool, tell me—how like you my *Court Gazette?*"

The shorter man-at-arms yawned square in the Jester's face. Red-hair offered himself as spokesman for the two of them.

"I think it damnably dull, sirrah Fool," he said simply. "Without a jest, without a quip to break again in barracks for our fellows over our cups."

"So it is damnably dull," agreed Patenson. "To such as you, particularly. Virtue is always dull to a bawd. To a harlotry, whoreson rascal aught is dull but bawdry. But—what more nearly concerns me —it is damnably dangerous, too. My coxcomb should be in danger of the block, were the King to get wind of my making so free of Mistress Boleyn's name—as free, in faith, as he of her person. But he is the King, and can make and break poor Jesters as easily as he can make and break rich Cardinals. So to my last entry:

"*Item:* The great bell wether, which has led our flock so many years, is fallen at last. This very midnight past, but two short hours ago, my Lord Cardinal Wolsey delivers over his Great Seal of Office, after stamping his last state paper thrice: *Finis. Finis. Finis.* Wolsey is down, and no one to mourn him. And even now, in his Speaker's inner chamber—which is why I watch so late this night—my master, Sir Thomas More, meditates his succession to the Chancellorship."

This time it was Henry Patenson, and not the men-at-arms, who yawned so elaborately and stretched his parti-colored arms. Limping a little for the cold and the long vigil, he crossed to the embrasure of one of the great windows, drew the curtains, and looked out. It was black as pitch in the sleeping courtyard. A bell tolled twice from Westminster clock tower.

"Two of the clock," announced Patenson with a shrug, "Sir Speaker, my constant master still up, and the moon, my inconstant mistress, not yet up. No wonder we poor lunatics, her followers, are so horn mad with love and desire. It is she who cuckolds us. What says the poet?"

The Jester took up his lute and began to sing:

> *"The moon embraces her shepherd,*
> *And the queen of love her warrior:*
> *While the first doth horn*
> *The stars of morn,*
> *And the next the heavenly farrier."*

Even as he hummed over the verse a second time, the strumpet object of his singing peered—not boldly at all—shyly round the curtain and into the antechamber. If Master Patenson's imagery this night were not so unfailingly erotic, he might have decided that, under the black domino of darkness, the whey-faced October moon wore something of the rice-powdered look of one of Monseigneur du Bellay's new Pierrots who nightly strummed their own lutes at the French Ambassador's table; or even, from still another point of view, like one of the white-faced, staring-eyed little French altar boys who, in extravagant scalloped surplices, served the Bishop of Bayonne's morning Mass.

No fire burned at all in the freezing inner room where, in his Speaker's gown of office, Sir Thomas More paced back and forth, turning over and over again, in sore perplexity of mind, the greatest riddle of his life. His beard was thinner now, in his early fifties, than when Erasmus had last seen him; his auburn hair began to be plentifully flecked with gray. As he walked—a mannerism that was to grow on him, pitiably—his scholar's right shoulder rose above the left one. The complexion was still clear; and the serene gray eyes. Only the eyes were clouded now with the agony of his thought. In the long hours he had come, increasingly, to spend in the gallery, the library, and the chapel of Chelsea New Building, More had grown used to praying and meditating aloud. More than once Henry Patenson had come across his master speaking thus to himself; and so had Margaret Roper broken in on his self-communings. They both had found it an embarrassingly delicate experience so to behold a soul stripped. Patenson, of course, did not rationalize his embarrassment. Margaret knew the why and the wherefore of hers. It was not only that the man who kept these tortured vigils was her father. It was rather that he reminded her of another Man who had also prayed aloud once in a garden. Now, as he paced back and forth in front of a blackened, stone-cold hearth, his freezing feet as if shod in marble, Thomas More, with no one to hear but the chill moon, once again thought aloud and at length in the Gethsemane of Westminster's Chapter House:

"So. The great wether of the flock is fallen for his crafty juggling with the King. Had he not juggled so craftily, would he have fallen sooner, later, or not at all? Sooner, I fear. At any rate, sooner or later, all must fall out with Henry. I, too, if I take this great office proffered me; and at once, if I do not. Besides, England is my country; Henry my King; and Catherine my Queen. It may mean an earlier death by some years or months or days. But what of that? I owe the great Lord of Death the little present of a life. It matters little when or where one dies. How one dies is, rather, the great point at issue. Without the Chancellorship Mistress Alice might one day bury me with some honorable burying, with the delight of a goodly and seemly funeral: so many torches, so many tapers, so many black gowns, a gay hearse, and so many merry mourners laughing under black hoods. But, supposing I put aside my present pleasant life of quips and quillets and gay gauds, and, in place of fantasies and sports and merry tales, take up stern office, what manner of honorable burying am I likely to find in the end? But what odds? All men are under sentence. I am a man. I am also a judge. Death is a graver judge even than King Henry's Master of Requests in the Court of Poor Men's Causes. Let me put it to myself thus:

"Suppose there were two men, both of them condemned to death, and both carried out at once toward execution. If one were sure that the place of his execution were within a single mile, and the other twenty miles off—yes, or a hundred, if you will—why, he who stood in the cart to be carried a hundred miles would not, I think, take much more pleasure in the ride than his fellow, notwithstanding the greater length of his road to the gallows. No, not though it were a hundred times as long as his fellow's, and he had thereby a hundred times as long to live, since, of a surety, and out of all question, he had to die at the end anyway. We are all in this plight. We all of us stand in that black cart, and hangman Death waits by his high gibbet for us all. Now let me put it to myself another way:

"What if you should see a lout in a pageant wagon at Yuletide, earnestly proud of the wearing of a gay golden crown, while, poor lorel playing lord, he strutted and preened in his stage play—would you not laugh at his folly, considering you know that, when the play is done and all the Christmas candles snuffed out, the silly knave will climb down from his guild wagon and walk away in his tattered old coat? You and I, and all men, are in that pageant wagon. While the gay comedy is being played out, we are proud of our players' garments, forgetting, for a moment, that, when the play is done, we shall go forth as poor as the knave I told of in figure. But, leaving off this ensample of plays and players as too merry a comic rout for the tragedy men act in life, let me put to myself a third and last and more earnest, unfeigned image of our condition, and true figure of our worshipful estate here in the world.

"This round world is a prison; and of this one thing we can be very sure that, early or late, old or young, man or woman, prince or page, all the while we live in our green cage, the earth, we are but prisoners in a sure prison out of which can no man escape. Some of us grow proud and overweening of the arms our ancestors, forgetting, in their folly, their mortality, have set up in the prison. But all our pride is because, for a little hour, perhaps, we are able to forget it is a prison. For, if we take the matter aright, the place we live in is naught but a prison, and ourselves condemned to death from the instant of birth. So should we reckon, then, this idle gear of titles and offices as worshipful as if a gentleman thief, when he should go to hang on Tyburn

Tree, should leave behind for a prison memorial the arms of his ancestors painted on a post in Newgate Gaol."

As the weary man paused at last in his ceaseless pacing to and fro, the great bell of Westminster boomed out the hour of three.

"My passing bell tolls its first dull strokes," he said aloud again in sad resignation, while a smile traveled over his tired face. "Signor Giustinian told me once of Pope Julius that it was his greatest joy to be *lord and master of the game of the world.* Not for such a poor reason do I take this heavy cross of state upon me. I count the game of the world the sorriest of all worldly games, without savor or merriment in it. Nor do I crave power—no, nor knowledge, either. I remember what Italian Pico said in the little book I translated: *Behold, my well-beloved, what madness holds us? Love God we rather may than either know Him or by speech utter Him. In loving Him we may profit ourselves. We labor less and serve Him more.* Love is the law and lord of life. What I do, I do for love. I take up this dolorous cross of state for my country and my King; and most of all, I think, for that gracious lady, my Queen, that I may aid her somewhat in her coming travail. Henry, my puissant liege, you have a Chancellor! But would God your new Chancellor lived in Amaurot which lies in the pleasant land of Nowhere!"

The meditation had, as so often before, ended in a joke. Nevertheless, when Thomas More came out into the cold gray dawn, there were new lines graven about his mouth. Henry Patenson put on his master's cloak in silence. Then the two of them set wearily out for Chelsea where Dame Alice had also kept the lonely night watch, kneeling on her *prie-dieu* before the great More *Corpus* on its bed of crossed wooden staves.

CHAPTER IX

EXIT A CARDINAL

ENTER AN ARCHBISHOP:

Night, November, 1530

To an offstage accompaniment of thunder and lightning, of hail and sleet and wind, one of the fools was getting ready to leave the stage forever. As the savage gusts swept round the spires, and the driving sleet lashed the corbels of Norwich Cathedral, a pious canon thereof remarked to his fellow that one of the Devil's own must surely be dying this night of tempest, for the Prince of the Air himself strode the storm-rack and the driven clouds. Whether Thomas Wolsey, Cardinal Archbishop of York, was one of the Devil's own or not must be left to the Great Assizes to reveal. But this much was sure: for two long days now Thomas Wolsey, Cardinal Archbishop of York, had been dying; and now, as the hands of the clock drew on toward eight in the evening, the last sands in Wolsey's gold-chased hourglass were fast running out.

Onstage at Leicester Abbey, whither his retainers had borne their dying master in a litter, there was a great stir and bustle. Wax tapers burned brightly at the head and foot of the sick man's pallet. In their chapel the monks, in serried rows, chanted the Office of the Dying. The medical fraternity had been busy all day long, plying their herbs and Galenicals: gentiane, fennel, poppy, belladonna, foxglove, camomile, mint, thyme, vervain, chicory, lavender, St. John's wort, witch-herb, and the eldritch mandrake which, begotten of a hanged man's sperm, grows only under gallows; unicorn's—if the truth be known, narwhal's—horn, mummy powder, toadstools, frog's eggs, viper's fat and viper's blood, steamed pigeon dung; pills rolled into the shape of mice excrements. The acrid smell of smoking guaiac wood brought smarting tears to the eyes of watchers in the death chamber. Never had the Abbot of Leicester Abbey seen so many rich gilt rings and so many learned red robes; so many fur hats and cloaks edged with the costly miniver of the Doctors' guild; or, hanging on the first hook in the porter's cell, so huge a sword, the gift of Master Paracelsus to a fellow practitioner, now attendant on my Lord of York. Men said it had once been the sword of execution of a German hangman, and that its magic pommel contained the mystic elixir known to alchemists as Azoth of the Red Lion. This lately come German doctor had been recommended to Erasmus, when the Dutch scholar was living at Basle on the upper floor of the house of Froben the publisher, by Paracelsus, born Theophrastus Bombastus ab Hohenheim. Master Paracelsus, Herr Froben's personal physician, had told Erasmus that this learned colleague of his knew how to generate *homunculi* from horse dung—a thing Erasmus scoffed at in his inner heart—and that, while a prisoner of the Tartars in the Ukraine, he had been initiated into the secrets of the Siberian shamans. On the strength of this latter, and more credible piece of information, Erasmus had been willing to prefer Paracelsus' friend to Wolsey's court. But not even that quintessential extract, Azoth of the Red Lion, not even the deepest *arcana* of the shamans, could help the Cardinal Archbishop of York any more. Plucking at the coverlet, drowsing off by fits and starts, by fits and starts awaking and asking for a drop of water, the dying man's glazing eyes stared at the whitewashed ceiling, and the dying man's fevered memory looked, with the terrible clarity of the deathbed, into the past. Behind stage there, in the theater of the mind and heart and conscience, behind the sweat-beaded, once bland brow, the scenes were changed at lightning speed and in kaleidoscopic variety.

What passed before the dying Cardinal's mind's eye, as the great cold crept up from his red slippered feet; as the eyelids became transparent and the nose began to sharpen? He saw first the little tableau in his Cawood Castle bedchamber, three days before the time appointed for his formal installation in good earnest as Archbishop of York in the York Cathedral he had never visited, and now was fated never to set foot in. Like Moses, the Cardinal Archbishop of York, great statesman and bad priest, was destined never to behold the promised land of his mighty bishopric. The wheel of fortune had come full circle there at Cawood when the Earl of Cumberland, whom he had received hopefully as a guest, laid timorous hand upon his scarlet arm and stammered out an embarrassed: "My Lord of York, I arrest you for high treason." Henry Percy still stuttered—in matters of state now, as once, long before when he had courted Mistress Boleyn, in matters of love. Once the first shock of the arrest was over, Wolsey had wearily wondered if the balding Coldspur, as he had called him at the time when the Cardinal had been Henry's emissary to warn the youngster off the royal preserve of venery, realized the irony of the reversed roles. Probably not, he had decided. It was even possible that, in retrospect, the boy, grown older, had been grateful to the Cardinal for his meddling. As it turned out, Anne had been a fatal snare set for the destruction of many. No, it was not Harry Percy who had lost by Mistress Nan's promotion to the royal bedchamber. It was the Cardinal himself.

For Wolsey knew who had caused his fall from high estate. Henry, give the King his due, had seen fit to spare him the ultimate charge of attainder. But, after the confiscation of York House, Anne's implacable vengeance and the vengeance of her family had harried him from house to house to that last burrow of his at Cawood in the north. First had come the remove to Esher; next to Richmond; and then, had not old Norfolk growled out an interdict, he would have made his pilgrimage to Exeter. But Anne's grizzled uncle had no intention of allowing the red-robed necromancer any further access to a King who might still be swayed, by ninth-hour blandishments, against the Boleyn faction. He snarled to Cromwell that, if the Cardinal did not go north at once, he would tear him with his teeth like a cur. Nor had it done the Cardinal any good at all to attempt to placate Mistress Nan and her henchmen. He regretted now the begging letter he had sent to turncoat Cromwell the previous December:

Night, November, 1530

If the displeasure of my lady Anne be somewhat assuaged, as I pray God the same might be, then it should be devised that by some convenient mean she should be further labored, for this is the only remedy. All possible means must be used for the attaining of her favor. . . . I commit me to your wise handling.

The one possible means, the achievement of the divorce, had been beyond his power, thanks to the staunch will of the Spanish woman and to the steadfast support my Lord of Rochester, John Fisher, had provided her. And, in the end, Thomas Cromwell, too, had proved recreant. Everyone had deserted him except his Fool, Patch, and him—who was the fool here? reflected the Cardinal bitterly—he had sent away, a craven gift, to Henry.

Bribes were equally ineffectual. Anne's raffish brother George, Viscount Rochford, pocketed his annuity of two hundred pounds sterling from the Bishopric of Winchester, and a second two hundred pounds from the Abbey of St. Albans. Rochford's hell-for-leather friends, Henry Norris, Sir John Russell, Sir Henry Guildford, Lord Sandys, and Sir William Fitzwilliam were also pensioned from the Wolsey benefices. But it did no good. The Cardinal got in return naught but cynical grins. Mademoiselle Anne continued to embroider the Cardinal's rich copes, cloth of gold and cloth of silver, which she found in the carven chests of York House. His damasks, velvets, and sarcenets were given to her maids-in-waiting.

Yes, Anne had been the lurking pebble over which the subtle diplomatist had stumbled. The first and oldest of men's snares had meant his downfall; and—most bitterly ironic thought of all—she, who had undone him, had not even been his woman. He remembered the evening at Richmond when, alone with Cavendish, his usher, he had noticed the wall tile with Cadwallader's dun cow, the Welsh Tudors' emblem, burned in color into it.

"Look you, friend Cavendish," he had said, bitterness welling up and spilling over in his heart. "Upon this cow there hangs a prophecy a wandering Irish harper, who sang of the Cow of Cooley and the wars of Maeve and Conchobar, once told me:

Exit a Cardinal. Enter an Archbishop:

*"When the cow doth ride the bull,
Then, priest, beware thy skull."*

To make the Irishman's rhyming epigram tell, the sexes had to be reversed, of course. Here the bull was the bull of the Boleyns, and the cow the house of Tudor. Well, the Boleyn bull had gored him well; and the Welsh cow gave no more milk to its one-time first minister.

Charles the Emperor, in whose behalf—at least, in part—he had arranged the French war, had also deserted him at the last. But, after all, all was fair in love and war; and he really did not resent either Charles or Anne. What really wounded him to the quick was the defection of Cromwell, the squat toad he had warmed to political life in his own bosom. A nervous twitch tugged the dying man's mouth awry as he thought on Thomas Cromwell. There, in sorry truth, lay the worst of all his works. The rape of the Church he had served so badly was already far advanced; and Cromwell, putting into effect the lessons Wolsey taught him, was the Church's chief assailant. Under duress, the Convocation of Canterbury voted one hundred thousand pounds sterling, and the Convocation of York an additional nineteen thousand, to the Crown. The King had accepted the monies with alacrity, but he had forthwith informed the Lords spiritual he could not pardon their breach of *Praemunire* unless they formally recognized him as *sole protector and supreme head of the Church and Clergy of England*. What that elastic formula might mean for the future Wolsey shuddered to contemplate. Weakly the clergy qualified their acceptance of the brutal demand by stipulating, at Archbishop Warham's suggestion, that the King was *their singular protector, only and supreme Lord, and so far as the law of Christ allows, even Supreme Head.*

Meanwhile, under the pretext of attainder, the great spoliation went on, with Cromwell, looter, bribe-taker, blackmailer, in the van. The Abbeys of Barling, Kirkstead, Bridlington, Whalley, Jervaux, and Furness were suppressed. Glastonbury, Colchester, Reading were in mortal danger. Mock auctions disposed of monastery treasures to the greedy new and craven old nobility which did not scruple, from this point on, to drink its stolen wine out of consecrated chalices. As Cromwell swore once, with a mighty oath, provided only the wine were of a good vintage, he would not boggle to drink from the Holy Grail itself. The holy bells were melted down; the lead stripped from convent roofs; the glorious wood of rood screen and choir stall piled on a midden bonfire. One of Cromwell's most relentless pursuivants, Dr. Legh, had gone so far as to commit sacrilege at the tomb of St. Cuthbert who, before the coming of Cromwell's venal minion, had slept, incorrupt and inviolate, for more than eight and a half centuries. The dying Cardinal groaned aloud at the thought that it was he, an ordained priest of God, who had opened these floodgates of impious destruction.

The Boleyns had, on the whole, barring Mistress Anne, no particular love for Cromwell, either. So the canny creature had had to linger on in the Cardinal's entourage until he was able to make his deal with the new masters of the Court. The price paid was Wolsey's head on Tower Hill—or would have been, the dying man reflected, while a sardonic *rictus* twisted his features into a mask of agony, if another sergeant had not laid bony hand on his shoulder first. It had been, like most betrayals, fatally easy to arrange. Wolsey had been indicted under *Praemunire* for illegally exercising powers in the service of a foreign Prince, the Pope; but, nullifying the charge in law, was the awkward fact that he had in his possession the King's express license, sealed with the Broad Seal, for the wielding of those same powers. On the Eve of All Souls, but a year ago, Cromwell had filched the precious document. On All Saints' Day he presented it to the King in London. The second act in the treacherous drama was even simpler. With the aid of a hundred pounds' bribe from the Duke of Norfolk the Cardinal's Venetian physician, Signor Agostini, was induced to testify that Wolsey was in treasonable communication with both the Pope and the Emperor. It was on these trumped-up grounds that, hard on the heels of Harry Percy, Sir William Kingston, Constable of the Tower, had arrived at the Earl of Shrewsbury's house to take charge of Percy's prisoner. The amiable bearded giant who was Kingston tried to soften the blow with many protestations of good will; but there was no necessity. Thomas Wolsey had always been the most clear-sighted of men in political matters; and the last thin scales had long since fallen from his eyes. He knew Henry like a book. Henry Tudor was what Thomas Wolsey had made him. Putting his hand on Kingston's, he sadly told the Constable:

"Do not try to bring me into a fool's paradise, for I know what is provided for me."

But, as it happened, death had cheated all three of them: Henry Tudor, William Kingston, Thomas Wolsey. Even as, grimly thought the dying priest, death would one day cheat Thomas Cromwell. Gasping for breath, he remembered the last day he had seen Cromwell, on that year-old Halloween of his betrayal, standing at a window and reading, from an illuminated Book of Hours, the Little Office of Our Lady. Prescient of the end already destined for him, the Cardinal had asked the man, who had even then betrayed him, if he would see to it that his natural daughter by Mistress Larke was entered as a nun at St. Mary's of Shaftesbury. As for Mistress Larke herself, she had long since been provided for, and to the best of the Cardinal's ability; for Thomas Wolsey had always been a generous master. One of the articles in the Bill disabling the Cardinal had charged him with marrying off his uncanonical wife to Mr. Lee of Aldington. God grant she be happy in the life left to her! It had all been the Cardinal's fault, not hers. Mistress Larke had ever been as soft and gentle and kindly as a lark. God grant, too, that Thomas Cromwell remember and honor the pledge he made that All Souls' Eve in regard to Dorothy Clansey, daughter of a cardinal. If he kept faith with Mistress Larke's child, then let the slate be wiped clean between the Cardinal and his creature. Lying there on the Abbey pallet, on coarse sacking, not his own crisp monogrammed sheets, Wolsey saw again, as he had seen them in their last Halloween meeting, the queer lambent eyes in the great jack-o'-lantern's head of Thomas Cromwell.

He remembered other things, too, while the Abbot anointed his chill limbs with the sacred oils of Extreme Unction: how, the night of his leaving York House forever, a thousand boats filled with sullen citizens of London had waited along the Thames to see the tyrant Chancellor rowed to the Tower; how, for once, he had revolted against Mistress Boleyn's machinations when he refused to appoint as Abbess of Wilton the licentious nun, her sister-in-law, Eleanor Carey, she who had been the open paramour of two priests and a lord's steward; how he had been given the lie direct by John Fisher, Bishop of Rochester, at the Queen's first hearing at Blackfriars, as, clad in his legatine scarlet, he sat on the dais beside Cardinal Campeggio.

It was this memory, more than any other, which now burned its brand of shame into the Cardinal's soul. It was not alone that Fisher's defection, as Henry called it—even at the time Wolsey knew there was a better word—drove the last nail into the coffin of the Cardinal's ambitions; for, from that point on, Henry knew that Wolsey could no longer serve his purpose in the matter of the divorce. Wolsey was long past caring for worldly failure. No, he burned hot with shame at the memory of John Fisher's heroism and the heroism of Queen Catherine. There could be no possible shadow of doubt any longer. The Spanish woman, the English Bishop, and the lawyer who had succeeded my Lord Cardinal in the Chancellorship were worth the whole lying Court and the entire venal bench of time-serving Lords Spiritual put together.

Before the trial opened, he had accompanied Campeggio's litter to visit Queen Catherine. There the two canonists suggested that the Queen resolve the parlous coil by abdicating her throne and going into a convent. The resulting scene had been terrible. The high-spirited Aragonese in Catherine replied proudly that she was willing to do so on the single condition that Henry thereupon enter a monastery. Next day, while the two defeated legates sat on their Blackfriars dais, with Henry under a gold-brocaded canopy on their right, and, on their left, under a similar canopy, but on a lower level, the stiffly passionate Queen, John Fisher had thrown the court into turmoil by his icy denial of Warham's and Wolsey's representations.

At the end of Henry's formal statement that the Bishops of England, assembled in conclave, had granted him the license he asked to come to this court; and, on the very heels of Archbishop Warham's lackluster assent to the King's categorical assertion, the Bishop of Rochester had coolly risen to his feet.

"There is some mistake here, Sire," he had said, standing there, gaunt and hollow-eyed. "I gave not my hand nor seal to such an impious document."

Shaking, Henry faced him, as Herod must once have faced another John, the man of Jordan.

"Is not this your hand and seal?" the King asked, displaying the document.

"No, Sire," said Fisher, "not mine. I told the Archbishop of Canterbury I would assent to no such act."

"So you said at first," intervened my Lord of Canterbury, "but, at the last, you were persuaded. Is that not so, my Lord of York?"

Trembling, Wolsey agreed. Then the burning eyes were turned on him; and it was as if Sahara entered his soul.

"Under correction I speak, my Lord King, my Lords of York and Canterbury," came the icy voice. "But there is nothing more untrue than what my Lord of York has just now stated. I say there is either forgery or grave mistake here."

The silence that fell then on Blackfriars flowed again into the chamber where my Lord of York now fought for life. He knew that his fellow of Rochester had signed his own death warrant in that speech. Feebly Wolsey groped for the beads a monk held out to him.

"My Lord Abbot," he said faintly. "Pray for my Lord of Rochester, John Fisher."

One thing the Cardinal Archbishop of York did not choose to remember; and perhaps this act of abnegation meant his salvation. He did not choose to remember how, in this last twelvemonth of his travail, when men and Kings proved recreant, he had drawn closer to the God he had neglected over so many years. Every Sunday, for a year now, he had ridden to a new parish in his Yorkshire Riding, there to say Mass, while one of his chaplains preached on an acceptable text. Afterward, with his own Cardinal's hand, he would administer the Sacrament of Confirmation; and, in the evening, provide a dinner for the squires of the district at his own expense. He arranged Love Days to compound differences in the Shire, with himself as arbiter, and all his incomparable skill in resolving diplomatic coils at the service of any rustic Darby and Joan who happened to have fallen out with one another. When the Cathedral chapter of York consulted him on arrangements for his long-deferred installation, he insisted that he would not emulate his predecessors who had walked on thick-piled carpets from St. James' Chapel to the great Minster of York.

"We intend," he said simply, "to go on foot without any such pomp or glory."

Now, shod only in the holy chrism and fortified by viaticum, the Cardinal Archbishop of York set out alone on that last journey all other mortal men must go alone as well as Thomas Wolsey. Among the shadows that, in the light of the death tapers, flared huge upon the wall, the dying man made out the shapes of Cavendish, his usher, and of Sir William Kingston, Constable of the Tower. Cavendish was troubling him about the matter of some fifteen hundred pounds the King required from him, but the Cardinal waved him away impatiently. Here was no time for pounds sterling when an immortal soul yet wavered in the balance. But Wolsey felt a twinge of pity for the officer. He knew his death would mulct Kingston of a mission. The Cardinal beckoned to the giant. Even as he did so, a priest took Cavendish by the sleeve and whispered something in his ear.

"My bones will lie here, Master Kingston, in Leicester Abbey, if the King allow," said the Cardinal feebly. "If it be so, I thank my Liege. And, Master Kingston, it may be I can give the King's ministers advice I never followed myself in life. Let me counsel you, then, if you be one of the Privy Council, as by your wisdom you are most fit to be, take heed what you put into the King's head, for, once a thing is in, you can never get it out again."

"My Lord," said Kingston respectfully. "Do not tire yourself."

Wolsey smiled a wan ghost of a smile.

"No need now for courtiers' speeches," he said. "I go where they will advantage me no whit—though, Master Kingston, they do your good heart credit. I tarry but the will of God. My disease is such I cannot live. If there come no alteration soon, then must either ensue frenzy or else present death; and the best thereof is death."

"But the doctors," began Kingston.

Wolsey raised his hand with something of the old courtly grace that used to win men's hearts.

"The doctors prate," he said, smiling wistfully. "In the end we all suffer from the same thing. Not from *ens astri* or *ens veneni*—diseases of the stars, diseases of poison—but from *ens Dei*. Diseases sent from God—His last disease of death."

"I am afraid, my Lord," said Kingston respectfully, "that you are in such dolor and pensiveness because you fear that very thing that indeed you need not fear; and it is that same fear which makes you much worse than you need be."

"I thank you for your courtesy, Master Kingston," said Wolsey. "But it is no use. I see how the charge against me runs, and why and how and by whose hand it is framed. But, Master Kingston, if I had served my God as diligently as I have done my King, He would not have given me over in my gray hairs."

It is given to few men, as it was given to Thomas Wolsey, to pronounce their epitaphs. He never spoke again. The watchers at the bedside put the Cardinal in mind, then, of the passion of Jesus. The Abbot shrived and annealed him. Incontinent, upon the stroke of eight, he yielded up his troubled spirit. The great bell of Leicester Abbey began tolling in the night. Cavendish and Kingston took horse together and rode through the darkness toward London.

Henry, with a green feather in his velvet cap, and Anne, in her hunting suit of green, were at the butts in the park at Hampton, wearing out thus pleasantly a soft day of St. Martin's Summer, when Cavendish, spattered with mud, bone-weary, rode into Hampton courtyard. The westering rays of the sun gilded the still green turf with a mellow golden light. The trees shone crimson in a last heraldic defiance in the face of winter. The Cardinal's usher made his

way at once to the archery range where he stopped, leaning against
a tree, while the King sighted his longbow. The string twanged. A
shaft quivered to its mark in the clout. Thomas More and Henry
Patenson, who were in attendance, clapped politely. So did my Lord
of York's Fool, Patch, contented enough now in the King's service,
though it had taken six of the Court's brawniest yeomen to drag him
away from his old master's home on the day of the Cardinal's disgrace. Patenson, who could appreciate fierce feudal loyalties, no
longer though of Patch as poor Patch. From that day on he was stout
Will Patch to his fellow Jester.

Patenson was the first to notice Cavendish. He nudged his master's arm, gesturing in dumbshow.

"My Lord King," said Thomas More, as Henry discharged the
last arrow. "Master Cavendish is just now come."

Henry tossed the long bow to his Yeoman of bows. Cavendish
sank upon one knee.

"Sire," he said, "my Lord of York is dead. I saw him die at Leicester Abbey."

The King did not move a muscle.

"Yes?" he said indifferently, mumbling his lower lip with his teeth.
"And the money he was holding for us?"

"It is with a priest I know," said Cavendish. "He came to me as
the Cardinal was dying."

Henry turned to Anne.

"You shall sup alone this night for once," he said to her in a low
voice. "I have now much business to discharge. The Cardinal's death
signifies it is high time we were about it."

Then to More:

"Master Chancellor, summon the Privy Council to meet at once."

Patenson watched them go in silence. Patch's thin shoulders
quivered. A tear rolled down his long horse's cheek. Patenson
clapped him roughly on the back.

"Never mind, friend Patch," he said fiercely. "Nature has spared
your old master a blood-letting on Tower Hill. Now he can be buried
in his own head, with his own Cardinal's hat still sitting on it. But we

owe Master Cromwell a debt, you and I, for the scurvy work of this twelvemonth. And someday the headsman will claim it for us."

Henry Patenson was not altogether a chancy creature. He had been born with a caul, for one thing. For another, old Mother Maude used to say that the Jester had second sight. One of his Scots ancestors had been known as a warlock; and once, before he first came to Judge More's upright household where such fantods were unknown, he had walked widdershins in a driving snowstorm round a church. Now, in a cold fury of passion, he cursed the name of Cromwell—from its obscure beginnings to what he hoped would be its bloody and unlucky end.

"Snutit gomeral," he said, relapsing, as was his custom when deeply moved, into the broad Scots of his grandfather, "wheechy, doited, havering gowk, glaikit, foutering tawpie! A curse upon all roundheads, say I. Ye are the death of what is left in England of honor and of beauty. May your headsman be a botchering butcher fit only for felling steers and slitting the fat throats of swine—on second thought, may he be a headsman of Kings and unused to slaughtering pigs. In that case he will bungle the disgusting job of removing your cropped head from its stunted trunk!"

But William Patch was beyond this kind of consolation. Weeping, he straggled toward the back quarters of the palace. Always a philosopher once his infrequent bursts of passion were spent, Henry Patenson shrugged his shoulders and sat down to wait, his back against a beech bole. If the Privy Council had been summoned—and he had heard the summons with his own ears—then that meant another long vigil for the Chancellor's Jester who, meanwhile, could console himself with his old solaces of soliloquy and the even more efficacious contents of a swag-bellied bottle.

"What cannot be mended must needs be endured," he said to himself, "and death is one of those unfortunate things that rarely get mended in this vale of tears. Besides, it is the Cardinal and not Henry Patenson who lies cold in death. The Cardinal, if the King and Mistress Anne have left him anything at all, has the wherewithal to have Masses said for his delinquencies. Still, I could wish that friend

Patch were here drinking with me instead of whimpering in his tower room."

The evening bugle blew from the ramparts. A faint mist curled up from the ornamental sheet of water that lay, like a comely mirror, on the green ground of the King's turf. Two deer came out of the covert and, poised on delicate hoof, lapped from the little lake. Thunder muttered far off. A tongue of distant lightning licked the western sky. Patenson hiccoughed sleepily as a drop of rain pattered in the beech leaves above him.

"Far off," he yawned, stretching his arms up and along the smooth bark. "And why should it not be far off? Henry Patenson is but a Jester and a lover of good wine—though, when good is not forthcoming, he is quite ready to drink bad. My Lord of York was a Cardinal, and is now a corpse. Jupiter's thunderbolt is leveled at Titans, not at Fools. What is it Master More says the Latin poem says?"

He wove a drunken forefinger magisterially in the air.

"*Et procul a Baccho fulmen abesse solet.* Lightning is wont to give Bacchus a wide berth. If Master More says it, it must be true. So—"

He tilted up the flask till the last dregs gurgled in his throat, and began to sing.

> "Who killed Cock Robin?
> I, said the sparrow,
> With my little arrow,
> I killed Cock Robin.
>
> "Who saw him die?
> I, said the fly,
> With my little eye,
> I saw him die.
>
> "Who'll be chief mourner—?"

Patenson broke his song off suddenly. It was a dangerous song, and a barren one. Cock Robin, of course, was my Lord of the Cardinal breast. As for the sparrow, Venus' lecherous bird, Henry was an eagle, and Cromwell a mole—no treason there, surely. But what of Mistress Boleyn? Could the archer sparrow be Mistress Boleyn habited in green for the butts? A dangerous surmise, as things were going now, and one that winged straight to the heart of the clout. And the fly? Master Cavendish, though a courtier, was no water fly. There was a minor mystery here. But there was no mystery at all about who would be chief mourner. Will Patch would be chief mourner. Will Patch would be sole mourner, except for another little bird nowhere mentioned in his song. A lark. A Mistress Larke.

The Jester had had enough of his dirge. Also, he had another song to sing-o, now that Scarlet-breast was dead. The mock falsetto quavered into the darkness.

> *"Sing a song of sixpence,*
> *Pocket full of rye,*
> *Four and twenty blackbirds*
> *Baked in a pie.*
> *When the pie is opened,*
> *The birds begin to sing.*
> *Is not this a dainty dish*
> *To set before a King?"*

Glossing this was all too easy, thought Henry Patenson. He had neither sixpence in his purse nor rye in his pocket, but Cromwell, portly old rook that he was, was the baker; and the blackbirds he baked were the canons and curates, the monks and abbots, the beneficed priests under Wolsey's protection. They were a dainty dish indeed. And so, in another connection, was Mistress Bol—but there! With tipsy elaborateness the Jester put one unsteady finger to his lips. Singing was bad enough; but thinking was even more perilous than singing. Draggingly this time, for the wine was taking effect, the song struck up again.

> *"The King was in his counting house,*
> *Counting out his money.*
> *The Queen was in her parlor,*
> *Eating bread and honey.*
> *The maid was in the garden,*
> *Hanging up the clothes,*
> *When along came Henry Patenson*
> *And—"*

Night, November, 1530

Henry Tudor was not the only Henry who fancied himself a snatcher of maidenheads. But Henry Patenson, *joculator*, would have to pursue that clover-sweet, lavender-scented laundress through his dreams. The empty bottle rolled out into the moonlit glade. A snore rose, quivered and fell, under the bronzed leaves of the pavilion of beech. In London one of Queen Catherine's maids-in-waiting, prim-mouthed Jane Seymour, in whose cool veins flowed the blood of Edward III, bore a silver ewer to her mistress.

The Jester's song was more prophetic than he knew. The King was in his council chamber, not his counting house. Queen Catherine, upright as any funeral monument, prayed now amid the cold gold blaze of her Spanish chapel. But Queen Nan, uncrowned or not, ate bread and honey with the other Boleyns in her Hampton parlor. Monseigneur du Bellay's successor as French envoy, the Seigneur de la Guiche, was invited to the revels; and Anne's father, the old Earl of Wiltshire, who had a gallows' taste in humor, commissioned a farce, *Of the Cardinal's Going to Hell*. While the French lord looked on in granite disapproval, the wild Boleyn clan roared out its approbation, and Mistress Anne herself, bouffant skirts kilted up to her white thighs, danced a swirling *rigaudon* in honor of their great enemy's passing.

In the King's council chamber four men sat late after all the others, including Chancellor More, had left: Henry himself; Stephen Gardiner, the strong-jawed young Bishop of Winchester and the King's sworn man among the Bishops of England; Thomas Cromwell in the act of putting a new plot in train; and the Cambridge canonist, Thomas Cranmer. In Gardiner's presence Cromwell set about spinning the new web by asking my Lord of Winchester if he thought the Common Law superior to the Roman. Taken aback for a moment by what he rightly suspected to be a test, Gardiner answered swiftly that the Common Law was superior, because it was English and not foreign. It was not at all the answer Cromwell had expected. His quick wit detected at once that Gardiner had mistaken a test for a trap. But, in a way, they were the same thing.

"Try again, my Lord of Winchester," he said with a short laugh, while Stephen Gardiner froze into immobility at the explicit and insulting familiarity in the thick voice. "Translate for me this maxim from the Civil which is the Roman Law: *Quod principi placuit legis habet vigorem.*"

Henry's little eyes watched closely. The sweat stood out on Stephen Gardiner's forehead.

"It means," he said after a little, "that whatever pleases the King's will has the force of law."

"Come, then," said Cromwell, after a short pause of his own. "What think you of the maxim? Is it true law?"

"My Lord King," said Gardiner, addressing the King directly. "I have no doubt that you can make your will law, nor that your will is a good will. But it is ever better for Kings to make the laws their will, instead, for the laws have behind them the wisdom of generations."

The reply may well have saved the Bishop of Winchester's unsteady soul. It certainly lost him the Primacy of Canterbury.

The King stood up, fat thumbs hooked in his broad baldric, and swayed back and forth on the Turkey carpet.

"We thank you, my Lord of Winchester," he said with a formality that had also a kind of mockery in it. "You may go now."

Cromwell smiled to himself as he watched Henry teeter on his heels. The game proceeded according to plan. He had been Wolsey's creature once, and it had served his turn well enough. Now Wolsey was down; and, in horrid parody of the Gospels, where the body was, there the vultures gathered. This time Thomas Cromwell would have a creature of his own: a pliant clever creature with a beautiful voice and strangely pale eyes; one who yesternight had brought him a book as, long ago, he had brought *Il Principe* to Wolsey.

"You have a book under your arm I see, Master Cranmer," he said with heavy humor.

Cranmer looked at Cromwell out of his curious pale eyes.

"Yes," he said, in the beautiful voice, so low-pitched, so perfectly modulated, so almost feminine. "Master Tyndale's *The Obedience of a Christian Man.*"

182

"I thought,'" said Henry, smiling a little, "that the Archbishop of Canterbury had denounced Master Tyndale and all his works as heretic."

Cranmer turned his pale eyes and courteous voice toward the King.

"You will remember, Sire," he said with melodious respect, "that Archbishop Warham is now eighty-two years of age."

This time it was Cromwell who wore the little smile.

"I should suggest, Master Cranmer," he said, "that you read aloud before our Lord the King those marked pages you showed me yestereve."

So the mellow cadences rose and fell in the yellow candlelight as Master Thomas Cranmer, fellow of Jesus College, Cambridge, husband of German Margaret, niece of the Nuremberg Lutheran divine, Hosmer, and chaplain of Anne Boleyn, expounded for the first time in England, before the ready ears of Henry Tudor, the seductive doctrine of the divine right of Kings:

> *"Neither may the inferior person avenge himself upon the superior, or violently resist him, for whatsoever wrong it be. . . . Hereby seest thou that the King is, in the world, without law; and may at his lust do right or wrong, and shall give accounts but to God only. . . . Though he be the greatest tyrant in the world, yet is he unto thee a great benefit of God, and a thing wherefore thou oughtest to thank God highly. . . . As the law is a terrible thing, even so is the King: for he is ordained to take vengeance and hath a sword in his hand and not peacock's feathers. Fear him, therefore, and look on him as thou wouldst look on a sharp sword that hanged over thy head by a hair. Whatsoever is done to us by Kings, that doth God, be it good or bad. . . ."*

Cranmer looked up from his reading.

"Shall I go on, my Lord King?" he asked.

Henry stared at him, bemused.

"Go on," he said.

Exit a Cardinal. Enter an Archbishop:

"In time of judgment the King is minister in the kingdom of Christ; he preacheth no gospel, but the sharp law of vengeance. . . . That clerics should rule the state is a shame above all shames and a monstrous thing. . . . Let Kings rule their realms themselves. . . . Let the King's first care be to disregard the oaths he has sworn to protect the liberties of the Church. . . . Let him put down the tyranny of the clergy and lay hold of their ill-gotten wealth for the common good. . . . Let him reverse the verdict of the traitor à Becket. . . . One King, one Law is God's ordinance in every realm. . . . Let the King determine for the people what is and what is not heresy . . . Let the King cease to be a mere hangman for the Bishops and the Pope. . . ."

Long after Cranmer had taken his soft-voiced leave, Henry sat in a brown study which Cromwell was very careful not to interrupt. Finally he heaved his great bulk upright, and brought one heavy fist crashing down upon a table.

"By God," he said hoarsely, "your newest divine hath the right sow by the ear!"

"Said I not so?" asked Cromwell insinuatingly. "And what think you of Master Tyndale's book?"

"Master Tyndale is the philosopher for me," said Henry. "He is as much better than Machiavel even as—"

"As Luther is than Clement?" supplied Cromwell quickly.

Too quickly. It was almost a mistake. The royal author of the *Assertio Septem Sacramentorum* retained his distaste for the German heresiarch. But Henry was in no mood to argue with the man who, even before he expressed a wish therefor, supplied him with the requisite weapons his every whim desired.

"Let us say rather," conceded Henry, "as a German is than an Italian when it comes to the iron hand. But come, Master Cromwell, you have a purpose in this jugglery. What do you wish for Master Cranmer?"

"Give him the Primacy, Sire," said Cromwell bluntly.

The sheer audacity of the suggestion took Henry's breath for a moment.

"But Archbishop Warham," he began.

"Archbishop Warham," said Cromwell, striking blow after blow now on the hot iron of the King's bending will, "hath resisted *Praemunire*. If you wish to be severe, you have your remedy at hand. If you wish to be clement—well, it will do no harm. As Master Cranmer pointed out, Archbishop Warham is in his eighty-third year. Also, he grows daily more infirm."

The King said nothing more. After a time he made a sign with his hand and, bowing, Cromwell took leave in his turn. The silence continued unbroken while Henry thought. with growing satisfaction, on Tyndale's dictum that the King need account but to God. Then, from the direction of Hampton Park, there rose a reedy voice. Henry Patenson was awake again. With a muffled oath, Henry flung wide the window and listened.

> *"I had a little nut tree, nothing would it bear*
> *But a golden nutmeg and a silver pear;*
> *The King of Spain's daughter came to visit me*
> *And all for the sake of my little nut tree."*

Henry clicked to the leaded casement in a passion. He was not yet alone with God, after all. No, not by a long shot. There was still the King of Spain's daughter—and the Emperor of Spain's aunt—to reckon with. There was still the Chancellor whose drunken Fool sang at midnight in a King's park. And, but for a bastard boy and a puling girl child with a long Aragonese face like her mother's, the Tudor nut tree yet remained barren.

The King slept alone that night, snoring stertorously from a surfeit of wine. Thomas Cranmer, a trifle restless at the prospect of his great expectations, slept a bit less quietly than was his wont. But Thomas Wolsey, who in life had often slept uneasily, now slept most peacefully of all, his strong statesman's hands folded decorously on his breast, at the end of all his great expectations and, perhaps, at their true beginning also.

Exit a Cardinal. Enter an Archbishop

In the cold aisles of Leicester Abbey Minster the monks waked the mortal remains of the Cardinal Archbishop of York, prior to laying him in the grave prepared alongside that of Richard Crookback who fell on Bosworth Field before the craft of the first Henry Tudor. In after years the people called them the "tyrants' graves."

CHAPTER X

HANS HOLBEIN PAINTS A PICTURE:

Chelsea, Afternoon, Spring, 1531

MASTER HANS HOLBEIN was troubled. He had left this portrait till last, because he wanted it to be his best; and it was not going well at all. And the time had come for leaving England after his two years' pleasant and profitable stay in the Chelsea home of Chancellor More. Putting down his palette, he clenched strong teeth on the brush he had been using, and, eyes narrowed as in his apprentice days, stared at the elusive subject who sat so patiently before him, a half smile on his lips. Why should the Chancellor be so elusive? Erasmus had not eluded Holbein's quick eye; nor Paracelsus; nor the many rich commissions Master More had obligingly secured for him here in England where the King was so wealthy he could afford to allow a German painter thirty pounds a year for the mere privilege of calling him his court painter. Master Holbein rapidly ran over in his mind those same lucrative English commissions: old Judge More; Dame Alice Middleton; Margaret Roper; Nicholas Kratzer; Archbishop Warham; Sir Henry and Lady Guildford; Sir Thomas and Lady Elyot; Sir Thomas Wyatt; Sir Henry Wyatt; my Lord of Rochester, John Fisher; Master Thomas Cromwell; Mistress Anne Boleyn; and the King. Above all the King. He'd more than enough to buy that timbered house in Basle now; and the two years' leave the jealous burgesses of Basle had granted their famous son was almost over. If he did not wish to forfeit his citzenship in their city, he would have to leave England in a month.

Master Holbein had first sought leave to come to England when Oecolampadius' reforming iconoclasm made it impossible, for the time being, for any painter to secure a living in Basle. Oecolampadius himself, a humanist and friend of Zwingli and Melancthon, was no fanatic; but his partisans, the small craftsmen of Basle, went so far in their zeal for the new religious idea as to smash statues and deface paintings in church and private house alike. Desiderius Erasmus, then living in Freiburg where Holbein had done a portrait of him, knew a good artist when he saw one; and in Hans Holbein he detected not only a good but a new thing in the long history of painting. The German was more than a painter of portraits; he was an historian of the soul. What was more, he was akin to the Erasmian Humanists in his tolerant understanding of human nature. Where they were humanists with the pen, he was was a humanist with pencil and brush. So Erasmus wrote a letter to the Thomas More who could refuse him nothing.

England had been fruitful beyond all expectation. The King's patronage was literally golden; and Holbein owed it all to the King's good friend, Sir Thomas More. And now he was failing at what should have been the best portrait of all, his token of gratitude to the generous English statesman who had made a German painter's prosperity possible. Hans Holbein sighed and took a fresh stance. It wasn't that he was tired. He wasn't tired at all. His mind was electric; his long fingers tingled to get on with their task. One of the things that baffled him, he thought, was a stubborn preconception that these grave, seldom smiling lips should be quicksilver with swift smiles. And it wasn't only his painter's intuition that directed thus. There was also the evidence of a letter from Erasmus which bore witness that More's *countenance is in harmony with his character, being always expressive of an amiable joyousness, and even an incipient laughter, and, to speak candidly, it is better framed for gladness than for gravity and dignity.* But Erasmus had not seen his friend since he became Chancellor. He would hardly say now that Master More's countenance was better framed for gladness than for sadness.

Holbein resorted to a painter's trick. He would let his mind rest for a time, and, in the interval, allow trained eye and supple wrist go their own course. He would concentrate, for the nonce, on the technical problems of reproducing the living sheen of raiment: the deep

188

green of the courtepy; the warm fur of the collar; the breathing, pulsing crimson of the sleeves; the massy gold chain emblematic of More's post as Chancellor of the Duchy of Lancaster; the velvet lawyer's cap; the silver pouncet box on the table; and, beside it, the silver seal of the Sub-Treasurer, its handle a *fleur-de-lys*, with its Moor's head crest, its chevron engrailed between three cocks, a second chevron between three unicorns' heads couped. For the first time that day, as his quick, nervous fingers blocked in a Moor and three unicorns, the painter's eyes began to twinkle. Here, at last, was waggishness at work somewhere! He relished the pun on *Morus;* and the utter extravagance of the three heraldic beasts. This was more like the author of *Utopia* for whose delicate jests he had carved out woodblocks in the House of Froben ten years back and more.

But there! His mind was beginning to work again; and, when you came right down to it, to let one's mind repose was more easily said than done. Holbein could not help but contrast his present plight with last week's entirely dissimilar predicament. Today, in his portrait of Sir Thomas More, he was struggling with might and main to put in what he knew instinctively must be there but which, for the life of him, he could not prize out of the sensitive mobile mouth and grave eyes. Yesterday, at Hampton, he had had to restrain himself lest he put in too much of what he saw without half trying to see. Then his task had been subtraction; now it was addition. At Court too much candor will always be construed as *lèse majesté*. Here anything more or less than the absolute truth would be a disservice to the kindly patron who counted no labor, however heavy, lost, if it would advantage a friend.

But he hadn't taken out too much at Hampton, either. Hans Holbein laughed a little to himself. He was a prudent German who knew what side his bread was buttered on. He was also an artist and needs must tell the truth to shame the devil. Posterity would be able to recognize the royal bull, Henry Tudor, for what he was, thanks to the eye and brush of Hans Holbein. *Taurus Regalis* was what he would have liked to label the finished picture, if he had had an entirely free hand in such matters, and if there were no such uncomfortable things as blocks and gibbets in the world. Henry the Minotaur in cloth of gold and velvet, poising his brutal-shouldered, massive-headed bull's torso on columned legs; the low-hanging taurine dewlaps; the dangerous eyes. The eyes gave Henry away. Except for those alert, heavy-lidded eyes, one could be taken in by the man's fat joviality. Holbein, looking back, was greatly pleased with himself. Like a skilled matador he had, for days at a time, faced down the great bull and won. The bull would never know it; but the people he ruled, like some fabulous monster, had only to look at a portrait signed *Hans Holbein pinxit,* and they would know their King for what he really was.

Like many great portrait painters, Master Holbein was a philosopher of history. He lived, moreover, in an age which beheld anew the central confrontation of history: Christ facing Caesar. Christ and Caesar always stood face to face somewhere in an artist's consciousness. Now, once again, they stood face to face before the world. Since Constantine's day the contrast had been complicated by Caesar's effort to play Christian, and by an occasional foray of Christ's Vicar in the direction of Caesar's throne. Holbein remembered how Julius had essayed the role of warrior-Pope. He also remembered what Erasmus had told him, while he touched up the Dutch scholar's prim mouth and delicate hands, of Constantine's placing the Cross upon the shield of his Romans and having his warhorse's bit forged from a nail of the True Cross. It was a detail that bore much thinking on.

Well, there were still some quarters of the world where illusion of this dangerous sort, self-begotten as it was, did not blur the ancient separation of function. Henry might not be entirely clear in his mind as to what were the things of Christ and what were the things of Caesar. But Master More knew, and my Lord of Rochester, if Henry didn't. Holbein had listened to what they were saying at court about Henry's attempt to rule on the morality of his own marriage, and about his recent decision to usurp the Pope's prerogatives in England. He himself had seen the great pig-faced Priapus—Phoebus! one of these new Italians should paint him as the lewd garden god!—buy relics as good-luck talismans while the plague raged in the streets of London. Relics against bubonic infection! And such relics as they were! Holbein smiled cynically as he thought on the fantastic cheapjacks who had hawked them and, beyond any doubt, had also bottled these precious chimeras from the nearest green, scum-mantled, standing pond. For the relics in question were of the liquid variety: a vial glistening with the sweat of Michael exuded when he wrestled with the black archangel, Satan; a tear shed by Christ over Lazarus, kept by an angel and handed on to Lazarus' sister, Mary Magdalene. No German peasant would be so credulous as this English King.

Hans Holbein put down a brush abruptly. The sleeve could wait. Was the elusive quality he found it so hard to ensnare something Christlike? That rare essence had not eluded him when he painted the fleshless features and delicate bird bones of John Fisher; but my Lord of Rochester was basically simple. This man was not. His intellect, at least, was subtler, if his personality was as simple. Possibly here lay the essential clue to More's complexity: simplicity conjoined with subtlety. If so, Holbein had not encountered the combination in any other of his many subjects.

Very rapidly he went over in his mind the faces of the subjects who had sat before him since his coming to England, beginning with the royal bull and ending with the royal bull's patient Chancellor. Mistress Boleyn did not detain him long. Her cool ambition was a commonplace at every court in Europe. There was a Nan in the Escorial. There was a Nan in the Louvre. There was a Nan in more than one *Château* along the French King's swan-haunted Loire. Her patience was greater; her will was stronger; and she played for somewhat higher stakes. That was all. She was still a whore. Nor did he linger long on the sodden greed and saurian gaze of Master Cromwell. It was all there for posterity in Cromwell's portrait; but Holbein did not choose just now to think on Cromwell's portrait. The reckless, appealing sensuality of Sir Thomas Wyatt flashed through his mind; and the exquisite calm of spirit that stamped the tranquil face of More's daughter, Margaret Roper. But not even Margaret's serenity bore the seal of acceptance that marked her father's countenance.

Holbein thought next on certain of his Continental subjects. Desiderius Erasmus was all mind; all lucid reason. He was the essential ash of the fires of life, his ironic features burned transparent clear of all fear, all hope, all exaltation. There was not even room for despair in that ironic repose. Someday, God willing, Holbein hoped to do the face of Doctor François Rabelais, licentiate of Montpellier, whom he had met in one of Orléans' famous tennis courts. As Erasmus was all mind, so was Rabelais all body: shrewd, earthy, kindly; not gross at all. Master John Calvin was living in Orléans at the same time. He did not frequent tennis courts, but Holbein had an introduction to the godly Master Calvin secured from the Paracelsus who, in his turn, had received it from one of his many patrons, the reformer, Oecolampadius. Master Calvin had not been in the market for a portrait at the moment; but he would have been an interesting subject all the same, with his precise mouth, his thin nose, and the cold fire of his eyes. Mind had burned Erasmus away to essential irony. Mind had fined and thinned and rinsed Calvin into essential idea.

As for Dr. Paracelsus, thought Holbein, here, if anywhere, was the man of the future. He talked his share of nonsense about the alchemic steps: about distillation, calcination, sublimation, fixation, separation, coagulation, tinction. But there was something in it all the same; something that was not all nonsense by a long shot. The alchemists might not be getting at the Philosopher's Stone; but they were getting at something. In his capacity as "new man," Paracelsus' hard-bitten cynicism was almost overwhelming—even to so tough a customer as Hans Holbein plumed himself on being. He had, for example, no respect for Clement. But, then, he held no brief for the Reformers, either. As Holbein set down in paint Paracelsus' strong, undistinguished features, he registered the abysmal indifference to theology reflected in the Doctor's remark that Luther and the Pope were like "two whores discussing chastity." Dogmatic controversy, such as the one Master More was carrying on with Master Tyndale, meant less than nothing to Paracelsus. He did not take sides in the religious controversy convulsing Europe for the simple and sufficient reason that, in his laboratories, out of his smoke-blackened alembics and evil-smelling retorts, he was, almost without realizing it, evolving still a third attitude toward fundamental reality, one different from both the incandescent rationalism of Calvin and the traditional faith of Catholicism. Yet he was by no means without a kind of religion, a species of mysticism of his own. It had both repelled and attracted Hans Holbein, lover of women, to hear this advanced German Doctor theorize on Eden from the pages of his *magnum opus,* the *Philosophia Sagax,* the *Great Astronomy or Sagacious Philosophy of the Macrocosmos and Microcosmos.* Where and what is Eden? asked the learned Doctor of the new learning. It is the mother's womb and the lover's lap, and fallen man rediscovers it twice—once at birth, and again in the marital embrace. The idea was shocking. The idea was heterodox. But again there was something in it. Speaking as a man of the world and a student of affairs, Master Holbein could not tell yet about Henry, or the Pope, or his host-subject, Thomas More. But he would wager his last guilder that, in the long run, Dr. Paracelsus, though he might not live to see it, would be on the winning side. There was a new wind beginning to blow through old Europe. The cat of history was getting ready to jump again. And Master Holbein had placed his bet.

But, reflected the painter impatiently to himself, all this philosophic maundering was getting him absolutely nowhere. The sleeve was finished; the essential More continued to elude his brush. There was a kind of simplicity that, in the last analysis, was subtler than the serpent. And also, in the last analysis, this kind of simplicity was not a painter's business. Saints should be honored by shrines, not portraits. A saint should have no truck with courts and chanceries. A saint should not have a Mistress Alice Middleton for his second wife. If there was one thing harder to catch than a saint, it was a fool. But Master More, whether or not he was a saint, was certainly no fool. And, to go a step further out of his present fruitless labyrinth of aimless speculation, Master More's Fool, Henry Patenson, whether or not he was a fool, was just as certainly no saint.

As if in answer to the painter's unspoken thought, the family Fool strolled into the New House library where the sitting was taking place. Patenson could barely read, but he carried a French book under his arm, the third volume of Maître Rabelais' *Gargantua et Pantagruel,* which Rabelais had sent to More by Holbein in pleasant atonement for the scurvy trick his Panurge had played on Thaumast—as Rabelais jestingly chose to call More—in the second volume. As he listened to Margaret Roper reading it aloud, this third volume, superseding even the *Praise of Folly*, had become Patenson's favorite book, chiefly for the honor in which it held fools in general and, in particular, those two fools extraordinary: Seigny John, Chief Fool of the City of Paris, the famous great-grandfather of the Court Fool, Caillette; and Triboulet who advised Panurge on marriage. Patenson had already been able to make sly harvest out of the sumptuous list of presents a grateful Panurge gave Triboulet: a wooden sword magnificently gilded; a dainty purse of tortoise shell; a crusted bottle of old Breton wine in a wicker casket; a peck of red Blandureau apples; and a jacket of cloth of gold with escalloped edges. He had lived for a sufficient length of time in the household of Sir Thomas More to realize that Master Rabelais was right when he assigned to humor the important role in life of *pempte ousia*, the quintessence or fifth essence, the fifth being of beings in created things. He had, finally, been hungry and thirsty often enough, and often enough sick of a surfeit of food and drink, to appreciate why Rabelais preferred Master Gaster, the stomach, to all the miniver-hooded philosophers of Montpellier, Orléans, and Paris. After Master More, in Henry Patenson's scheme of things, came Master Gaster, importunate professor in the stomachic Sorbonne. Keep that clamorous pedagogue, Master Gaster, quiet, and the world rolled on wheels like the pageant wagon empowered to show forth Pentecost. Master Gaster was the Master for him.

That afternoon good-natured Margaret Roper had been indulgent enough—and, if the truth were known, amused enough herself—to read over, until he had got it by heart, Panurge's and Pantagruel's Tribouletinal litany of the fool; and, when the right time presented itself, Henry Patenson intended to pluck a make-believe foolscap from his doublet, and intone aloud this chorus anatomizing the perfect and impeccable, the proper and total, in a word, the pure fool. Perhaps the same propitious hour was even here and now. Hans Holbein put down his palette and brushes, stretching and yawning the while.

"You may relax now, Master More, an it please you," he said courteously. "Possibly Master Patenson would entertain us while we catch our breath for a second sitting. What say you, Master Patenson?"

"I am willing," said Henry Patenson. "How would you like Maître Rabelais' *Litany of a Fool* from the third volume of *Gargantua and Pantagruel?* It is hot from the Paris printers. No one at Court, even, has yet heard it."

"I should like it very well," said Hans Holbein, munching an apple and sprawling back in his chair. "A thorough knowledge of the *genus*, fool, would be of some advantage in my business."

"In mine, too," said Thomas More. "I, too, must read faces for a living."

"In that case," said Henry Patenson, curling his legs under him, "I shall be glad to oblige my learned colleagues of the College of Fools."

And he began droning out his *Litany of Fools:*

> "*Fool fatal.*
> *Fool natural.*
> *Fool celestial.*
> *Fool Jovial.*
> *Fool Mercurial.*
>
> "*Fool Caesarean.*
> *Fool imperial.*
> *Fool royal.*
> *Fool original.*
> *Fool loyal.*
>
> "*Fool Talmudic.*
> *Fool commendious.*
> *Fool abbreviated.*
> *Fool hyperbolical.*
> *Fool pleonasmical.*
> *Fool liverish.*
> *Fool cerebral.*
> *Fool splenetic.*
> *Fool lymphatic.*
> *Fool distilled.*
> *Fool complaisant.*
> *Fool in panic.*

Hans Holbein Paints a Picture:

"Fool high-toned.
Fool in B sharp and Fool in B flat.
Fool terrestrial.
Fool wild and Fool merry.
Fool jolly and Fool sportive.

"Fool papal.
Fool consistorial.
Fool conclavist.
Fool synodal.
Fool episcopal.

"Fool prognosticating.
Fool Summist.
Fool abbreviating.
Fool who morris dances.
Fool titular.
Fool cantankerous.
Fool well-hung.
Fool crosspatch.
Fool aziminic.
Fool baritonic.
Fool speckly.
Fool gun-proof."

Henry Patenson drew breath.

"Now," he asked, "what think you of my *Mirror for Fools*? Cannot every condition of fool find his fool's face reflected therein?"

"It is indeed a long list," conceded Thomas More.

"Yes," said Henry Patenson. "You are in it. Master Holbein is in it. We are, all of us, fools natural. Henry is fool royal. Clement is fool papal. The Emperor Charles is fool imperial. Will Patch, it is true, is too much of a fool pleasant to be termed fool crosspatch. But he is there with all the other fools, nonetheless. Have you ever seen Will Patch dance the morris? Will Patch is fool who morris dances."

"So I am in it, am I?" asked Master Holbein. "Where, an it pleasure your Foolship to answer?"

"And I?" asked Thomas More.

"You, Master Holbein," said Patenson, grinning, "like all Alemains, are fool well-hung. I, as I live and die, am fool fatal; and, as I hope to attain immortality when time is not, fool celestial as well. At the risk of stamping myself fool prognosticating wrongly, I should say, my Lord Chancellor, that you were once fool merry, and now are both fool episcopal and fool—"

"Fool episcopal, Master Patenson?" cut in Thomas More. "How so?"

Patenson answered vehemently in swift counter-thrust; and there was no levity in his voice now.

"That is easily answered, my Lord Chancellor," said the Fool. "Do you not play the monkey part of your own marmoset and pull their episcopal chestnuts out of the fire, lest my Lords spiritual soil and singe their dainty hands with their own proper work? Do you not, Sir Monkey More, monk it more than the monks themselves? Do you not nightly spoil your rest and waste your eyesight with scrivening replies to Masters Tyndale and Luther? What's Dom Luther to you or—"

A knocking at the door broke off the passionate harangue. Holbein, who had been listening to the Fool with vast interest, opened the door and took from the hands of one of Master More's watermen a letter sealed with the seal of the Duke of Norfolk.

"What is it, friend Holbein?" asked Thomas More.

"A message from the Duke of Norfolk," answered Holbein.

"Read it to me, an it please you, friend Holbein," said Thomas More.

Holbein slashed the wax with a palette knife, raked the missive with his eye, then set it hurriedly down. Life at certain ducal courts in the Germanies had made the painter wary of other people's secrets.

"It is a private communication," he said. "Not one intended for my eye or ear."

"Read it, Master Holbein," urged Thomas More courteously. "My Lord of Surrey and Norfolk is an old and frank and loyal friend of mine. You need not fear treason."

"It is not treason I fear, Master More," said Holbein, reluctantly picking up the letter. "It is against my judgment. But, since you wish it, I am willing to read."

And, very slowly, he read aloud the Earl of Surrey's ominous warning to Thomas More.

"Dear friend: It has come to my ear that the spoiling of shrines goes on apace, especially in the south. St. Cuthbert's at Durham, Our Lady of Walsingham, are suppressed as superstitious; and hence heretical. Belief in Our Lady and heaven's hallows is now, it seems, become the new heresy. But worse follows.

The martyred saint of Canterbury—your namesake, à Becket; *absit omen, care* More, but one can never be sure—has been exhumed, tried for treason, and for heresy, and his long-dead bones burned.

Another thing: Master Cromwell, who lords and clerks it above all others now with our Lord the King, has written his creature Pollard, at Hyde, 'to sweep away all the rotten bones that be called relics; which we may not omit lest it be thought we are more for the treasure than for avoiding the abomination of idolatry.'

You have friends in Flanders; and you have a family. Also you are reckoned a wise man. Show yourself one. The Emperor esteems you, and the French King. I dare write no more. Already I take my life in my hands by writing thus much; but I could do no less for my dearest More who, upon receiving it, will do well to burn this letter incontinent.

Norfolk."

Holbein looked up questioningly at Thomas More who never moved a muscle. Only he seemed older all at once.

"My Lord of Norfolk's suggestion is a good one, Master Holbein," said Thomas More at last. "Hold his letter to the candle flame."

While the crackling parchment curled into black ashes More turned to Henry Patenson.

"You were about to tell me what second variety of fool I am, friend Patenson," he said. "Besides fool episcopal, of course."

"Yes," said Henry Patenson, shaking with emotion, "yes. Does my Lord of Norfolk reckon you a wise man? You are fool Caesarean— Caesar horns you as well as the Bishops—and, to cap the list, you are, above all else, fool loyal."

"It may be, it may be, Master Patenson," said Thomas More, still as a graven image. "If it be as you say, you have complimented me."

Then to Holbein:

"Shall we resume the sitting?"

As Holbein prepared his easel again, Henry Patenson craned over the painter's shoulder at the unfinished portrait of his master.

"What think you of the likeness?" asked the painter.

Henry Patenson stared hard and long at the canvas.

"I think," he said, with no vestige of mockery in his tone, "I think the sleeve is admirably well done."

So, thought Hans Holbein to himself, as he set about his task once more, so the Fool has seen it, too. He sighed a little. Well, at least the sleeve was good. He had never painted a better sleeve.

CHAPTER XI

THE MARCHIONESS OF PEMBROKE

PAYS A VISIT:

Westminster, Evening, November, 1531

THE LEAN COURSING hounds of wind and rain were in at the death of the year. But, at least in island England, this year of 1531 had died gloriously; not ignominiously, as happens to men. Autumn had come much earlier than usual. That ruffling late-comer to August, the grasshopper, autumn's harbinger and outrider, had this year laid down his brittle *défi* to summer early in July. Across the Channel in France Dr. François Rabelais, waxing more poetic than was his wont, set pen to paper and wrote of how early the grasshoppers seemed to grow hoarse this season—*lors que les cigalles commencent à s'enrouer.* Braggart sword at guardsman's hip, the grasshopper strode high on insolent Gascon boots, affronting the busy burgess spider, spurring steel song into September's sorrel nights, predicting loud the purple wine of autumn occupation, October's subject sheaves, the winter defeat of the year. But, as the woods and groves fell into their tranced crimson sleep, wearing gonfanons instead of hatchments, winter still held off strangely. Fall's cardinal laid his legatine scarlet interdict over the fields of England. Under her heraldic coverlet of deep gules leaves Nature slept her vermilion sleep. At Chelsea, in his water-bright, water-sweet, water-loud, wood-hung demesne, Thomas More's beeches turned dark copper. The mellow old brick of the spiral chimneys flushed the redder for the reddening ivy that mantled them. The herb garden stayed aromatic under the gentle pestles of cool morning and hot noon. As he walked there, between the old silver of the river and the soft red of his Chelsea brick, looking out over the yellow fields and fallows, Chancellor More thought of England as some Oriental bird—like, for example, the resplendent Chinese pheasant, gold gorget on crimson body, a ship's captain, who plied China waters, had brought him for his ménagerie.

The change came with the last week of November. Rain lashed the leaded panes of Whitehall, streaming down the glass and heavy cames, while the King looked sullenly out, at loose ends, biting his nails for sheer vexation that tilt-yard and archery range had grown too sodden to use. Fog, cloaked like a pardoner, crept up the river past Bucklersbury, Blackfriars, Bridewell, the Temple, to Westminster, where, in the giant grates, fires were now kindled early and burned late into the chill nights. For my Lord Chancellor More refused to see no suitor, no matter how humble.

This night they burned especially bright in the antechamber of my Lord Chancellor's state office. For today Mistress Anne Boleyn, new-made Marchioness of Pembroke, had taken her impatient way to Westminster to pay a call on my Lord Chancellor More. It proved to be a long call. The two of them had already been closeted together in the inner office for more than two hours; and still the slow minutes ticked away into the lengthening shadows of the gray November evening.

The fire burned red in the fender. A suitor, muffled in a dark cloak so that his face remained hidden, came in, and, nodding to the guards, took his place on a bench against the wall, at the other end of the room from where Mistress Anne's maid-in-waiting sat, chaffing with two guardsmen—the same two guardsmen who used to keep the antechamber for Master More in the old Chapter House when he was still but Master Speaker and not yet my Lord Chancellor. They were old friends on and off duty, the precious pair of them, quite inclined, in casual encounters such as this one, to share the lists of love together. With common strumpets there can be no rivalry; and, for all her air of gentility and rich perfumes, Mademoiselle Renée was a common strumpet. The cloaked suitor, lithe and arrogant, still young, watched the guardsmen's clumsy overtures with contemptuous amusement.

"La, Sir Guardsman!" said the maid-in-waiting, pulling away from the redheaded guardsman's grasp, but taking care not to tug so firmly that he would lose his hold in earnest. "I have but to cry out and my mistress will hear."

The maid-in-waiting slurred her r's like the French woman she was. She had been serving-maid in the service of Queen Claude, and, later, of Marguerite, Duchesse d'Alençon, when Anne Boleyn was herself maid-in-waiting to those two French princesses. Mademoiselle Renée, as she was called, had, on a certain memorable occasion when Louis XII had deigned to pay impetuous court to the English girl, been able to rescue her from a most compromising situation; and, when Mistress Boleyn returned to England, she had taken the clever French-woman with her.

As neither redhead nor his fellow showed the slightest inclination to honor her warning, Mademoiselle, with a soft rolling of gutturals, for all the world like some pouter-breasted amorous pigeon, renewed it. Red-thatch only laughed.

"She will hear, I have no doubt," he said, "but will she heed? Master More, who sometimes seems half monk, is concerned about the chastity of serving-maids and serving-men in his halls. Do not cry so loud his monkish ears will hear, else our pleasant sport is like to have a sudden termination. As for Mistress Boleyn, however, I am told on authority she herself is quite expert in the ways of a maid with a man."

Mademoiselle Renée flirted her front of false curls.

"Be more respectful, if you please, Monsieur Leroux," she said saucily. "My mistress is now Her Grace, the Marchioness of Pembroke."

The shorter guardsman, with an expertise born of long practice, took her plump hand in his very suddenly.

"They say," he remarked, "that your mistress gives Henry love phil-ters."

The Frenchwoman's grin was halfway between monkey and tiger.

"If so," she answered coarsely, "they are better than the pox his Spanish nun gives him."

"They also say," pursued the shorter guardsman, "that your mistress has something more about her person than most other women. Than you, for example."

"*Comment? On dit?*" shrugged Mademoiselle Renée. "And just what is it they say she 'ave?"

"A sixth finger on her right hand," said the shorter guardsman, stroking the maid-in-waiting's palm. "My old nurse told me once that was an infallible sign of a vampire."

Mademoiselle Renée came from Normandy where, in the twilight hour between the dog and the wolf, the awful *loup-garou* walks the cold moors. So she did not altogether like this talk of vampires. After all, one never knew for sure. Mistress Anne was very good to her, but, when she was angry, her slanted eyes glinted greenly.

"It may be so," she said, laughing uneasily. "I do not know. I have never seen Mistress Boleyn without her French gloves. She keeps them on always."

"That is proof then," said red-thatch, slipping a deft arm round her waist. "For my part, I have heard she has other things as well about her that Christian maids are not in the habit of possessing. Things that make her a troll as well as a vampire. Andres, our Norse comrade in the guardsman's mess, saw her bathing once in Hampton Park at midnight, and he says she is no mortal woman but a Stavanger troll."

His practiced hand stole upward toward her tight-laced bodice. She laughed into his flushed face.

"*Et cela, Monsieur de la garde du roi?*" she asked provocatively. "What is it, Sir Guardsman, that trolls are so fortunate to 'ave, and not Christian women?"

The guardsman secured a firmer hold on her ample breast.

"Guess," he said, mocking his captive. "But first let me give you a clue. Mademoiselle Renée Dubois, maid-in-waiting to a vampire troll, has the customary number of the feminine appurtenances in question."

"And very fetching ones, too," added the shorter comrade-in-arms, pressing home his amorous advantage on her unprotected other flank.

Again the French woman laughed shrilly. But this time her strident laughter was cut short by the sudden intrusion of the cloaked suitor who, up till now, had been a sardonic onlooker, without comment, of this bucolic *tableau à trois*.

Now, standing up, he cut across their laughing scuffle.

"Perhaps," said the unknown in a voice that rasped disconcertingly,

"perhaps, my friends, I can resolve these little metaphysical diffi-
culties of yours. At the very least, I can satisfy your curiosity and give
the lie direct to friend Andres who has such accurate information
about Stavanger trolls and such inaccurate knowledge of the contours of Mistress Boleyn. I, too, have seen Mistress Boleyn bathing at
midnight, but not at Hampton Park. And I can assure you, *messieurs
de la garde du roi, et mademoiselle la femme de chambre,* that the
Marchioness of Pembroke possesses the usual quota of not inacces-
sible breasts, and no superfluous finger on either hand. Nor does she
brew love philters, for she does not need to."

He broke off as suddenly as he had begun, while the startled trio,
quailing a little, shrank back toward the lee of the fireplace. They
were willing enough to talk loosely, in all conscience, but this fashion
of wild, whirling utterance went far beyond the bounds of common
prudence. It smelled of the ax and the fagot. Then, before they were
able to recover their scattered wits, without warning the eerie suitor
almost shouted aloud in a burst of crazy laughter.

"Nevertheless," he cackled, laughing till he choked, "you are not
altogether wrong. Mistress Boleyn *is* a vampire, and a damned Nor-
man-Irish witch of the Ormonds. She sucks men's souls out of their
breasts. The sorceress, Morgan le Fay, is her godmother. The Greek
carline, Circe, breathed over her cradle. But she will harm me no
longer. She wears diamonds now about her swan's neck that spell
out the simple posy: *Caesar's I am.*"

And the sardonic gentleman flung back the muffling cloak to stand
before them in a rich suit of black sarcenet, one hand on the pommel
of a grimly serviceable Italianate rapier that looked as if it had seen
more than a little use. At once the two guardsmen sprang to their posts,
leaving the maid-in-waiting face to face with this eccentric and, apparently, dangerous suitor. As he let fall the folds of his cloak, mademoiselle Renèe gave vent to a little gasp of fear.

"*Mon dieu!*" she said, dropping him a distracted curtsey. "Sir
Thomas Wyatt! You have followed Mistress Anne here!"

"Not so, my dear," said Wyatt with another grating laugh. "Not I.
For a change, the boot is on the other foot. If anything, she followed
me. I was in the hall when you twain entered. But, I am ready to con-

fess, this is to engage in the veriest quibbling. I do not flatter myself that Mistress Anne gives her former *ami* a second thought nowadays. Nor must you, friend Renée, let her flatter herself that Thomas Wyatt any longer slinks, like a love-sick schoolboy, in her imperial train. We are both of us, I believe, grown too old for that. No, I wait here to see Master Patenson, the Chancellor's wise Fool. He is a great connoisseur of my verses and can sing them most dulcetly to the accompaniment of his lute. But make no mistake, *mon amie*, Renée. I am done with the kind of foolery you hint at. I lost my heart for love once, it is true. But a man may live without a heart. I think better of my head. I sent Mistress Anne a rhyming *billet* to this effect, and we parted friends after a fashion. Whatever she may wish me, I wish her well. You may tell her so again, if you choose."

His harsh tone softened a little.

"Mademoiselle Renée," said Thomas Wyatt, "you did me the honor in the old days of liking my verses—more, l believe, than Mistress Boleyn, who was always more for the dance; for the rebeck, not the lute. Would you care to hear my *billet*? It hath a pretty moral, and Master Patenson will not object if we borrow his lute for a space."

Wyatt took down the Jester's lute from its hook in a chimney embrasure, and began to sing in a pleasing baritone that was curiously at variance with the angry rasp of his previous speech—almost as if poetry released all the tensions in him:

> *"Madame, withouten many words,*
> *Once, I am sure, ye will or no:*
> *And, if ye will, then leave your bourds*
> *And use your wit, and shew it so.*

> *"And with a beck ye shall me call,*
> *And if of one that burneth alway*
> *Ye have any pity at all,*
> *Answer him fair with yea or nay.*

> *"If it be yea, I shall be fain.*
> *If it be nay, friends as before.*
> *Ye shall another man obtain,*
> *And I mine own and yours no more."*

The Marchioness of Pembroke Pays a Visit:

As the last words' baritone timbre bronzed into resonant silence, Wyatt prolonged their echo with a sweep of his fingers over the lute strings. Then, very softly, he struck up another strain:

"Now cease, my lute, this is the last
Labour that thou and I shall waste,
And ended is that we begun;
Now is this song both sung and past:
My lute be still, for I have done."

The door of the inner room opened, as the singer gently hung the lute up again on its hook in the chimney embrasure. My Lord Chancellor More, in his official robes and wearing his great gold chain of office, stood framed in the entrance. Beside him was Anne, Marchioness of Pembroke, clad in her familiar hunting habit, a scarlet feather in her green page's cap. Evidently the long interview had not progressed as Mistress Boleyn wished, for her face was flushed and she kept nervously smoothing the chamois hunting gauntlets on her long fingers. Intent on their own concerns, neither of them noticed the tall singer in black; nor he them. Not even when he turned and spoke again to Mistress Boleyn's maid-in-waiting did the trio confront one another.

"Yes, Mademoiselle Renée," said Wyatt to the French woman, "we are quits at last, Mistress Boleyn and I. And I've no complaints. She answered me fair enough with nay. For Mistress Anne is very honest in her way—there, I have another rhyme, one for which I can no longer have any use in the world. She said she preferred a crown to a sonnet. And who will gainsay that? Already she wears a ducal coronet on account."

Suddenly, as he heard the Chancellor's grave voice, Wyatt became conscious that others were in the room. He whirled around at once.

"I will clear the room of suitors, Mistress Boleyn," said Thomas More to his visitor. "It will be warmer waiting here by the great fireplace till your equerry arrives."

He stopped as Mistress Boleyn gave a perceptible gasp. She had come squarely in front of Wyatt.

"Wyatt!" she said.

Then, turning to her host:

"Sir Chancellor! I demand to know what this may mean! Do you set spies on me in the King's own precincts of Westminster? Or do you mean this man to annoy me? It is a grave and calculated offense in either case."

More wore a troubled look.

"I am sorry," he said, "if you are discommoded, Mistress Anne. I have never seen this gentleman before, nor do I know his business. But each and every one of His Majesty's good subjects has a right to seek out His Majesty's Chancellor in the precincts of Westminster."

Mistress Boleyn regained control of herself. Except for a lip that would not leave off trembling she was as icily composed as ever.

"His name is Wyatt," she said stiffly. "I did know him once."

Thomas Wyatt bowed mockingly to her, his right hand on the pommel of his rapier which, as he inclined exaggeratedly low, stiffened the cloak out behind him into a rooster's tail.

"Sir Thomas Wyatt, poet, at your service, Sir. The lady speaks what is only right. I did know her once, as she knew me—centuries ago by the stars and moon. As for my business in your antechamber, I do wait on that wise gentleman, your Fool, who is not, however, so prompt as he is wise. For he appointed to meet me here, and is already late by a good hour and a half. But if I am troublesome to Mistress Anne, I can as easily wait in the corridor."

Anne Boleyn's white features did not alter. She said nothing. Wyatt shrugged.

"I think it would be better, Sir Thomas," said Thomas More very courteously. "And, by the bye, Sir Poet, I much admire your verses." Wyatt inclined his head again and withdrew. At a gesture from Mistress Boleyn, her maid-in-waiting accompanied the poet and the two guardsmen. Thomas More watched the dumbshow quizzically. Another piece of the royal puzzle clicked into place in his mind.

So this was the wild courtier who, with young Henry Howard, Earl of Surrey, had introduced Petrarch's sonnet into England. Master More was far enough removed from his own salad days to prefer

Wyatt's satires to his love poems; but he could recognize, nonetheless, the fire of passion and anvil plangency of utterance in the love balettes. The man wrote out of his heart's blood. "I grant I do not profess chastity," was Wyatt's proud statement at his trial before a timeserving Bishop of London. "But yet I use not abomination." No man who rode so hard as Wyatt did with Henry's Vicar of Hell, Sir Francis Bryan, could profess chastity without hypocrisy; and Thomas Wyatt was no hypocrite. He broke his marriage oath to Elizabeth Cobham, even as she had broken her sworn troth to him. But he did not neglect their children. He lived in plain concubinage with Mistress Boleyn, and so he told the Privy Council when the King's great matter was first bruited openly. But, when Henry, in his besotted brutishness, elected not to believe the circumstantial story and banished Wyatt from the Court, the bitter gallant did not false his King. From his first distinguishing himself at Court in the Christmas tournament of 1525 to his escape from the Emperor's crack Spanish troops the year before his banishment, his hall marks were courage and honesty. Now that his term of exile was over he shunned the Court, and foregathered in taverns with such noncourtiers as Will Patch and Henry Patenson.

The Chancellor sighed and drew a brocaded chair up to the fireplace for Mistress Boleyn. Now that Sir Thomas was gone, she shivered a bit and chafed her hunting gauntlets as if the hands underneath were mortal cold. More stood observing her, compassion in his glance.

"I am sorry, Mistress Boleyn," he said at last, "that I cannot accommodate you or conform my mind to yours in this great matter of the King's divorce and remarriage. I will not oppose it publicly, I promise you. Nor will I support it either publicly or privately. You have had your say and given me your reasons at great length for the course you and my Lord King are bent on following. Now, in justice, you should also hear me out while I detail the reasons why, in conscience, I may not go your way. I should never have sought you out for this purpose, Mistress Boleyn, but, since you have sought me out, I do not think that, in all fairness, both as your Chancellor, your elder by many years, your fellow Christian, and your friend, I may let this present opportunity slip."

The slight figure by the fire left off rubbing her hands.

"Friend, my Lord Chancellor?" she asked, the penciled brows arching above the green eyes. "This is but cant and prating. I do not think you are my friend. Certainly I am no friend of yours, nor can be, after what has just passed between the two of us in talk there in your inner room."

"I am the sorrier for that, Mistress Anne," said Thomas More.

Now the slender shape in its sheath of Lincoln green took to tapping chamois fingers on the brocaded arm rest.

"I might, however," she said, "point out an important and relevant detail, while we are about this same matter of friendship. I am not your friend, it is true. But neither am I yet your enemy. Whether I become your enemy, my Lord Chancellor, rests with you and you alone."

"Again I am sorry, Mistress Anne," said Thomas More. "What you have just now said makes what I am about to say even harder, and it would have been difficult to say at best. Do you know Jane Shore?"

Mistress Boleyn seemed puzzled. The name of Jane Shore swung slow, like faroff fairy bells, in her memory. It rang of ballad love and of ballad hate; of beauty and scandal and defeat. Pictures formed in her mind of a poisoned cup and a ball of shining silk; of a song like Blondel's; and of a death. But surely that was wrong. Those bright images clustered, rather, about the ill-fated name of Rosamonde Clifford, the mistress of Henry II, the rival for the King's love of that fairy-tale Queen, Eleanor of Aquitaine, she who was mother of the Lion Heart. Rosamonde lived in a bower in the midst of a maze at Woodstock, bore William Longsword to the King, and died in Godstow nunnery where Hugh of Lincoln marked her grave with the two simple words, *Tumba Rosamondae.* Henry's rose of the world lay in a tomb. Where, then, was Jane Shore, whose story was as poignant as Rosamonde's? Anne Boleyn came out of the mists of reverie with a start. Now she remembered who Jane Shore was. How dared this meddling Chancellor call back to life memories of dead Kings' mistresses? Henry VIII yet lived and loved; and Anne Boleyn meant to be his Queen. Her eyes narrowed in anger. Sir Thomas More, watching, saw them narrow. It seemed to him that all the eyes that watched him nowadays narrowed in much the same way. The eyes of Henry, the sensualist; of Cromwell, moneylender and courtier; of Mistress Boleyn, gambler for a crown.

"You mean the leman of Edward IV?" she asked icily.

"Yes," said Thomas More.

"Do you consider this a seemly question, my Lord Chancellor?" asked Anne Boleyn, bridling. "I am not Henry's mistress."

The Chancellor sighed.

"Rumor belies you there, Mistress Anne," he said. "But I believe you. Nevertheless, I put my question once again: do you know Jane Shore?"

"I saw the woman once," said Anne Boleyn shortly. "Some ten years ago and more, I believe. She was aged even then, and begged alms at the Court."

"Mistress Anne," said Thomas More almost pleadingly, his hand on her shoulder, "Jane Shore was in these chambers yesternight, even as you are today."

Anne Boleyn shook off his friendly touch.

"She is living still?" she asked with an affectation of indifference; but her voice quivered. Master More's quiet shaft had flown straight to its mark. "I heard she had died years back."

"She lives," said Thomas More, pressing home his advantage. "She lives, but she is no longer goodly to gaze on. She is old now: lean, withered, and dried up. Nothing left of her but riveled skin and hard bone. Can an onlooker guess the beauty of one long departed by her skull taken out of a charnel house? It would be as easy to do that as to estimate what Mistress Shore was in the days of her glorious youth. My old master, Cardinal Morton, told me once she was the bonniest woman then he had ever laid eyes on. So said Sir Thomas Malory who drew the fair ladies, Guinevere and Nimue, in his *Book of the Table Round* which I read as a boy. Passing bright were his Guinevere and Nimue; but they were no brighter than Jane Shore while, as Master Chaucer puts it, she had the world an in her day. They were a glorious pair, she and Edward. Proper she was and fair, nothing in her body that you would have wished altered, unless, perhaps, you had wished her somewhat higher—as tall as yourself now, Mistress Boleyn. Edward the King was her goodly fere: of visage lovely, of body mighty, strong and cleanly made."

Now the slippered foot began to tap even as the gloved fingers left off.

"I congratulate you on your sermon, my Lord Chancellor," she said. "Master Colet could have done no better. Henry has told me more than once you were early bent on being a monk. It is a pity you did not follow the cowled profession in earnest. But tell me this, my Lord Chancellor: what has Jane Shore to do with me, or Henry with Edward?"

The Chancellor began to pace up and down the antechamber. He had not really meant to say so much; but, once started, he could not stop.

"What has one human being to do with another?" he asked her. "We are all fellow travelers through this valley of sorrow. As for you and Mistress Shore, Mistress Boleyn, it is a sin to belie even the devil. And Mistress Shore never showed herself a devil. In her own way and her own day Jane Shore was a good woman. When in his merry mood, Edward used to say he had three concubines who all excelled in three different fashions. One was the merriest, another the wiliest, the third the holiest harlot in the realm. For no man could get this third one lightly out of the church to any other place, unless it were to the King's bed. The merriest was Master Shore's wife in whom the King took special pleasure, for many women he had, but her he loved, and she never abused his favor to any man's hurt, but, on the contrary, to many a man's comfort and sure relief would she often solicit the King's good grace."

"My Lord Chancellor," said Anne Boleyn, biting her lips now till the blood showed. "I find your discourse offensive. I ask you again: what have I to do with a dead King's whore?"

Thomas More raised his hand to stop her, as she began to rise from her chair.

"A moment more," he said, "and I am done. This dead King's whore was a merciful woman. When the King took displeasure as Kings will sometimes do—even the best and truest of Kings, Mistress Boleyn—she would mitigate and appease his mind. Where men were out of favor, she would bring them in his grace. For many that had highly offended, she obtained pardon. Of great forfeitures, that threatened to ruin whole families, she got men remissions. And, finally, in many weighty suits she stood many men in great stead, either for none or for very small rewards, and those rewards rather gay than rich. A gewgaw, a flower, a ribbon, a smile would be enough. And she did what she did for these woman's reasons only: either that she was content with the deed itself well done; or else that she delighted to be sued unto and to show what she was able to do with the King; or else, at the very least, because certain wanton women, when they are wealthy, are not always covetous. Mistress Shore was, as you say, a whore. But, like another whore in history, much will be forgiven her because she loved much."

Anne Boleyn got to her feet, white as death. A pink tongue, viper-quick, licked lips that had grown parched with fury.

"I believe, my Lord Chancellor," she said, "that there is a writ expressly forbidding blasphemy."

She stopped, fighting hard to control herself. Then continued:

"But, if Mistress Shore be thus saintly, why do you not press her cause for canonization? If you will not aid at Rome Mistress Boleyn, living, why may you not assist Mistress Shore, dead? Or, at the very least, see to it that the Court historians set her high in the chronicles of that time?"

"I do not jest, Mistress Boleyn," said Thomas More quickly. "We are none of us saints. Also, I doubt not that court chroniclers will think this woman too slight a thing to be much written of and set among the remembrances of great matters. But I think far otherwise. I think her the more worthy to be remembered for the very reason that she is now in a beggarly condition; unfriended and worn out of acquaintance, after good substance. Unfriended after great favor with the Prince. Unfriended after as great suit and seeking to on the part of all those that had business to further—after as great influence as had many other men in their times who are famous now only by the infamy of their ill deeds. Her doings were not much less than theirs, though nowadays her deeds are much less remembered because they were not so evil. For, if men but do their fellow men an evil turn, we inscribe it in marble. Good turns are written in the dust of windy London Town. It is well demonstrated by poor Mistress Shore. Today she begs in vain of many living who, in her day, had been beggars, had she not lived. Yesternight she begged a guilder of me. I gave her fifty."

Anne Boleyn was mistress of herself once more.

"It was generous of you," she observed ironically. "And the moral of your long-winded *exemplum*, my Lord Chancellor? You spell me a puzzle. Let me see if I may riddle it for you a-right."

She touched one slender finger to her temple, and stood locked in mimic thought. Then she clapped gloved hands together as if in great delight.

"How is this, Sir Chancellor?" she asked him mockingly. "Mistress Shore was beautiful. Mistress Shore was good. Mistress Shore is nothing. There! Do they riddle better than that in the schools of Oxford?"

"That is one way of reading her history, Mistress Boleyn," said Thomas More as coolly as herself. "I have no doubt that, by her forbearance in the days of her power, Jane Shore saved her soul."

"There is another way of reading her history, then?" asked Anne Boleyn, continuing to mock. "What of this interpretation, then, Master Exegeticist? Mistress Anne Boleyn, do thou go and do likewise—become the harlot of a King!"

More's face was every bit as inflexible as the white mask that stared into his own.

"I do not say so," he said stiffly.

"I tell you, my Lord Chancellor," hissed the angry woman, bringing her suddenly contorted face close to his, "I will be no King's harlot! I will be Queen of England or nothing!"

Thomas More caught her gloved hand in his. For the first time in his life he felt an impulse to strike a woman.

"Mistress Boleyn," he said with equal vehemence, "my mistress and yours, Queen Catherine, is a great and good gentlewoman. See to it that you steal no more that is hers!"

"I will be Queen, I tell you!" raged Anne Boleyn.

He let fall her hand, his quick passion spent.

"Then," he said sadly, "I tell you, Mistress Boleyn, in the end you will be far worse off than that good harlot, Jane Shore."

Anne Boleyn stared venomously at the Chancellor. Her breast rose and fell. She smoothed down her long gloves and plucked at the archer's bracer on her arm.

"Now," she said slowly, measuring the weight of every word, "now, my Lord Chancellor, you are my enemy. We shall meet no more."

The outer door opened, as the men-at-arms admitted Mistress Boleyn's equerry, an arrogant spurred and booted cavalier, insolently ruffling it in the new livery of the Howards. Mistress Anne swept proudly to the threshold where her equerry fell upon one knee.

"Your Grace, the Marchioness!" he said.

Regally she gave him her hand, looking backward the while at Thomas More.

"You may get up, my Lord Manners," she said lightly. "Your present posture better becomes a church than a court. You should have come earlier. It would have been more in keeping then. Master More had the tedious taste to favor us with a long and boring sermon on the subject of death and virtue. A *memento mori*, my Lord Manners. Are not *memento moris* going out of fashion?"

The cavalier took his cue from his mistress' tone and manner.

"*Memento mori?*" he parodied in a coxcomb's voice. "'Tis almost a pun—but a vile one. Shall we *remember More?* Doth my Lord Chancellor see fit to engage in Latin puns, since his elevation to the

Chancellorship? It is a presumption that doth ill fit a family sprung from the lowly purlieus of Cripplegate. But, to pun somewhat more aptly, *honores mutant mores.*"

And the besworded popinjay snuffed up a huge whiff of scent from his jeweled pouncet box. But he had made one mistake. One does not measure swords of wit with the author of *Utopia,* and come off scot-free.

"Your Latin proverb is apt enough, my Lord Manners," said the Chancellor, eyes twinkling. "But you forget one thing in your assignation of horses to eager beggars. Honors *do* alter men's behavior, it is true. But *mores* in English is not *More* but *Manners.* But, perhaps, since he is become equerry to Her Grace, the Marchioness of Pembroke, my Lord Manners grows so exalted that he no longer speaks English. I should advise him to make her re-acquaintance. Mother tongue is the nurse of mother wit."

The equerry gave More a black look as they left. At that very instant Henry Patenson capered in astride a hobbyhorse, belled cap jingling, his Fool's bladder bobbing almost in Mistress Boleyn's face. Reining in his wooden steed, he gazed quizzically after the entourage; then, as quizzically, at his master.

"Lord-a-mighty! Master Chancellor!" he observed. "What means that Medusa stare?"

"Which one?" asked Thomas More with a smile. "My Lord Manners'? Or the Marchioness of Pembroke's?"

"The lady's, of course," said Henry Patenson. "My Lord Manners looks baleful enough, but he is a cipher in a court suit. Mistress Anne looks like a wivern or a cockatrice. It is a basilisk look she favors you with."

"It means, friend Patenson," said More more seriously, "that I have made a mortal enemy. I am sorry for it, and I am sorry for her, too."

"I am sorry for you," said Henry Patenson. "But, at any rate, you are in good company. Or bad, if you count my good friend, Wyatt."

"You are not prompt upon your hour," said Thomas More. "Master Wyatt cooled his heels some two turns of the glass before you came."

"Some two turns of the glass?" asked the Fool scornfully, snapping his fingers in disdain. "No more than that? Foh, say I! What has a Fool or a Poet to do with time? But, speaking of Thomas Wyatt, here is a song Master Wyatt bade me give you, since you like his poems so well. He wrote it yesternight at the Golden Pineapple, with Will Patch sitting on his lap, since, as he tells the world, Mistress Boleyn no longer will."

He took a scrap of foolscap from his jerkin. It was all spotted with candle grease and the heel-taps of Canary wine. Despite himself, Thomas More had to smile. He sat down by the fire.

"Read it to me, friend Patenson," he said.

Patenson peered closely at his bit of paper as if he found it hard to make the writing out. It was one of his less inspired devices, since he read but little anyway. But Thomas More, who had seen the dodge a thousand times before, endured it patiently for the thousandth and first time. He folded his hands as if in great expectation.

"It is dedicated," announced Henry Patenson, "to one Mistress Anne Boleyn late of the Court; now translated as Marchioness of Pembroke to the Court that is above the Court. Do I know her?"

Henry Patenson paused in his make-believe reading and peered over the edge of his foolscap.

"We both know her now, friend Patenson," said Thomas More; and now his faint smile had turned wistful. "But go on. Read more, I pray you."

"It needs my lute and Master Wyatt's melting voice," said Henry Patenson. "But Master Wyatt is neither here, nor has he yet set an air to it. However."

And he proceeded to recite Sir Thomas Wyatt's leave-taking from a lady the poet had no need to name.

> *"With serving still*
> *This have I won,*
> *For my goodwill*
> *To be undone.*

216

"And for redress
Of all my pain
Disdainfulness
I have again.

"And for reward
Of all my smart,
Lo, thus unheard
I must depart.

"Wherefore all ye
That after shall
By fortune be
As I am, thrall,

"Example take
What I have won,
Thus for her sake
To be undone!"

Henry Patenson cocked his head like some giant rooster.

"How like you Master Wyatt's new song?" he asked. "Is it not, Sir Thomas, a sad lament for a false love?"

"It is, in truth, a sad song, friend Patenson," said Thomas More. "But, you know, I think Sir Thomas Wyatt is a lucky man. A very lucky man, friend Patenson. There are others I could name not nearly so lucky as he."

"Who, for example?" the Jester prodded him.

"Who, for example?" asked Thomas More, a faraway look in his eyes. "Why, King Henry, Mistress Anne, and the King's Chancellor, Sir Thomas More, to draw but three names out of strumpet Fortune's cap."

Sometimes, it seemed, the gods were more than good to Jesters. Henry Patenson's cup of satisfaction overflowed as Momus smiled. The best openings were always the ones you did not have to maneuver for, but the ones which opened up as unexpectedly and as rewardingly as a Jack Horner Pie at Christmas, or a child's Jack-in-the-Box. Henry Patenson grinned from ear to ear as wide as Jack himself, and got ready to spring out in his master's face. Quick as a wink, from among the many comic properties he kept convenient to hand in the chimney embrasure, he placed a cardboard crown on his head.

"Now speaking of strumpet Fortune and of caps, my Lord Chancellor," he said, brandishing his Jester's bauble like a scepter, "see—I am transmogrified! I wear a crown. How like you my king's cap, Master?"

"It fits you handsomely, my Lord Fool," said More, entering into the spirit of the game.

Patenson took off the mimic crown and replaced it with a prodigious paper miter—one of the carnival miters that, in the old days, used to be worn by the Boy Bishops for the Feast of Fools.

"Aha!" he said. "*Chimera bombinans in vacuo! Presto!* I wax in glory. I promote myself. This time, how like you my Pope's cap, Master?"

Thomas More's face grew longer. The Fool was acute. He caught every flying rumor in the streets. The Chancellor saw which way the game was tending.

"Not quite so well, perhaps," he said slowly. "There are many ways of playing King. There is but one true road to Peter's chair."

The Jester took off his swollen miter, and scrutinized it close by.

"So you say, at least," he commented. "And so it has been for centuries. But what if the rules of the game are changed? What then, Master? I would not say aloud, my Lord Chancellor, such things as you have just now said to me."

He scrambled the miter onto his head again and gabbled out some mumbo-jumbo, one hand upraised in grotesque benediction.

"You are safe with me, of course, friend More. *In sigillo confessionis*—under the seal of shriving. But Master Cromwell's pursuivants—those that have not taken orders, those he picked up in the stews and prisons—violate their vow of secrecy and silence without so much as a second thought. Confess not to them, if you value your neck. There are rumors going round the taverns about a certain Act of Supremacy Master Cromwell is hatching in his noisome nest of rooks and daws. Have you heard of this, my Lord?"

Thomas More's eyes were leaden.

"Yes," he said heavily.

He had more than heard of it. At that very moment there lay on his desk a corrected draft in Cromwell's handwriting of the Supplication of the Commons against the Bishops, and the first draft of a new bill, which would surely pass, demanding the banning by law of the ancient custom of paying annates to Rome. Master Cromwell had still a third and more devastating act in pawn: a Statute of Appeals which would utterly preclude from henceforth any appeal to Rome whatsoever in the vital matters of marriages, wills, rights of tithes, oblations and obventions. In a few short months, as things were now going, papal jurisdiction in the island of Britain would be a thing of the past. The threat of royal usurpation of the papal prerogative was now much more than a threat; it was rapidly becoming an accomplished fact.

And still the cunning architect of these royal and parliamentary aggressions against the *Ecclesia Anglicana* continued to wax in pelf and power, and to draw into his spinner's hands more and more strands of the complex web that he was weaving. Not only was Master Cromwell now the most trusted member of Henry's Privy Council. He was also Master of the Jewels, Master of the King's Wards, Chancellor of the Exchequer, Master of the Rolls and Secretary to the King, Vicar General and Visitor General of the Monasteries. Both the marriageable and the well-endowed celibate paid heavy tribute to his subtle self. My Lord Chancellor More of the realm of England might still wield the Great Seal. My Lord Chancellor of the Exchequer Cromwell held the key to the Treasury, loosed and unloosed the purse strings of the commonwealth. It was not hard to tell which of the two Chancellors controlled the greater power. Nor did all these increased political responsibilities put any stop to Master Cromwell's reading of those first loves of his, the Italian political philosophers. He had lately come across a two hundred-year-old treatise, the *Defensor Pacis*, by a compatriot of Messire Machiavelli, Marsiglio of

Padua, which argued, simply and cogently and, to Cromwell at least, irresistibly, the King's supremacy in spiritual matters over the Pope within the boundaries of the King's own domain. At his own expense Cromwell had the book bound in expensive white vellum and even more expensive crimson velvet and given to the King as a Christmas present.

But Henry was beginning to advance far beyond a mere legist's arguments. He blithely wallowed now in the seductive quicksands of mysticism. Taken by the sublime idea of the Church as the Mystical Body of Christ, Henry had evolved, in labored counterpart, a secular *mystique* of the realm as the mystical body of the King. The King's majesty, he argued ponderously, is the head and soul of the people. In the King's majesty all subjects are constrained to suffer together. The pains, the insults which the monarch suffers, are equally the affair of every man jack in the kingdom. All England, from Land's End to Canterbury, was thus stained with the awful stain of the King's incestuous union with Queen Catherine. Thomas More groaned aloud at the thought. The ironist, no less than the moralist in him, was revolted by the egomaniac effrontery of the concept. When Henry Patenson had first heard of the King's "mystical body," he had given vent to a much earthier comment than a groan. And now my Lord of Canterbury himself, old Archbishop Warham, was sick even unto death of an apoplexy suffered only last evening, within a few hours after his valiant defiance of tyranny in the Upper House. And, Thomas More knew, Cromwell had designated Thomas Cranmer as his successor in the Primacy. Thomas Cranmer! A man not even a Bishop! A man living in open concubinage with his German paramour! Or, worse yet, with his German wife! A man who consorted with avowed heretics at the White Horse Inn in Cambridge! A man who daily prayed for the overthrow of the Pope's authority! The Chancellor laid his heavy head in his hands.

Henry Patenson watched his master anxiously.

"You have heard of this new arrangement, then?" he asked again.

Thomas More roused himself from his lethargy of despair.

"Yes, friend Patenson," he said as heavily as before. "I have heard of it."

"A very neat and tidy arrangement, I should say," said Henry Patenson, touching, in his earnestness, the Chancellor's arm. "When Henry is Pope, then he can both divorce and wed himself again. And again. And again, if the fit so takes him. Bed and wed. Shrive and wive. Or, rather, wive, then shrive. Everything but bury himself. For hugger-mugger in mother earth even a King must needs call in another monk like the rest of us. But what odds, Master? No need to look so hangdog. It is but one oath the more. I, for one, will not stick to swear, if the King's sergeants approach me."

Patenson's voice quivered. This was what he had been leading up to all the time. The Jester feared for his loyal fool of a master.

"I will not stick to swear," he repeated. "Will you, my Lord Chancellor?"

"I am afraid I must, friend Patenson," said Thomas More. "The King is my lord temporal, and I his faithful vassal. If he will make Mistress Boleyn Queen, I will serve her and her issue, even as I serve him. It is only right and proper for the sake of peace within the commonwealth that the succession to the throne be secured. Even if the King and Parliament decide to fix the succession on Henry Fitzroy, my Lord King's natural son, I shall comply, though with much regret that the legitimate heir, Princess Mary, is passed over. But I may go no further than this. The King, who is my lord temporal, may not be my lord spiritual. If the Oath enjoins renouncing the Pope as head of the Church in England, I shall never swear that part of the Oath."

"Even so? You will not swear?" asked Patenson softly, pathos and affection and anguish and, above all else, the most terrible resignation in his voice.

Then the Jester sprang into the air, caracoling in desperate gaiety.

"In that case, nuncle," he cried, giving More his coxcomb, " in that case, I abdicate my high office. The Fool is dead! Long live the Fool! Since I have no dunce cap, do you take my fool's cap, my Lord Fool, and get you a snug berth somewhere safe outside of England. As for Henry—"

Patenson tossed his grotesque miter into the air.

"Heighho!" he crowed. "The King may have my Pope's cap, and with a will, so that he lets me keep my head! And, do you know another secret, nuncle? I wager a stiver you will find the Bishops of my way of thinking."

"You will win your wager, friend Patenson," said Thomas More tonelessly.

His head fell upon his arms again. As he watched his master's nocturnal agony, the Fool's eyes filled with tears.

CHAPTER XII

MY LORD CHANCELLOR MORE
WRITES A LETTER TO OXFORD:

Chelsea, Afternoon and Evening, May 1, 1532

THE WHEEL of Fortune was coming full turn; the sands were fast running out of the hourglass. Thomas More knew he did not have overmuch time left him to do the little things that, later, could not be done. Like taking leave of his library, for example, with all its goodly books. The English ones, rolled, stamped and bound by the Worshipful Company of Bookbinders resident in his old parish of St. Giles, Cripplegate; his own shield, the Moor's head and unicorns, imprinted clear and clean on the first leaf. The costly presentation copies in their brave white vellum and deep crimson velvet; presents from Erasmus and Archbishop Warham and my Lord of Rochester, John Fisher; from my Lord of York, the great Cardinal that was; from the King. Old treasures from Flanders, found for him by his friends, Vives and Peter Giles: illuminated Flemish Books of Hours, with their Calendars of Saints, their lovely devotions for the Canonical Hours, their order of service for Baptisms and Burials. Heaven was so near and dear in them, so small and precisely colored, as if, in sober earnest, He had suffered these childlike painters of the middle age to come closer unto Him than the great artists who were even now making the Vatican resplendent. A quaint medieval Bestiary. An even quainter and more endearing translation of Pliny's *Natural History*, with its improbable but delightful "clement lions," and its Ethiopian dragons, "ten fathoms long."

It was even more important to take leave of his beloved garden. And what better day for a garden leave-taking amid the pleasant meads of Chelsea than May Day, the day of Mary the Mystical Rose? Since early morning the groves and thickets had been alive with lads and lasses swarming over the woods and fields to collect birch boughs and plaited flowers for their May arbors. Ribbon-decked Maypoles stood on every village green: in Holburn and Bishopsgate, in Charing and Islington, in St. Giles' Fields. The morris dancers and the hobbyhorse pranced among the other dancers. And Thomas More walked alone, and for the last time, in his garden beside the silver Thames, where the King's swans, the enchanted daughters of the old Celtic god, Lír, arched their proud white necks and swam imperiously by.

Farewell, then, to the violets and orchises and lilies of the valley. Farewell to the pink and silver anadyomeneal foam of pear and apple and cherry blossom. Farewell to the gillyflowers, the daffodils, the primrose and narcissi, the sweetbriar and honeysuckle. The roses were still folded in the bud; but he bade them farewell, anyway. Farewell to these velvet-textured Queens of English June gardens. He would have liked once more to smell these roses of his. Roses brought all the world into Chelsea: the perfumes of Persia; the troubadour songs of Provence; the wilder mountain air of the nomad Caucasus; the bronze gongs and incense of Cathayan temples; the twin ensigns of the Red and White Rose. Yes, each man's and each woman's garden life was, in its own way, a *Romaunt of the Rose*.

Farewell, too, to the beasts: to the peacocks and the weasel and the marmoset. Most especially to the marmoset. Master Monkey was far and away the most amusing of his many animal friends. And they were good friends, too, mused Thomas More, as he paced the sanded walks of his ménagerie. And a great mystery as well. Man knew more about the nature of the angels he could not see than he did about the nature of the animals he lived with and, in a certain sense, belonged to. There were hints here and there in Scripture; but no

more than hints. John of Patmos, for example, saw godhead prefigured in animal splendor rather than human rationality.

It was something Thomas More had always envied Adam, the
great prime-Father. He, Thomas More, Knight of Chelsea, Christian
from the sixth day of his birth, knew Christ as Adam did not. But
only Adam, among men, had met the beasts face to face. One of the
Chancellor's recurrent dreams that no one else knew—not Henry
Patenson, not Mistress Alice, not even little Jane Colt—was meeting
with Adam in eternity and talking with him of the animals suppliant
at the Tree. His reticence was not due, however, to his being in any
way ashamed of the dream. After all, who knew what heaven would
bring? And did not all men, in their several ways, desire to get back
to the Prime, to the condition of those Dante called the *prima gente,*
the first people of the Garden? Most men tried to achieve this adorable impossibility through love of women, under the auspices of
Venus, the *fair planet which hearteneth to love, making the whole
East to laugh,* as great Dante, again, put it in limpid Italian that
shimmered to the ear even as the serene star rays of Venus to the eye.
But love, though the best, was not the only way. The astronomer,
watching the wheeling stars from his lonely tower, knew another
means. So did the maker of ménageries. Except that, when all was
said and done, every way was the way of love. Farewell, then, to the
beasts who, like the flowers and the books and the laughing lips of
women, were also the way of love. He regretted Chelsea had had no
accommodations for an elephant. Then, with a certain grim satisfaction, he remembered there were lions in the Tower. It was well. In
the Place of the Lion he would not be alone.

Henry Patenson, who had grown too rheumatic of late years to go
a-Maying anymore with the neighborhood Corinnas, watched his
master from a mullioned window. Intuitively he understood what the
Chancellor was up to; and, as a man of sentiment, the Jester approved.
If the sword of Damocles that now hung by a thread over Master
More's head hung over his own, why, Henry Patenson, *joculator,*
would also have certain matters of leave-taking to attend to. Only,
thought Patenson wrily, it would not be books and flowers he would
bid adieu to. He was a city man. He would say farewell to the tav-

erns of his election. Nostalgically he thought on the cozy creaking of their gay-colored signs: the Parrot, the Angel, the Saracen's Head, the Black Boy, the Mermaid, the Ship, the Gun, the Green Dragon, the White Horse, the Brindled Cow, the Black Bear, the Red Fox. He had drunk enough in his day to sink the Ship. Once he had almost been so indiscreet as to think of marrying the horny-fisted nixie who kept the Mermaid; but, luckily, a veritable merman in the shape of a sailor from the London wharves had taken her off his hands in the proverbial nick of time. He had straddled more than one hogshead in the White Horse; and pulled many a Christmas snapdragon out of blue-burning brandy at the Green Dragon. The Brindled Cow ran beer instead of milk. As for the Gun, he had not visited that excellent hostelry of late, for the good and sufficient reason that he had not paid his shot there. The Jester fairly crowed for joy as he made this silent play on words within the vinous interior of his mind.

Thomas More had done now at long last with leave-taking. But he still had business on hand. Business for the King who was, as yet, his royal master, and, so far as he knew, his great good friend as well. He walked into his private closet in New Building library and sat down at his desk. A manuscript lay open on top—part of his reply to Martin Luther's demand that all relics of the True Cross be thrown on a bonfire, and the golden reliquaries enclosing them melted down and sold, and the proceeds thereof given to the poor. It was ever the revolutionist's oversimple expedient for wiping out poverty and social injustice. Mohammed had made much the same sort of suggestion once; and, where the hooves of his leveling horsemen passed, the grass and trees grew not again and the parched springs dried up. The Chancellor smiled as he remembered to what base uses the Utopians relegated gold and silver. They made of those precious metals chamber pots and chains for slaves and criminals. Now, there was a revolutionary idea for Master Luther if he was really serious about getting rid of gold. But he remembered, what Erasmus had informed him, that Master Luther possessed scant sense of humor. The Chancellor looked at the last sentences he had written:

Chelsea, Afternoon and Evening, May 1, 1532

"How small a portion were the gold about all the pieces of Christ's Cross, if it were compared with the gold that is quite cast away about the gilding of knives, swords, spurs, arras and painted cloths; and, as though these things could not consume gold fast enough, the gilding of posts and whole roses, not only in the palaces of princes and great prelates, but also right mean men's houses! And yet among these things could Luther espy no gold that grievously glittered in his bleared eyes, but only about the Cross of Christ."

The great prelates who had commissioned his retort to the German heresiarch would not much relish this reference to the gold in their splendid palaces. But Thomas More cared not a whit for their displeasure. He was their sharp sword in controversy. A good falchion had two cutting edges. If they got hurt, handling their sword of the spirit, so be it. An honest brand did not shrink from wounding. And, man of peace that he was, Thomas More knew himself for an honest brand in the warfare of the mind and soul. *Magna est veritas et prevalebit.* It was a law as immutable as the laws of the old Medes and Persians. If the Bishops chanced to read upon the gilded walls of those same episcopal palaces of theirs the ancient warning, *Mene, mene, tekel upharsin,* why, he had no mind to stop them. He had not put the handwriting there. He certainly would not erase it, nor pretend, as too many prelates had been pretending for too many years, here in England and the Germanies, that it was not there at all.

But this afternoon the Chancellor had other business. At the request of the Bishops he had fought heretics. Now, at the request of the King, he would fight bigots. Thomas More did not know which of the two he detested more. At Easter he and Henry had ridden together down to Abingdon, whither the Court made a practice of removing when the plague threatened London, as it did last spring. From Abingdon he and the King had journeyed to Oxford, there to enforce the sanitary regulations which directed that all infected houses be marked with a wisp of hay, and that every doctor or nurse, who had attended those sick, identify themselves, when they went out, by carrying a white wand. But, as it turned out, a plague of another kind altogether was raging in Oxford. The King and his

Chancellor were utterly dismayed to find the University almost torn in two between the warring factions who called themselves Trojans and Greeks. The quarrel was the old quarrel over the new learning which still divided Erasmus and his fellow Humanists, on the one hand, from, on the other, the University conservatives who thought that Universities should be seminaries, and that all other studies but theology were carnal snares set by the devil for the souls of unwary intellectuals. The undignified squabble had irritated Henry who expected, at the very least, the illusion of harmony on his royal Progresses. It had alarmed Thomas More who knew that the little flame of bigotry which, in some souls, burns as steadily and constantly as a vigil lamp is very easily fanned into a devouring conflagration. A personal reason, too, entered into the Chancellor's reaction of distaste. John Clement, his protégé and former secretary, was professor of Greek at Oxford, preferred to this honored post by my Lord Cardinal Thomas Wolsey in the days of his power.

Hence this last of my Lord Chancellor More's state papers in behalf of the realm of England. Wearily he picked up a quill and set down the salutation:

"To the Fathers and Proctors of the University of Oxford: Greetings."

More put aside the pen and thought a space. The rebuke he intended to administer was hardly a politic act; but it was richly deserved. If the Bishops at large would rankle, John Fisher, who had once sent Erasmus to Cambridge, there to lecture on Greek studies, would not—though my Lord of Rochester had scant influence any more. And what he was about to do was for the good of the realm and in the best interests of Christendom. Not that the Universities had no faults whatsoever; not that they did not need certain reforms. The Provost of the University of Paris had recently issued a writ enjoining all resident *scholares* from throwing stones or horse dung during lectures; from bringing the women of Montmartre into the class rooms; from *actum Veneris exercere in publico;* from begging, telling fortunes by the stars, and hawking horoscopes at fairs. So much for student delinquencies. As for the professors, many of them had degenerated into apes of their intellectual betters; and their betters were the subtle scholastic thinkers of Aquinas' great century. Erasmus had written him from Basle on this very head:

> "They spend their time in questioning, dividing, distinguishing, and defining. They divide the first part into three, of which the first part again is split in four, and so on. Vulcan's chains cannot bind them; they cut the links with a finely tempered distinction, as if with an ax. They will tell you through just which crack in the earth's surface, and just which aperture in the human body, Sin crept in to corrupt man. They will explain anything and everything with their extravagant qualifications: how God can be a woman, or an ass, how He can assume the substance of the Devil or of a pumpkin, and how, under these latter circumstances, such a pumpkin can preach a sermon, work miracles, or be crucified."

And it was mere tumblers of the mind, mere gymnasts of futile paradox, fantastic pedants such as these who would close the windows of Oxford on the clean air of Greek studies! More thought the professors' obstructive idiocies much worse than the skylarking of the undergraduates. Take this fool in a cowl, now, who preached the Abingdon Lenten sermon against all liberal arts and all secular studies. The Chancellor had met the obscurantist priest before, when the two of them were appointed to debate this same topic before the King. Then, worsted in the unequal duel of wits, the enemy of Greek, instead of admitting defeat, had knelt in front of Henry and affirmed, in his own excuse, that, while preaching, he had been directly inspired to say what he had said against Greek. Henry had laughed at the priest's obduracy. "The spirit which inspired you, sirrah priest," the King had said, "was certainly not that of Christ, but rather that of folly. For your folly, I lay this fool's penance upon you: to read the *Encomium Moriae*, the *Praise of Folly*, by that great lover of Greek, Desiderius Erasmus. And remember this, friend monk, I tolerate no speaking of folly at my court—unless it be from the lips of my friend More. My *Morus* may utter what *Moria* he will. For his divine folly transcendeth other men's deepest wisdom." Yes, the King could be most gracious when it pleased him.

My Lord Chancellor More Writes a Letter to Oxford

But bigotry and malicious folly die hard, thought Thomas More bitterly. His old antagonist was in the lists again. And this time he would have to fight out the good fight alone. Erasmus was in Switzerland. Bishop Fisher, Chancellor of the sister University of Cambridge, was out of favor. Henry, besotted by his sodden lust for a woman who was worse than merely light, gulled by the sinister schemes of Thomas Cromwell, was no longer an effective ally, even though it was the King who had commissioned this present letter. But, in the very midst of his depression, the Chancellor found himself breaking into a smile, as he recalled the present Hans Holbein had brought him from Maître Rabelais who, surely, must be lightening the French University which had the good fortune to reckon him among the number of its faculty. That good giant, Gargantua, writing in praise of Greek to his philosophic giant-son, Pantagruel, had dated his famous chapter on liberal education from Utopia, the seventeenth day of March. *Witness Greek,* the giant had written, *without which it is a shame for anyone to count himself a scholar. Before all other studies, first master Greek.* It was an auspicious omen. The eloquent, ironic pen began to scratch quickly across the pages.

"At the very outset, *illustrissimi doctores et magistri in artibus,*" he began, "I must apologize for my insufficiency of knowledge, when measured against yours, and my great temerity in addressing so illustrious an academy. Whatever small learning I have I owe to Oxford. In her groves I suckled at the tender *ubera tuae sapientiae.* So I would far liefer encounter the reproach of arrogance in thus presuming to speak than the infamy of ingratitude for keeping a cowardly silence when the best interests of the University are at stake.

"I heard lately at London that, either in some fool's frolic, or else from a rooted and inveterate dislike of the study of Greek, a clique had been formed among you, calling itself Trojans, and that the object thereof was to throw ridicule on the Greek language and literature. It was reported that the leader was called Priam, the captain under him was Hector, a third Paris, and so on. This action of yours is foolish in itself and gives an unpleasant impression of your general intelligence. I was sorry to hear that men of learning were making so poor a use of their leisure, but I had reached the conclusion, nevertheless, that, in any concourse of scholars, there would always be a certain fixed number of blockheads, and that all this to-do was but a passing madness.

"Since coming to the town of Abingdon, I have been informed, however that this same folly has grown into the very ecstasy of moon-crazed lunacy, and that one of these same Trojans, who mistakenly plumes himself on being a genius of sorts—a man wise in his own esteem, and merry in the judgment of others, but who must be accounted insane by all who consider his conduct—has seen fit to preach a course of public sermons during the sacred time of Lent, denouncing not Greek classics only, but Latin classics, too, and, indeed, all liberal education. Most liberally has this jack-in-a-hood raved against all liberal arts. A fool's speech comes out a fool's head; and this was the speech of a very fool. And, moreover, that all his folly might be of one piece, he did not comment on a complete passage of Holy Scripture, after the manner of the ancients, nor even take a Scripture text, after the modern fashion, but, instead, took for his text some old wives' saws in English. I am sure his listeners were deeply offended by such unseemly doings. For who could have a spark of Christian feeling in his breast, and not lament to see the majesty of the preaching office, which had gained the world to Christ, degraded thus by one whose duty it was to adorn and guard it? What greater indignity could be offered the preacher's holy function than that the preacher himself, in the holiest time of the ritual year, before a great assembly of Christian men, in the very temple of God, from a pulpit's lofty eminence as from the throne of Christ, Himself, in the venerable and adorable presence of the sacred Body and Blood of Christ, should turn a Lenten sermon into a gross Bacchanalian farce?

"As to this Lord of Misrule's attack on all secular studies, it is not as if the good man had long withdrawn from the world and, like an eremite, spent years in the desert, and, suddenly coming from his solitude, had urged his hearers to give themselves over to watching, to praying, and to fasting, saying that by such means only could they gain heaven, and that all other earthly concerns were but the merest trifling. Saying that the study of literature was the forging of fetters. Saying that the rude and unlearned fly to heaven unhindered by the dead weight of such idle sophistication. I will not gainsay that there is more than a modicum of truth in such holy counsel. From such a preacher, as I have here imagined, such a sermon might have been endured. His simplicity might have gained him forbearance. Some kind hearers might have called it sanctity. Even those hearers who liked it least might have found it in their hearts to excuse it as the excess of piety and devotion.

"But, illustrious Masters of the University of Oxford, we have not to do here with a latter-day Elijah or John the Baptist come again. He does not live on cold water, on locusts and wild honey, but on good wine and the daintiest cates gold can buy anywhere in Christendom. What sort of man was it his Abingdon listeners saw mount into the pulpit he proceeded to disgrace? A fool for God? Not so. A fool for God is holy. This man is a malicious fool. A man dressed in the rough skins of beasts? In Lenten sackcloth and ashes? Again, not so. They saw a man ascend the pulpit elegantly dressed in fur mantle and in the academic regalia of that same learning which he attacked so traitorously. There, in the very midst of a University to which no one comes but for the sake of learning, his listeners heard this obdurate, unfaithful, and ungrateful professor openly rail against almost every kind of literature. Now who can deem these insensate and unnatural actions anything but the merest malice and the sheerest envy?

"What right has a man like this, whose livelihood is learning, to scoff at learning? What right has he, who should, in truth, know better, to denounce Latin, of which he knows little? Science, of which he knows less? Or Greek, of which he knows nothing? He had done far better to have limited his witless discourse to the seven capital sins with which, I have no doubt, he has an intimate acquaintance. In fact, one might, without much fear of error, call him licentiate of those same seven sins. Since he is so ill-disposed that he prefers to blame what he is ignorant of rather than to put himself to the pains of learning it—is not this Sloth? Since he slanders those who, by their talent and industry, happen to know what he is prevented from knowing by his own indolence and incapacity conjoined—is not this Envy? Since he would have no science esteemed except what he falsely fancies himself to possess—for a fool of this deep stripe possesses exactly nothing save his folly—and, since, in reality he vaunts his ignorance rather than his knowledge—is not this the height of Pride?

"We all of us know, forsooth, what he labors so hard to prove: to wit, that without secular learning a man can save his soul. Yet even secular learning, as he contemptuously styles it, prepares the mind for, and disposes the mind to, virtue. But what bearing has this simple fact of universal knowledge and acceptance on the point at issue? Learning is still a positive good even if the unlearned are able to merit heaven without it. And, in any case, it is for learning, and for learning alone, men come to Oxford. Any good mother can teach her child at home rude and unlearned virtue. Students come to Oxford to receive a liberal education. They do not go there to learn Theology alone. Some go to learn law. Other some are in search of a knowledge of human affairs, a branch of knowledge so useful even to a theologian that without it he may possibly sing pleasantly to himself but will certainly not sing agreeably to his congregation. Still other some seek for knowledge of human nature in general, a form of knowledge of no small utility to preachers, if their audiences are not to think them fools. And both these latter knowledges can nowhere be found in such abundance as in the classic poets, the classic orators, the classic historians.

"Others again go to Universities to study natural science, philosophy and art; and lo! this Daniel of our condemns the whole of their eager pursuit under one general condemnation. Nothing, he says, is of importance except Theology. It is not so, illustrious Masters. He contracts God the Creator and His glorious creation. Knowledge of either is both a good and an end in itself. But, agreeing thus far with our Doctor's thesis, to wit, that Theology is the radiant Queen of the sciences, even then this holds good: there are some scholars, and they not a few, who make the knowledge of things natural a road to heavenly contemplation, as once did Abraham, old star-watcher in Ur of the Chaldees, and those holy astronomers who knelt beside the Crib. Now scholars of this sort pass on from philosophy and the liberal arts—subjects of study which this man of whom I write condemns out of hand under the general head of secular literature—to Theology, thinking it no unfitting task to despoil the women of Egypt, who are handmaidens of divine knowledge, in order better to adorn the lovely Queen who is Theology herself—a secular flower of rhetoric I plucked from the garden of a great Greek scholar whom this Doctor has calumniated only too often in his day.

"And as regards this same Theology, which alone he seems to approve, if indeed he approves even that, I do not see how he can ever attain it without the knowledge of languages, either Hebrew, Greek, or Latin, unless, indeed, in his fondness for English fables, he has persuaded himself that he will find it amid old wives' country tales of firedrakes, puckles, hobgoblins, Tom Thumbs, and other such fireside bugs as these. Or perhaps he thinks that the whole of Theology is comprised within the limits of those set questions on which such pedants as he are always disputing, for the understanding and phrasing of which, it must be admitted, little enough Latin is wanted. Scholastic conundrums are games for grown-up children, and, I freely concede, can be learned without any particular effort. But Theology, that august Queen of Heaven and Earth, that crowned Empress of human knowledge, demands an ampler scope. The knowledge of God can be gathered only out of Scripture—Scripture and the early Catholic Fathers. That was where for a thousand years the searchers after truth looked for it and found it, before these modern paradoxes were heard of. And if he fancies, in his ignorant presumption, that Scripture and the Fathers can be understood without knowledge of the language in which the Fathers wrote, he will not find many to agree with him.

"He will pretend, beyond doubt, that he was not censuring learning itself, he was censuring only an excessive devotion to it. I do not, however, see so great a disposition to sin in this particular direction, so headlong a rush of men toward the ascetic pleasures of study, that these manifestations need to be checked by a public sermon. But, in sober truth, this pious reformer of other men's manners had no such moderate design in view. He calls those who study Greek, heretics. The teachers of Greek, he says, are full-grown devils, the learners of Greek are lesser devils, and he names with the name of devil-in-chief a certain celebrated professor of Greek whom, I think, the veritable devil of devils would be very loath to see in a pulpit. He did not call this person by his own honored name, but everyone, who heard, knew that this great fool meant the sage author of the *Praise of Folly*.

"It is not for me, illustrious Masters, to defend Greek or the liberal disciplines in general. You know yourselves, from your own wide wisdom and experience, that Greek needs no defense. The most glorious of the world's writings, Theology included, are in Greek. Is truth only to be found in Gothic Latin? The Romans had no philosophers save those two disciples of the Greeks, Cicero and Seneca. The New Testament was first written down in Greek. Your wisdoms will freely acknowledge that not all Greek scholars are fools, and you will not tolerate that this admirable study be put down by the public sermons of bigots or the private cabals of fools and knaves. Make these same precious gentlemen of the cloth understand that, unless they promptly cease from such factious doings, we outside will have a word or two to say about it.

"Remember, too: Oxford is something more than today's faculties, and today's administrators. It is yesterday's students, and tomorrow's professors as well. Every man who has been educated at your University has as much interest in its welfare as you who are now at its head. The body of great Oxford belongs to the Christian Community of Sinners. Ye are its stewards—an honored post, it is most true; and a heavy charge. See to it, illustrious Masters, that ye be good and honest stewards; that ye honor your godlike trust. Your Primate and Chancellor, my Lord of Canterbury, and your King, Henry of England, are not likely to commend unjust stewards. With its lordly colleges and its goodly endowments there is nowhere in the world a place of education so richly furnished as Oxford; and the object of these munificent foundations is to support students in the acquirement of knowledge. Your wisdoms, therefore, will seek out means to silence these foolish contentions. Let these latter-day Trojans call to mind that, were it not for a blind old Greek called Homer, the very name they assume to keep their bigotries in countenance would not be known. Useful learning, of whatever kind it be, shall be protected from ridicule and shall receive due honor and esteem. Be you diligent in so doing. Improve the high quality of your own lectures and so deserve the thanks of your Prince, your Primate, and your Chancellor.

"I have written thus candidly out of the deep regard I feel for you. Know, illustrious Masters, that you can command my own poor services whenever you feel you need them. God keep you all in safety, and make you increase daily in richness of learning and godliness of life.

> Thomas More, Chancellor
> From Chelsea, this first day of
> May, 1532"

Thomas More was very tired. He flexed his cramped fingers. Even as he wrote, the afternoon had waned and the soft spring evening drawn on. Yawning, he rang for a serving man to fetch him a cold collation. He had dated his letter to the Fathers and Proctors of Oxford from Chelsea, which was a trifle irregular. Official documents really should be dated from his office in Westminster. But he had done so deliberately. He had wanted this Oxford letter on liberal education to carry the liberal imprint of the Chelsea home where he had kept his family school without threat or ferule. It would all be official enough once the Great Seal was affixed to the document, no later than tomorrow morning.

It was, he decided, a good enough letter in its way: clear, logical, direct, unflinching. It was more than he knew; or any man of his time knew, either. It was liberal education's great charter of rights; modern education's earliest mellow manifesto; England's first idea of a university.

Yawning again and stretching, Thomas More lit one of the fine wax tapers which were his only real luxury; or, as he preferred to think, a necessary tribute to the Muses who required decent light to show off their comeliness properly. There was just room before bedtime to look at a new map Master Rastell had last week sent over from his home. The Chancellor noted, with amused interest, that the monsters were beginning to disappear from the latest mappemoundes. There were fewer mermaids and spouting sea beasts. The pictured whales did not gape nearly so widely as before. Fewer sea serpents writhed their scaly lengths across the *terrae incognitae;* and those same *terrae incognitae* were fast contracting in extent. Mother Maude would not have liked it at all; but, in his clear-sighted rationality, King Utopus would surely approve. It was, Thomas More supposed, partly the doing of Nicholas Copernicus, the Polish astronomer. There, at any rate, he conceded with a smile, was a modern European who knew more than an ancient Greek; more, actually, in his own line, than great Aristotle himself. But it did not really change things so very much, after all, to learn that the earth was not the fixed center of the universe, and that the sun and the stars did not really revolve about it. If, in the light of all this new flood of scientific knowledge, the earth was diminishing, the universe outside was expanding. If man began to find out more and more about the macrocosm, he did not thereby necessarily know more and more about the microcosm, though, of course, he might think he did. In fact, Thomas More had a shrewd suspicion that man was actually beginning to forget certain essential things about his own nature. The monsters might be vanishing from the parchment margins of the mappemoundes; other monsters would not therefore sound the less deep within the haunted soul of man. Not even in this year of grace, fifteen hundred and thirty-two years after the Incarnation of our Blessed Lord, was Leviathan to be taken with a hook. And, so long as books continued to exist, certain of the lesser monsters would still swim about endearingly in the shallow depths of Pliny's *Book of the Little Beasts*. With a smile of affection he read again Pliny's description of the dolphin:

> *The dolphin is the swiftest fish in the sea. . . . Above the nature of other fishes they love young children, and the sound of stringed instruments. . . . They live three hundred years. . . . They rejoice when one calleth them Simon, and they love the human voice.*

That night Thomas More had a strange but soothing dream. He stood on the shore of a lake, its wavelets sparkling like the ἀνήριθμον γέλασμα, the "numberless laughter" of the old Greek poet. Men, dragging their nets near the edge of the rocky shale, were taking a great draught of fishes; and One who stood in their midst, hand raised in benediction, spoke these odd words to a great porpoise gamboling just off shore: *Blessed art thou, Simon bar Dolphin, for thou hast known Me in the days of thy gamboling; and thou delightest the children of men.* Then, on a sudden, as happens in dreams, the lake was gone, and in its place grew a goodly garden, moated round by a silver stream. Somehow Thomas More knew it was not merely a garden. It was the Garden of all men's desire. Out of its fresh green meadows towered a castle, like the *nobile castello* in Dante where dwelt in eternity the masters of them that know, the great poets of antiquity, the great philosophers, the virtuous pagans. There were people in the grove, gathered round the heroic figures of two men: one an old man, wearing a white beard, who was numbering the beasts; the other a hero with noble brow, herculean breadth of shoulder, and grave glance, who was appointing for the animals their names and orders. Without being told, Thomas More knew that the patriarch's name was Noah, and the hero's name Adam.

My Lord Chancellor More Writes a Letter to Oxford

Among those chosen few who aided Adam in his glorious task of naming the beasts was one in the vestments of a Greek slave, with black-pointed beard, and quick brown face like the profiles one saw on old vases dug up in the Troad. More recognized him as Aesop. He also recognized the Phoenician profile of Il Poverello, a bright nimbus of birds, in avian cloud of witness, circling about his tonsured head. The others he did not know at all, except that there seemed to be English among them; among the frisking rabbits, the little country beasts of hedge and river, a great black panther paced like a King. He sensed also, that in the place to which he had come there was no such thing as time. Past and future were a single timeless present there, though he could tell, in some obscure fashion or other, that he was witnessing what had been and what would be as well as what already was.

Thomas More smiled in his sleep. Mistress Alice, watching him by the yellow light of a solitary candle, relaxed. He had not slept so peacefully in months. She noticed, with a twinge of pity, how the stubble on his chin shone silver in the candlelight. It made him look old and drawn. Then, as the door latch rattled, she stiffened in sudden fear. Even as she watched, the door swung open, and a chattering little ball of fur hurled itself onto the bed.

"Drat the beast!" Dame Alice said to herself, vexed, yet amused.

The sleeping man did not awake. He smiled again. The little monkey face seemed to contort in pleasure. The marmoset slipped a protective black paw into his master's hand, and snuggled down between them, burrowing into the warm coverlets. Dame Alice sank back on her pillow with a sigh. In five minutes she, too, slept. And she, too, began to smile. Somewhere, far off in the empyrean's *nobile castello*, Plato's face was also wreathed in smiles, while the Stagirite frowned. Let Aristotle win all he liked by daylight. In Utopia and in the nighttime soul of Master More great Plato reigned victorious.

CHAPTER XIII

MY LORD CHANCELLOR MORE

GOES TO MASS:

Westminster, Morning, May 16, 1532

THOMAS SURREY, Duke of Norfolk, was no politician. He was a soldier, and a good one, the best English Captain in Henry's realm; slow, faithful, dogged; a braw man to follow the proper leader, but a bad man to lead. He did not shrink from the butchery inherent in his martial trade; nor would one really have looked for overmuch fastidiousness in the son of the grim victor of Flodden. He had cut down the errant apprentices on Evil May Day without a single grain of compunction. Eyes narrowed, peering from the saddle, he had drawn into his lungs the acrid smell of burning French villages without turning a hair. Like most professional soldiers worth their salt, he was closer to Malory than to Machiavelli. Again, like most professional soldiers, he was at once an historical anachronism and an historical necessity. The kingdom could not well do without this grizzled warrior who, legs bowed from a life spent on horseback in the open field, now walked impatiently up and down my Lord Chancellor More's firelit antechamber at Westminster. But he looked the while as if he belonged to the reign of the sixth Henry, not that of the eighth. He looked, as a matter of fact, very much like one of the great Captains who warred against Joan the Maid; like Warwick or Talbot. It was already a quarter past eight in the morning. My Lord

My Lord Chancellor More Goes to Mass:

Chancellor More was still at his devotions in Westminster Chapel. The Duke of Norfolk, perforce, must wait. And the Duke of Norfolk did not like waiting.

As Surrey strode back and forth across the stone-flagged chamber, irritably kicking aside the rushes, he tossed his gloves from hand to hand and played restlessly with the gilded hilt of his dagger. My Lord of Norfolk's gloves, no matter how sumptuous, had a habit of looking like gauntlets; and, style or no style, Italianate and French-ified rapiers with their basket hilts and ornamented hangers were not for the likes of him. In battle he wanted a broadsword for the heavy work and a shortsword for any infighting that might be necessary. In undress he felt at home only with a dagger to turn, back and forth, in his belt. For Norfolk life was a matter of cut and foin and slash. He left thrusting in the new fashion to the braggart fops who fol-lowed in the train of his niece, Mistress Boleyn. Norfolk detested that scheming niece of his, and most of the other Boleyns, too. They were an unregenerate tribe, all of them. They forced him to play pol-itics, to cool his heels in antechambers, and fawn in council rooms. Politics and soldiering did not go well together. Short words, like barked commands, and the evasive periphrases of politics made uncomfortable bedfellows. No, decidedly, politics were not for a man of Norfolk's kidney. He was the first peer in the realm; and Anne's father, my Lord of Wiltshire, his pretentious brother-in-law, who had crept like a cuckoo into the Norfolk eyrie, was a damned, huck-stering cheapjack who bought offices and sold them. Yet he found himself, like any ambitious young squire on the rise, dancing atten-dance on these Boleyn latecomers to greatness.

Norfolk growled low in his throat and spat on the hearthstone. It was all the Boleyns' fault that he was about this morning's dirty busi-ness of the Chancellorship. For dirty business it was. If the King's great matter had now progressed so far that it began to touch my Lord Chancellor More's honor, then, he supposed, his old friend had no other recourse but to resign his high office. Norfolk understood considerations of honor; and he was quite willing to allow Thomas More his own individual construction of that sensitive point, the *punto d'onore.* As it happened, Norfolk's somewhat fiercely limited concept of what honor constituted did not extend to matters of religion. He was a good enough Catholic, as he was a good enough conservative and a good enough knight. But he would not raise his little finger for an Italian Prince like Clement. If Henry wanted to be Pope in England, let him and welcome. If he wanted to draw the sharp teeth of a few Bishops or clip the rook wings of a parcel of thieving monks, why, my Lord of Norfolk had no objection to that course of action, either. Things would go on as they always had. The day would still begin with Mass and end with Vespers. So, on the whole, he thought his friend More a great fool to stand upon this particular *point d'honneur.* A woman was one thing; a duel another. But to risk the King's displeasure for a caprice like this!

Still and all, it was a dirty business; and the Boleyns, with his precious niece at their head, were to blame for it. Norfolk's sinewy fingers fairly itched to stripe the girl's ambitious backside so hot and long that Mistress Anne would fain seek out a soft, cool pillion somewhere away from Court and nothing so regal-hard as the throne of England. But Henry had quite other plans for the lithe, free-striding Boleyn hips than my Lord of Norfolk's old-fashioned remedy for female wantonness. And, in his own toad's turn, Thomas Cromwell, too, had his own deep-laid plans for the Chancellorship. The Duke swore fluently to himself as he thought on Cromwell's candidate for the vacant office: that urbane and handsome nonentity, my Lord Audley, who had already followed close upon the heels of Thomas More in the two offices of Speaker of the Commons and Chancellor of the Duchy of Lancaster. Audley was just the sort of colorless politician any bluff soldier would hate worst, because he would always feel disarmed and helpless before this sort of majestic blandness and hollow comeliness. Neither villain, fool, nor hero, Thomas Audley was the eternal and essential tool of government; the facade of respectability and plausibility which makes tyranny seem both plausible and palatable. His handsome eyes were as empty of passion as those of a marble bust. Again Norfolk spat vehemently into the fire. Less than three full years ago, when Thomas More first took the Seal in the great hall of Westminster, he had declared, on the King's behalf, how "all England was beholden to Sir Thomas More," and how worthy this son of a London commoner was "to have the highest room in the realm." Perhaps it had been conventionally uttered at the time. But, by God, it had turned out true. Sir Thomas More was the best Chancellor England had ever known. And, if Thomas More insisted on playing Amadis of Gaul for a religious scruple, then my Lord Audley bade fair to be the worst.

The men-at-arms grounded their halberds in salute. Norfolk wheeled to see my Lord Chancellor More come in the door, a surplice caught across his robes of state, still humming a snatch of *O Salutaris Hostia* from the Benediction service which had closed the Mass. He bowed cordially to Norfolk.

"Welcome, my Lord of Norfolk," said Thomas More, slipping the garment over his head with the assistance of the red-haired man-at-arms.

Norfolk stared at the Chancellor, dumfounded. Suddenly a great wave of bitterness welled up in his practical soldier's throat. He tasted bile. What futility, what folly was here!

"God's body! God's body, my Lord Chancellor!" said Norfolk testily. "A parish clerk! A parish clerk warbling in a surplice! You dishonor the King and your own high office under the King!"

"How so, my Lord Duke?" asked Thomas More pleasantly, taking no offense. He was used to his old friend's asperities. "How so? I am the King's good servant, I trust. But God's first, surely. And I am a better liege of His Majesty's for that very reason. Your Grace should not think that the King, your good master and mine, will be offended with me for taking an early morning hour to don God's livery and do God's holy service."

"God's body, my Lord Chancellor!" said Norfolk, still growling. "No one objects to your attending Mass. But the surplice, man! That is neither the King's livery nor yours. It is the sexton's or the altar boy's. It sets you lower than the chaplain who droned out the Mass."

Thomas More began to laugh. He laughed long and heartily.

"Your pardon, friend Norfolk, if I offend you," he said at last, still laughing. "I see it is not God's service you object to, but mine own humble part therein. You would have me play Mary, not Martha. I grant you your spiritual perceptions must be reckoned far finer than mine, for it cannot be gainsaid but that Our Savior Christ accounted the Blessed Magdalen's sitting at her ease and hearkening a far better business than the busy stirring and walking about of His good hostess, Martha. Yet there is something to be said for poor Martha, too. We cannot all be Marys in this world, else would the world wag on but badly. Of all worldly business Martha was yet occupied about the best. If she was busy, she was busy about alms and hospitality, and the guesting of the best Poor Man and most gracious Guest that ever yet was guested in this world. No, friend Norfolk, you are wrong. You and I and Henry are men as well as masters. Martha's Poor Man is our master—the King's master no less than yours and mine. Henry thereby cannot account my office dishonored."

Norfolk looked appeased; and he was not at all the kind of man who easily tolerates having sermons read to him. But one did not long stay angry with Thomas More.

"Perhaps, my dear old friend," he said, taking More by the shoulder, "perhaps you do not know Henry very well, after all—after all these years of close acquaintance between the two of you. And I am afraid he does not know you at all."

Norfolk dropped his hand. He looked More square in the eye.

"Sir Thomas," he said, "I come here in peril of my head to warn you that you are in grave danger unless you subscribe your hand to the Oath of Supremacy, and at once. If you are still bent on resigning the Great Seal, the King bids me inform you that he will reluctantly accept your decision. But I tell you, Thomas mine, it is a perilous course you intend to follow. Henry does not easily take rebuffs. Make no mistake: your resignation is a mortal rebuff to the King. Nor will it save you from the Oath. The Oath must be subscribed, willy-nilly, sooner or later. It will be administered to everyone in the realm. The Commissioners are appointed—Master Cromwell had their appointing. Master Secretary Cromwell has himself drawn up the instrument, and Master Audley has had the amplifying of it for him. Master Cranmer has argued in Council that you should be spared the article demanding renunciation of all papal authority in England. Master Cranmer, give him his due, is a kindly man. He has acted as your friend. But Master Cromwell denied his petition, saying that there may be no exceptions. You can guess what Mistress Anne has been whispering into Henry's ear."

"I am the more bounden to Master Cranmer," said Thomas More. "Do you thank him for me for acting as my friend. But Master Cromwell is right. There should be no exceptions in these matters."

"Sir Thomas!" said Norfolk sharply. "You are blind to your dire peril. Master Secretary Cromwell comes here to Westminster this very morning to sound you out. Yesterday, in Parliament, the most part of the Bishops signed. The Abbots will be asked next."

Thomas More never moved a muscle.

"Not John Fisher," he said tonelessly.

"No," agreed Norfolk. "My Lord of Rochester did not sign, it is true. But what is one among so many?"

"One can be right," said Thomas More, "and many wrong. My Lord of Rochester is right. My mind is made up. I follow his course. I accept the divorce. I accept the remarriage. I accept Mistress Anne as my Queen and the lawful wife of my King. I accept whatever means of succession the King and the Parliament see fit to settle on. But I cannot accept the King as my lord spiritual. I cannot renounce the Pope. Straight on his coming here this morning, I will surrender the Great Seal to Master Cromwell, that he may bear it to the King. Or, if my most gracious liege wishes to see me once again, I shall bear it to him myself wheresoever and whensoever he wishes."

Norfolk stared, speechless, at his friend.

"So be it then," he said, stepping back a pace, spreading his hands out in a hopeless gesture.

More, in his turn, looked compassionately at Norfolk. It was almost as if the roles were now reversed; as if, from some vantage point high above the bright tumult of men and affairs, the Chancellor were consoling the Duke.

"My Lord of Norfolk and my friend," said Thomas More. "You are a layman, a soldier, a good servant of the King, and, somewhat against your will, I know, a politician. But I tell you the Bishops are blind. They connive in their own destruction. Can they not see that, in the end, they cannot purchase immunity by selling principle? Can they not see that this present plunder, great as it is, is yet but the beginning of plunder? Everyone else is able to see it, but they alone. Do they not remember à Becket and another Henry? There I have said it! Is it treason to remember the martyr of Canterbury and his royal executioner? Do they not remember the great ensample of à Becket? I have here a letter in cipher taken from the pouch of one of the messengers of the French Ambassador. Do you read for yourself this English translation of what it says."

He handed a parchment to Norfolk who ran his eyes over the ominous communication.

Now that my Lord Cardinal Wolsey is some years ruined, and Chancellor More, too, totters to his fall, the great Lords here in England mean to attack and plunder the Church. It is hardly needful for me even to pretend to write this species of intelligence in cipher any more, for the Lords proclaim it openly in boast and in jest. I expect they will soon perform fine miracles here in this douce realm of England.

Norfolk handed back the missive without comment. Thomas More looked at him.

"You see, my Lord of Norfolk," he said. "Your kind message is no great surprise to me."

At that the Duke of Norfolk lost his patience altogether.

"God's body, Sir Thomas!" he rapped out in utter desperation. "Do me the grace to regard it as something more than a mere message! It is a warning—one delivered at great peril of my own head! You are a much bigger fool than I had bargained for. Why, think you, did my Lord Reginald Pole remove to Padua this January past? England is no longer safe for him, as it is no longer safe for you. Yet he is the King's own cousin, and a clergyman of God. By the Mass, man, it is perilous striving with Princes! Either get you out of England, with your whole family, and at once, or else subscribe the Oath. If you mean to remain in England, you must incline yourself somewhat to the King's pleasure. For, by God's body, my Lord Chancellor, *indignatio principis mors est.* You are a good enough Latinist, I believe, to be able to translate that maxim."

"Yes," said Thomas More. "I have enough Latin to puzzle it out. It is a favorite maxim of Messire Machiavelli whom Master Cromwell is forever quoting. *The wrath of the Prince is death.* But what of that?"

"What of that, my Lord Chancellor?" echoed the Duke incredulously, purpling in passion. "What of that, you say?"

"Yes, what of that?" repeated Thomas More. "Is this all you have to say to me, my Lord of Norfolk? Then, in good faith, there is no more difference between Your Grace and me—or between Henry and the two of us, for that matter—but that I shall die today, and you twain tomorrow."

Thomas More stopped speaking as he noticed Norfolk's ghastly face. The ugly flush faded. Now it seemed as if the Duke's whole body were drained of blood.

"But, my more than friend," said the Chancellor very softly, "this is showing you but scant gratitude indeed for the great favor you do me, and for the great risk you run in so doing it. I thank you heartily. There! My hand upon it! My right hand upon it in heartfelt thanks! And now, friend Norfolk, Westminster bell tolls nine. It would be wise for you, I think, to leave by the inner door. It is close upon Master Secretary's hour. And it is one of Cromwell's virtues to be prompt."

The two friends exchanged handclasps at the inner door. The iron throat was still hawking hoarsely when, punctual to the minute, a clashing of halberds signaled the arrival of Master Secretary Cromwell. More had not met the man face to face since his appointment to the Secretaryship. So he scrutinized him a bit more closely, perhaps, than courtesy warranted. Success and advancing years combined had dealt hardly with Master Cromwell. Never what the most charitable would call a pretty man, he was now sleeker than before. The heavy face had grown heavier. The little eyes were more deeply lodged in their enclosing pouches of fat; but their sharp glance was not, thereby, the less steely-cold. The hard mouth had, if possible, set more firmly than ever. But, to tell the truth, the Chancellor could sense no increased aura of menace. What hostility there was, was impersonal, almost departmental. As Cromwell's power to hurt increased daily, it seemed, and truly, as if his capacity for hatred diminished. Men were no longer friends or enemies to him, but, instead, mere integers in a political equation. More shuddered inside. Anne Boleyn's malignant hatred toward him appeared more human than this icy detachment. If it consumed one to ashes, at least it did not freeze one to the very marrow of one's innermost soul.

On his own side, Thomas Cromwell looked with equal narrowness at the man he had now to deal with. The Chancellor had been right in his intuitive surmise. Cromwell felt no vestige of animosity whatsoever toward him as an adversary. He was, rather, an obstacle to be removed from the path of inevitable progress. For, if Thomas Cromwell had a private theology, it was that he was an emissary and functionary of fate, which he liked to think of as progress. And it was a pity, too, in a way, that Thomas More had to be an obstacle. Insofar as Master Secretary Cromwell could experience either affection or respect, he felt both for Thomas More. He rather liked More's humorous lucidity. If indulgence were still feasible at all, then Master More should have indulgence. It all hinged on the Oath. Cromwell put out a friendly hand to the Chancellor.

"Well met, Master Secretary!" said Thomas More cordially, advancing to meet his visitor. "My heartiest congratulations upon your entering into office as Secretary to His Majesty. May I, as your elder and an old friend, say a word to you?"

Cromwell nodded a cynical assent. He knew what was coming. Master More had served notice that he understood who was Audley's master, and that he intended to give some advice to the power behind the new Chancellor's chair. The man was clever and courageous. A great pity he so misdirected his splendid acumen and courage.

"You may," he said, settling himself comfortably in a chair and locking hands across his bufonian stomach.

"You are now entered, Master Cromwell," said Thomas More, "into the service of a most noble, wise, and liberal prince. If you will follow my poor advice, you shall, in your counsel-giving to His Grace, ever tell him what he ought to do, but never what he has the power to do. So shall you show yourself of a truth a faithful servant, and a right wise and worthy counsellor. For, Master Secretary, as you well know from your readings in Messire Machiavelli, if a lion knew his own strength, hard would it be for any man to rule him. Do you find me over sententious?"

Thomas More stole a glance at Thomas Cromwell who, he thought, had not expected this last very Machiavellian thrust in tierce. Cromwell sat his chair, motionless, heavy lids drawn over the little eyes. Nevertheless, the shaft had gone home. The ironic Utopian in More was well satisfied with his little counterpoint in Machiavelli.

Reaching into his Chancellor's drawer, Thomas More carefully took out the Great Seal of the realm of England. Enclosing it in a soft bag of white doeskin, he placed this inner receptacle inside an outer pouch of crimson velvet, and laid it on the desk within reach of Cromwell's hand.

"And now, Master Secretary," he said, "the time has come for me, through your gracious instrumentality, to render up to my most puissant King the Great Seal he has entrusted to my keeping these three years past. You have been successful in securing me an audience?"

"Let us say my Lord of Norfolk has been successful," said Cromwell, and More found his inflection bafflingly enigmatic. "The King grants audience to you twain at three o'clock this afternoon in the garden of York Place."

Thomas More felt uneasy for Norfolk. There was a sinister ambiguity in Cromwell's way of putting the matter of the audience. For Norfolk's own sake, he decided, the two old friends must have no further communication.

"Master Cromwell," said More, after an uneasy pause. "I have a further favor to ask of your good graces. Will you carry a message from me, his good and faithful servant, to our Lord the King? I have written down somewhat of my private feelings touching this great matter of the Oath in this letter to him."

The obsidian eyes unlidded.

"I should like first, Sir Thomas," Cromwell said, "to know what the letter contains, that it touch not my loyalty too nearly."

"That is easily done, Master Secretary," said Thomas More. "Here. Do you take and read it. I have not sealed the letter yet."

Cromwell, impassive, stretched out his hand for the letter. He read it carefully to himself:

> I thank my Liege lord for his favors to me. I am sorry I may not, in conscience, touch the matter of the Oath more nearly than I have heretofore done. However, as God is my help, touching this same matter of the Oath, I shall never wittingly draw any man away from it, nor advise anyone to refuse it, nor shall I ever put any scruple in any man's head regarding it, but leave every man to his own good conscience. And I beg Your Grace that you see fit to accept my protestation of good faith and that you think it just that, in return, every man leave me to my good conscience. I have now, in all good faith, discharged my mind of all matters pertaining to your Kingdom.
>
> Never, were it to have the whole world given me, shall I meddle in the world again. I shall withdraw to mine own house, there to make my whole study upon the Passion of Christ, and on mine own passing out of this world. Never mean I to dispute Kings' titles or Popes'. But the King's true faithful subject am I, and will be, and daily shall I pray for him and all his, and for all that are of his honorable Council, and all the realm.
>
> I pray Your Grace accept my pledge and promise. If I lose your good opinion, nothing else shall give me any further meed of pleasure in this world. In such an unhappy event, my only comfort would be that, after my short life and Your Grace's long one, I should once again meet Your Grace in Heaven, and there be merry with you, as we were wont to be merry together on earth. In Heaven where, among mine other pleasures, this should yet be a chief one, that Your Grace should surely see there, with your own eyes, that I am your true beadsman now, and ever have been.
>
> Thomas More, *eques,* from Westminster,
> this sixteenth day of May, 1532

"It is all written down in order on the parchment, Master Secretary," said Thomas More, a trifle of uncertainty and anxiety in his voice. "Do you think it fitting?"

My Lord Chancellor More Goes to Mass:

Thomas Cromwell pondered the letter. He had known beforehand that More was an extraordinary man, but not till this present reading had his eyes been opened to just how extraordinary a man he really was. Why, the man was actually in earnest about wanting to retire from the world and think on the Passion of Christ! And it was precisely this moral and spiritual seriousness that made him so dangerous an obstacle to the plans Cromwell had now in train. Unlike Norfolk, he was in no hurry to apply the epithet, "fool," to More. Cromwell's chill sophistication of intellect had gone so far that the verbal counter, "fool," had almost disappeared from his vocabulary. This same detachment conferred a cold integrity, a glacial chastity of motive upon his actions. His own fixity of purpose in regard to the royal supremacy, for example, made him capable of appreciating fixity of purpose in others and for other reasons. More than any clash of arms that had yet taken place between them, more than any of the exigencies of Henry, more than all the importunities of Anne, the reading of this letter riveted Cromwell's resolve that More must be done away with. There could be no question of indulgence any more, though it would be politic to pretend that redress was still possible. Again his cold worldliness recoiled, appalled, before More's purity of intention. My Lord Chancellor, who would soon no longer be my Lord Chancellor, must subscribe the Oath in full. Or die.

"Do you think it fitting, Master Secretary?" More asked a second time.

"A most dutiful document, certainly, Sir Thomas," said Cromwell, turning toward him. "But it is much too late in the game for dutiful documents to serve your turn. The King is no longer to be played with. Since you have been good enough to honor me with a small piece of advice, do you allow me to return the favor. Subscribe the Oath; and that shortly."

"I am sorry, Master Secretary," said Thomas More. "I cannot."

"Why not, pray?" asked Cromwell. "It is well worth the little price you pay. The theologians, remember, have not stuck at the divorce from Catherine. Oxford, Cambridge, Paris, Orléans, Angers, Toulouse, Bologna, Ferrara, Pavia, Padua—every University in Christendom. All of their faculties, Doctor and Rabbis alike, have agreed, at twenty-four crowns a head, that it is foul incest for Henry to sleep with his dead brother's wife. They will render a similar favorable verdict about his new Act of Supremacy—and this time, I wager, we can have their learned suffrages for twenty crowns a tonsured poll."

"So say you," said Thomas More sadly. "And it may well be so. But I may not swear the Oath, nevertheless. How may a layman be head of the Church in England? It is not suitable. It is not reasonable."

"Reasonable?" asked Cromwell, bleak contempt creeping for the first time into his thick voice. "Reasonable, Master More? What is reason, after all? Reason is power and possession. Reason is what the Prince allows to be. What says Master Luther on the subject in his excellent advice to Princes? *You must wring the neck of the beast, reason.*"

Thomas More's eyes flashed at the mention of Luther.

"You will find, Master Secretary," he said passionately, "you will find—and Master Luther, too,—that, once you twain begin your task of wringing, reason will prove herself a hydra-headed beast. No one shall ever wring all of reason's necks."

Cromwell shrugged. He never lost his temper. It was a luxury he had not yet found himself well enough off to afford.

"One can but try," he observed. "But there are other less violent ways, too. *How may a layman be head of the Church in England?* you ask. Easily. We shall have a Cardinal ordain him. Cranmer will do it in a trice."

"Cranmer is not a Cardinal, Master Secretary," said Thomas More.

"Granted," said Cromwell shortly. "Not yet at least. But he will soon be an Archbishop, and that is sufficient."

The Secretary leaned forward in his chair.

"Sir Thomas," he said menacingly, "we are paltering. And there is no longer time for paltering. I tell you, there will be little difference in the end whether one is burned by the Pope or beheaded by the King. The thing to do is to make terms with the more immediate danger. And, in your case, the King is the more immediate danger."

However hectoring tactics might succeed with other men, they made no impression on Thomas More.

"I am sorry, Master Secretary," he said. "I am more afraid for my King's soul than I am for my own neck."

"So it is the King's soul which is at issue now?" asked Cromwell contemptuously. "He can have Masses said for that if he so chooses."

More flushed in anger.

"Where?" he asked vehemently, becoming utterly impassioned for the first time. "Where, Master Secretary? Where shall he now have Masses said for his soul—he or any man? Chantries are every day confiscate to the greed of the great Lords. Prayers for the dead cease all over England. By God, I cannot see why any Christian man— yourself included, Master Secretary—should, in his heart, think it labor lost to pray for all Christian souls. No thank you, Master Secretary. I am sorry we do not agree. But we do not agree—not in anything. Take the great Seal, I pray you. I have other business to attend to, before this afternoon's audience with the King. And my watermen await me."

Without so much as rising Cromwell accepted the Great Seal and parchment from his hands, and More went out with a hurried bow. No sooner had the Chancellor gone than, as if at a signal, the men-at- arms admitted Mistress Boleyn. Cromwell at once left off his frowning over the document More had given him, and offered her a chair next to the desk.

"Well?" asked Anne Boleyn, one slim hand disposing her rustling skirts.

The Secretary looked at her covertly a moment before replying. Among Cromwell's other qualities was an almost utter indifference to women as women. He had, early in life, married quiet Elizabeth Wykys in order to gain her father's shearman's business. After the death of his wife and their two daughters of the dread sweating sick- ness in 1528, four years before, he had neither solaced himself with another wife, nor sought irregular consolation elsewhere beyond an occasional tavern rutting for, as he put it, the sake of his body's ease. The one woman he now maintained in his household was for the practical and prosaic purpose of providing a governess for Gregory, the near idiot who was his only son. This woman, Margaret Vernon, was an increment from the Secretary's new monastery speculations.

Before the dissolution of the nunnery at Little Marlow she had been
Lady Prioress there. Now she was reduced to teaching the drooling
child the bare rudiments of letters out of a horn book.

But, like the scent of musk, Anne Boleyn had a way of exciting
Cromwell's sluggish senses. He lusted for her, as it were, vicariously.
She knew it; and was not ill-pleased, though somewhat disdainful.
Of recent weeks their colloquies together almost took on the aspect of
an obscenely sinuous dance, with, as on the present occasion, Cromwell, like some squat and uxorious familiar, smiling over the Marchioness of Pembroke's white shoulder.

"Well, Master Secretary?" asked Anne again, impatiently.

"He has refused, Your Grace," said Cromwell. "I told you he would
refuse. Here is the Great Seal of the realm, and with it a letter for
Henry."

"So much the better then," said Anne Boleyn, balancing the velvet
bag in one gloved hand. "My Lord Audley should prove more pliable.
As pliable a Chancellor as Cranmer an Archbishop."

She ran her eyes down the parchment.

"Sir Thomas likes to write passing well," she said indifferently.
"He should be a scribe in a monastery."

Then, as another kind of thought struck her, the apparent indifference disappeared. A faroff evil light came into Mistress Boleyn's eyes.
She wet her upper lip with the tip of a pink tongue.

"Sir Thomas," she said slowly, as if savoring every word, and find-
ing their taste pleasant. "Sir Thomas likes to write. He writes other
things as well as letters of resignation from the highest office in the
land under our Lord the King. But always they are sermons. Only
yesterday this other pretty morsel was brought to my attention.
Hearken to Sir Thomas sermonize on an old Bible King and Queen."

With dreamlike grace and deliberateness, as if moving through
the elaborate steps of some formal pavane, Anne Boleyn took a paper
from her embroidered pocket. As she slowly recited the contents, it
was very evident she had them by heart. For not once did she refer
to the little paper:

"St. John Baptist was, ye wot well, in prison, while Herodias sat full merry at the feast, till with her dancing Salome danced off St. John's head. And now sitteth John with great feast in Heaven at God's board, while Herod and Herodias full heavily sit in Hell, burning both twain, and to make them sport withal the Devil with the damsel dances in the fire afore them."

Anne Boleyn fell silent, a strange, wicked smile on her face.

"The Devil with the damsel dances in the fire afore them," she repeated in the same dreamlike cadence. "Would it not make a subtle dance for one of the French Masques Marguerite commissions at her court?"

The rationalist in Cromwell shrank from this eldritch talk about the devil.

"In justice to the man, Mistress Boleyn," he informed her, "I should point out that he can have meant no possible offense to you by that particular piece of writing. It was written full ten years ago and has no conceivable connection with you or yours. I know. It is my business to know such things. The King pays me well for my knowledge. My Secretary's office has a full file of what Master More has written and does write. I must confess he is lately very circumspect with his pen. Save for state matters, of which the King has full intelligence, he toucheth nothing nowadays but the heretical doings of Master Luther, Master Tyndale, and, most recently, Master Simon Fish's *Supplication for the Beggars*, a leveling pamphlet Henry doth most heartily abhor."

"Nevertheless," said Anne Boleyn, still smiling, her slanted green eyes half closed like a drowsing cat's, "I like not what he has written here, no matter how long ago, no matter where or why he wrote it. The people know nothing of dates. What if this were one day hawked about the streets of London?"

The police agent in Cromwell awoke at the question. Mistress Boleyn had a point there, he admitted to himself. Well did he know the power of rumor and canard. This was the kind of document that could be used indifferently either by an *agent provocateur* to incriminate some person the government found in its way, or, with equal cogency, by someone in opposition bent on embarrassing the government. It was borne in upon Cromwell with increasing force that More's very existence was becoming troublesome. But this kind of delicate discrimination was usually beyond a woman's wits. He wondered if Anne Boleyn nursed a more fundamental and earthy anxiety about the calendar. In spite of himself his eyes traveled to her girdle. Anne noticed the direction of his glance and laughed a trifle shrilly.

"Have no fear, Master Cromwell," she said in the midst of her mirthless laughter. "I am no nun, it is true, nor ever have been. But I yet carry not Henry's seed within my body. But I grant you it is a hard contest, and becomes daily more unequal. My woman's weapons grow blunt before his hot siege. We must cut this coil and soon, if we are to win at all. It is not so much that my rooted resolve flags, but that my nerves sicken. And Henry's appetite grows daily more importunate."

"Things progress apace," he reassured her. "You need be patient but a short time longer. And, touching Master More—there is a remedy. There is a remedy, if you choose to avail yourself of it."

"Well?" said Anne Boleyn. "I do so choose. Well?"

The squat familiar moved closer to her slim, crimson-sheathed figure.

"Read again," it suggested, pointing to the scrap of paper. "Says it not something about dancing therein?"

Anne Boleyn looked at the saurian lids, bewildered.

"The Devil with the damsel dances in the fire afore them," she said, faltering a little.

"No, Mistress Boleyn," whispered her familiar softly, pointing out the line it meant with one damp, podgy finger. "There."

Then, with a sharp intake of breath, Anne Boleyn understood the monstrous suggestion.

"Ah," she breathed, hissing through white teeth. "Ah. Yes. *Till with her dancing Salome danced off St. John's head.* Yes. There is indeed something about dancing herein, Master Secretary."

"St. Thomas hath a head as well as St. John, hath he not?" Cromwell asked her, snuffling through nose and mouth in mounting excitement. "Hath he not? Can you dance, Mistress?"

The Secretary's amorous reflexes were twitching now like a toad's legs when they are tickled by mischievous boys. Having seen her dance excellently well, he knew that Mistress Boleyn could talk with her whirling body. He had a sudden gratifying and distracting recollection of white thighs flashing in a rigadoon, and a sudden intimation of the buoyant hips that wove their provocative message above them. For the first time, perhaps, Master Cromwell realized all at once the haste and importunate urgency of Henry's suit.

"I shall dance tomorrow even," said Anne Boleyn softly, as if speaking to herself. "Tomorrow even I make the King a great banquet at Hanworth. He shall have pastime and dalliance. He shall also promise me a certain head for a wedding present. What think you of that, Master Cromwell?"

A grin creased the sodden gray planes of Cromwell's face. If guardsman Andres had seen the two of them at that moment, he would have said some elf-woman from his Norwegian mountains held parle with a Dovre troll.

"I think," said the troll familiar to the Norman witch, "I think you will need a platter for it. A silver one. A great altar vessel came into my possession only today from the inventory of Durham Monastery. Those monks will need it no longer. I have seen to that. May I give it you as a wedding gift?"

"Yes," said Anne Boleyn, almost whispering as she gave him her slender hand on the bargain. "But the wedding must needs be soon. I have not danced for Henry in over a year. Never have I danced for him as I shall dance tomorrow eve at Hanworth."

"Have no worry," whispered the familiar. "I promise you it will be soon."

CHAPTER XIV

MY LORD CHANCELLOR NO-MORE

GOES TO VESPERS:

Chelsea, Evening, May 16, 1532

As THOMAS MORE's eight sturdy watermen rowed upstream from Westminster to Chelsea, the silver shield of the Thames turned a heraldic cloth of gold under the armorer's brush of the westering sun. More's son-in-law, William Roper, was waiting anxiously at the water stairs; and, as his Chancellor's great state barge swung to the landing stage for what he knew was its last Chelsea moorage, Thomas More's heart turned to cold water in his breast. His resignation from office would be a sorrow to Meg and a perplexity and annoyance to Dame Alice; but to William Roper and the other young men of his household it would be a bitter setback to great expectations long nurtured and already bearing fruit. They were young men on the rise—in a sense, pensioners of the Court; and they owed their present enviable positions not only to their own abilities but to More's influence with the King. He wondered sadly if John Clement would remain Court physician now; if John Heywood would continue to receive the Court pension he earned for his prowess on the virginals; if William Roper would stay on as Protonotary of the Court of King's Bench. Because of his intensity of temperament, son-in-law Roper did not take easily to disappointment. That same impetuosity was what had made him, for a time, so hot a Lutheran, praying, fasting, tiring his eyes over Master Luther's *De Captivitate Babylonica* instead of over his law books, arguing theology with the contentious merchants of the Still-yard. No, thought Thomas More with a sigh, young men were rarely philosophers at best. But son Roper appeared never even to have heard of Horace's *aurea mediocritas*. With him it was feast or famine, never the old Stoic-Epicure's golden mean. Well, today and for some time to come, it would have to be famine. Thomas More heaved a second great sigh as the mooring rope was looped about the iron post.

His lead oar handed him out at the water steps. When the man turned to go again, Thomas More caught him by the arm.

"One moment, Hodge," he said, the slightest trace of a tremor in his voice. "Old friends ought not part without some semblance of a leave-taking. And we have become old friends, you and your fellows and I. We part now for the last time. I do not like this parting any more than you. But I trust that our new master, my Lord Audley—as new Chancellor of our realm he is my master, too, remember, under our Lord the King—will be as kind to you as you have always been to me and to the great barge we all sat merrily in together, and which my Lord Audley will now have. I give it him, a free gift from an old Chancellor to a new. I shall miss you, my good friends. Hodge will take this purse and give you your Christmas vails some months ahead of time, for I do not know if this year I may keep my usual appointment with Father Christmas. He will open yon slim purse as you row downstream again."

"It is not so slim as all that, my Lord Chancellor," said big Hodge stoutly, unshed tears in his voice. "It is as right plump a jingling purse as any Duke would give!"

"Would it were ten times fatter, friend Hodge," said Thomas More, rallying him. "There will be enough in it, at any rate, to buy a toast or two to your old Lord Chancellor. So it's farewell, friends, and huzza for Thameside! Huzza for the brave boys of *Westward Ho!* and *Eastward Ho!* as well! Farewell!"

Hodge led the crew in a rousing round of cheers.

"Farewell, my Lord Chancellor!" they cried. "Farewell! And huzza for the Moor's head and the unicorns of Chelsea!"

Long after the oarsmen's cries had died away over the sunset water and only the light *legato* of the barge's passing still sent tiny waves lapping against the water steps, Thomas More stood silent there in the Venetian glory of the sunset. The Moor's head and unicorns would still mark the More tomb in Chelsea church and the first page of his books in the library of Chelsea New Building; but no later than tomorrow they would be rubbed off the side of the Chancellor's barge to make way for my Lord Audley's crest. Chelsea church tower, chiming, tossed a silver coin of sound into the golden well of evening silence. Roper folded his father-in-law's cloak gently about him. Again Thomas More sighed in the gathering twilight.

"Good even, son Roper," he said. "Thank you for your arm."

"I waited your coming here before turning home," said William Roper. "Meg is very anxious about you and will be right glad of any news I can bring. What luck, Sir? I like not what you told the boatmen just now."

Thomas More smiled wearily at his son-in-law.

"Good son Roper! Good daughter Meg!" he said. "It may be I sound tired. It may be that the night air begins to take me by the throat a little. Son Clement says my chest is no longer sound as a nut, and that the spring mists may trouble now and then. It must be that. For I have every reason to be merry now. Son Roper, I thank our Lord the field is won."

"Sir," said Roper, and his voice held no assurance, "I am very glad of that. But I am not sure I take your meaning fully. You are sometimes, Sir Thomas, in the habit of being merry without trying. I trust, Sir, that all is well."

"It is so, indeed, son Roper," said Thomas More. "I thank God therefor."

"Have you, then, taken the Oath with the others?" persisted Roper. "And do you still bear the King's Great Seal? You did not speak so to the watermen."

"By my troth, son Roper," said More very gently, "I was not thinking on such matters at all."

"Not thinking on them, Sir!" said Roper sharply, hostility edging his tone. "And we, your family, sick almost to death with anxiety over them for your and our own joint sakes! I am sorry to hear you say so. Why should you be merry when all goes ill?"

"I am sorry I grieve you, my dear son," said More apologetically enough. "One should be merry in weal or woe. But will you know, friend Roper, why I should be merrier now than at any time these past six months? These past six years, perhaps, if the truth be told?"

"That would I gladly, Sir," said Roper, but his voice remained stiff and hurt.

"Because," said More, tightening his grasp on Roper's shoulder till his fingers almost clenched the bone. "Because, son Roper, I laugh in my heart, as I never laughed before, that I have this day given the devil a foul fall, and that I went so far this day with His Grace and Master Cromwell as, without great shame, I can never go back again."

In spite of himself Roper was shaken by his father-in-law's fierce exultancy. Never had he seen Thomas More so moved as now.

"So you did not sign," he said, uncertainly, "and my Lord Audley is Lord Chancellor in your place."

"No, son Roper,' said Thomas More, "I did not sign. And my Lord Audley now bears the King's great Seal in my stead."

William Roper looked disconsolately down at his feet.

"I think it all scant cause for rejoicing, Sir," he said dully. "And I think your daughter, Meg, will find it but slight reason for joy as well. We grieve for your fall from favor, Sir Thomas."

More clapped his son-in-law affectionately on the back.

"Boy, boy," he said gaily. "I will answer for Meg, and I would that you could answer so confidently for Mistress Alice. But she is my cross. *Coniugium mali remedium est.* I made my bed—I must lie in it. Do you go now to Meg, son Roper, and be my advocate as best you may. And I shall wend my way to Alice and there, in her sterner court, say what can be said for myself—if anything. Good even."

"Good even," said Roper, turning away, at the top of the water stairs, in the direction of his own house.

William Roper had as much as accused his father-in-law of feigning merriment. Now as, shoulders sagging, he dragged his steps slowly toward the parish Church of All Saints, it seemed as if there really might be something in the angry intimation. Thomas More did not appear so very merry any more. He stopped before the south side door where, on his coming to Chelsea in 1528, he had built a chapel for the Church. Hans Holbein had drawn the designs for the carven capitals of the arch. On the western capital were the conventional ecclesiastical symbols of tapers, candlesticks, Gospel book, holy water pail and aspergillum. The eastern capital bore his Moor's head and unicorns and the secular symbols of his profession: a crossed sword and scepter and the Chancellor's truncheon. In the sanctuary, to the right of the high altar, stood the More tomb, a sarcophagus of gray stone, erected after Sir Thomas' own design, and with the inscription he wrote incised into a polished slab of black marble that extended up to the spring of the arch. Little Jane Colt already slept therein; and places awaited the coming of Dame Alice and Thomas More. Dame Alice was able to see the monument from the More pew in the south chapel. It irked her somewhat that Jane Colt should, as it were, possess the place of honor beforehand; nevertheless, she liked to look on the shields and graven foliage of the spandrell, because, in the central shield, were the Moor's head and the unicorns.

The tapers were lighted now on the high altar, and the music of Vespers could be heard through the open doors. More took up his stand in the shadows beside the south portal where he could see the altar and hear the choristers. He knew that Mistress Alice knelt within; but he would not disturb her till the short service was over. Except for the singing and the drowsy household arrangements of night-nesting birds, all was silent in quiet Chelsea.

When Mistress Alice finally came out into the murmurous spring darkness, Sir Thomas stepped forth from the church shadows and made a low obeisance before her. She gave a little cry of fright.

"Madame," he said, "my Lord is gone."

It was the gentleman usher's ritual salute, at the end of services, to the Chancellor's wife; and it was Sir Thomas' gently ironic way of announcing that there would no longer be a gentleman usher to perform this courtly service. But it only frightened Alice Middleton.

"My Lord Chancellor More!" was all she could say.

"My Lord Chancellor no-more," he corrected her from the very nadir of his elaborate bow. "Your husband only, Alice, naked and unadorned."

"*Bone deus*, man!" said Dame Alice crossly, regaining her self-possession, but paying no attention whatsoever to his punning correction. "You will be the death of me someday with these daft japes of yours! Where is our gentleman usher that, like Sir Marmoset, you must play his part? He did not unlock our stall tonight. I made my devotions on a *prie-dieu.* Is that fitting, think you, for the wife of a Chancellor of the realm?"

"Alice," said More with compassionate seriousness, thinking hard on how she prized the velvet gowns and gold beads of her rank, "did you not understand what I just now said? My Lord Chancellor that was is just now gone from our house and resides henceforward at my Lord Audley's. You cannot be oversurprised. You must have known what would finally proceed from my refusal to swear the Oath. I must be your gentleman usher from this time on, my Alice. All must go now from a poor man's house, even friend Patenson. Henceforth I must make shift to play the fool alone."

Mistress Alice's acceptance of the news was not at all what her husband had expected; but something infinitely more pathetic. She only fell in upon herself like a scarecrow in a field.

"I did not think it would come to this, my husband," she said at last. "Was it not but New Year's last our Lord the King sent you the walking-staff wrought with gold? Was it not New Year's last, Thomas? I think it was. But sometimes I fear my wits become mazed."

"Yes, Alice," said More gently. "It was New Year's last. The King's gold-wrought walking stick was a portent. With it I walked myself out of the Chancellorship and back again to Chelsea. We shall see much more of one another from this time on."

A little of the old Alice awoke.

"I did not think it had to come to this," she said, "were it not that my husband is a stubborn fool. But since it has, we will make out."

She pulled his sleeve with clumsy tenderness.

"We will make out, eh, Thomas?" she asked gruffly.

For answer Thomas More kissed her.

"We will make out, Alice," he said, "even if with bags and wallets we go a-begging together at every man's door to sing *Salve Regina,* like the little waits at Yuletide, and so to keep company and be merry always."

Henry Patenson's quizzical face peered out of the church door on their colloquy.

"So we keep merry together, you and she, eh, Sir Thomas?" he asked, and the bitterness in his voice was unmistakable. "That is the important thing always. Keep merry together, though the heavens fall."

For once Thomas More was startled.

"Good even, friend Patenson," he said, recovering. "I did not know it was your habit to hear Vespers."

"It did not use to be, certainly, my Lord Chancellor no-more," said Patenson. "But if habits change, one thing, at least, remains the same. You may lose the Great Seal, friend More, but you still know how to steal a Jester's jokes before he makes them. It is enough to drive a conscientious *joculator* to hang himself in his foolscap—or to drive him to Vespers, which is equally uncomfortable and even more tedious. Since you thus press me on the subject of my putting off the old Adam, I may freely admit I do not find Evensong very amusing. But we change our habits nowadays, you and I. You doff the King's livery. I don the Lord Mayor's. Henry Patenson, Fool for two Mores, is the Mores' Fool no more now. Since you, my Lord, will play the fool in earnest, I must even fall to praying. And, faith, at the Lord Mayor's, where you were good enough to send your cast-off Fool last night, they do so little praying, a prayer rings rarer than a jest. That way, if things keep on as they have begun, I make my fortune without racking my brain, and to the convenience of my soul, perhaps. But it was not kindly done, Sir Thomas."

More was troubled. He did not wish Henry Patenson to be bitter about a necessary arrangement for his own good.

"It was kindly meant, at least, friend Patenson," he said. "Even Fools must eat now and then, for all their chameleon propensities otherwise. And I have all too few pennies these latter days. But I indenture no man against his will. You may break the articles without fear of penalty."

Mistress Alice plucked at her husband's sleeve, gesturing privately the while to Patenson. She knew that the Fool's bitterness was not directed against her husband, but against the world of knaves which had betrayed him.

"What little there is to eat tonight will be spoiled, if we do not hurry," she said. "Good even, friend Patenson."

"Good even, Mistress Alice," he said, understanding. "Good even, my Lord Chancellor no-more, but still my Lord Chancellor to me."

The Jester watched them go, his old master dragging his feet a little, and stumbling at intervals; his old mistress with a protective arm thrown across her husband's drooping shoulders.

"I lied in my teeth," he said to himself, "when I said it was not kindly done. It was done so kindly the tears yet stand in my eyes to think upon it. There it stands, written down in my articles till the Giants of London leave off their sleepless watch, or till I choose to drown myself in my Lord Mayor's turtle soup: *My Lord Chancellor More*—he was not yet my Lord Chancellor no-more yesternight when these articles were devised—*signs over his good merryman, Henry Patenson, joculator to my Lord Mayor of London Town, provided it be here enacted as an instrument of law that the aforesaid Henry Patenson become Fool Hereditary, so long as he lives, to all Lord Mayors of London Town in succession.* Well, if the beam go down, the beam must needs fly up as well. What says my *Court Gazette* tonight?"

Patenson struck an antic posture in the shadow of the parvis.

"*Item:,*" he intoned. "The best and noblest Chancellor in the realm— no, let me start again. The best and noblest Chancellor the realm has ever known succumbs to the intrigues against him of Master Secretary Cromwell and Her Grace, the Marchioness of Pembroke. And why? Because he was too honest a fool to heed a Fool's advice. Because he read his Books of Hours and not my *Court Gazette.*"

The Jester grimaced in sudden grief against the crumbling masonry of the church porch. It was as if a gargoyle had climbed down off a gutter spout and made mows before the south door of Chelsea Church.

The night candles burned far into the morning hours in the library of Chelsea New Building. For Thomas More had some unfinished business on hand. His work for the King was over; now he would de-

vote a little time to the matters of one Thomas More. He knew that
the news of the resignation would fly on the many wings and many
tongues of painted Rumor; and he was enough a man of his day to
wish his escutcheon kept clean of slander and lying report. Honor
and Christ walked hand in hand up to a point. More followed Honor
as far as this crossroads but no further. What he had to do now lay
well within the confines of this common borderland. He was very
conscious of the fact that, for all his era's moral and spiritual infirm-
ities, he yet lived in a more spacious air, a *largior aether* than the world
had heretofore known. What Erasmus wrote to Budé back in 1517
still held good: *Immortal God! what a world I see dawning! Why am I
not young again?* Thomas More would not want to be young again;
but Erasmus had written truly nonetheless. Old Alcuin's great insight
that there is in men a royal mind had born strong fruit. Everywhere in
his age he saw this *mens regalis* in man. For the first time since the
Fall, probably, man was cognizant of his full stature as man. *Fama,*
glory, and *virtú*—for that untranslatable word the original Italian
must stand—belonged to this high idea of man. Master Luther would
like nothing better than to supplant *fama* and *virtú* with the crude
concept of brute power, which was an additional reason why Thomas
More disliked Master Luther so heartily. Rather than a heresiarch he
seemed to More a leader of the rabblement, a brutal Friar Tuck of a
monk who had found his wanton Maid Marian in the shameless nun
he had married.

Thomas More knew how irrevocable his act of resignation had been.
It was, beyond all doubt, the last act of his public life unless, as was
all too likely to happen, there should come a bloody sequel on Tower
Hill. Nothing remained for him to do now but to measure his shroud
and make his soul. Nothing but one thing. There was also incumbent
upon him the proud obligation of preparing his *apologia*. Like Horace
he, too, had built a *monumentum aere perennius*: his life. Let him
now inscribe his name on the last page in lapidary letters so that
there should be no conceivable mistake. Let him stop the foul
mouth of calumny before it so much as opened. He had set
right his wife, his son-in-law, and that wise man who, till
yesterday, had been his and his father's Fool. He had set them right

at the sacred time of Vespers, the evening hour that marked the *Recessus Dei,* the departing of God. But God did not depart without first leaving the words He spoke graven in the minds and hearts of His followers. Vespers also marked that glorious evening time when the Lord made Himself known in the breaking of bread. He would have communion, too, with the great scholars, the great Humanists with whom he had broken the sweet white bread of noble idea. Let him now, then, while there was yet time—and with Cromwell master of the hounds there might not be much time left—let him now set Europe right. For a space, at least, it might be hard to tell the truth to England. But, at the very outset, Europe—and, after Europe, the rest of Christendom—should know.

When, in 1515, the already aged Archbishop Warham had resigned the Chancellorship to make way for Wolsey, Thomas More had taken it upon himself to send my Lord of Canterbury this message:

> "I ever judged your paternity happy in the way you exercised your office of Chancellor, but I esteem you much happier now that you have laid it down and entered on that most desirable leisure in which you can live for yourself and for God. Such leisure, in my opinion, is not only more pleasant than the labor you have forsaken, but more honorable than all your honors. To be a judge is the lot of many, and sometimes of very bad men. But you possessed that supreme office which, when relinquished, is as much exposed to calumny as it formerly conferred authority and independence; and to give up this willingly is what none but a moderate-minded man would care, and none but an innocent man dare, to do."

What he wrote of Warham in 1515 was perfectly applicable to his own position seventeen years later; except that the surrounding circumstances had changed. Henry was different. Instead of Wolsey, there were Anne and Cromwell, and their creatures, Cranmer and Audley. But, considering only his *fama* and *virtú,* the same tactic might well work again, if he should write to the right man. And surely there could be no question who was the right man. Surely the right man was that uncrowned king of Europe's scholars; the conscience, the wit, the common sense of his century: Desiderius Erasmus. If

More could defend Warham, Erasmus should defend More. Whatever his darling More should write him, Erasmus would publish to the four winds and the four corners of the habitable world. Single voice, weak reed that he was, Desiderius Erasmus yet wielded a power Henry Tudor did not command: that of the pen. Here More winced humorously as he remembered that he would have to tell a white lie about his relations with the King. But that was all part of the game. Loyalty to one's liege lord was still a virtue, even if lying would never be anything other than a sin. He had been a diplomat too long, perhaps, and he was still and would ever be a King's man. On the whole, Thomas More thought God would forgive him on this score. He took up his pen and, in a mingled mood of calm resignation and proud insistence, began to write:

"From the time of my boyhood, dearest Desiderius, I have longed that I might some day enjoy what I rejoice in your having always enjoyed—namely, that, being free from public business and affairs of state, I might have some time to devote to God and myself. This, by the grace of a great and good God, and by the favor of an indulgent Prince, I have at last secured. I have not, however, obtained it quite on the terms for which I hoped, for I wished to reach this last stage of my life in the world in a state which, though suitable to my age, might yet enable me to enjoy my remaining years healthy and unbroken, free from disease and pain. It remains in the hand of God whether or not this wish—perhaps an unreasonable one, Desiderius—shall be fulfilled. A disorder, I know not of what nature, has attacked my chest. I suffer less from present pain than from fear of future consequence. For when it had troubled me continuously for some months, the physicians whom I consulted, headed by our dear John Clement, gave their opinion that any long continuance in this disease was dangerous, and any speedy cure impossible, but that it must be dealt with by proper diet, medicine, and, above all other panaceas, by time. Neither could they fix the period of my recovery nor ensure me a complete cure. Considering all this, I saw that I must either lay down my office or fail in the performance of its many and arduous duties. I could not carry out all the tasks imposed by my high position without endangering my life, and, if I were to die, I should have to give up my office as well as my life. So I determined to give up one rather than both!

My Lord Chancellor No-More Goes to Vespers:

"Therefore, for the benefit both of public business and my own health, I humbly appealed, and not in vain, to the goodness of my noble and excellent Prince. . . ."

Thomas More put down the quill for a moment, and reflected. The demands of decorum had now been complied with, but hardly those of history. Something more was needed. Erasmus, it is true, could easily read between the lines. But the first lawyer of Europe was the first to recognize that reading between the lines was hardly evidence for either the present or for posterity. If Erasmus were to defend his darling *Morus'* reputation effectually, he would have to be in a position to quote More's own words; and those same words must be both uncompromising, so far as the truth was concerned, and, at the same time, unswervingly loyal to Henry. Thomas More thought a space, brow furrowed. Then he smiled. He had it! In his last letter Erasmus had asked for a transcript of the epitaph in Chelsea Church that he might send it to his dear friend, Bishop Johann Faber of Vienna, with whom he had lately been in earnest correspondence over a libelous charge, then circulating in the Germanies, that Chancellor More persecuted the new heretics. He opposed them vehemently and successfully, Erasmus had explained, but, far from persecuting them, in the first two years of his Chancellorship there had been no burnings for heresy at Smithfield. (There were no less than three executions for this crime in his last six months of office, Thomas More said to himself, but they had been Henry's doing, not his—Henry's and Bishop Stokesley's. He would keep on fighting heresy with the pen, and without quarter; but not with the sword or the fagot.) Erasmus had gone on to point out to Faber that More had even thrown open his Chelsea house to Dr. Simon Grynaeus, the Lutheran Professor of Greek and Latin at the University of Heidelberg, and the close friend of Melancthon and Oecolampadius. He had made Grynaeus free of the libraries of Oxford and Cambridge, insisted that he sit next to him at the Chancellor's table, and loaned him the secretarial services of Master John Harris for the time of his stay in England. Erasmus then went on to liken More's house and household on the Thames to the Platonic academy of some Christian Plato, and, in jesting defense

268

of his friend's orthodoxy, after he had thus demonstrated his intellectual tolerance, concluded a letter to Faber thus:

"In the Church of his village he has constructed a family tomb, to which he has translated the bones of his first wife, so little does he approve of any divorce. On the wall he has placed a tablet, with the record of his life and his intentions. I see, my Lord Bishop, I have been too talkative. But it is most pleasant to converse with a friend about a friend."

It was indeed most pleasant. Delighted, Faber had immediately written back for a copy of the funereal tablet, and Erasmus, amused and more than a little flattered, too, had sent the correspondence to More with a request that John Harris transcribe two copies of the epitaph, one for himself, and one for my Lord of Vienna. So here was a golden chance to kill two birds with a single stone; to gratify Erasmus, and to place in the hands of this eloquent apologist for truth and friendship the best possible brief he had been able to contrive against the vicious innuendoes of Court. Thomas More took up his pen again:

"Do not, dearest Erasmus, have any reservations about publishing this next part of my letter to you which is also, in a sense, a letter to the world. Some gossips, here at Court, have for months been spreading it about that I was being forced to resign against my will, no matter how hard I might pretend it was not so. So, when the time came to set up my tomb, I determined to state the matter as it really is in my epitaph that any one who wished might refute this libel. As soon as these courtiers, of whom I speak, had taken note of my graven tablet and the contents thereof, as they could in no way show it to be false, they found fault with it as vaunting overmuch. I preferred this charge of boasting to letting the other rumor gain ground. Not, indeed, for my own sake, Desiderius, for I do not care at all what men say of me, provided God approves of what I do. But, since I had written in our own tongue some little books against some defenders of contentious doctrines, I considered that I ought to defend the integrity of my name. And, that you may know how boastfully I have written, you shall receive a transcript of my epitaph in this letter. By this you will see that, in my security of conscience, I by no means flatter these sycophants in order to prevent them from saying about me whatever they please. As yet no one has come forward to attack me in public. Either I have been so innocent or else so cautious in my epitaph that, either way, my opponents must allow me to take credit for one or other of these same qualities. But my resignation is yet new; and we shall see what the morrow may bring.

"As regards this same business of my resignation from the Chancellorship, the King has spoken of it many times privately, and, so far, twice in public. For yesterday afternoon, in words which I am ashamed to repeat, when my successor was installed, the King, by the mouth of my old soldier friend, the Duke of Norfolk, Lord High Treasurer of England, ordered an honorable testimony to be given that with difficulty had he yielded to my request to retire from public office. And not contented with this, the King, out of his singular goodness to me, will have the same thing repeated by my successor, Lord Audley, in his own presence, at the solemn assembly of the Peers and Commons of the realm when they are convoked to confirm Lord Audley as Chancellor of the realm of England.

"Here then, Desiderius, is my epitaph. It is conceived *more Romano* which may serve to excuse the bravado of *More Anglicano*:

" 'Thomas More, a Londoner born, of no noble family, but of honest stock, somewhat brought up in letters. After that, in his young days, he was a pleader in the laws of this Kingdom for a certain span of years, was one of the Under-Sheriffs of London, was of noble King Henry the Eighth (who alone of all Kings worthily deserved both with sword and pen to be called Defender of the Faith, a glory afore not heard of) called into the Court, and there chosen one of the King's Council, and made Knight. He was then made Under-Treasurer of England, after that Chancellor of the Duchy of Lancaster, and, last of all, with great favor of his Prince, Lord Chancellor of England. In the mean season, he was chosen Speaker of Parliament, and, besides, was divers times in divers places the King's Ambassador, and, last of all, King's Ambassador at Cambrai, did there join fellow and companion with Cuthbert Tunstall, chief of that embassy, then Bishop of London, and, within a short while after, Bishop of Durham, who so excelleth in learning, wit, and virtue, that the whole world scant hath at this day any man more learned, wise, or better. There, at Cambrai, he both joyfully saw and was present King's Ambassador when the leagues between the chief Princes of Christendom were renewed again, and peace so long looked for restored to Christendom, which peace may Our Lord establish and make perpetual.

"When he had thus gone through this course of offices and honors, in such a way that neither his gracious Prince could disallow his doings, nor was he odious to the nobility nor unpleasant to the people, but yet to thieves, murderers, and heretics grievous, at last John More, his father, Knight, and chosen of the Prince to be one of the Justices of the King's Bench, a civil man, pleasant, harmless, gentle, pitiful, just and uncorrupted, in years old, but in body more than his years would warrant lusty, after that he perceived his life so long lengthened that he saw his son Lord Chancellor of England, thinking himself now to have lived long enough, gladly departed to God. His son, then, his father being dead, to whom as long as he lived being compared was wont both to be called young and himself so thought, too, now missing his father departed, and seeing four children of his own, and of their offspring eleven, began in his own conceit to wax old; and this affection of his was increased by a certain sickly disposition of his breast, coming on him by and by, as a sign or token of old age creeping upon him. He, therefore, irked and weary of worldly business, giving up his offices and promotions, obtained at last by the incomparable benefit of his most gentle Prince, if it only please God to favor his enterprise from now on, the thing which from a child in a manner he had always wished and most desired: that he might have some years of his life free, in which, little by little withdrawing himself from the business of this life, he might continually remember the immortality of the life to come. And he hath caused this tomb to be made for himself, his first wife's bones brought thither, too, that both might every day put him in memory of death that never ceases to steal on him as it doth on all men. And that this tomb, made for him in his lifetime, be not in vain, nor that he fear death coming upon him, but that he may willingly, for the desire and love of Christ, die and find death not utterly death to him, but the gate of a wealthier life, help him, I beseech you, good reader, now with your prayers while he liveth, and when he is dead also.' "

The irony of his having resigned in monumental stone before he did so in fact should please Erasmus vastly. It was a Utopian joke. Thomas More smiled. He might as well enclose another Utopian joke, too—the Latin verses he had attached to his marble brag. Whether or not he died laughing, as Erasmus had predicted, his grave, at any rate, should laugh through the centuries. Slowly, painfully now, for his hand was very cramped, he copied down the lines:

> *"Sir Thomas More's dear little Jane lies here.*
> *For Alice and myself this tomb I rear.*
> *By Jane I had three daughters and one son*
> *Before my time of prime and strength was gone.*
> *To them such love was by Dame Alice shown*
> *As is, in mothers even, rarely known.*
> *The world believed the children were her own.*
> *So dear was Jane, in Alice I so rejoice,*
> *It's hard to judge which was the happier choice.*
> *If Destiny or Law our prayers could grant,*
> *To join us three, we should no blessings want.*
> *One grave shall hold us, in Heaven we shall live,*
> *And Death grant that which Life could never give."*

Day was breaking as the tired man at last affixed his Moor's head seal to another epistle to Erasmus. Matins were already over, and the lark song of Lauds rose from the choir of Chelsea's Church of All Saints when Thomas More got down upon his knees to pray for his friend, Desiderius. He had always thought him more like Pierre Abélard than any other man. As in the case of Abélard, he knew that wit and logic had gained him the hatred of men—*perverse perverters of truth,* as Abélard called them, *for whom Wisdom is a kind of Hell.* But he did not pray against Desiderius Erasmus' many enemies. That was not Thomas More's way. He prayed, instead, that his friend retain humility in the midst of his wisdom; and that he never succumb to Abélard's besetting sin of intellectual pride.

He prayed, too, that, at the last, Erasmus would have the grace to keep in mind Abélard's great profession of faith:

> *I do not wish to be an Aristotle if this means I shall separate myself from Christ. I adore Christ who reigns at the right hand of the Father. I clasp Him with the arms of faith, when, by the divine power, He performs glorious works in a virginal flesh born from the Paraclete.*

Chelsea, Evening, May 16, 1532

"This is the faith in which I live and from which my hope derives its strength. In this refuge I do not fear the noise of Scylla. I laugh at . . the maelstrom of Charybdis. Nor do I dread the Sirens' fatal song. Let the tempest come. It will not shake me! The winds may blow, but I shall not be moved. The rock of my foundation is sure.

The ancient Vikings, who ravaged dark-age Christendom, swore by the god of their own *meginn;* their own might and main. The new assault, seizing the initiative from four centuries of Christian rationalism, took its oath on the sovereign power of unaided human reason. More did not wish the razor-sharp intellect of Erasmus to fall into this latest pit dug for the sons of men. And, remembering how Peter Abélard had listed *risibilis,* the faculty of laughter, as first among the purely human attributes, Thomas More, who loved laughter next to God, now prayed for the living soul of that unhappy, long-dead great clerk of the Schools of Paris.

CHAPTER XV

POMEGRANATE SEED:

Greenwich, Night, Shrove Tuesday, 1533

IN ONE of Greenwich's turreted bowers Snow White tended Rose Red. Golden-haired Jane Seymour, one time maid-in-waiting to Queen Catherine, now in attendance on Her Grace, the Marchioness of Pembroke, combed out the Marchioness' long black hair. The Marchioness seemed ill at ease. She tossed and flirted and jerked her head under the maid-in-waiting's skilled fingers. It was Shrove Tuesday night. Within an hour the King's board would groan with dainties, piled high on the massy plate, that had once been my Lord Cardinal Wolsey's service, for one last Court revel against the long Lenten fast which would begin with ashes and penitential psalms on the morrow. But the Marchioness could not wait out that hour. She had a burning craving on her. Like Solomon, she wished to be stayed with apples, weary, as she was, of the first fruits of love. For, since the night she danced at Hanworth for a head, Anne Boleyn had forsaken the slow waiting game of chess for the dicer's reckless throw. No more for her the long fencings on the threshold; the stolen moments in the bower; the potions, after, and the sequent weeks of sick anxiety. Anne Boleyn was now with child by the King. She put down her gold-embossed mirror.

"Mistress Seymour," she said peremptorily. "Fetch me that gentleman, whoever he be, who is now on duty in the corridor."

Jane Seymour's golden eyebrows raised the merest trifle. Sir Thomas Wyatt was on duty in the corridor; and the maid-in-waiting knew full well that Mistress Boleyn was quite aware of the fact. But she did as she was told. Wyatt, lounging in the turret hall, was startled into speechlessness by her unexpected message. For a wonder, he had been that morning to Mass; and the King's Chaplain had preached on the patristic text: *The Sirens are endowed by the Devil with the faces of women, because nothing so estrangeth the heart of man from the love of God as the faces of women.* As the priest warmed to the congenial task of developing his misogynist's theme, Wyatt found himself gloomily agreeing. He wondered now, as he received the Marchioness' bizarre directive, what new devilment was working in his old Siren's mermaid loins. He soon found out.

Anne stared at him, imperiously, her black hair down her back, the lace filigree that filmed her white breast sending out distracting little whiffs of perfume as she breathed lightly in and out.

"Sir Thomas," she said in a sudden spate of words, "I yearn for an apple. For three whole days now I have thought on nothing but apples."

Her voice rose and broke in a semihysterical trill of laughter. Wyatt only looked at her, astounded.

"Do you know what the King says?" she asked him, tears of joyless mirth running down pale cheeks. "He says it is an infallible sign I am with child. And he wishes me to go on pilgrimage to Our Lady of Walsingham where the holy milk that nursed the Savior is preserved in a crystal vial. But how may this be, Sir Thomas, since I know not the King? Do you think it is a miracle?"

Sir Thomas Wyatt had managed to recover himself by now. He did not think it was a miracle. But he knew both the King and Mistress Boleyn; and the whole Court had been buzzing for months with rumors of a secret marriage.

"Madame," he said, in stiff formality, "it is not the time of year for apples. The ones we have at Greenwich, at the very bottoms of the fruit bins, are wormy and musty after the long winter. I should suggest, instead, a pomegranate. We have in the cellars fresh baskets full newly shipped from Spain."

"As you say," she said, a little sullen now, all laughter spent for the moment. "As you say. You would spare me Eve's fate, I see, Sir Thomas. Well, if you refuse me Eve's fruit, it is only right I try your apples of Granada."

After the crimson fruits had been borne in, Wyatt watched Anne tear, with her white teeth, the succulent red flesh of the pomegranate. A different but no less dangerous light in her green eyes now, she followed the direction of his brooding glance.

"Pour Master Wyatt a goblet of Canary wine while he waits," she instructed the maid-in-waiting. "We shall return one Spanish favor with another."

"No thank you, Your Grace," said Thomas Wyatt, every bit as stiffly as before.

"No?" asked Anne Boleyn, pausing in her greedy rending of the fruit. "You fear what Ovid says of wine in the book you gave me on my birthday once—that it lights the torch of Venus? So, Master Wyatt, it is true what they fable in the Court: that you turn monk."

Thomas Wyatt was white-lipped now.

"Again, not so, Your Grace," he said, striking in his anguish, where he knew it would hurt worst, and repenting sore the moment he had struck. "Not so. I live with my wife again."

But perhaps Anne Boleyn was beginning to live beyond the range of such once deadly shafts. The high laughter ran through an arpeggio once more. Sir Thomas looked on the sorry spectacle, his face stony. After the paroxysm was finished, Anne Boleyn returned to eating off the silver salver he had presented her on bended knee when the serving man first bore in the pomegranates.

Later, on his way across the courtyard Wyatt encountered Henry Patenson who had escorted his master, the Lord Mayor of London, to the King's *Mardi Gras*. The courtier stalked past him, unseeing.

"Aha!" called the Jester, whistling ribaldly after him. "Art thou possessed of Afernoch, the demon of melancholy, that thou knowest not an old drinking comrade? Or hast thou seen a ghost?"

"Much worse," said Thomas Wyatt, recognizing Patenson. "I am just now back from a visit to the Queen of Hell. So I am in haste to expel the spirit pythonis that belongs to witches and Sirens by taking in as much strong drink as I can, and as fast. Will you join me?"

"Agreed," said Henry Patenson. "But, Master Wyatt, you whet not only my appetite but my curiosity. What is it you carry under your right arm?"

Wyatt exhibited the salver. It shimmered into cold argent life under the moon's silver pencil.

"Only the tray on which I bore Persephone her pomegranate," he said magniloquently.

Only the silver salver of Persephone! But, for all his sardonic bravura, the poet in Thomas Wyatt groaned aloud. It was all wrong. Persephone left six pomegranate seeds on the plate of Pluto, which meant that the dancing daughter of Demeter might spend six months out of twelve under the sun in the upper air of men. With his own eyes he had seen Anne Boleyn's white teeth daintily crack each seed, one by one, till none remained upon the salver of her servitude. Persephone had gone down into the dark in winter—as was almost fiting, if death can ever be said to be fitting. Anne Boleyn was entering on her captivity in spring, the time of daffodils and violets, of budded lime trees and wild roses, of April dusks and May morning dews. Summer would come, and with it the white of beehives resonant in clovered gardens, the dark of rain-wet boxwood, the fragrant hay of June, the sun-warmed wheat of September, August's crushed mint that is trodden into sharp midnight perfume by the unheeding passion of young lovers' embraces. Autumn would come, and with it the hunter's moon. Winter would come, bearing in its ice-chased chalice of cold night Christmastide's winter-wafer moon. But Persephone would not rouse her in her prison-cavern. Spring would wheel round again, and all the world awake to resurrection, but not Persephone. Earth's changeling must lie quiescent, bound to her Plutonian lover. Of a sudden Wyatt spat savagely on the ground. To Pluto? To a gross Silenus! To a disgusting Priapus, all swollen belly and phallus! Satyrs held the stage of fools. And already the pageant wagon was moving into the shadows of the underworld.

"On second thought," Wyatt said aloud, "I withdraw my invitation. He who has just supped with the Queen of Hell is no fit boon companion for an honest Fool. Friend Patenson, I have no further stomach for drinking this night."

Aha! said Henry Patenson a second time, but this time to himself. So the old worm yet works in Master Wyatt's blood. There is no fool, in this weary world of fools, like a fool for love.

"As you wish, Master Wyatt," he said to him aloud. "But if you have no further stomach for drinking this night, perhaps you do have a stomach for a page or two of my *Court Gazette*, which the Lord Mayor, my present master, is too witless to understand, and my old master, Sir Thomas More, too far out of earshot to hear. It is, I assure you, a clyster against dyspepsia. For my *Gazette*, you must know, is part gossip, part invention, part prophecy, and all truth. You will listen, friend Wyatt? It begins with bagatelles. It ends with bagatelles. In between are more bagatelles—all excellent ones."

"I will listen," said Wyatt indifferently, folding his arms.

The Jester took up his stance.

"*Item:*," he began, taking out his omnipresent blank scroll. "Monseigneur du Bellay ailing of the gout. Dr. Rabelais prescribes viper soup three times a day. The prescription works.

"*Item:* Master Ulrich von Hutten ill of the pox, a most unseemly disease for a scholar; but a most human disease for a Humanist. Dr. Paracelsus prescribes a regimen of guaiac wood to burn in his room all day and all night. The prescription does not work.

"*Item:* Mistress Anne Boleyn is fond of dainties. The pantries at Greenwich overflow with marchpane, hippocras, almonds, quinces, dates, prunes, white sugar, saffron, ginger, nutmeg, cloves, cinnamon, mace and cream. The lady Anne continues thin on her rich diet. Not so her royal protector, Henry.

"*Item:* Old Archbishop Warham dies; the See of Canterbury lies vacant. It will not lie vacant long.

"*Item:* Mistress Nan created Marchioness of Pembroke.

"*Item:* The Marchioness of Pembroke visits France with Henry. *Monseigneur le Roi de France* receives her. *Mesdames les Princesses de France* do not. Other things happen, too. She is not given a *tabouret* to sit on at Versailles, an affront our Lord the King brooks but ill.

Marguerite of Navarre is polite enough to say that Mademoiselle Anne may be in a new chapter of her *Heptameron,* but may not be in her house. When Madame la Duchesse de Vendôme receives the Marchioness of Pembroke, Marguerite further remarks that it is only right and fitting one whore should receive another. She suggests that the old country saw be amended at Court to read: *One bad whore deserves another. Monseigneur le Roi d'Angleterre* is mortally offended at this polite exhibition of *esprit Gaulois.*

"*Item*: One Thomas Cranmer, onetime chaplain of the Boleyns, recalled suddenly from abroad. Arrives in England without his German wife whom Master Secretary Cromwell declares contraband on the reasonable and patriotic grounds that English priests, who violate their vows of chastity, should cleave to good English flesh for their doxies. Any other arrangement is heterodoxy and a flagrant breach of *Praemunire.* England for the English is the watchword.

"*Item:* Thomas Cranmer receives from Rome his Bull of Confirmation as Archbishop of Canterbury. The more fool Clement.

"*Item:* At long last Henry anticipates his great felicity. The Marchioness of Pembroke is with child by the King.

"*Item:* The Marchioness hawks and hunts no more, but sews a fine seam by the fire.

"*Item:* My Lord the King hath great expectations. Anything less than the arrival of a stout boy will be construed *lèse majesté.* He commissions, from the shop of a French goldsmith, this lavish commemorative toy for his expected son: a miniature room, gilded, screened by an iron grill, furnished with a bed, a dresser, a pier glass, an escritoire, and armchairs. About the room in most cunning wax, *in petto,* stand those good fairies of the divorce, Master Cromwell, Master Cranmer, my Lord Audley, and, of course, my Lord the King.

"*Item*: The Marchioness of Pembroke is secretly wedded to the King by an Augustinian friar of the distinguished name of Brown.

"*Item*: Queen Catherine in seclusion. Mistress Nan of Boleyn and Pembroke receives a solemn pledge from her royal bedfellow that, no later than Easter Eve, she shall attend public Mass with him as Queen of England.

"*Item*: My Lord of Canterbury is now on the point of pronouncing the King's old marriage with Catherine, Princess of Aragon, invalid, and his new marriage with Anne, Princess of Nowhere, which is Utopia, correct. *La reine est morte! Vive la reine!*

"*Item:* My Lord Chancellor More surrenders the Great Seal. My Lord Audley is named Chancellor. But I woolgather. This is stale news. Yet cannot I believe it even yet.

"*Item:* All the Lords temporal and Lords spiritual, save Master More of London and Bishop Fisher of Rochester only, accept the Oath of Supremacy naming Henry Head of the Church in England.

"*Item:* My Lord Chancellor no-more receives an invitation to attend Mistress Anne's Coronation at Westminster Abbey."

Henry Patenson cast down his roll of paper and trod upon it with a curse.

"I am sick unto death of my *Court Gazette,* Master Wyatt," he said bitterly. "It is false and stupid and wearisome. Mother Maude told better tales by the score. I mind me of one whose moral you and Henry both know now: *All cats are gray in the night.* I mind me of another in which a certain Mistress Anne married a certain great Lord with a blue beard."

The Jester fell silent for a moment, his pale face working. Then, staring up the lighted tower where the Marchioness of Pembroke slept, he cried out in an eldritch falsetto that made Wyatt jump and two guardsmen race into the courtyard till they saw it was only the Lord Mayor's Jester:

"*Mistress Anne, Mistress Anne, what do you see from your tower?*
"*Mistress Anne, Mistress Anne, what do you see from your tower?*

Wyatt took his friend by the arm.

"Come," he said roughly. "I find it in my heart to drink, after all."

From her tower Mistress Anne saw the future. There had come to her hand from one who wished her good or ill—she could not tell which—a certain book of prophecies about the Queens of England yet to sit upon the throne. One page was marked with a red rubric; and, not liking what she thought she read thereon and saw in the accompanying picture, Mistress Anne had sent in secret for a wise woman of the neighborhood: one skilled in the casting of horoscopes and shuffling of Tarot cards. The white witch had some minutes gone now; and, staring at the book on her lap, sat Mistress Anne, never heeding that the fiddles were already struck up in the great gallery in the banquet hall and that the Court waited her coming.

"What did the wise woman say, my Lady?" Jane Seymour asked her after the waddling, wheezing, horribly goitrous old woman had left.

Anne Boleyn looked queerly at her maid-in-waiting.

"She told me something about you that I greatly mislike," said the Marchioness to her maid.

Jane Seymour crimsoned.

"What said she, my Lady?" she asked in a low voice.

"Nay," said the Marchioness, "I tell you not that."

Anne Boleyn plunged down a gloved finger on the pictured page.

"She said of me," said the Marchioness, "that here is the King, with a third wife; and here am I, with my head cut off; and here is our child on the throne of England. What do you think of that, Mistress Seymour?"

The flush did not leave Jane Seymour's face.

"I think, my Lady," said Jane Seymour coolly, "that, were I in your place and believed that to be true, I should flee to France. Do you believe it true, my Lady?"

"Aye, Mistress," said Anne Boleyn, haggard. "For I now know my Lord the King. But, at least, I shall have been Queen. And my blood shall now run in the veins of those who after come to rule in England. Think you I am a fool?"

"I said not that, my Lady," said Jane Seymour, the blood finally ebbing from her cheeks.

CHAPTER XVI

THE FORT IS BETRAYED:

Westminster Abbey, Morning, June 1, 1533

ON FRIDAY AFTERNOON, the 30th of May, at Greenwich stairs, Anne Boleyn, Marchioness of Pembroke, entered the great Queen's barge, whose sides were now gilt-embossed with her own pinchbeck Boleyn heraldry instead of with Catherine's ancient Aragonese arms, and traveled by water to the Tower of London, there to wait her crowning on Whitsunday. In front of the barge went a huge float in which stood a mechanical dragon, continually moving its head and casting wildfire in the direction of the throngs which lined the banks of Thameside. Comic devils tended the stoorworm; but the great crowds, which usually took devils to its collective heart, did not seem to find these fiends amusing. The onlookers were curiously silent for so festive an occasion as the coronation of an English Queen. It was natural enough. The people had dearly loved their Spanish Princess; and, though obliged to accept, were in no mood to cheer the usurper. But, natural or not, Anne did not like their sullen silence. She whispered something to her Jester who then proceeded to grimace and shake his bauble at the watching multitudes. "You must have the scurvy," he shouted. "Else why are you whoreson clods afraid to uncover your scald heads?" "Not so," called back a mocking voice from the river bank. "We whoresons have the pox like your mistress. Pray look under her own whore's hennin." It was Henry Patenson. The crowd roared for the first and last time during that water Progress.

Mistress Boleyn's black eyebrows set in a frown. But the Tower guns boomed out their official salute; and the King was waiting at the Tower.

On Saturday, the 31st, the royal procession made its stately way from the Tower to Westminster. Anne rode in a litter, drawn by palfreys white as unicorns, caparisoned in damask that was whiter than new-fallen snow. Over her head waved a golden canopy fringed with silver bells that rang each step the white-maned palfreys paced. A Cheapside 'prentice, who was new to the ways of the world and took Anne for the virginal maiden her white garments so brazenly proclaimed her to have been, noted down that "she shall make music wherever she goes." Every churchbell in London rang; the spring air glinted bright with music. New-made that day, the Knights of the Bath sat their horses, splendid in blue gowns purfled with white. Four knights in scarlet, Knights of the Cinque Ports, were the new Queen's personal attendants. Her twelve maids-in-waiting wore cloth of gold. The black-habited dowagers of Norfolk and Dorset certified the bride's respectability. Conduits poured red wine and white in the streets. Heralds flung gold to the watchers along the way. The children of St. Paul's piped complimentary songs in childish treble as the samite litter passed. And still the London crowds were silent.

Next morning, Whitsuntide, the day of the Coronation, Mistress Anne rose early. It would take much time and care to set the jewel-constellations, like glimmering stars, in the dark fragrant night of her hair. The surcoat of white cloth of tissue, furred with pure white ermine, must be kept stiff and crackling so it would not wrinkle in unseemly wise. The purple velvet underneath must have its imperial nap cunningly fitted to the rounded contours of her figure—except, of course, about the already thickening waist; there the gown must be made, instead, to bell away and fall, in billowing waves, into a regal Tyrian train. The child would be born in September, if all went well. And, since the divorce decree had not been promulgated by Cranmer till the week before the Coronation itself, it would not do for the salty, earthy cynical London crowds to learn that their new-married Queen had been bedded ere she was wedded like any country Malkin with questing loins; and that she was now many months big with child. But the crowds knew anyway. And this day, unlike the two preceding, they did not intend to keep silent. Before the long ceremonies should be over, Mistress Anne would wish, with all her heart and soul, that they had stayed mute as before.

By quarter to eight in the morning all was ready; and Mistress Anne walked on a fresh-laid crimson carpet from Whitehall, where she had slept the night and which had once been my Lord Cardinal Wolsey's York House, to Westminster Hall, there to be received by Archbishop Cranmer, his brother Bishops of England, and the great Abbots of the realm; and by the Earls of Suffolk and Norfolk and their brother Earls who, bearing on a cushion her crown, scepter, and ivory rod, holding a golden canopy above her, would escort her to the Abbey where the Crown of St. Edward awaited. But early as was the Lady Anne at Westminster Hall, one was there before her; one who came by water from his house at Chelsea, past the festal buildings tapestried with arms and festooned with green boughs; one who had been invited to the Coronation by the King himself and who, in keeping with his own quirky sense of irony, even had a wedding dress therefor; one who, nevertheless, for certain reasons of his own, had refused to attend.

Sir Thomas More had other reasons of his own for coming to Westminster Hall this first morning of June. It would, to some small degree, at least, oblige those good friends of his on the Bishops' Bench: Bishop Gardiner of Winchester; Bishop Tunstall of Durham; Bishop Clark of Bath. These three had come to his house the night before, pressing upon him the absolute necessity of his putting in some kind of appearance at the Coronation. It was a friendly gesture on their part; and, no matter how utter his opposition to their present policies, he was very grateful to them for this demonstration of friendly solicitude in his behalf. In the second place, he craved an opportunity to explain to the Bishops, in full conclave met, just why he might not take the purse they offered him for his writings against heresy. Finally, and above all, he did not think another chance very likely to offer itself for him to have his say out about what was happening to the Church in England. And have his say out he meant to do—as a good subject of the King, as a faithful member of the Universal Church, as a loyal defender of the rights and privileges of the people's Parliament.

For, day by day now, Caesar was crushing out Christ within the polity of the realm. Centuries ago, in his *Sermon against Auxentius,* St. Ambrose had reminded Caesar: *Imperator intra Ecclesiam non supra Ecclesiam est.* The Emperor is within the Church, not above it. Only yesterday my Lord of Rochester, John Fisher, had pronounced this harsh judgment on the work of his apostate colleagues: *The fort is betrayed even of them that should have defended it.* The work of sixteen centuries was undone. The keep of Christ had been delivered over to the enemy by the subtle legists and ambitious canonists who sat upon the Bishops' Bench in England.

Within the great Hall of Westminster all was hubbub and stir. Thomas Cranmer, all doe-eyes and rabbit-face under the huge Archbishop's miter, was being vested by attendants. Other servitors tested the heavy censers by swinging them back and forth. Most of the Bishops were already in their gorgeous vestments and waiting for the procession to form, when Stephen Gardiner led Thomas More up to Cranmer.

"My Lord of Canterbury," said Thomas More, bowing low. "I come to return the purse you sent me yestereve by the gracious hands of my Lords of Winchester, Durham, and Bath. They know my reasons at length, and will deliver them to you in good season. But, to prove I am no curmudgeon and that I appreciate your great courtesies to me, I accept the lesser of your gracious gifts—this camlet gown which I purchased with the twenty pounds you sent me as a vail at this festive season of my Lord the King's marriage to the Lady Anne. As for the five thousand pounds you offer, though, my Lord Bishops, I am exceeding sorry to have to refuse. But refuse I must. I cannot accept the purse."

Archbishop Cranmer bowed without speaking. The five thousand pounds in question were no concern of his. Archbishop Warham had commissioned and appropriated the sum before he died. And, to tell the truth, what with his Lutheran sympathies and the clouded circumstances of his accession to the Primacy, Cranmer was not at all ill-pleased that such a tidy amount should revert to the Bishops' treasury. But Stephen Gardiner was not so easily satisfied on this especial head as my Lord of Canterbury.

"I think you are wrong, Sir Thomas," he said impetuously. "The money is offered you in good faith by the grateful clergy of England, and no strings attached. You have done our own proper work of fighting heresy better than we could have done it ourselves. It took time and strength—much time and much strength—to answer the pernicious errors of Masters Luther and Tyndale. And you are no longer either a young or a rich man, Sir Thomas. If not for your own sake, then, accept our gift for the sakes of Dame Alice and your children."

"I am sorry, my Lord of Winchester and my Lords Bishops," said Thomas More, "that you thus force me to be as firm in language on this matter as I am in heart. Harsh as it may sound to you, I would far rather see these same monies cast into the Thames, to no one's fruit or avail, than that either I or any one belonging to me should enjoy the worth of a penny thereof. For, though your offer, my Lords, be indeed very friendly and honorable, yet set I so much by my pleasure and so little by my profit that I would not, in good faith, have lost the chance of so many a merry jest or the solace of so many a night's sweet sleep as was spent upon this toil, for much more than your generous gift. Nevertheless, for all that, as I look back into the past and forward into the future, upon condition that all heresies were suppressed, I could find it in my heart to wish that all my books were burned, and all my labor utterly lost. I tell you, my Lords, all of us, heretics and faithful alike, could occupy our minds more profitably with Thomas à Kempis' *Imitation* or Bonaventure's *Life of Christ* than with either my barren wits or Master Luther's and Master Tyndale's graceless inventions."

Here and there, among the smooth-shaven, patrician faces, a lip curled in disdain and, indeed, in positive dislike. Every bit as much as my Lords temporal my Lords spiritual were used to command. In the best of times—and today was not the best of times—Thomas

More had always been too stiff-necked for the Bench's taste. What meant this jack-out-of-office now by haranguing them at such length on this day of all days? A murmur arose from among the surplices and miters. Archbishop Cranmer noticed it uneasily.

"I am sorry for this refusal of yours, Sir Thomas," he said placatingly to More. "But I trust all is well otherwise. I take it, from your new camlet gown and your coming hither, that you will attend Queen Anne's Coronation?"

Thomas More drew himself up to his full height. He had their arrogant attention now and, God willing, whether they liked it or not, he meant to hold them fast for the few minutes necessary to have his say out. He had written their reply to Luther. Now they should listen to his reply to them. The clamor lulled a little, as the adversaries stared at one another. More at the Bishops; and the Bishops at More. All their Lordships of the Bishops' Bench of England: my Lord Thomas Cranmer, Archbishop of Canterbury; my Lord Edward Lee, Archbishop of York; my Lord Cuthbert Tunstall, Bishop of Durham; my Lord John Stokesley, Bishop of London; my Lord Stephen Gardiner, Bishop of Winchester; my Lord Robert Shirburn, Bishop of Chichester; my Lord John Longland, Bishop of Lincoln; my Lord John Kyte, Bishop of Carlisle; my Lord John Veysey, Bishop of Exeter; my Lord Thomas Goodrich, Bishop of Ely; my Lord Rowland Lee, Bishop of Coventry and Lichfield. And with them my Lord John Taylor, Master of the Rolls; and my Lord John Chambre, Dean of St. Stephen's; and all the great Abbots and Priors of the Kingdom. After he had done saying to them what he had to say, they would all be his enemies, however reluctant Stephen Gardiner, for example, might be about it; or Cuthbert Tunstall, his old comrade in arms in the diplomatic lists of Cambrai, where the two of them had saved England's honor. He was sorry. But he could not help it any more.

"You ask me, my Lord of Canterbury," he said to Cranmer, "if I will attend Queen Anne's Coronation? Not so, my Lord. This is my second refusal. I wish King Henry well of his new Queen. And I wish Queen Anne well of her new crown. I will be their loyal subject and beadsman. But I may not attend her Coronation. Since, my Lords Bishops, in the letter accompanying your gift of the twenty pounds, you asked two things of me, I felt the freer to deny your second request, since I had been so well content to grant your first. I took you for no beggars and knew myself for no rich man, so I was right glad to pocket your twenty pounds. The invitation, however, put me in mind of a certain story I read once in Roman Tacitus. You have some time yet, my Lords, before the Procession forms. May I tell my story?"

The stir grew louder and more menacing at what the press of great churchmen considered their former Chancellor's gratuitous insolence. But Stephen Gardiner, in all the strength of his personal ascendancy, was able to quell it. Impelled by his innate decency as well as by his old fondness for More, he held up a staying hand.

"I say yes, and with a will, Sir Thomas," he said, looking sternly at his brother Bishops. "No one tells such tales as yours in the King's Council nowadays. I, for one, sorely miss them."

In Parliament Thomas More had well known how to ride the waves of bitter opposition. This was not so unlike Parliament that he was to be easily daunted.

"It is a long story, my Lords spiritual," he began, "but a good one. And we have time to listen a space while we wait the coming of the Lady Anne. Let us say we while away a quarter hour together. No more."

He drew a breath, carefully measuring them with a practiced parliamentarian's eye.

"There was a certain Emperor," he began again, "who ordained a certain law to the effect that whosoever should commit a certain heinous offense—its nature, I confess, I have forgotten; nor does it much matter—should suffer the pains of death, unless the offender in question happened to be a virgin. This great Emperor, you see, unlike certain other great Emperors we know of, had a great reverence for virginity.

"Now it so fell out that the first committer of that offense was in very truth a virgin. When the Emperor heard this, he was in no small perplexity, since he was strongly bent on putting that law in execution by some striking example. Whereupon one of his counsellors, a good, plain man who, like some good, plain counsellors amongst us, had read Messire Machiavelli to good effect, and who had long sat still debating this matter in his mind, suddenly rose up in the midst of the Council and said: 'Why do you make so much ado, my Lords, about so small a matter? Let her first be deflowered, and then after she may be devoured in all legality and good faith.' "

The familiar voice the Bishops had heard so often arguing for justice on the floor of Parliament stopped. Stephen Gardiner flushed, and hung his head. Rowland Lee's face was white-lipped in rage. Cranmer delicately dabbed at his lips. If one looked closely, my Lord of Canterbury's hand was shaking. For the most part, the Bishops' Bench sat inscrutable as rows of Sphinxes in lace surplices.

Then the quiet, cheerful, inexorable voice began again:

"Now you men of the Church in England are virgins by profession and by your consecrated oath. And though so far, by the grace of God, in this matter of the King's matrimony you have, in the main, kept yourself pure virgins, yet take good heed, my Lords Bishops, that you keep your virginity still. For there are some counsellors in our Kingdom—I name no names; you know them—who seem strangely desirous of deflowering you, my Lords spiritual. They have advanced already more than a little distance toward their goal by first procuring your Lordships to be present at this Coronation. Next they will have you preaching in its favor. Finally they will set you writing books to all the world in its defense. And when, by these gentle degrees, they have deflowered you, then will they not fail soon after to devour you. First your virginity will be confiscate; then—a far lesser loss, though you may not think so—your benefices.

"As for me, my Lords spiritual, it may not lie within my little power to keep them from devouring me, but, as God is my good Lord, I shall so provide that they shall never deflower me!"

Thomas More's voice rang out proudly on his final syllables. Cranmer's liquid eyes had been distractedly seeking the corners all this while. Now he caught sight of what he had been searching for. One of Master Secretary Cromwell's pursuivants—nowadays the man's eyes and ears were everywhere—was busily noting down in a tablet what Sir Thomas said. My Lord of Canterbury nervously took his cue.

"An eloquent parable, Sir Thomas," he said, taking care to raise his musical voice so that the pursuivant should be sure to hear. "And —shall we say?—a dangerous one. More dangerous, even, for what you left out than for what you put in. If I remember my Tacitus aright, the little maid who was deflowered was the daughter of Counsellor Sejanus, and the Emperor in question was Tiberius. Am I right? If I am, I can think of a parallel your ill-wishers might well construe as seditious."

More bowed to Cranmer, cool contempt evident in his manner. He, too, had seen the pursuivant at his task of writing down information for his own and Cranmer's master, Master Secretary Cromwell.

"I congratulate my Lord of Canterbury on his memory," he said ironically. "And even more on his acumen. And now, my Lords, it is close upon your hour. I may detain you no longer. If we meet not again, I wish you well."

As Thomas More came out of the cool, underseas cavern of Westminster's great Hall, where bloomed today the gorgeous sea-anemone hues of vestment and ducal mantle, the bright air winced with the sounding of many silver trumpets. That part of the Procession, which would include the great Abbots and Priors, was already formed. Thomas More watched the Church Militant in its serried ranks and orders; in its black and brown and white and white-and-black hoods: Thomas, Abbot of Shrewsbury; John, Abbot of Hyde; John, Abbot of Welbeck; William, Abbot of Westminster; Thomas, Prior of Canterbury; Christopher, Abbot of Newhouse; John, Abbot of St. Augustine's; Thomas, Abbot of St. John's; Richard, Abbot of Winchcombe; John, Abbot of Battle; John, Abbot of Cirencester; William, Abbot of Hulme St. Benet's; Robert, Abbot of Walden; Robert, Abbot of Waltham; Robert, Abbot of Bermondsey; Richard, Abbot of West Dereham; Henry, Abbot of Grace Dieu; Stephen,

Abbot of Bildwas; William, Abbot of Stratford; John, Prior of Merton; John, Abbot of Bury. And many, many more he did not know. Many had come to the Coronation. Too many, thought More sorrowfully to himself. But not a few were absent, too. His heart leaped for joy in his breast when he noted that, conspicuous among the missing, were the Priors of the three Charterhouses of London, Beauvale, and Axholme; Dr. Richard Reynolds, Prior of the Bridgettine monastery of Syon; and the six Priors of the Observant Franciscans whom Henry's father had introduced into England.

A hand out of the crowd plucked at his sleeve. It was Henry Patenson. More warmed toward his old friend come across in this chance meeting.

"What do you here, Master More?" asked Patenson. "The Carthusians are not here. If you would enter the Charterhouse again, you must seek out the Prior in his cell. He is a fool like you. He stays away from Coronations."

For all the bitterness of the observation, Thomas More felt grateful to the Jester for thus serving notice how closely he could yet read his old master's thoughts. He smiled. The day was not entirely lost —no, nor the fort utterly betrayed—when one could still come across such honest English salt as this.

A new skirling of silver trumpets gave sign that Mistress Boleyn, in a blaze of jewels, conspicuous among them the Glastonbury Sapphire which Abbot Whiting had brought up as a wedding gift culled from the Abbey treasures, was entering the portals of Westminster Hall. Master Cromwell walked at her elbow. As they came together into the vesting room, his pursuivant stepped up to Cromwell and, without comment, handed him the paper on which he had been writing. Cromwell read its contents swiftly, also without comment. Then he motioned that the Queen's attendants fall back a space, so that the two of them, the Lady Anne and he, might have privacy for conversation.

"So, Master Secretary," said Anne Boleyn, looking about the Hall and nodding her head in satisfaction, "among your many other talents, you are also an admirable Major Domo. I congratulate you on the smoothness of the day's arrangements thus far. It was a capital thought to wait here, out of the heat and the press, until the rest of the Procession forms."

Cromwell bowed in answer to the compliment, and handed her the note.

"I am also," he said coolly, "an admirable Captain of Archers. Read here what Master More, replying to your gracious invitation, just now said to the Lords spiritual assembled in full conclave for your crowning."

Anne Boleyn read the paper through. Then she angrily crumpled it into a ball and hurled it to the floor.

"Insult!" she said, green eyes flashing, the narrow dints of her nostrils distending. "I shall not brook it! It ill becomes a reverend knight, like Master More, to prate so glibly of deflowering!"

Cromwell's slow senses reeled at the perfume of her proximity. He took her gloved hand and kissed it.

"Perhaps," he said, a cold relish of cruelty marring his face, "perhaps we cannot deflower him. I think myself it is much too late for any such attempts as that. But there are ways of insuring it that he will do no deflowering on his own part ever more."

"I am not sure," said Anne Boleyn slowly, "that I take your meaning, Master Secretary."

The cold unwinking eyes gazed meaningly into the green cat ones.

"Think a little, my Queen," he said. "What is the sentence they execute on traitors to the Crown?"

Anne moved her lips as if forming to herself the awful words of the full capital sentence. Then, as she had done in Wyatt's presence on Shrove Tuesday evening, Mistress Boleyn threw back her head and gave vent to a terrible, mirthless, high-pitched laugh.

"I think I take you now, Master Secretary," she said. "It is an odd portent for a wedding morning, is it not? For, Master Secretary, I look on Coronation Day as my real wedding morning."

The silver trumpets shrilled again outside. Henry, from his vantage point in the cloisters of St. Stephen, stirred restlessly, shifting from foot to foot. A herald stepped respectfully forward, as the twelve maids-in-waiting, in their cloth-of-gold, took up Anne's train. "The Procession is formed, Your Grace," the herald said.

At the Abbey Archbishop Cranmer lifted the massive crown of St. Edward from the new Queen's head. It was too heavy for her to wear long; her swan's neck arched under the weight, and she grew faint. His consecrated hands replaced it with the lighter crown Henry, in his uxorious solicitude, had commissioned for her. It was something new in Coronation procedure; and Henry Patenson had a phrase for it. That night, by the red light of bonfires, the London crowds roared out Patenson's newest quip: *A light crown for a light woman!* But Anne did not hear. Lying next to Henry in the King's bed at Whitehall, she felt the child stir in her womb. Yawning, replete with food and love, Henry found himself sleepily remembering the prim mouth and tight but modest bodice of Mistress Seymour. He wondered how it would do to lie with a slim little Puritan like her. There was something to be said, he thought, for ice after fire.

CHAPTER XVII

THE FIELD IS WON:

Lambeth, Morning, April 13, 1534

THE long jousting was over at last; and the blunt lance of Master Secretary Cromwell had finally prevailed. It had, Cromwell thought, looking back over the field, been a much harder struggle than he had reckoned on at first. For Henry had shown himself strangely reluctant to proceed against his old Chancellor. Several times, when Cromwell and Anne both thought the game was won, the King had stayed his Secretary's over eager hand. But, in the end, the logic of events had hurried Henry on as well—almost, as it were, against his will. The Moloch jaws of tyranny are insatiable. They cannot discriminate. They dare make no exception. If all the world should yield but More—and almost all the world had yielded but Thomas More—then victory would not be complete. And the King's nature, like the archetypal nature of tyranny, was such that it required complete victory. Now Cromwell had but to close his hand—thus—and the quarry was taken.

It had been, all things considered, a long and devious course to the kill. For the first six months after the Coronation Cromwell suffered his quiet foe to live peacefully at Chelsea, reading, writing, meditating, going out but seldom, seeing hardly anyone. Then, at Christmas, the King's Council issued a book of nine articles justifying the King's marriage. Someone published an anonymous pamphlet in answer. Master Secretary—if, indeed, in his role of *agent provocateur* he was not responsible for the pamphlet, authorship and all—saw his chance and took it. He charged More with having written the retort, and his nephew, William Rastell, with having printed it. Quietly, dignifiedly, efficiently, the master lawyer, who was Thomas More, cleared the two of them of the absurd accusation. Cromwell and his pursuivants were as wax in his advocate's fingers. Thwarted for the time, and rankling under the easy way in which he had been balked, Master Secretary and his ugly pack of thief-takers cried off the chase. But only for a time.

Immediately afterward another and better opportunity presented itself. When, on February 21, 1534, a Bill of Attainder, in connection with the case of the Holy Maid of Kent, the nun, Elizabeth Barton, was introduced into the House of Lords, More's name was included in the Attainder along with that of my Lord of Rochester, John Fisher. The Holy Maid of Kent might well have been a maid—the Bill of Attainder did not bother to impugn her chastity. But she was most certainly not holy. After listening to her public confession at Paul's Cross on November 23, 1533, the lucid rationalist in More contemptuously dismissed her trancelike revelations as hysteria or even malignant invention. He called her "a lewd nun," and "the wicked woman of Canterbury"; and stamped her so-called prophecies relating to the King's death as mischievous and, indeed, traitorous nonsense. John Fisher, unfortunately, had not been so discreet. In entire good faith, but mistakenly, he had allowed himself, as More had not, to be put in communication with the woman and with some of her less moderate adherents, like Friar Peto, Franciscan Observant of Greenwich, who, preaching before the King and the assembled Court, had warned Henry the dogs would one day lick his blood as they had licked the blood of the impious Hebrew monarch, Ahab.

The Bill proceeded to its third reading before the Lords, with More's name still in it; but even Cromwell was convinced, by this time, that they had overplayed their hand for the moment. A special committee, composed of Cranmer, Audley, and the Duke of Norfolk, waited on the King, begging him to remove More's name from Attainder. For, they said, in this case of the nun he was acccounted "so innocent and clear that, for his dealing therein, men reckoned him far worthier of praise than reproof." Henry assented with bad enough grace. Cromwell, acting as secretary to the Committee, duly noted the King's display of pique, and decided—as events were to prove, correctly—that next time Sir Thomas would meet with short shrift at the hands of the King.

Next time followed as close upon the heels of now as Cromwell's great gift for arrangement could reasonably contrive. In March the Act of Succession and Supremacy was amended and strengthened by Parliament in such a way that no further evasion of the full Oath was any longer possible. Heretofore the Commissioners, on the King's and Cromwell's express direction, had left the reins purposely slack, so that dissenters might have their head. Now this policy of relative tolerance was to be altogether jettisoned. The reins were to be just as purposely tautened so that all dissenters, having been for some time allowed their due meed of rope, should now be caught in them and strangled. The penalty of refusal to make a full corporal oath was, first, misprision of treason, involving imprisonment and confiscation of goods; and then, after a trial, whose result was a foregone conclusion, execution on Tower Hill.

On the Sunday after Easter, the Sunday of April 12, 1534, the long-awaited blow fell. Notice was served on More by the King's officers who came upon him in his old house at Bucklersbury where John Clement now lived with his wife, Margaret. William Roper was in the company of his father-in-law when the summons to appear on the morrow before the Commissioners at Lambeth was served. They had come up together to hear the sermon at St. Paul's; and they returned together at once to Chelsea. There, on Sunday evening, More took tender leave of his family. Next morning he walked to Chelsea Church, was shriven, took the sacrament, and, again with Roper to accompany him, went by water to Lambeth.

Over the week end the King's Commissioners throughout the length and breadth of England had done their unyeomanly work right well. The Dominican Priors of King's Langley and Dunstable, the Carmelite Prior of Hitchin, the Franciscan Guardians of Bedford, Aylesbury, and Ware, all added their names to the 6500 secular clergy and 1470 monks who were already signatories. The Bishops and Archbishops had previously subscribed their episcopal hands: Cranmer, Gardiner, Clark, Stokesley, Goodrich, Longland, Kyte, Lee, Salcot, Shirburn, Tunstall, Veysey, Nykke, Booth, Rawlins, Standish, and Rowland Lee, so designated to distinguish my Lord Lee of Coventry and Lichfield from my Lord Lee of York. Only four of the twenty-one members of the English hierarchy resisted the royal demand: Athequa of Llandaff; Campeggio of Salisbury; Ghinucci of Worcester; and Fisher of Rochester. And of these latter four only one was an Englishman resident in England. Well might my Lord of Rochester mourn that the fort was betrayed even of them that should have defended it.

What grieved More most of all, perhaps, was the way in which his old diplomatic associate, my Lord of Durham, Cuthbert Tunstall, acceded to the royal fiat. Not only did he subscribe his hand to the Oath; he threw himself into this new matter of the King's as if into a Crusade. Commissioner Legh wrote Cromwell that Bishop Tunstall, in person, had gone up and down the length and breadth of his great diocese, preaching and setting forth "the Primacy and the King's high authority of Supreme Head, and that marvelous discreetly and clerkly." The ill news traveled by letter to Reginald Pole in exile on the continent. He wrote Tunstall a scathing rebuke; and, in reply, Tunstall asked Pole why—as Pole seemed to suggest he should have done—he should have laid down his life for an Italian Prince, a foreign power that would not have "lost one penny" to succor him. Pole wrote back at once:

"Good, my Lord of Durham, tell me of my Lord of Rochester and of Master More? Have these twain subscribed the Oath? If not, do they think the Pope will send an host to deliver them from death? These words you write in extenuation of your cowardice: what words be these in so great a matter? And it is a great matter you engage in, my Lord of Durham. Make you the matter as light as you will, the better to lighten your heavy-burdened conscience, it will not avail. There was never a matter of more importance to the health of the realm and of the whole Church than this one you are betraying."

If ever pride could be forgiven one, More did not know. But, grievous sin or not, he was proud of what my Lord Pole had said of him and John Fisher. The praise did not, however, serve to remove his deep depression over Cuthbert Tunstall's defection. It was one thing for my Lord Stokesley, the stammerer of London, who, for his speech impediment, had never preached before in his life, to enter a pulpit in the Act's behalf. Knowing Stokesley, as More did, that ultimate enormity might almost have been predicted. It might also have been predicted that Rowland Lee, bloody Lord President of the Council of Wales who, in his day, had slain Welshmen like so many noxious flies, should, in his new capacity as Bishop of Coventry and Lichfield, back to the hilt the Henrician tyranny. But his old friend, Tunstall! Tunstall, who had denounced Tyndale and Luther, who, so recently as February of 1531, had resisted Henry's usurpation of the spiritual power by supporting John Fisher's saving clause of qualification introduced into the first form of the Act: *In quantum per Christi legem licet.* That is: *As far as this is lawful in accordance with the law of Christ.*

But Thomas More could allow himself no such slender refuge; nor did he think the Commissioners would, either. He must be harried and hunted down. So must John Fisher. So, from all appearances, must Queen Catherine, immured and under guard as she was in her distant castle of Kimbolton in Huntingdonshire. But this attempt to suborn a Queen's honor had recoiled upon itself. All England rang with Catherine's proud words to the Commissioners who had threatened her with instant death for not signing the Oath: *If one of you has a commission to execute this penalty upon me, I am ready. I only ask that I be allowed to die in the sight of the people.*

Brave words, thought Thomas More, as the rowers' oars grided in their oarlocks at the foot of Lambeth's water stairs. High words, like those of maid Antigone to tyrant Creon. Only sweetened by the great promise of Christ that one does not go down into the dark alone. More wondered if he would fare as bravely in the coming ordeal as had the Princess of Aragon.

When Thomas More was ushered into the upper room of the Archbishop's palace at Lambeth, where the special Commissioners for London were holding their sittings, Hugh Latimer had just been sworn, and Cromwell, who could be very pleasant when he chose, was thanking him for his compliance. My Lord of Canterbury, Archbishop Cranmer, Master Secretary Cromwell, and my Lord Chancellor Audley sat in high-backed ecclesiastical chairs at a long table cluttered with pens and papers and the newly-cast seal of the Royal Commissioners. Master Secretary sat in the middle, with Cranmer on his left and Audley on his right, facing the deponent who was being interrogated. While still on the stairs More could hear Cromwell's thick utterance, as the door leading from the judgment room to the antechamber was swung open by two men-at-arms, and Dr. Latimer, his bluff face flushed with relief, came out to be familiarly greeted by an ecclesiastic of the Archbishop's service. He bowed to More, as the two of them passed on the stairs; and More bowed back. He liked Hugh Latimer well enough, if he did not respect him. Latimer was a lover of wine and laughter. When he preached, which was often, he had a racy English tongue in his head that helped make him vastly popular. And, judging by his demeanor at the moment, he had made no bones at all about the Oath.

"Now, my Lords," Cromwell's voice was saying through the open door, "we come to the heart of the matter. *Item:* touching the learned man of Chelsea, whilom my Lord the King's man, now Queen Catherine's chief supporter in the realm. Summon Sir Thomas More."

More could not decide whether this brutal impropriety were calculated or a careless slip on Cromwell's part. In either case, it was an ominous sign that, for the first time in his knowledge of the man, Master Secretary's arrogance appeared to wax with his ever-growing power. As the men-at-arms escorted him in, he noticed that Cromwell was noticeably fleshier. Master Secretary did not bother to rise. Nor did he ask More to sit down during the course of the inquisition.

"Good morrow, Sir Thomas," said Cromwell with the kind of brutal joviality which, with him, passed muster for good nature. "We

are at the old game again, you see. And we wish to ask you the same
old question. Will you swear the Oath?"

It was an abrupt enough opening in all conscience. More, who was
skilled in interpreting such gambits, realized at once that Master
Cromwell did not care much any more whether or not he subscribed
his hand to the Act. Well, he said grimly to himself, this last time the
hare would see to it that he gave the hounds a good run, if only for
the honor of that high profession the hare had graced in his day and
these hounds were presently disgracing.

"I will not stick," he said equably, "at the Act of Succession. Let
Anne be Queen, and gladly. And let the infant, Elizabeth, inherit.
Otherwise, I cannot swear the Oath."

My Lord of Canterbury seemed nervous. His liquid eyes looked
uneasily from side to side. Thomas Cranmer did not like bloodshed
or violence. He even deprecated argument as a species of bad taste.

"Dr. Latimer has sworn," he interposed in conciliatory fashion.

"I thought as much," said More with the suspicion of a smile.

Master Secretary Cromwell did not like this gay ghost of a smile.
"You thought as much?" he snarled. "How thought you as much?"

"I thought as much," said More, "when he passed me on the stairs
just now. He was wondrous merry and relieved, too, I thought. For
he flung his arms around the neck of my Lord of Canterbury's Chaplain so familiarly that, had they been women, I would have thought
he had grown wanton of a sudden. He was dry, too, he told the
other. So he strode up to the buttery bar of the palace and called for
drink."

"I can sympathize with Dr. Latimer," said my Lord Audley
blandly. "Ours is dry work indeed for a warm spring day. The Vicar
of Croydon swore before him. You know the Vicar of Croydon, I
believe, Sir Thomas."

More knew the Vicar of Croydon for one of the veriest fools on
God's earth. He must one day ask Master Patenson just where to fit
the Vicar of Croydon into the Litany of Fools.

"I know Master Phillips of old," he said drily. "But I trust you had
him scrutinize the document in question very closely. One cannot be

too careful in these matters. Sometimes the Vicar of Croydon mistakes the meaning of a text. It was in my Lord Cardinal Wolsey's time, I remember, that he wrote asking to be preferred as first Bishop to the new territory of Utopia."

My Lord of Canterbury and my Lord Chancellor Audley both laughed right merrily. For a moment, it was almost as if they were both More's guests in Chelsea. As a connoisseur of the more civilized essences in life, Cranmer even found himself regretting that a mere difference in ideology prevented More's Attic salt from seasoning nowadays the somewhat flat sessions of the King's Council. But Master Secretary Cromwell did not laugh. He had not remembered this man could be so annoying.

"We have scant time for jesting today, Sir Thomas," said Cromwell impatiently. "Everyone has sworn but you. All the Lords spiritual and temporal of this realm: Tunstall of Durham, Stokesley of London, Nykke of Norwich, West of Ely, Clark of Bath, Kyte of Carlisle, Veysey of Exeter, Longland of Lincoln, Standish of St. Asaph. But why go further? All, without exception and without cavil, all have subscribed their hand."

"I do not hear my Lord of Rochester's name amongst these many others," said Thomas More very quietly.

A dead silence fell then on the Archbishop's upper room there in Lambeth. A paper rustled as my Lord Audley moved his sleeve. Cranmer shuffled his feet a little. But Thomas Cromwell flushed in anger. It was quite apparent that, at long last, Master Secretary felt himself sufficiently entrenched to indulge in the expensive luxury of outbursts of temper.

"Bishop Fisher," he said, reddening to the nape of his short neck, "Bishop Fisher appears before us later this afternoon."

"I do not think he will subscribe his hand, Master Secretary," said Thomas More evenly.

Cromwell leaned forward, hunched over the desk, supporting himself on two moist splayed palms that left damp marks on the polished wood. The old uncanny resemblance to a toad was accentuated by his present posture.

"You are privy, then," he said, raising his thick voice in a hectoring tone, "to my Lord of Rochester's plans? You exchange seditious letters with him?"

"We exchange letters, Master Secretary," answered Thomas More quietly. "There is no sedition in them. Last New Year's Day he sent me a gift of oranges and apples and an image of St. John; and, in return, I sent my Lord of Rochester a present of wine and a panel of the Magi visiting the Infant Christ. That is the sort of correspondence that passes between us."

Cromwell ignored the new bird this line of questioning had flushed, and doggedly reverted to his previous point. More could not help but admit that Master Secretary's tenacity in cross-examination made him a formidable opposing lawyer.

"Supposing," said Cromwell, with an admirable assumption of good-natured reason, "supposing Bishop Fisher does not sign? What odds, then? What is one against so many?"

"One," said More simply, "can be right, and many wrong. It has happened before in history."

Cranmer's delicate fingers left off playing with a quill.

"Tell me, Sir Thomas," said the Archbishop persuasively, shielding his white brow with one soft hand so that he would not have to look into More's face. "Why do you stick thus to swear?"

More turned away from Cromwell and toward my Lord of Canterbury.

"My Lord Archbishop," he said, "I believe that, in your heart, you already have the answer you seem to seek. Moreover, in strict legality, I need not reply to this question of yours. I have the King's pledge I need not be molested in this matter, provided I keep my own good counsel and good conscience and do not molest other men on this same point. But do you tell me something, instead? Why do you insist so earnestly I swear?"

It was Chancellor Audley's turn to enter the discussion. But first he went to a window that opened on to the street and stood beside it, his hand on the latch.

"From the standpoint of practical politics," he said, "your question, Master More, is easily answered. You are known to the people as Queen Catherine's friend, and she is still popular among them. Also, she has a daughter, the Lady Mary, whom the people have known longer than they know Queen Anne's new daughter, the Lady Elizabeth. The succession must be made secure. Listen!"

And he swung open the casement. A sullen roaring came up from the street below. One high-pitched voice could be heard above the ugly tumult, singing what had lately become a popular tune of the day:

> *"Nan is a ribald! Her child but a bastard!*
> *Eliza's a bastard! Her dam but a ribald!"*

Chancellor Audley closed the casement with an eloquent shrug of his shoulders.

"You see, Master More?" he asked. "And hear? There is a very practical reason for our attitude and our insistence, is there not? You are become a symbol of resistance to a régime. Witting or unwitting, innocent or guilty on your own part, that is an undoubted fact. Your subscribing the Oath will go a long way toward removing the unfortunate impression that you oppose the King's policies."

"I am sorry, my Lord Chancellor," said More, "for the unrest in the streets. But it is none of my doing. Nor can I accept any responsibility for it. I repeat again: willingly will I swear that part of the Oath which has to do with the Succession. But no more. On peril of my immortal soul, I touch not on that which has to do with renouncing mine allegiance to mine own true superior in the realm of things spiritual, the Pope, who is first Bishop of Christendom."

Cromwell smashed a fat fist down on the table in the most abysmal disgust.

"God's blood!" he growled. "Do you want me to tell you, Master More, why you thus stick to swear? You are the Pope's man, the creature of the ruler of an Italian Princedom, and have been since the beginning, ever since that day when, against his interest and better judgment, you seduced our gracious King, by sinister subtle slights, to set forth a book asserting the Seven Sacraments and maintaining the Pope's authority. You thus put an English sword into the Pope's Italian hand to use against our King to the dishonor of his Grace and his Grace's realm of England throughout all Christendom. Sir Thomas More, Knight recreant to his sworn oath, I formally charge that never was there servant to his sovereign so villainous, nor subject to his Prince so traitorous as you."

Thomas More did not move a muscle during Cromwell's bitter diatribe. As if he still sat in judgment upon the King's Bench, he looked squarely at his three inquisitors in turn; then let his cold glance return to Master Secretary Cromwell.

"My Lords," he said contemptuously, "these are terrors for children, not me. King Henry will never lay to my charge that I procured or counseled His Majesty to the book you speak of. After it was finished, by His Grace's appointment I was a sorter out and editor of the matter therein contained. No more. In fact, I call to your own and His Grace's attention my former feeling, then vehemently entertained, that, in his book, he defended the Pope's authority far too strongly. I reminded King Henry that the Pope was a Prince, like himself, and in league with other Christian Princes; and that, in case of breach of amity between them, his book in the Pope's favor might one day hurt the King's good cause. King Henry cannot but remember this of which I speak."

Again Cromwell returned to the point at issue.

"If what you say be true, Master More," he said in a more friendly voice than before, "then why do you still stick to swear?"

Thomas More's voice was still knife-edged with cold contempt.

"Because, Master Secretary," he said, "because—since you thus force my utterance—I have studied this matter of the Primacy for some ten years now and more, and I think today King Henry was right upon that point, when he wrote his book, and that I was wrong. In the past I did not believe that the Primacy of the See of Rome was begun by the institution of God till after I had read what the King's Highness wrote against the heresies of Dom Luther. Now, after ten years' study, I cannot deny that the Primacy was provided by God. Even you, Master Secretary, must see, at the very least, that that same Primacy is accepted by the corps of Christendom. And, since Christendom is one corps and one body, I cannot conceive, even in reason and prudence, setting aside matters of faith, how any member thereof may, without the common consent of the whole body, depart from the common head."

Ah! It came at last. Cromwell took his palms off the table and, leaning back, relaxed in his chair. The game was won. The dog would not be whistled to heel; but, when the time came, he would be hanged, anyway. Even now he had made the necessary admissions.

"Come, Master More," he said expansively. "You were Lord Chancellor once. You know of practical politics. Surely you must see that, when the King wrote his book, it suited his best interests in his war against the French to gain favor with the Pope."

"I know somewhat of practical politics, Master Secretary," said Thomas More. "Was I not at Cambrai? But something must stand above politics. Truth, for example. And justice. And God."

Master Secretary's temper flared again. He grew irked nowadays with the mention of God and justice. It was all whining cant. But it would not go down any more with either him or Henry.

"We woolgather, Master More," he said savagely. "We split hairs. Let us play our little pageant through and be done with it. I make this final appeal to reason. May you not well be mistaken, since it is your opinion and yours alone against the opinion of all the Bishops and, indeed, of all Parliament, the great Council of the realm?"

So easy was his attitude now, Thomas More might have been standing on the floor of Parliament, in the old days, before the King's great matter was so much as thought on. His voice soared into peroration.

"I do not think so, Master Secretary," he said. "I have on my part as great a Council, and a greater one, too—the Council of all Christendom. I am in no wise bound to the Council of this realm of England that I love so well above all other realms of the earth, and against the universal opinion of Christendom."

"By the body of Christ, man," swore Cromwell, jerking himself forward in his chair, "you put me beside myself! I will try one last tack, and then we are done, you and I. Done forever."

Cromwell turned to two of his pursuivants who, tablets in hand, stood in the background recording the proceedings.

"Summon Master Rich," he said to them.

Master Richard Rich, Solicitor General of the realm of England, was another of Cromwell's creatures. Lean, sallow, clever, Cicero's day would have called him a *novus homo*. He was a bird of prey well versed in the shabby art of feathering his own nest from the misfortunes of others; a scavenger living on garbage in the courtyard of the Temple of Themis; a foregatherer with turnkeys, bailiffs, and such summoners as were able to put him in the way of the greasy business he battened on. Men like Rich—and there were many of them today as well as yesterday and would be tomorrow—dealt not with the living body of Justice, but with the cold corpses they were able to cut down from the gibbets of litigation. More had known the man in his student days; and, sitting in the Court of Poor Men's Requests, had ruled against him on more than one occasion before Rich's sudden rise to power under Master Cromwell. As the men-at-arms ushered him into the Archbishop's inner chamber, he bowed to the three Commissioners and to More.

"The Solicitor General," said Cromwell, "has a legal conundrum to propose to you, Master More. See what you make of it."

He settled back in his high ecclesiastical chair and fixed his small eyes on the two of them.

"Sir Thomas," said Rich, joining the tips of his fingers, "you are a man of law as I am. We sat together once in the Middle Temple. Will you, in memory of our ancient fellowship, suffer my putting to you this case? Admit, for the sake of argument, there were an act of Parliament that the realm should take me for King. Would you, then, Master More, also take me for King?"

The fellow's sickening hypocrisy and even more sickening assumption of previous intimacy well nigh nauseated Thomas More. He saw, too, that a cunning gin had been laid. But, in a sense, he no longer cared. The end was in sight; and he was almost glad thereof.

What he had left to do now was to fight clean and hold fast.

"I see no manner of difficulty there," he said courteously, despite his physical revulsion at the sight of Rich's vulture-shaped head and curving finger tips. "In that case I would take you for King, Master Rich."

"I put my case further, then," went on Rich. "That there should be an act of Parliament that all the realm of England should take me for Pope. Would you not also, then, Master More, take me for Pope?"

The insinuating voice as much as whispered in his ear. More had to fight down a mounting nausea over the monstrous yet childish malice of the proceeding. He saw their drift quite clearly. Rich's treacherous function was to trap him into a technical admission that the King could not be Primate, which would be against the letter of his commitment to Henry not to prejudice men's consciences on the Act. But he would evade this newest pit digged for him. His adversaries might gain their point in the end. But he would force them into perjury to gain their point. Thomas More set his jaw grimly.

"I answer you thus, Master Solicitor," he said, raising his voice so that the three Commissioners should hear. "As for your first case, the Parliament, Master Rich, may well meddle with the affairs of temporal princes. As for my answer to your second case, I put you this other case in turn: suppose the Parliament should make a law that God should no longer be God. Would you then, Master Rich, say that God was no longer God?"

"No, Master More," conceded Rich. "That I would not. No Parliament may make such a law."

"You are an apt pupil," said More, eyeing him with evident distaste. "You see, then, do you not, why, in conscience, I must stick to swear?"

The cat-and-mouse game had not ended quite as Master Secretary Cromwell had wished it. But it had ended, nonetheless; and Cromwell was ready to pounce upon his prey at last.

"So, Master More," he said, getting to his feet. "We penetrate to the quick at last. You have stated that the Parliament may not make the King the Supreme Head of the Church in England."

The Field Is Won:

Thomas More faced Thomas Cromwell across the length of the Archbishop's table.

"I said not so," he answered steadily, every syllable chiming clear as a pebble dropped into a well.

"Nevertheless," said Cromwell, "that is your manifest meaning. And the Solicitor General now stands ready to bear witness to your open admission."

The other Commissioners had now risen to their feet as well. Cromwell turned to the pursuivants.

"Summon Sir Richard Southwell," he said, "to convey to the Tower, as an accused traitor to His Majesty of England, Sir Thomas More, Knight of Chelsea. There deliver him into the custody of the Lord Lieutenant, Sir Edmund Walsingham, that he may stand further questioning, and there await his day of trial."

Sir Thomas More heard the clashing of grounded halberds as the pursuivants delivered the message to the men-at-arms; and then, a little later, a measured tramp in the corridor of a contingent of the guard under the command of Sir Richard Southwell.

As it happened, Sir Richard Southwell had other business for the King which detained him till almost evening. But, once the Tower barge got under way, the journey downstream was very rapid. When the boat pushed off from shore at last, Thomas More's glance lingered wistfully on the towers of Westminster across the crepuscular water from Lambeth. Past Whitehall and its orchards the great barge swiftly glided; past the Temple, Whitefriars, Bridewell, the cloacal reaches of Alsatia's underworld, where those sinister purlieus debouched into the river; past the splendid palaces of the Strand; past Blackfriars, Paul's Wharf, Tower Hill, its scaffolding standing out black against the blood red sky. It was nearly floodtide, but Southwell's sturdy rowers made easy work of shooting between the timbered starlings of London Bridge. The boat rushed beneath the arch of the gatehouse tower which guarded the middle drawbridge where stood, on their haggard poles, the rotting heads of executed traitors. It was sunset when the barge came out of the dying light into the black shadow of Traitor's Gate where the Lieutenant of the Tower, Sir Edmund Walsingham, waited to receive them.

Sir Richard Southwell lightly touched the gold chain More was wearing over his camlet gown.

"You know the customs and usage here, Sir," he said as delicately as he could manage it. "I should be very glad to convey the chain to either Mistress More or Mistress Roper."

"No, friend Southwell," said Thomas More with a little laugh. "I came not in a wedding garment to Queen Anne's Coronation. But I wore my best to this morning's trial of arms. And gladly do I abide by the rules of the field of honor. I have been, in my day, a diplomat, not a soldier. But, since I am taken in battle by my adversaries, I would that they should somewhat fare the better for me. Let it not be said I am no prize at all. And yet, friend Southwell, I am not at all ill pleased. For, in a way, the field is won, not lost."

In the White Tower the bell of St. John's Church had finished ringing Compline. Its humming bourdon still throbbed like a great heart against the sunset air as Sir Edmund led Sir Thomas More into the Beauchamp Tower which was to be the place of his confinement. The prisoner's lips moved in Compline's *Nunc dimittis* and, even as he left the sunlight, in the glorious inner music of *Te lucis ante terminum.*

Rosemary grew thick and bees boomed loud in Chelsea. The trumpet vines and morning glories sounded their tiny elfin retreat each morning as the mists rose out of the river and life began once more in Master More's house. The great mulberry tree in the garden bloomed hale and strong again. Meg brought him one of the leaves only yesterday, and he had carefully pressed it between the parchment pages of his new Meditation on the Passion. *But the man in the Tower had scant time now for remembering the past. Nor did he think on the future, either. Time no longer hurried on winged pinions nor dragged leaden feet. It was narrowed to an arrow point; but the Lord of time kept His finger on the tautened string, and the great bow of time, which would one day launch a shaft to slay itself, stayed still. The man in the Tower had time only for the timeless present; and that, if one took it aright, meant that he was already half out of time, halfway on his journey to what Boethius described as eternity: to hold and possess the entire plenitude of life in one single moment, here and now, past and present and to come.*

Strangely enough, it was the easier to do now that his Mass privileges had been withdrawn, though that, of course, had not been his jailers' intention at all when they forbade his visits, turn and turn about each alternate morning, to one of the two churches within the Tower precincts: St. John's in the White Tower, and the Church of St. Peter ad Vincula. It had not been Sir Edmund Walsingham's doing, but the doing of Master Secretary Cromwell. Sir Edmund was an old friend who, in a privy moment, told the prisoner he would gladly make him good cheer in honor of their ancient fellowship, but that he dared not incur the anger of the King which grew daily more terrible to those about him. The man in the Tower thanked his friendly jailer. He would not like to involve good Master Walsingham in any manner of political difficulty. So, when he was moved from the Beauchamp Tower in the western ward, first to the dank crypt, well named Little Ease, in the White Tower, and then to the circular bastion of the Bell Tower, overlooking the postern and the Byward Tower, he said nothing in answer to my Lord Lieutenant's shamefaced apologies. Thus, gradually, communication between the Lieutenant and his prisoner fell off, too. The human universe was fading.

Another thing that made it easier for him to stray out of time was the fact that the London bells were fewer. For the sake of his fellow Christians out in the world, however, the man in the Tower regretted the passing of the bells, and, most of all, the reason for their passing. The Angelus bells must go, advised a new royal writ, "lest the people do hereafter trust to have pardon for the saying of their Aves." But, thought the man in the Tower, fingering his rosary, his lips moving through that part of the Lord's Prayer which concerns forgiving our trespasses, what the weary world needs is more pardon, surely, not less. Pardon was sorely needed, certainly, for what was going on in London. The great gilt Cross of Cheapside had been defaced; the image of our Lady stabbed in the breast, and her crown removed. At Austin Friars the ancient funeral monuments were being removed and sold. The Charterhouse, the convent buildings of St. Mary Overy, the Abbots' houses of Bury, Tortington, and Salisbury, were turned over to sundry of the great nobles. The Minories was become an armory; St. Mary Grace a naval storehouse; the abodes of the Black, White and Crutched Friars no more than glass houses. St. John's, Clerkenwell, had gone to the Master of the Revels.

In the country the monasteries, large and small, were being dissolved. Their passing was attended by no fanfare, no heroism. Master Secretary Cromwell knew his hangman's business too well for that. While the Duchess of Suffolk lunched in a monastery garden, the monks of Butley Priory trudged forth under the sharp eye of Cromwell's overseers, with naught but their cowls upon their bent backs. The Commissioners sealed the cells. The fox was hunted across Staverton Park. Her Grace of Suffolk poured wine in the garden. Another monastery was dead. And the world wagged on.

Pardon was needed, too, for what had been done at Oxford. The man in the Tower remembered the rich peace of the English countryside as, over the water meadows of Oxford, the great bell of Osney Abbey pealed the Angelus that now would ring no more. He remembered his own Canterbury Hall; sturdy Merton; the spires of Magdalen, St. Mary's, St. Frideswide's. He remembered William of Wykeham's great foundation: the College of our Lady for men of the south country; Exeter for men of the west; Jesus for men of the Welsh marches.

Now the goodly necklace of monasteries from Godstow to Rewley no longer clasped the comely neck of Thames. Durham's and St. Bernard's College, the Austin Friars, the Carmelites, the Grey Friars, the Dominicans—all, all were gone now.

Pardon was needed, above all, for what had been done at Oxford to Duns Scotus, the great thirteenth-century Franciscan philosopher of Love and Poetry, and of the Immaculate Conception. Dr. Layton, far and away the most diligent of all Master Secretary's very diligent thief-takers, had, stretching across three centuries, laid a sergeant's heavy hand upon the stooped shoulder of a dead philosopher. Layton had written, jovially boasting of this exploit to Cromwell, and the dismal ripples of the deed had even seeped through the thick masonry of the Bell Tower: "We have set Duns in Bocardo, as they call the town prison in this place, and have utterly banished him from Oxford forever. The second time we came to New College, after we had declared your Injunction, we found all the great quadrant court full of the leaves of Duns, the wind blowing them into every quarter."

The man in the Tower could not rid his fancy of that vivid picture of Layton's. Like Sibyl's leaves at the entrance of the Cumaean cavern, he saw the wind blowing the leaves of Duns into every Oxford quarter. Whirling them up against the glorious stained glass Thomas and John Glazier had long ago glazed for William of Wykeham in Winchester and New College. Against the five south windows of the Choir. Against the Tree of Jesse in the great west window of the Antechapel of All Souls. Against the southeast window's Virgin of whom Duns Scotus had sung. As he pondered in memory what Duns had written, the great quadrant court of his own personality was filled "full of the leaves of Duns." Duns knew the imagination, as Augustine had known the heart and Aquinas the intellect. Duns saw the Maker's hand working within the mind, there sculpting metaphor and image. He was no philosopher for fools—at least, not for the fools of power. The fools of God and the fools of beauty were another thing. The man in the Tower sighed.

No, Duns Scotus was no philosopher for fools; but now that subtle, fire-swift, air-keen brain was become a byword for a sodden fool. And his writings were foolscaps gone with the wind; dunce caps the dolt-

ish present knew not it was too stupid to wear. Again the man in the Tower fetched a heavy sigh.

Like the water standing on the glistening walls of Little Ease, other news trickled in slowly from outside. In September of 1534 Pope Clement died, and, in his place, Paul III came to the throne of Peter Fisherman. The man in the Tower prayed for the repose of the soul of the aged Pope and—with something of his old waggishness, but in utter seriousness, too—asked God to grant His new Vicar not only virtue, which Clement had possessed in abundance, but courage and wisdom and strength of mind, qualities in which Clement had been sadly lacking. Paul sounded an auspicious name; but, then, so had Clement. The man in the Tower remembered how he had replied to Master Luther's assault on Pope Julius:

> It is far more to be wished that God may raise up such Popes as befit the Christian cause and the dignity of the Apostolic office: men who, despising riches and honor, will care only for Heaven, will promote piety in the people, will bring about peace, and exercise the authority they have received from God against the "satraps and mighty hunters of the world," excommunicating and giving over to Satan both those who invade the territories of others and those who oppress their own.

Beyond these few rumors of the outer world the man in the Tower saw and heard naught but his own soul and the face of Christ. His daughter Meg came at longer and longer intervals. That Master Secretary allowed her to come at all was not so much out of a sense of humanity as out of hope that her presence, after long absence, would help bring the prisoner to the breaking point before he came to trial. Cromwell himself and his chief pursuivants paid more frequent calls. They were four in number. Two priests: the foul-mouthed, filthy-tongued, immensely able, Dr. Richard Baskerville Layton; that coarse prebendary and infamous spoiler of women, Dr. John London, now Warden of New College, Oxford, where had gone on the scattering of Scotus' leaves. And two laymen: a dry Welsh pedant, John ap Rice, who, for a wonder, was a man of pristine honor; and the venal cousin of Bishop Rowland Lee, Dr. Thomas Legh, whose own share of the

monastic plunder had been the Cistercian house of Calder in Cumberland and the great Priory of Nostell in Yorkshire. So far they had not
put him to the question, to the peine forte et dure, though Cromwell
threatened the extremity of torture on more than one occasion: the
rack; the thumbscrew; the poire d'angoisse; the infamous cage bind-
ing neck, hands and feet together, and known as the Scavenger's
Daughter.

Short of these, however, Master Secretary Cromwell had his own
exquisite notions of just how to turn the screw a notch higher on the
shrinking mind and wincing imagination of his prisoner. After one
particularly strenuous visitation he sent the man in the Tower, in his
own Secretary's hand, an itemized list of the expenses attendant on
a Canterbury execution for treason: so much for the half ton of wood
for the gallows; so much for the carpenter who built them, the laborer
who dug the holes, the four men who set the heavy engine in place;
so much for the cartage of the timber for the hurdle from the stable
to the prison; so much for hiring a horse to drag the prisoner on his
hurdle; so much for two men and a woman to tend the parboiling
kettle; so much for straw and halter; so much for the executioner and
for the four messengers who, after the drawing and quartering, were
commissioned to bear the dismembered quarters to the city gate; so
much for beer all round after the thirsty work was over. It made a
tidy sum. The man in the Tower, setting his jaw, wrote back to Master
Secretary Cromwell that executions must come cheaper at Tyburn,
since there government maintained a permanent gallows and a regular hangman. He had said once he was not to be daunted by terrors
for children. He would abide by that resolve.

The man in the Tower turned his unicorn ring so that the white
heraldic beast caught the last rays of the sun on its single horn. The
unicorn, that high Utopian animal! It, at least, would outlive Master
Cromwell. So would, in the end, those other old strong things: Mary,
the Mass, and love and friendship. Laughter, too. Had he not once
written: "The Devil, the proud spirit, cannot endure to be mocked?"
And then proceeded to mock him most unmercifully? Well, one could
save one's soul with laughter, even as one could lose it through pride.
All would yet be well with Oxford. And with England. And the world.

CHAPTER XVIII

THIS VALLEY DARK:

The Tower, Evening, Late June, 1535

HE no longer thought much on time; but time had laid a heavy hand on Thomas More.

A year's imprisonment had stooped and bent his body. His once auburn hair—but graying a short twelvemonth's span ago—was almost white. He halted when he walked. The weakness in his chest had grown steadily more disabling. One leg was almost crippled with rheumatism from the damp of the Bell Tower. He voided in pain; for stones and gravel had beset his kidneys, and the burning strangury contorted him for hours at a time. This evening the long June twilight still held the radiance of day. Enough light to write by came in through the small cell window that was set into the stone just above the ramshackle desk kindhearted Master Walsingham had managed to find for him in the Tower lumber room. It, and the few books stacked on the wooden bench against the wall, were his last remaining privileges. For some reason or other Master Secretary Cromwell had not yet seen fit to withdraw them. But he knew that the few grains of sand still left in the hourglass were fast running out. So Thomas More, who otherwise no longer took time into account, now wrote against time as swiftly as he could. The King and Master Cromwell would not stay their hands forever. Meanwhile he had certain things that still needed to be set down on paper.

"Let me see," he said to himself, laying down the pen. "How goes my new prayer?"

This Valley Dark:

He had grown so accustomed to the sound of his own voice over the past twelve months he could not tell how terribly it quavered when he read the beginning of the prayer aloud:

> *"Give me Thy grace, good Lord, to set the world at naught,*
> *To set my mind fast upon Thee,*
> *And not to hang upon the blast of men's mouths. . . ."*

He set the paper down again, satisfied. He liked his new prayer well—at least in its beginnings. It was not bad for an old Utopian to have written. Though, in sober truth, he could claim no great credit for setting the world at naught here in the Tower. To be precise, both as a penitent and a man of law, it was rather the world which had set him at naught. Nor did it allow him much scope to hang upon the blast of men's mouths any more. No one was any longer suffered to visit the Bell Tower. Not Alice. Not son Roper. Not even Patenson. Only Meg, and she not often. He had a chill foreboding that perhaps this evening's would be the last visit allowed her as well. Dear Margaret! It was close upon her hour now; and his *Treatise on the Passion* was not far advanced over what it had been last time she visited him. He should not have very much to read her this evening. But, then, this evening he had other business with Meg than reading her the latest chapter from his *Treatise on the Passion*. He had certain things to say he had not said, and might not be able to say again.

Nevertheless, he thought Meg would like his latest chapter, except, perhaps, that it seemed to fit his present plight all too nearly. But they had no secrets from each other, Meg and he. Never had there been reservations between them. This time he picked up a sheet of foolscap from another pile and read aloud again:

> *"And, therefore, but if he be a fool, man can never be without fear that, either on the morrow, on on the selfsame day, the grisly, cruel hangman, Death, which, from his first coming in, has ever drawn aloof, and looked toward him, and ever lain in wait for him, shall, amid all his royalty, and all his main strength, neither kneel before him, nor make him any reverence, nor with any good manner desire him to come forth; but rigorously and fiercely gripe him by the very*

breast, and make all his bones rattle; and so by long and divers fierce torments, strike him stark dead, and then cause his body to be cast into the ground, into a foul pit, there to rot and be eaten with the wretched worms of the earth, sending yet his soul out further unto a more fearful judgment, whereof at his temporal death his success is uncertain."

Thomas More was not sure whether or not he much liked this part; nor even whether or not it was very good. The King of Terrors deserved better at his hands, he felt, than this child's tale of grave-yard bogles. Death, after all, was much more than what Henry Patenson, quoting his Scotch ancestors, used to call a "cauld grue." But there was no escaping the "cauld grue," either. Still, true or not, what he had written was a bit too much like the pictured bonemen that capered on the walls of French charnel houses. It was common, as Death was common. But, twist it how one would, it fitted. It fitted Henry as well as himself. Maybe it fitted Henry better than it did himself. An icy premonition made More's bowels like water. For he knew he was very like to come headless to the feast of the residuary worm, the legatee in ordinary of man. What would the Master say to those who came headless to His feast? For a short space he set to writing again. Then, for the third time that evening, read aloud what he had written:

"To this great glory can there no man come headless. Our head is Christ: and therefore to Him must we be joined; and as members of His must we follow Him, if we will come thither. He is our guide to guide us thither. Know you not that Christ did suffer Passion, and by that way did enter into His Kingdom? Who can, for very shame, desire to enter into the Kingdom of Christ with ease, when Himself entered not into His own without pain?"

No, nor without great fear, either, thought Thomas More, if he could read Scripture aright at all. Yet He was very God. God's bloody sweat of fear and His great cry of desolation upon the bitter tree of Crucifixion consoled the man in the Tower. He feared the scaffold much, the knife more, the painful question most of all. They racked the Charterhouse monks before they hanged them at Tyburn. With his own eyes he had seen their bruised bodies dragged forth from the Tower to their hurdles of pain. Should he stand firm as they in the gaunt shadow of the rack? Even the French Maid, he had heard, faltered for a time and, for a time, stood not firm when first they showed the engine of torment to her. He dreamed of nights, sometimes, that consent to the Oath would be extorted from his weak flesh by duress and hard handling. If it should come to that final pass, he prayed that God, of His free grace and through the prayers of his friends, would give him strength to stand fast as, in the end, had stood the Maid and the Fathers of the Charterhouse.

With a little sigh, he fell to writing again. Even faster now, for his sense of dreadful urgency was growing. It was going well, he thought, turning a page and pausing to scan his handiwork:

The Lord is my shepherd. I cannot fail. Christ speaks to me, His errant sheep: "Pluck up thy courage, faint heart. What though thou be fearful, sorry and weary, and standest in great dread of most painful torments? Be of good comfort. For I myself have vanquished the whole world, and yet felt I far more fear, sorrow, weariness, and much more inward anguish too, when I considered My most bitter, painful Passion to press so fast upon Me. He that is stronghearted may find a thousand glorious valiant martyrs whose ensample he may right joyously follow. But thou now, O timorous and weak, silly sheep, do thou think it sufficient for thee only to walk after Me, who am thy shepherd and governor, and so mistrust thyself, and put thy trust in Me. Take hold on the hem of My garment, therefore; from thence shalt thou perceive such strength and relief to proceed."

Thomas More lifted his head to listen. His ears had grown attuned, over the long months, to every whisper in the stone and every little chuckling ripple of water that lipped and lapped the Tower moat. But there was nothing. He fell to writing again, only to pause immediately and read aloud once more the last sentence his pen was destined ever to set down on paper:

"There were torches in the garden. They laid hands on Jesus."

The Tower, Evening, Late June, 1535

So. There *was* something after all. He had been right about the noises in the Tower a little back. Now there came a clashing sound of wards rasping in the keyholes, and a griding squeak as unoiled bolts were shot. The door to his cell opened. Master Secretary Cromwell, his thick-set figure muffled in a dark cloak, entered with a guard. The gray-faced prisoner, who did not rise to greet his unwelcome visitor, looked more essentially human, despite the squalor around him, than did the well-nourished toad in man's mantle who now confronted him. It suddenly occurred to Sir Edmund Walsingham, standing with a lantern in the corridor, that it was not the prisoner but his inquisitor who bore the ineradicable dungeon mark upon his brow.

"So," said Master Secretary Cromwell, strong distaste apparent on his clay-colored face, "we write again this evening. I should think, Master More, you would have had by now enough writing in your learned belly for two lifetimes. But, for the moment, let that pass. I have more important things to say to you. Master More, this may well be our last conversation. The King's patience has worn thin before your stubborn contumacy. He asks you plainly either to swear, or to utter your malignity so that all men may hear."

The man in the Tower sighed.

"I have no malignity, Master Cromwell," he said gently, "as I have told you many times before. Therefore I can utter none. I have always, from the beginning, truly used myself in his Majesty's service, looking first upon God and next upon the King, according to the lesson that His Highness himself taught me at my first coming into his noble service."

The toad mouth drew down at the corners, The toad hand threw back the cloak over one rounded shoulder.

"Have done," it spat, leaning toward the prisoner. "Have done with your perpetual paltering about God. Master More, till this day no man has charged you with cowardice. I charge you now with cowardice and with imbecility. You know what must be the end of all this, and soon, if you persist in your stubborn contumacy. Why, then, if you will not swear, will you not speak out unequivocally against the statute?"

Here was a new tack. Thomas More thought he knew what it meant. His captors had given up all idea of his recanting. Now they wanted no more than public confession of his guilt. His voice grew stronger.

"Master Secretary," he said, and now there was no quaver apparent in the sick man's tone. "You and certain others seem bent on my destruction. But I am like most men in that I do not rush gladly to death on the way. Let him come at his good time. Moreover, I have not been a man of such holy living as I might be bold to offer myself to death, lest God, for my presumption, might suffer me to fail."

The toad eyes did not blink. They stared balefully and fixedly at More; then, with no perceptible change of expression, turned, unwinking, to the guard.

"Remove his books and papers," said Cromwell. "There shall be no more writing or receiving of writings before the trial. Master More, the day therefor has been appointed. You shall be heard the first day of July. Till then, I wish you joy of your contumacy."

The guard gathered up the pen and ink, the books and the papers. Again the bolt was shot home. The echoing footsteps left the bastion to silence. Dazed, Thomas More looked about his cheerless cell, now emptier even than before. And it had been very empty before.

One more consolation was gone, then; another piece of harness hewn from him. Books were always, and from of old, among his best friends. Even the Scriptures were taken away now. But no one could take away their head and hero, Christ. And had not that patient angler for souls, my Lord of Rochester, John Fisher, said somewhere once that Christ on the Cross was like a book? He bent the sinews of his once peerless memory to recall when and where and how my Lord of Rochester had said it. It was hard, hard work. And he was tired unto death.

Wearily Thomas More's memory groped after pictures of the days he had spent in the company of Bishop Fisher. Pleasant days, most of them. Gradually, like beautifully colored miniatures in a Book of

Hours, the scenes grouped themselves again in his mind: riding on horseback together down green Kentish lanes; watching white sails on the Medway outside the windows of the Bishop's study in the great episcopal palace that, inside, was as austere as any fighting captain's tent in the field; the golden afternoon my Lord of Rochester, knowing his fondness for a jest, had told him of the punning inscription he had ordered engraved on his tomb: *Faciam vos fieri Piscatores hominum. I shall make you Fishers of men.* Bishop Fisher was a true Utopian. He saw no harm in a man's being half a giglot and more. He approved of honest mirth and honorable laughter, first agreed that man's chief comfort must be in God, and that with Him one must begin and with Him continue and with Him end as well. He did not mind, when talking of heaven, refreshing his friends and hearers with a merry foolish tale, knowing full well that, whatever heaven was, it was not heaviness. It was as strange as anything he knew to reflect on the fact that Bishop Fisher was his fellow prisoner now; in the Bell Tower which, like the Beauchamp Tower, was situate in the west ward of the great Tower of London. Never had they twain lived so close in life as they now dwelt side by side in the life-and-death of imprisonment; never seeing, never hearing one another; as far apart, in fact, as the distance separating the earth from the moon.

Yes, that had been a golden afternoon when Bishop Fisher had stamped himself a true Utopian with the jest about his tomb. The tomb was to have been in Rochester Cathedral—More's memory lit up with an altar lamp. What he was searching for had to do with Rochester Cathedral, too . . . a sermon, perhaps? Yes. It all came flooding back in a radiant surge of recollection. A sermon preached after Bishop Fisher's having been preferred to the See of Rochester by the King himself who, in better days, had been much taken by the holiness of his mother's, the Lady Margaret Beaufort's confessor. A Good Friday sermon on a text of Ezechiel: *Lamentationes, Carmen et Vae.* There! It was all stamped now, clear as a die, on his mind's eye and his mind's ear. He saw again the towering Yorkshireman in his pulpit; saw the large bones and great jaw and blue veins show-

ing everywhere under the tanned skin. Heard again the silvery voice
—so startlingly musical coming from so gaunt a frame:

> *But you marvel, peradventure, why I call the crucifix a book? The*
> *two boards of this book are the two parts of the Cross, for when the*
> *book is opened and spread, the leaves be couched upon the boards.*
> *And so the blessed body of Christ was spread upon the Cross.*
>
> *The leaves of this book be the arms, the hands, legs and feet, with*
> *the other members of His most precious and blessed body.*
>
> *Never any parchment skin was more straightly stretched upon the*
> *tentors than was this blessed body upon the Cross. And so they*
> *reared up this body aloft against the sun, even as a parchment skin is*
> *set forth before the heat of the sun to dry. It was set up aloft to the*
> *intent that all the world might look upon this book.*
>
> *This book was written within and without. First within was written*
> *but one word: the second Person in the Godhead, the son of God*
> *which by the Holy Ghost was written in the inward side of this parch-*
> *ment. For the Godhead of Christ was covered and hidden under the*
> *likeness of man. The Godhead was the inward side and the manhood*
> *was the outward side.*
>
> *Furthermore, when a book is spread, you see that in the leaves are*
> *many lines drawn. And many letters, some red, some black, and some*
> *blue. So in this book—the most blessed body of Christ—were drawn*
> *many lines, for it was all scourged with whips, so that everywhere the*
> *print of the cords of the scourges was left behind, and that in every*
> *place, from the neck downward unto the soles of His feet, so that there*
> *was no margin left in all this book. So that there was no void place in*
> *it anywhere to be seen. . . .*

The best book of all, then, no one could take away from him,
unless he so chose; and never would he so choose. It was written on
his heart and soul; on the baptismal bond; in the indentures of the
Eucharist. As for pen and paper, there was a coal lying in one corner,
and four corners to the cell he lived in. Poising the coal in his hand,
Thomas More thought back over the decades. What should he write
now with his pen of coal on his slate of stone? Thirty years before he
had written some verses for his *Book of Fortune.* Now that the last
page of that ill book lay open before him, it might be good sport

again to look upon those verses written when the world lay a ball at his feet, and springtime rioted in his veins. If he tried hard, he was sure he could recall them still. Slowly, haltingly, his lips moving over the remembered syllables, summoning back what had once been, Thomas More scrawled on one wall those lines so faroff in time and space and mood they might almost have been written by another person. Nevertheless, however altered his face and gait, he was still the same person he had been. Even as he wrote the lines, he recited them to himself:

> *"But, an thou wilt needs meddle with Her treasure,*
> *Trust not herein, and spend it liberally.*
> *Bear thee not proud, nor take not out of measure,*
> *Build not thine house on height up to the sky.*
> *None falleth far, but he that climbeth high.*
> *Remember, Nature sent thee hither bare.*
> *The gifts of Fortune—count them borrowed ware.*
> *The head that late lay easily and full soft,*
> *Instead of pillows, lieth after on the—"*

He paused, and repeated this last incomplete line, completing it in the process:

> *"Instead of pillows, lieth after on the block."*

Now there was a pretty mawmet for his pastime! He feared, though, there was something awry with the final rhyme. But the meaning fitted all the better, perhaps, for the imperfection. In that way his verse was like life. His life, at least. He had climbed high and fallen far. But he had climbed high against his will, and fallen far with his own free consent. So it was well. If he lost, he won. Strumpet Fortune's wheel had come full circle, and he was on the bottom now. Another revolution,, and she would fling him off into the abyss. It was still well. All men played at dice with her, and all men lost in the end. He, poor fool, had needs challenge her to chess, the King's game; and she had won there, too. He was checkmate now. But still he won. And he had even one Utopian weapon left: the lance of laughter. If sometimes Fortune smiled, she never laughed.

Laughter was left to Utopians. He would checkmate her with his chalk.

Snail-slow, again pausing to read each line aloud, Thomas More drew on the wall a new and final stanza with his coal:

> *"Eye-flattering Fortune, look Thou never so fair,*
> *Nor never so pleasantly begin to smile,*
> *As though Thou wouldst my ruin all repair,*
> *During my life Thou shalt not me beguile.*
> *Trust shall I God, to enter in a while*
> *His haven of Heaven, sure and uniform;*
> *Ever after Thy calm look I for a storm."*

The coal fell from More's listless hand. Nodding a little, he stretched out on the bench. But sleep would not come. Instead, other echoes and other images of the past came thronging into the little cell. Thomas More may have thought he had done with the past. The past had not yet done with him. Jane Colt's demure and winsome presence was in the room. Old tunes sang in his head; old words. Words of those contrapuntal stanzas on divine and human love he had affixed, in his distant youth, to his translation of Pico, Count of Mirandola. Coughing a bit—for a miasma was rising from the moat now in the night damp—he began to hum what few verses he could remember. Two of the stanzas, he called to mind, Henry Patenson had liked to sing. He used to say they went with the mood of that lovely ballad, *Greensleeves.* Sadly, reedily, for the man in the Tower had never sung well at best—Erasmus and Bishop du Bellay used to jest with him over his tuneless voice—the words of his youth hung on the air a moment, and were gone:

> *"If love be strong, hot, mighty, and fervent,*
> *There may no trouble, grief, or sorrow fall*
> *But that the lover would be well content*
> *All to endure, and think it eke too small,*
> *Though it were death, so he might therewithal*
> *The joyful presence of that person get*
> *On whom he hath his heart and love yset.*

The Tower, Evening, Late June, 1535

"Thus should of God the lover be content
Any distress or sorrow to endure,
Rather than be from God his love absent,
And glad to die, so that he may be sure,
By his departing hence, for to procure
After this valley dark the heavenly light,
And of his love the glorious blessed sight."

After this valley dark the heavenly light. But first the valley dark. It was the law of life. No lover could be exempt from that immutable law. Not Tristram of Lyonesse. Not More of Chelsea. Not Alice Middleton. Little Jane Colt was happier than they. She alone of them had passed through the dark valley. She only had her heart's desire. The drowsing man in the Tower sleepily wondered why his thoughts ran so this night on the little maid he had wed so long ago, and had called in fun *uxorcula Mori.*

Suddenly Thomas More sat bolt upright. The sliding bar rattled in its slot. The wards clashed. Sir Edmund Walsingham was inside the cell again, dazzling his prisoner's eyes with the white hot light of his lantern. And Jane Colt was with him! It was impossible! But it was true! After so many years of separation in the grave he saw again the little wife of his bosom!

"Father!" said Margaret Roper almost in a scream.

Thomas More stared, unseeing, at his daughter. Then, suddenly, he understood. It was not Jane Colt at all. It was his and her daughter, Margaret. Only Meg had grown to look so like her mother! He put out his arms to her.

"Father!" said Margaret Roper, embracing him. "You are grown pale and old! Do they mistreat you here?"

Gently Thomas More disengaged himself from her loving grasp, almost as if girding himself for the combat that must now take place between them. For combat it would be; and he feared it would be hard. But he would win this reluctant war with Meg, even as he would win his other war with Cromwell and the King.

"There are, Meg," he said, "two answers to your question. Speaking as a citizen of the realm, a Judge and a man of law, I may tell you that they who have committed me hither, for refusing of an Oath, are not by their own law able to justify my wrongful imprisonment. And surely, daughter, it is great pity that any Christian Prince should, by a flexible Council ready to follow his whims and desires, and by a weak clergy lacking grace to stand steadfast constant in their clerisy, with flattery be so shamefully abused.

"But, speaking as a Christian soul, Meg, and one no longer young in years, I have an altogether different answer. I believe, daughter, that they that have put me here think they have done me a high displeasure. They wrong me as a citizen and a free Englishman, it is true. But I assure you on your father's faith, my good daughter, Meg, if it were not for my wife and you, my children, whom I account the chief part of my charge on earth, I would not have failed, long before this, to have shut myself up, of my own free will, in as strait and narrow a room as this—and a straiter and narrower one, too, for that matter. But since I am come hither not of my own deserts, I trust that God of His great goodness will discharge me of my care, and with His gracious help supply my lack among you. For myself alone, I thank God, Meg, I find no cause to reckon myself in worse case here than in mine own house. It seems almost as if God makes me His wanton, and sets me on His lap, and dandles me, as a child her moppet."

Margaret Roper wrung her hands in anguish. She had not come to the Tower this night for long legal lectures. She was patient, beyond most women, in the face of male unaccountableness. But something purely feminine rose now from the depths of her innocent and tractable nature in mute protest against this masculine futility of her father. Men were so maddening; and her father, for all his excellence and nobility of heart and mind, was, in the end, no more than a man and, as such, a slave of illusion. That mistress of reality, who is woman, sat now, in Margaret Roper's soul, in judgment on her judge father, and condemned him to freedom. Freedom from his scruples, his ideals, his fantastic *points d'honneur.*

"Father! Father!" she moaned. "You must take the Oath at once.

Even now there is scarce time for that. They killed my Lord of Rochester two days ago. His head is stuck on London Bridge."

"So," said Thomas More, infinite sadness in his voice. "So Bishop Fisher is gone to his reward. I knew long since it must come to that with him. You saw him on the scaffold, Meg?"

"I scarcely knew him," said Margaret Roper, "so had he changed in prison. When last I saw him he was a slender, seemly person, tall, and of regal carriage. He stood there before the people, skin and bones, his flesh consumed. Death in a man's shape and using a man's voice. Father, you must sign at once! Subscribe your hand!"

"What, daughter Meg!" said More playfully, and his daughter's heart sank at the affectionate levity in his tone. Never had she or any other woman pierced man's armor of lightsome levity. "You, even you, a Mistress Eve, like all women, to play the serpent with a man? Margaret, we have been over this ground more than once, you and I. In the old days in Chelsea it did not take you thus long to get by heart a simple lesson. More than once have I answered you that, in this matter, if it were possible for me in conscience to do the thing that might content the King's Grace, and God therewith not offended, then no man would more gladly have taken the Oath than I."

"But," Margaret Roper argued hopelessly, "other good men have taken it. Why not you?"

"Meg, Meg," said Thomas More, and there was a ring of authority in his voice now. "Have done. I meddle not with the conscience of any man who has sworn. I take it not upon me to be their judge. But I may not swear."

It was Margaret Roper, not her father, who looked old and tired now.

"Father," she said, wearily sinking on to his bench, "you did not use to be so stubborn. Why may you not swear?"

More sighed. Here was the old impasse come up again—with Meg as well as with Cromwell.

"That question, too," he told her, "I have answered you more than once. The reason why I may not swear lies between me and my heavenly King, on the one hand; and between me and my earthly ruler, on the other. I have promised Henry never to reveal the reason, neither to you, nor to anyone else, unless the King's Highness should himself see fit to command me thereto. Or, unless at the very end, when naught is to gain but Paradise and naught to lose but my immortal soul, I may think it my duty to speak out, and no disservice to the King. But not till then, Meg. Not till the very end. And, if the King keep faith with me, never."

"The King will not keep faith, Father," said Margaret Roper. "You know that now."

She was silent for an instant. Then, passionately:

"But those who have sworn are so many, and those who have refused so few—yourself, Bishop Fisher, the Charterhouse Fathers, Sebastian Newdigate. And, except for these, no one else in all the Kingdom."

"Friend Newdigate, too?" asked Thomas More. "I did not know."

Sebastian Newdigate, brother of Lady Dormer, and monk of the Charterhouse, was an old tilt-yard companion of Henry's whose friends had been appalled at his decision to become a monk because, as his sister indignantly told Prior Houghton, he could not eat fish without vomiting. But he, too, in the day of his trial, had held firm against that greatest of fishes, Leviathan. Thomas More said a short prayer for the soul of Sebastian Newdigate, knight, courtier, chivalric lover, and priest of God.

Margaret Roper uttered a tiny scream of anguish. She beat her palms together.

"Take the Oath!" she cried. "Take the Oath, Father! Time runs out apace. It may already be too late to change."

Thomas More stroked her hair.

"It is already too late to change, Margaret," he said very gently. "Master Secretary Cromwell and the King have appointed me to stand public trial on the first day of July. But I thank God, my Meg, that it is now too late. Had I ever made such a change as you have wished, it would have been too late indeed by all eternity. Such a change would have come only from fear, and well I know that would have been but evil medicine for my sick soul. But now the field is won at last. Never trouble your mind more, my own good daughter, for anything now that can hap me in this world. Nothing can come now, but what God will. Are you not glad of that, Meg? Pray to God for me, and with a will, but trouble yourself no more. Even so shall I full heartily pray for us all, that we may meet together again in Heaven, where we shall make merry forever, you and I, and Jane, your dear mother, and son Roper, and Mistress Alice, and son John, and all the family, whom we dearly love, and Mistress Alice's monkey."

Tears ran down Margaret Roper's cheeks. For months she had held back grief in her father's presence. Now the floodgates were unloosed; and she no longer had the strength to care.

"Father," she said sobbing. "I cannot help it, but I cannot laugh."

"Perhaps not, Meg," More said compassionately. "It is often harder to laugh than to cry. And crying has its uses, too. Have your good cry out, Meg. And, when you are done, you can do me one last welcome service—if, that is, you have brought housewife's pen and ink along with the pins and scissors in your girdle. I have two letters to write before I come to trial, and today Master Cromwell gave order that my pen and paper be taken from me."

Still weeping, Margaret Roper sat down at her father's table. More continued to stroke her hair for some minutes. Then, striding up and down, his gait and bearing seemingly stronger, he began to dictate.

"The first letter," he said, "shall be to you, Meg, and, through you, to all the family. I can write things today I cannot say; and you, I have no doubt, read things it would unman you to hear. So, Mistress Secretary, the best man ever had—for the last time:

"Our Lord bless you, good daughter, and your good husband, and your little boy, and all yours, and all my children, and all my god-children, and all our friends. Recommend me when ye may to my good daughter, Cicely, whom I beseech our Lord to comfort. And I send her my blessing, and to all her children, and pray her to pray for me. I send her a handkerchief. And God comfort my good son, her husband.

"I cumber you, good Margaret, much, but I would be sorry it should be any longer than this day week. For then it will be the even of St. Thomas of Canterbury and the Utas of St. Peter. It is on that day I long to go to God. It were a day very meet and convenient for me.

"I never liked your manner toward me, Meg, better than when you kissed me last, which was but a little while ago. For I love it when daughterly love and dear charity has no leisure to look to ceremony and worldly courtesy. Farewell, my dear child, and pray for me, and I shall for you and all your friends, that we may merrily meet in Heaven.

"I send now to my good daughter Clement her algorism stone, and I send her and my godson, and all hers, God's blessing and mine. I pray you at time convenient recommend me to my good son, John More. Our Lord bless him and his good wife, my loving daughter, to whom I pray him be good, as he hath great cause. And I pray him, also, that if my land come to his hand, he break not my will concerning his sister, Dauncey. And our Lord bless Thomas and Austen and all that they shall have. And Alice, my beloved wife, whom I have loved these many years."

Thomas More fell silent. Margaret's pen stopped scratching. She began to sob aloud; great wrenching, convulsive sobs. Her father laid a protecting hand on her shoulder.

"Meg, Meg," he said brokenly. "But a moment more, and I am done. The second letter will be shorter."

Margaret Roper looked at him distractedly.

"The King," she said in sudden fierceness, "is evil as the Great Turk, and his false Queen is worse."

"Nay, Meg, hush," said More, soothing her. "Speak not against the King. Nor too much against the Turk, either. Is it wisdom to think so much upon the Turk that we forget the devil?"

"Then," said Margaret Roper, "I hate the Queen. She is a false Queen. Queen Catherine is my Queen."

"I repent me," said Thomas More, "I asked not earlier after Queen Anne. How is her health, Meg?"

"Never better, in faith," said Margaret Roper bitterly. "The evil thrive. Master Secretary Cromwell, too, waxes fat and sleek as a paddock, while you pine and peak here in the dark."

"Never better!" said More. "Alas, Meg! Alas! It pities me to think into what misery, poor soul, she shall shortly come. But to our letter. It is to Messire Antonio Bonvisi, gentleman mercer and scholar, in whose house I have been, almost these forty years now, not a guest, but a continual nursling."

Antonio Bonvisi, a "dry merry man," as Thomas More had once called him, was a merchant of Lucca resident in London, who in 1524, had bought the lease of Crosby Place from More. Since More's imprisonment in the Tower the faithful Italian had been his last link with the Europe he loved.

"So, Meg," said More. "We start again:

"Messire.

"I greet, through you, the Europe and the Christendom we both have loved so well. Will you greet for me, when you have occasion, Signor Luis Vives of Madrid, Peter Giles of Antwerp, Monsiegneur du Bellay, Cardinal of France, and, most especially, Desiderius Erasmus of Rotterdam, who has always been my darling? Bid them all: *Memento Mori*. Remember More, as he will also remember you, his friends, in that fair city, where we shall need no letters to pass between us, where no wall shall evermore dissever us, where no porter shall keep us from talking together, and where we shall have the fruition of the eternal joy with God the Father, and with His only begotten Son, our Redeemer, Jesu Christ, with the Holy Spirit of Them both, and the Holy Ghost proceeding from Them both.

"And, in the mean season, Almighty God grant both you and me, good Master Bonvisi, and all mortal men everywhere, to set at naught all the riches of this world, with all the glory of it, and the pleasure of this life also, for the love and desire of that joy. Thus, together with my Erasmus, of all friends most trusty, and to me most dearly beloved, and as I was wont to call you twain the apples of my eye, right heartily fare ye well. And Jesu Christ, friend Bonvisi, keep safe and sound and in good health all your family, which is as dear to me and me to it as their master is.

Thomas More

"I should in vain append, 'Yours,' for thereof can you not be ignorant, since you have bought that poor signature with so many

benefits, the second last of which, the French wine and the jelly, I
sent to Bishop Fisher the night before—though I did not know it then—
he died; and the last of which, the silk camlet gown, I wear now to
my death. It is a comely and a costly shroud, for which I thank you
heartily. Yours then, dear Messire, though I am no longer such a one
that it much matters whose I am."

More came softly up behind Margaret and kissed her on the
forehead.

"There, my Meg," he said tenderly, "you may lay down your pen.
I have taken farewell of those I love and have loved well in life. You.
My family. My friends. Music, letters, learning. My England. And my
Europe."

Almost beside herself with grief, Margaret Roper rocked back and
forth on the wooden bench.

"Father, Father!" she cried. "Why must you die?"

More drew his daughter to him.

"All men must die, my Margaret," he said. "Sooner or later we all
come to it. Why do I die betimes? Of late the face of Christ hath
dominion over my heart. You would die for husband Roper. Husband
Roper would die for England against the French or Spanish. Maybe
there was a time when Henry would have died for Catherine. Catherine, I think, would still die for Henry. And Anne for the baby Elizabeth. Those of us who are lucky die for love, Meg. Why do I die
betimes? I am one of the lucky ones. I, too, die for love!"

The great bell of the Tower struck eleven. Its deep toll was like a
death knell. When Margaret Roper came forth from the Tower, for
the last time, in addition to the letters, she carried, under her cloak,
a small parcel containing her father's hair shirt and the discipline
he used in secret on Fridays. Sir Edmund saw the pitiful little bun-
dle, but did not inquire into its contents. Whatever it was, he was
sure it had naught to do with treason. And, whatever it was, it could
not make much difference now—now that the day of trial was finally
appointed.

The Tower, Evening, Late June, 1535

"The conflict is over now," Thomas More had said to Margaret when he gave her the instruments of penance. "So I lay down my arms and send back my weapons." Between them, Messire Machiavelli and Master Cromwell had slain the last of chivalry. But, like Roland on the field of Roncesvaux, a knight of Chelsea, he of the Moor's head and the unicorns, still knew how to give back his glove to God.

CHAPTER XIX

STRANGE FASHION OF FORSAKING:

Greenwich, Night, Late June, 1535

Sir Thomas Wyatt had long been out of favor at Court; but his songs would never be out of favor so long as Queen Anne kept in her entourage connoisseurs like Mark Smeaton, her personal dancer and musician, who had been at Court now these three years and who, though, perforce, he still signed his name *sine nobilitate,* found himself comfortably enough fed and lodged in payment for his artistic talents. Smeaton thought Master Wyatt's muse improved year by year. Take this latest ballet of his making now. Its strange cadences and unaccountable broken rhythms lent themselves perfectly to the haunting ruminations of the recorder on which Master Smeaton specialized. Pensively he sang it then to the liquid accompaniment of his flageolet in the perfumed languorous darkness of Queen Anne's yellow-hung private closet. Even as he began to sing, the Queen came in, in ornate deshabille, carrying a massive candlestick in one gloved hand. No one but Henry saw the Queen without her gloves, though all the world and his brother might on occasion—and now was one of these occasions—stare his fill at half-draped bosom and shoulders. Smeaton's voice was perfectly attuned to the aqueous melody of his instrument and the wild longing of his song. The Queen watched him closely as he sang.

Strange Fashion of Forsaking

"They flee from me that sometime did me seek
With naked foot stalking in my chamber.
I have seen them gentle, tame and meek
That now are wild and do not remember
That sometime they put themselves in danger
To take bread at my hand; and now they range
Busily seeking with a continual change.

"Thanked be fortune, it hath been otherwise
Twenty times better; but once in special,
In thine array after a pleasant guise,
When her loose gown from her shoulders did fall,
And she me caught in her arms long and small;
Therewithal sweetly did me kiss,
And softly said, dear heart, how like you this?

"It was no dream: I lay broad waking.
But all is turned through my gentleness
Into a strange fashion of forsaking;
And I have leave to go of her goodness,
And she also to use newfangleness.
But since that I so kindly am served,
I would fain know what she hath deserved."

The warbling sighs of the flageolet faded away into silence. Queen Anne took her fingers from their place alongside her head.

"Another of Master Wyatt's, sirrah?" she asked Smeaton softly, the spell of the strange lines still powerful upon her. "I like it well. I like especially well the music of *strange fashion of forsaking*. It fits the lot of lovers, Master Smeaton, as you will one day learn, if you live long enough. But it is very late now. Get you to your bed, lad."

As Mark Smeaton went out the door, he met Master Secretary Cromwell, cloaked, coming in. A French clock was just striking the hour of eleven, one silvery ping succeeding another in rapid and precise succession.

"A dark night, Master Secretary," said the Queen, setting down

335

her candlestick on a credence table Queen Catherine had long ago brought from Spain in the faroff days when she first came to England to be the bride of young Prince Arthur. "Moonless. Not a star in the sky. What took place at the Tower this evening?"

Cromwell flung back his cloak. He found it close in the airless yellow room, with the perfume, and the flowers, and the disturbing presence of the Queen in her careless undress.

"What we expected, Your Grace," he said as casually as he could. "He refused to take the Oath."

Anne Boleyn smiled her cruel catlike smile.

"For the last time?" she asked, her small white teeth showing between her lips, as if in anticipation.

Cromwell looked at the Queen a little uneasily. One would not call Master Secretary the most fastidious of men. But, of late, the Queen almost daunted him.

"For the last time," he said, "unless—but that rests with you, my Queen."

"What rests with me, Master Secretary?" she asked him bluntly.

"The other Commissioners," he explained, "Audley and Cranmer, and the Dukes of Norfolk and Suffolk as well—my Lord of Norfolk has always been friendly to Sir Thomas, as his niece well knows—would qualify the Oath for him, as was done for the Commons, and for certain others of those swearing from among the laity. But for none of the clergy. Sir Thomas would then be asked to subscribe to the Oath of Supremacy with this formal exception noted:*As far as it would stand with the law of God.*"

The green eyes measured him appraisingly.

"Do you think," asked the Queen, "that Master More would swear the Oath under this guise of wording?"

"I know he would, Your Grace," said Cromwell with utter confidence. "He loves Henry more than enough for that. And the qualification leaves his conscience clear enough."

"Then," said the Queen drawing in her breath sharply, as if in fear, "he must not be offered the chance. Master More must die."

Of a sudden a nerve began to twitch in one of Master Secretary's plump cheeks. It kept on jumping throughout the rest of their interview together.

"Sometimes, my Queen," he said, speaking very low, "I fear you go too far. The King did love this man once."

"I know he did," said the Queen, grimacing, and Master Secretary found her grimace almost intolerable to bear. "It is but one more reason why I hate Master More the more."

Then Cromwell shrugged.

"You will square it with the King?" he asked, drawing on his cloak again.

"I will square it with the King," said the Queen, the strange smile on her face. "Never fear."

A flourish of trumpets sounded some corridors away. Startled, Anne took Cromwell by the sleeve and gestured to him to go quickly. Ever since the birth of the Princess Elizabeth the King's temper had been unpredictable. Cromwell knew it as well as she. He left at once a moment before Henry, taking leave of Suffolk and Francis Bryan, came in by the opposite door. Quite obviously more than a little the worse for drink, the King lurched a trifle when he walked. There was a dark winestain on the rich yellow of his banquet dress. At first he did not see the Queen in the musk-scented darkness, lit only by the single candle. Timorously, almost placatingly, she called softly to him.

"Henry!" she said.

And again:

"Henry!"

Henry Tudor stood stock still. So the Minotaur might have stood at midnight in his Cretan maze, snuffling the air for maiden flesh.

"Eh?" he said stupidly.

"It is past your bed hour," said the Queen.

It was a misstep. The King liked to repose on the strength of others well enough. But, at the same time, he did not like the uncomfortable sensation of dependency; of being led. The royal bull wanted to feel no ring in his nose. Besides, this woman in the night rail, this half-naked wench, whom he now recognized as his wife, was becoming troublesome to him in more ways than one. She got at him nowadays, and worried him worse, even, than the barren Spanish woman he had cast off for her.

Suddenly a stupefying thought inserted itself into the winy labyrinth of the King's mind. His new wife was a barren woman, too. As barren as his first one. No more, no less. They both had borne him daughters. Where was the son God owed him? Where was the son a man had a right to? Where was the boy he wanted? Where was the golden lad England needed, if the succession was to remain stable and the land stay secure? Was it for this unprofitable end he had huddled Cranmer into his uncanonical miter, blackmailed the clergy of the realm, risked excommunication from the Papacy whose staunch champion he had been beyond all other Kings of history, destroyed the monasteries, and defied the Emperor, his first wife's nephew, and the other Christian Princes of Europe? Was it for this he had sent John Fisher to the block—John Fisher, his sainted mother's holy chaplain? And just now sealed the death warrant of his old friend, Sir Thomas More? That was why he was drunk so often nowadays. He had to drink the day he sent a friend to death. And he seemed to be sending so many friends to death these days. Fisher; Newdigate; now More. It was all this woman's fault. She it was who wanted More to die. He did not want More to die, though things had gone so far now that necessity dictated More should die. He did not want More to die. Nevertheless, More had to die. The woman was an evil witch who had overlooked him in the two central sources of his being: in the creative powers of his bed; and at the Council table.

Henry found himself remembering the dark stories he had laughed at, in the first hot flush of his infatuation—that was part of the enchantment, he supposed now—stories of philters and love potions. *Jesu!* What if this green-eyed bitch had practiced sorcery upon him! Perhaps this was why God, who tolerated not abomination in high places, had opened her womb, like the Spanish woman's before her, only for female children. The Bible forbade witchcraft every bit as much as incest. What if he lay nightly with a witch? Was it not draining his energy of late, even as, in the latter years, Catherine had drained him? Almost with a crawling of his gross flesh, the King looked at the Queen's white breast, half exposed as it was in her filmy negligée. She was a wanton. Mistress Seymour, he would go bond for it, would not appear thus even before her husband. It was strangely exciting to think of the cool allure of Mistress Seymour. As the King remembered the way Mistress Seymour demurely moved under her full farthingale, his bull's reins stirred with an old familiar stirring. He looked again at the Queen; and his dislike was humiliatingly, terrifyingly apparent.

"I have been in Council," he said thickly, swaying on his heavy pillared legs.

"And what," asked the Queen, "of Master More?"

Henry looked at her out of bloodshot, wicked little eyes.

"He has refused again," he said. "The Council appoints his trial for the first day of July."

"And if he is found guilty?" asked the Queen, smiling, excitement in her voice.

The King did not like her smile; nor yet the excitement in her voice.

"He shall die," he said shortly. "And he shall be found guilty. Make no mistake about that."

Anne Boleyn laid her long gloved hand on his arm.

"How is Master More to die, Henry?" she whispered, biting his ear lightly with her little teeth.

For a moment he did not understand.

"Eh?" he asked dully, confused.

Then her meaning took him with a rush; and revulsion with it. He looked on her, aghast.

"How is Master More to die, Henry?" she asked, louder, nibbling his ear till the blood came. "Like the foul traitor he is? By hanging, drawing, and quartering?"

The King lurched toward her with a low, growling, animal noise deep down in his throat. He wrested the candlestick from her terrified hand and held it up before her white neck and breast. Then, with his free hand, he struck the Queen heavily across the face.

"Faugh!" he said, breathing hard. "You are the cause of this just man's death. He was my friend once. Perhaps, were it not for you, he would be my friend still. I do not have friends any more. Get to my bed, you Howard trull!"

The Queen lay where she had fallen, never moving, her dressing gown pulled away from her white body. When she did not stir, slowly, deliberately, the King kicked her. Then, with a cry, she got to her feet and scurried away in terror. Henry looked at the candle in his hand. He blew it out and cast it to the floor with a ringing clangor of heavy silver on stone. Then, in the smoky darkness, he threw back his head. Proudly, regally, bull-like always now.

"Sir Thomas," he said aloud, "shall die a clean death. By beheading."

CHAPTER XX

THE KING'S GOOD SERVANT:

Westminster Hall, Afternoon, July 1, 1535

THEY had taken John Fisher from the Tower to Westminster Hall by water lest, walking, he faint on the way and die; and the King's vengeance be thus cheated. But Thomas More, white-haired, gray-faced, long-bearded, leaning on a staff, his eyes blinking painfully in the blinding sunlight of July, was able to stumble through the streets, flanked by his escort of halberdiers, while the silent London throngs watched, pitying, the broken progress of their old Chancellor. As in the case of Fisher he was indicted under the Act of Supremacy rather than under the Act of Succession. The indictment, setting forth his offenses and misprisions, was of inordinate length. Standing in the well of the court, the Clerk of the court, in his strongly accented Latin, had droned it out sentence by sentence, article after article, till my Lord Audley, his robes heavy on his perspiring back, nodded on his hot Justice's bench, fancying some great bluebottle fly had gotten stuck in his inkwell and buzzed and buzzed and buzzed. The prisoner never took his eyes off the Clerk. It was strange how twelve months of imprisonment altered one's perspective, physical as well as moral. His eyes had difficulty adjusting themselves to the normal values of horizon and river and walls uncircumscribed. Everyone and everything seemed so miniature and far away; so tiny and, as it were, so unimportant. He rubbed his eyes more than once to help keep them in focus. It was of the utmost importance now that he see and hear what was going on. His life no longer depended on it, it was true. But what of that? His honor? He thought he was long past considerations of mere honor. But the truth! And his integrity as a Christian soul!

When one took away all the sonorous Latin formulae and all the old Law French, the charge More had to face was a dual one: that, after promising not to "meddle with such matters," he had thereupon, publicly and before witnesses, denied the Supremacy; and that, by letters exchanged between them, he and the executed traitor, John Fisher, clerk, had been confederates in this same treason. Both charges were patently false, of course. Not even to Meg had he declared his inner mind. But the cry was up. The hounds, baying in full voice, would be in at the kill. And he was the quarry marked down for their sharp teeth.

Now, as, with a winding of trumpets, the heralds declared the recess at an end and the great Hall began to fill again, Thomas More looked about him. Things were not so scarlet splendid as they had been at Blackfriars' first legatine hearing on the King's great matter. Then Cardinals Campeggio and Wolsey had sat in their crimson robes, and Henry and Catherine under their regal canopies. No churchman sat on this present bench of Oyer and Terminer for Middlesex, only the great lay lords, all of whom were now his enemies, plighted to his death, including even Norfolk who must, perforce, turn a face of marble on their previous intimacy. Well, he knew the rules of the game. He would not embarrass his old friend, my Lord of Norfolk. He would do his duty, and leave my Lord of Norfolk to his own.

Nor would he show any rancor or hostility to the twelve good men and true, who were this day his jury panel, recruited from the London inhabitants who dwelt within the liberties of the Tower. Whether they knew it or not, sitting in their docile rows, they were the emblems and champions of the English Common Law. The Common Law which he had one day administered within this very Hall of Westminster was a glorious thing; a great good English thing.

Omnipotence could have no fellowship with freedom; unless it were the omnipotence of a just and merciful deity. But royal omnipotence could not co-exist with the Common Law. The *lex regia* of the Civil Law aided and abetted the King's arrogation unto himself of omnipotence. It was no friend of the people's. The Common Law was. The Common Law was a broad shield of popular liberty, not an implement of government. The Common Law called the nation into consultation on the affairs of the nation. More remembered with affection how, in the century before his, blunt Sir John Fortescue had spoken up for the Common over the Civil Law:

> The King of England is not able to change his laws of his own sweet will. He does not rule his people with a regal rulership only, but with a rulership that is political also.

The City, then, was greater than any one man—even the man to whom the gods gave to rule the City. More found himself remembering Haemon in *Antigone*: *That is no City which belongs to one man*. Rome had, for a time, changed all that: the Rome of the Caesars. But Thomas More had always preferred the lucid Athens of Pericles to the heavy Rome of Augustus. Today's proceedings were, he knew, a tragic Roman farce. The *lex regia* prevailed; and the twelve jurors from within the liberties of the Tower were but a cruel masque intended to lend an English flavor to the inquisitorial transactions now going on. But it was an interlude merely. The tired man in the prisoner's dock felt confident the Common Law would one day resume its hard-bitten, canny, tolerant, reasonable—but not ultra-reasonable; the human personality was something more than reason—sway.

The Crier called aloud the names of the jurors, and each of the twelve men replied as he took the place appointed for him.

"Thomas Palmer, Knight!"

"Thomas Spert, Knight!"

"Gregory Lovell, Squire!"

"Thomas Burbage, Squire!"

"William Brown, Squire!"

"Jasper Leyke, Squire!"

"Thomas Byllington, Squire!"

"John Parnell, Gentleman!"

"Geoffrey Chamber, Gentleman!"

"Edward Stokewod, Gentleman!"

"Richard Bellamy, Gentleman!"

"George Stokys, Gentleman!"

The Court of King's Bench rose respectfully to its feet as the Judges entered in their gorgeous robes to take their set places on the raised dais. The Crier called the great names aloud, one by one:

"My Lord Chancellor Audley!"

"His Grace, the Duke of Norfolk!"

"His Grace, the Duke of Suffolk!"

"The Earl of Huntingdon!"

"The Earl of Wiltshire!"

"The Earl of Cumberland!"

"My Lord Montague!"

"My Lord Rochford!"

"My Lord Windsor!"

"Master Secretary Cromwell!"

"Sir John Baldwin!"

"Sir Richard Lister!"

"Sir William Paulet!"

"Sir John Porte!"

"Sir John Spellman!"

"Sir Walter Luke!"

"Sir William Fitz-William!"

"Sir Anthony Fitz-Herbert!"

The Lord Chief Justice had not entered yet. While the court awaited his entry, restive in the summer heat, conversation became general throughout the great Hall. At the entrance the same two men-at-arms, who used to keep the door for Thomas More when he was still my Lord Chancellor More, conversed together with pitying but cynical discretion.

"Poor Sir Thomas!" said red-thatch, his face as stiff as if he were not exchanging a single word with his fellow. "I greatly fear me it is but short shrift for our old Chancellor now."

"How so?" asked the shorter guard, never moving a muscle in his own impassive turn.

"It is a hanging court,'" said red-thatch out of the corner of his mouth. "See who sits below the Chief Justice. His Grace of Wiltshire, Queen Anne's father. My Lord of Rochford, Queen Anne's brother. What verdict do they want, do you think?"

The self-same thought was just passing through Thomas More's mind as he gazed on the faces of these two of his judges. On the reckless, dissolute, dangerous face of Viscount Rochford; sportsman, poet, duelist, and no indifferent statesman. On His Grace of Wiltshire; suave, weak, irresolute, time-serving, clever; the Mammon of iniquity in the robes of a Judge. On Sir John Baldwin, Chief Justice of the Common Pleas, and Sir Richard Lister, Chief Baron of the Exchequer. Able jurists both; but they would not count in the final verdict. They were included here for no other reason than to give a smack of legality to the sorry proceedings. On Master Secretary Cromwell. But he had seen enough of late of Master Secretary Cromwell. Thomas More turned his eyes away.

At last the Crier announced the entry of the Lord Chief Justice:

"My Lord Chief Justice, Sir John Fitz-James!"

After the Lord Chief Justice had seated himself on the top tier of the Justices' dais, with Master Secretary Cromwell and the two Boleyns, father and son, immediately beneath him, Chancellor Audley, speaking for the King, arose and addressed himself directly to the prisoner. Despite the excessive sultriness of the day, my Lord Audley, cool, composed, bland as ever, spoke with his usual impersonal suavity.

"Sir Thomas More," said my Lord Audley, while the dust motes spun about in a sun shaft just above his head, "before we recessed you heard the several heads of the indictment against you. It is a dreadful charge under whose shadow you now stand. And, if you are found guilty, the penalty that awaits you, as well you know, is a traitor's death. Now we are old friends in the law, you and I. You need not fence against me; and I need not fence against you. You may, then, shorten your disagreeable task and mine by pleading guilty. Or, if you will only choose to put aside your stubborn malignity for but a moment, there is still a last chance of pardon."

My Lord Audley cleared his throat and, raising his handsome head, looked round the great Hall a space before he resumed.

"Sir Thomas," he said impressively, "you have heinously offended against the King's majesty. Nevertheless, such is his great bounty, benignity, and clemency, we are here in very good hope that, if you will but revoke and reform your willful, obstinate opinion that you have so wrongfully maintained, and so long dwelt in, you may yet taste of his gracious pardon. And perhaps—who knows?— of his gracious favor once again."

While Audley's rounded periods rose and fell, Thomas More had risen unsteadily to his feet. One might see, for the first time, how pale his face was; and how straggly the great beard he had grown in prison. He leaned upon his staff. But that slight support was not enough. He stumbled, at intervals, and caught himself against the edge of the dock. He looked at the bench of Justices. My Lord Audley's speech had been mild enough in all conscience. But it meant no more than this: the honey first. And after, if the honey did not catch the fly's feet, the gall. Well, when all was said and done, it was no harder to reject honey than gall.

"My Lords," said Thomas More, faltering at first, but his voice gradually recapturing its old Parliamentary resonance, "I do most humbly thank your Honors of your great good will toward me. But I must once again refuse your gracious offer so often and so kindly proffered me. I make this my boon and petition unto God as heartily as I may, that He will vouchsafe to nourish, maintain, and uphold in me, even to the last hour and extreme moment that ever I shall live, this my present good, honest, and upright mind, and fixed intention to persist on the road I am going. Concerning now the matters you charge and challenge me withal, the articles are so prolix and long and many that I fear, what for my long imprisonment, what for my long lingering illness, what for my present weakness and debility, that neither my wit, nor my memory, nor yet my voice will serve to make so full, so effectual, and sufficient answer as the weight and importance of these great matters crave."

The great Hall whirled round him suddenly, and the floor came up to meet him. He staggered and almost fell. My Lord Audley, a look of pity on his classic features, nodded to a Sergeant who brought forward a chair. The prisoner sat down.

"Thank you, my Lords," said Thomas More, breathing deeply till the awful nausea retreated again. "Perhaps I may repay favor for favor, mercy for mercy, by making my defense as short as is consonant with clarity and truth, and with the great respect in which I hold my Lord the King. First, as to the charge of my having maliciously and traitorously deprived the King of the title of Supreme Head of the Church in England, let me say in answer that treason lies in word and deed, not in silence. For this, my silence, then, neither your law, nor any law in the world is able justly and rightly to punish me."

"Not so, Sir Thomas," remonstrated my Lord Audley, quickly getting to his feet again. "Not so. This very silence of yours is a sure token and demonstration of a nature maligning against the statute. Yea, there is no true and faithful subject that, being demanded his opinion, touching the said statute, is not deeply and utterly bound, without any dissimulation whatsoever, to confess the statute to be good, just, and lawful."

The amenities were done with, then, and the issue joined. My Lord Audley was a good lawyer—none better when it came to knowing every nook and cranny and fissure of the law. But, squaring off now, More knew he could match him precedent for precedent, word for word, urbanity for urbanity.

"May I remind my Lord Chancellor Audley," he requested with the utmost civility, "that, when we two went to school together, there was a legal maxim we both learned by heart: *Silence gives consent?* Silence, then, should be construed rather as ratification than rejection. But, my Lords, there is here a far deeper issue at stake than merely this. You must understand that, in things touching conscience, every good and true subject is more bound to have respect to his said conscience and to his soul than to any other thing in the world beside. A subject must be a loyal King's man, it is true. Says not Paul that we should obey God, honor the King, and love the brotherhood? But, from the beginning to this very moment, have I been ever a loyal King's man. Never have I given any occasion of slander, of tumult and sedition, against my Prince. I assure you, my Lords, that I have not hitherto to this hour disclosed and opened my conscience and mind to any person living in all the world on this matter of which we now speak."

A violent spell of coughing took him by the throat. My Lord Audley made a gesture that the Sergeant fetch More a glass of water.

"Again, my Lords, I thank you," said Thomas More, after the fit was spent. "As for articles two and three of the indictment, those touching on my letters written in the Tower to my Lord of Rochester before his death, let me say at once that never did I encourage him against the statute, nor he me. Bishop Fisher burned my letters, and I his. But I remember their contents sufficiently well, so recently was it we exchanged good wishes. In one of them there was nothing in the world contained but certain familiar talk and recommendations, such as was seemly and agreeable to our long and old acquaintance. In the other was contained my answer to my Lord of Rochester when he demanded of me what thing I answered at my first examination in the Tower upon the said statute. To this request of his I answered nothing but that I had informed and settled my conscience, and that he should inform and settle his. And other answer than this, upon the charge of my soul, made I none. These, as I have given them, are the tenors of my letters, upon which you can take no hold or handfast by your law to condemn me to death."

My Lord Audley turned to the Crier.

"Summon Baron Rich," he said.

"Summon Baron Rich!" called out the Crier.

Then, as Rich entered the courtroom.

"Baron Rich!"

It was Baron Rich now. But Rich's new-won honors made no appreciable difference in his tipstaff's face. None, at least, that one could notice as he took his stand beside my Lord Audley as witness for the prosecution.

"Baron Rich," said my Lord Audley, "on your oath as a Christian Knight, tell us what words, touching on the Oath of Supremacy, the accused did utter in your presence on the twelfth of June last in the Tower."

Rich gave More a sidelong glance before he replied to my Lord Audley's instruction.

"My Lords," he said unctuously, "on my sworn oath as a Christian Knight and good servant of King Henry, I tell you that the accused, in my hearing, said the Parliament could not make the King Head of the Church."

My Lord Audley looked over toward the prisoner.

"What do you say to Master Rich's testimony, Sir Thomas," he asked him courteously.

The Utopian awoke in Thomas More. Baron Rich's manner well became his manor—the Priory of Lighes, part of Master Secretary Cromwell's portion of the sack of the monastery lands. Maître Rabelais, who had endowed the world with the gay Abbey of Thélème, could, beyond any doubt, have made much of this fitting bequest to a thief-taker and a hypocrite. He would do his best, too.

"My Lords," he said, and More's gray eyes sparkled as they used to in the long Parliamentary sessions, whenever a merry jest was cracked, "not to my edification, I must admit, I have known Baron Rich for many years—long before, even, the King bestowed upon him the Priory of Lighes. But I tell you, my Lords, what you already know, that long before he became Lord of Lighes, this man was a great liar."

Sir John Baldwin and Sir Richard Lister smiled openly at the sally. There was loud laughter in the back of the court. Even my Lord Audley was hard put to keep a straight face. But Master Secretary Cromwell, discomfited in the discomfiture of his creature, looked up angrily.

"Master Sergeant," he said with an ugly snarl, "call the court to order."

349

The Sergeant thumped with his heavy halberd.

"My Lords and gentlemen," he cried, "the court will come to order!"

Beef-witted Charles Brandon knew a good thrust in the tilt-yard when he saw one.

"By God!" he said, close to Norfolk's ear. "He has yon gallow's kite on the hip!"

My Lord of Norfolk did not reply to his fellow of Suffolk, though he had long since gotten to tolerate him. Instead, as he looked on his old friend standing there, white as death, but smiling, the heart turned over in his breast. But he would not be warned. *Indignatio principis mors est.* The King was angry; so Sir Thomas More must die. Norfolk longed, with a sick longing, for an end of the degrading comedy.

"If, my Lords," said Thomas More, when the laughter had died down, "if I were a man that did not regard an oath, then I needed not, as you well know, in this place, in this case, at this time, to stand here as an accused person. And if this oath of yours be true, Master Rich, then I pray I may never see God in the face—a thing, were the truth otherwise than it is, I would not say to win the whole world."

Now Thomas More looked straight into the eyes of Baron Rich of the Priory of Lighes. There was no loathing in his own eyes, nor any compassion, either; only judgment: inexorable, ineluctable judgment. As the court watched the two of them confront each other, the court knew which man told the truth and which lied.

"As for you, Master Rich," said More, "in good faith, I am sorrier for your perjury than for my own peril. But I wish now the court to understand that neither I, nor any man else to my knowledge, ever took you to be a man of such credit as, in any matter of importance, I or any other, would at any time consent to communicate with you. And I have known you from your youth onward, for we long dwelt together in one parish. I am sorry I am now compelled to testify you were esteemed then very light of your tongue, a great dicer, and of no commendable fame or report. In your house at the Temple, also, were you likewise thus accounted. I am sorry, Master Rich, to have to disclose such things. But you drive me to it in my own defense."

More paused like the trained debater he was. He looked at the bench of Justices.

"Can it therefore seem likely to your honorable Lordships," he asked, "that I would, in so weighty a cause, so unadvisedly overshoot myself as to trust this Master Rich so far above my sovereign Lord the King, or any of his noble Counsellors, that I would utter unto him, and unto him alone, the secrets of my conscience touching the King's Supremacy, the special point and only mark so long sought for at my hands? To this Master Rich, of all men under the sun, when I never would reveal it to the King's Highness himself or to any of his trusted Counsellors, as is not unknown, my Lords, to some of my Judges sitting before me, they who, on several occasions, were sent from His Grace's own person unto me in the Tower for this very purpose?"

The utter silence in the Court of the King's Bench was answer enough. Master Secretary Cromwell looked uneasily up at the Lord Chief Justice.

"My Lord Chief Justice," he said, "the man maunders. Have we heard sufficient?"

Even for one of Master Cromwell's drumhead trials the cynicism implicit in that bald query was breathtaking. My Lord Fitz-James, however, was both well-trained and docile. He did not kick under the goad.

"We have heard enough," he said solemnly. "I charge the jury to reach a verdict."

While the jury conferred together, Thomas More sat apart, his head bowed, motionless. Conversation became general again in the court. The men-at-arms resumed their cautious colloquy.

"Our old Chancellor has defended himself bravely," said the shorter guard.

Red-thatch nodded sagely.

"Aye," he agreed, "but—"

And he nodded to where the two Boleyns lounged back upon the Justices' bench:

"The wolves gather and—"

This time he gestured to where the jury had their heads together: "The sheep scatter."

It took the jury but a quarter of an hour by the glass to reach its decision. After this bare formal show of conference the foreman, Thomas Palmer, Knight, rose to announce the verdict.

"My Lords and Justices," he said, stammering a little over the eminence temporarily thrust upon him, "we find the defendant, Thomas More, Knight, guilty of treason and misprision of treason against our high and puissant Lord and Majesty the King."

"In that case, gentlemen," said my Lord Audley, eager to get the bad business over with, "it is my duty to pronounce sentence."

But my Lord Audley had reckoned without Sir Thomas More, Knight of Chelsea, and once Lord High Chancellor of the realm of England. As if he had husbanded his slender physical resources for just such a contingency, the prisoner rose resolutely to his feet, interrupting the speaker. His composure of mien and resonance of voice were very marked now. But a short space ago, in the Tower, Master Secretary Cromwell had taunted him with cowardice for not speaking out. He would not be able to taunt him now. What he was going to say might make all the difference with Henry between a merciful beheading on Tower Hill and the barbarities of Tyburn gallows. He could not help it. The time he had spoken of to Meg had come; the time when he had naught to gain but Paradise, and naught to lose but his immortal soul. It was the very end. He would speak out at last. Henry had not kept faith. He would speak out.

"My Lord Chancellor Audley," he said, and his voice rang out over the hushed Court of King's Bench. "In the days when I was toward the law, the custom, in such a case as I am in now, was to ask the prisoner before judgment what he could say to show why judgment should not be given against him."

He paused, looking expectantly over toward my Lord Audley. The Chancellor bowed.

"You are in the right, Sir Thomas," he said in reply. "You show yourself a good lawyer to the end. Go on, say why judgment should not be rendered against you."

"My Lord Chief Justice," choked Cromwell, struggling to his feet. "I protest against this shocking irregularity! Silence the prisoner while judgment is pronounced!"

Sir John Fitz-James was no hero. He owed his office and his continuance in office to the sufferance of Master Cromwell; and Master Cromwell was a man who expected prompt payment on any note of hand. Nevertheless.

"It is the prisoner's right," he said coldly, "if he so chooses to exercise it."

Cromwell was in a fury now.

"It may be the prisoner's right," he said viciously, "but I do not think he would be wise to exercise it."

Thomas More knew what he meant; and so did every other person in the Court of King's Bench. Master Cromwell was holding out to him, as the price of present silence, the bribe of Tower Hill; and, as the penalty for speech, the threat of Tyburn gallows.

"I said to Master Cromwell once, and he well knows what I mean," said Thomas More contemptuously, "that these are terrors for children, not me. But, my Lords, we waste your time, Master Cromwell and I, with this fruitless bickering. And, since my Lord Chief Justice has ruled in my favor, I promise you I shall be brief."

He drew a deep breath, and turned to the Justices' bench. The die was cast, and he was glad.

"My Lords," he said, without preamble. "You sat in Parliament, many of you, when I first became your Speaker. I was your common mouth before His Majesty. I was also His Grace's man before you, his Commons. Only once did I speak as I really wished to speak, for you and for myself. And then I begged our Sovereign Lord the King, His Grace of England, for freedom of utterance for his Parliament, for every man to have the right to discharge his conscience in debate without fear of His Grace's dreadful displeasure. For every man to have the right to speak unafraid here in this fair City of Man, our sweet Kingdom, this goodly realm of England. For, as the Greek youth, Haemon, in a play I and King Henry once loved together, said to the tyrant Creon: *That is no City which belongs to one man.*

"Now, my Lords, the time has come for me to speak out again. I had pledged my self to King Henry not to broach my mind to anyone on this matter. But I think my present condemnation relieves me of that pledge. *Leges silent inter arma.* The laws are silent in the face of Mars. *Sed non in articulo mortis.* But I do not think they should be silent in the jaws of death. As the golden bowl breaks and the silver cord is loosed, so should be loosed the tongue of him who is to die. For you and for myself, then—aye, and for King Henry, too—and for the last time. And not now for our fair City of Man alone, which is England, but for that fairer City of God of which we are all also citizens. So, Lordings, seeing that I see you are determined to condemn me—God knows how; I know why—I will now, as I did then many years agone, in discharge of my conscience, speak my mind plainly and freely touching my indictment and your statute."

The great Hall of Westminster was as silent now as any tomb.

"My Lords," said Thomas More, looking into their faces, "this indictment is grounded upon an Act of Parliament directly repugnant to the laws of God and of His holy Church, the supreme government of which, or of any part whereof, no temporal Prince may presume by any law to take upon him. For it rightfully belongs only to the See of Rome, in whose regard the mouth of our Savior Himself, personally present upon earth, by special prerogative, granted spiritual preeminence only to St. Peter and his successors, Bishops of that same See of Rome. It is, therefore, insufficient in law, amongst Christian men, to charge any Christian man with what I have been charged.

"Remember, my Lords Justices, in the City of God this pleasant realm of England is but a member and small part of the Church. It may not make a particular law disagreeable to the general law of Christ's universal Catholic Church, any more than this dear City of London of ours, as but one poor member of a whole realm, may make a law, against an Act of Parliament, to bind the whole realm. *Magna Charta* yet stands as the statute of our land wrested by our fathers

354

from a despot at Runnymede. Do you know what our Great Charter says about the King and the Church? That the King may not touch the Church. *Quod Ecclesia Anglicana libera sit, et habeat omnia jura sua integra, et libertates suas illaesas.* That the Church in England shall be free, and shall maintain all its laws unimpaired, and its liberties unhurt."

Thomas More turned away from the Bench of Justices and toward those benches in the body of the Hall where the great Lords not sitting in judgment listened to his statement. Cranmer was there, without his robes. More fixed his eye, and spoke again.

"My Lord of Canterbury," he said, "you, of all those who hear me now, should surely remember whose bones used to lie under the high altar of Canterbury, and why the holy, blissful martyr, à Becket, died."

Cranmer bowed, gravely and uncomfortably. Again no one moved in the great Hall. Thomas More resumed:

"The Act of Supremacy, my Lords, is also contrary to that sacred Oath which the King's Highness himself, and every other Christian Prince, always, with great solemnity, take at their Coronations. No more may this realm of England refuse spiritual obedience to the See of Rome than may the child refuse obedience to his natural father. For, as St. Paul said to the Corinthians: *I have regenerated you, my children in Christ.* So might St. Gregory, Pope of Rome, through whose missionary agency, by St. Augustine, his messenger, we English first received the Christian faith, truly say of us Englishmen: *You are my children, because I have, under Christ, given to you everlasting salvation—a far higher and better inheritance than any fleshly father can leave his child—and by regeneration have made you spiritual children in Christ.* St. Gregory grew merry once over us English whom he loved so well. *Non Angli, sed Angeli,* he said in loving jest. Not Englishmen, but Angels, the great Pope called us. I tell you, Lordings all, this Act of Supremacy can turn Gregory's beloved *Angeli* into *Diaboli.*"

My Lord Chancellor Audley had long since recovered from his momentary shamefacedness. He saw his chance to interpose now, and took it.

"Before God, Sir Thomas," he said, raising his voice, "we have had enough and more than enough now of your prating presumption! Do

you think yourself wiser and better than all the Episcopate and Nobility of this Kingdom? Yes, and of Parliament, too? Seeing that all
the Bishops, the Universities, the Lords, and the best learned men of
the realm have assented to this Act, I much marvel that you alone
against them will hold out, will so stiffly stick to swear, and now so
vehemently argue there against."

"My Lord Chancellor," said Thomas More, "you raise again our
old topic of debate: why I stick to swear. It is long too late to go over
that ground again. But I do not make so great a virtue of mere number
as you. Still, if the number of Bishops and Universities be so material
as your Lordship seems to take it, then I see little cause, my Lord, why
that same thing should make any change in my conscience. For I
nothing doubt but that, though not perhaps in this realm, yet in
Christendom about, they be not the fewer part that are of my mind
therein of these well-learned Bishops and virtuous men that are yet
alive. But if I should speak of those that are already dead, of whom
many are now holy saints in Heaven, I am very sure it is the far, far
greater part of them that, all the while they lived, thought in this case
that way that I think now. A cloud of witness to my cause looks down
upon me as I speak. And therefore am I not bound, my Lord, to conform my conscience to the Council of one realm against the general
Council of Christendom. My Lord, for one Bishop of your opinion I
have a hundred Bishops and saints of mine. And for one Parliament or
Council of yours—and God knows of what kind!—I have all the General Councils for a thousand years. And for one Kingdom I have
France and all the Kingdoms of Christendom."

Master Secretary Cromwell had sat hunched down on his bench
for long enough.

"Master More," he interrupted harshly, "we have heard enough.
We now plainly perceive that you are maliciously bent."

As in the trial of my Lord of Rochester, the prosecution had placed
heavy stress upon the legal counter, *maliciously.* John Fisher had
shown this same panel of Justices how bad their law was by pointing
out that "by all equity, all justice, all worldly honesty, and civil humanity," it was absolutely impossible to charge him with denying the
Supremacy *maliciously* when he had only spoken out at the demand

of the King, and under the solemn pledge that his answer should be revealed to no one but the King. But neither law nor honesty had place in Master Cromwell's court. Now, at the ninth hour, the greatest lawyer of his day contemptuously waived argument over the technicality.

"No, Master Secretary," he said, "not malice, but pure necessity, for the discharge of my conscience, enforces me to speak thus much. I did not wish it so—and well you know it, you of all people in this court. I did not wish it so, but you and the King compel me in the end. I call and appeal to God, whose sight alone pierces into the very depth of man's heart, to be my witness to this truth. But never think you delude me, Master Secretary, nor you, my Lords of Rochford and Wiltshire, who sit high among my Judges. It is not so much for this matter of the Supremacy you seek my blood, as for that I would not condescend to the marriage between the Lady Anne and my King."

Truth of this towering stature had the power to move the marble composure even of my Lord Chancellor Audley. Shaken, he turned to my Lord Fitz-James.

"My Lord Chief Justice," he said, white-faced, "you have now heard out Master More on the heads of this indictment. Do you rule for us on its legality. Is it full and sufficient?"

If the Golgotha of Tower Hill lay ahead for Thomas More, at least the Tower's Gethsemane was now behind him. And, in that stone Gethsemane, he had been spared the crown of thorns and the flogging block. But he was not to be spared another of the Passion's immemorial gestures. My Lord Chief Justice may or may not have sold his soul to Cromwell. Now, his short revolt at an end, he would try to wash his hands.

"My Lords," he said, "it hinges on the Act of Parliament. If the Act of Parliament is not unlawful, as we know it is not, then, by St. Julian, the indictment is not, in my conscience, insufficient."

"Lo, my Lords, lo!" called out my Lord Audley quickly. "You hear what my Lord Chief Justice has ruled. And you have heard Sir Thomas say his say as well. Therefore, Sir Thomas More, I now adjudge you felon and traitor to our puissant Majesty Henry, and do hereby declare your life forfeit to the Crown, said forfeit to be paid in full by you

357

on the sixth day of this month, in the morning by ten of the clock."

A tumult arose in the court. For the first time my Lord of Norfolk got to his feet. Wishing to end his old friend's ordeal, and proffer him the gall-soaked sponge of this world's mercy, he spoke above the rising murmur.

"Sir Thomas," he said, "you have heard the sentence of the court. If you have anything further to say in farewell, we grant you the favor of that audience."

Coming as it did from that stiff soldier, Norfolk, it was a *beau geste* indeed. Thomas More understood and was grateful.

"My thanks, my Lord of Norfolk," he said while the din quieted. "But, my Lord, I have no more to say but this: Farewell. We part as friends, I hope—and you, too, Lordings all. Do we not read, in the Acts of the Apostles, that the blessed Apostle, St. Paul, was present at the stoning, and consented to the death of St. Stephen, and, indeed, tended the clothes of those who stoned him to death? Yet are they now, both twain, holy saints in Heaven, and shall continue there friends forever. I, it is true, am no Stephen, and you, I believe, no Paul. Yet I verily trust, and shall therefore right heartily pray, that, though your Lordships have now here on earth been Judges to my condemnation, we may yet hereafter in Heaven merrily all meet together, to our everlasting salvation, there to be merry forever and ever. Do you pray for me in this world, and I shall pray for you elsewhere. And I bid you carry one last message from me to His Grace. Tell him I remain his beadsman still. That I pray God to give him good counsel. That I die the King's good servant, but God's first."

The men-at-arms presented pikes. The escort of halberdiers regrouped itself. And Thomas More walked out of Westminster Hall for the last time, the head of the ax turned toward him.

When the Justices' Bench emptied itself, three Judges remained behind, lost in thoughts of their own: Master Secretary Cromwell; Sir John Baldwin; my Lord of Norfolk. Master Cromwell was the first to rouse himself and go of these last three. He caught Sir John Baldwin's eye, as he brushed past him with a muttered apology. Perhaps, for once, Master Cromwell was unduly sensitive. But he did not think he liked the expression on Sir John's face.

"A penny for your thoughts, Sir John," he said offensively.

He did not expect the answer he got.

"*Crito, we owe a cock to Aesculapius; pay it and neglect it not,*" the Chief Justice of the Common Pleas answered abruptly. "If you must know, Master Secretary, I think on Socrates."

"And I," said my Lord of Norfolk, who was in no sense a religious man, "I think on Someone else who also came to trial before a tribunal such as ours."

Putting his cloak before his face, Master Cromwell made his way out of Westminster Hall. The thing was over at last; and he had won. Or, he asked himself with his customary lucidity, had he?

CHAPTER XXI

STAGE OF FOOLS:

Tower Hill, Morning, July 6, 1535

MASTER ROGER HARLINGS, Mercer, of Wilberfoss, Yorkshire, cursed himself for a fool and a ninny. Here he was, a prosperous merchant and knowing man of the world, on his first visit to London, with his little lad with him, in addition, to take orders for the cloth goods the family looms specialized in: kerseys, shalloons and russets; bays and says, grogram and mockado. And, like any green countryman gawping at city wonders, he had suffered himself to be picked up by a press of people and, gasping, penned into this narrow enclosure right in front of the scaffold where some poor wretch—a man of some means, once, by the look of him—was about to pay the penalty for his crimes. It was an unsettling sight at best. But Master Roger happened both to be without his breakfast, and—the worse luck—to have his young son along. What would he say to the bairn, once the canny little mommet began to ask what was toward up there on the creaking gallows? The Yorkshire mercer groaned. If his shoon were thick with the yellow marl of Pontefract, he could not have shown himself a bigger fool. Not since, in his fourteenth year, a wandering Prigger of Prancers had gulled him of a horse, had he been so befooled. Was he a child to follow a bear-ward, or a woman taken in by some begging clapperdudgeon, that he should thus blithely go down a blind alley after a throng?

In point of sober fact, Master Roger Harlings, Mercer, did not know just how privileged a personage he really was this sixth morning of July in the year of our Lord, fifteen hundred and thirty-five, at ten of the clock by the bell of Westminster. Nor what high circles he currently moved in. Not even those first peers of the Kingdom, my Lords of Norfolk and Suffolk, not even the King's father-in-law, my Lord of Wiltshire, not even the Duke of Richmond, Henry's natural son, stood closer to the block in all that dense press of folk than he. And who were these two in masks right next to him—except, of course, for the halberdiers who fenced the masked pair in? A great bull of a man with a spade beard? And a squat man in a cloak, though the day was warm and sultry, with great thunderheads in the sky? A shorter man hunched close to his companion for all the world like some Yorkshire paddock come on in a field? Master Roger had no time at present to riddle it all out, for the child had begun his questioning. What was yon platform? Who were those on it? And those under it? Sweating in his effort to spare the boy, the Northern mercer had a sudden inspiration.

"It is a play, laddie," he said, "like the *Judgment Day* in the pageant wagon we Mercers acted out at York. There is Heaven in the sky, and Hell below, and we stand here on Earth, watching the while. Do you remember now, laddie?"

"I mind me, father," said the boy, satisfied by his father's improvisation. "Cousin Hoveden was the Christus and taught me the speech to the Good and Bad Souls."

Amid the stirrings of the great crowd the little lad's treble rose in the old Northern tongue of the Yorkshire Ridings:

> *"My chosen childer, come unto Me!*
> *With Me to dwell now shall ye wend.*
> *There joy and bliss shall ever be.*
> *Your life to liking shall ye lend.*

> *"But, cursed caitiffs, from Me flee*
> *In Hell to dwell withouten end.*
> *There ye shall never but sorrow see,*
> *And sit by Sathanas, the fiend.*

"Now is fulfilled all My forethought.
For ended is all earthly thing.
All worldly wights that I have wrought,
After their works have now winning.
They that would sin and ceased not,
Of sorrows sere now shall they sing.
And they that mended them whiles they might,
Shall shelter and bide in My blessing."

"Amen!" called out a Jester in the press of people, waggling his belled cap at the boy. Then the great ax rose in the air, poised, came cleanly down. A sigh went up from the huge crowd. Frightened, the lad dug his head into his father's coat.

"Father!" he whimpered, not looking up again. "Why did they cut off the old man's head?"

This time Master Roger had no answer ready. But help came from an unexpected quarter. The squat man in the mask, who looked so much like a paddock, stooped down to the child, grinning from under the black silk which creased as he smiled.

"Why?" he said; and the thick voice behind the mask seemed oddly unsteady. "Because he was a fool."

CHAPTER XXII

WEEP FOR A FOOL:

Thameside, Evening, July 6, 1535

THE crumbling gray parapet of Thames Embankment looked cooler
and grayer for the honey-colored air of evening and for the lithe figure in flame-hued motley that sat cross-legged upon it, looking pensively out over the silver reaches of the Thames. The crowd that had
been flowing past from Tower Hill all day since noon was ebbing
now, even as the tide of Thames on the other side of the wall reached
its neap and the state barges began moving up and down again to the
distant cries of the watermen: *Westward ho!* and *Eastward ho!* A
clock pealed a single note to mark the quarter hour; it lingered in the
stillness more golden than the twilight air. Henry Patenson, resplendent in the new livery the Lord Mayor had bought him to wear on
state occasions, sighed and shifted his position. As he did so, his hand
closed upon a halberd set aside by one of the three members of the
watch who kept the King's water stairs here at Greenwich and who,
at the moment, were gaming at cards a yard or so beneath his dangling toes. A Jester's reflexes are, perforce, always attuned to the time
and place he finds himself in. With an automatic grin Patenson stood
up on the parapet and struck an attitude very like that famous crown
prince of the playing cards, the Knave who stole the tarts from his
mother Queen. Then, remembering of a sudden what day it was and
why he sat there in the pleasant amber dusk, he stopped short in his
miming and let the pike drop with a clang to the cobbles below. It

was the octave of St. Peter and the eve of the feast of à Becket. Thomas More had had his wish. But Henry Patenson, *joculator,* had not had his.

The watch paid no attention to his pantomime with the pike. But it had not gone altogether unnoticed. Sir Thomas Wyatt, cloaked and spurred, on his way to the King's revel in the gardens of Greenwich, his domino in his pocket—Henry had never lost his taste for masquerade—stopped to watch the Fool play out his little game. When it was over, he swept the Jester a low bow with his cavalier's hat.

"*Monseigneur,*" he said. "*Le beau valet de diamants! Votre serviteur!*"

Patenson appreciated the compliment once it was translated.

"How is that, my friend the poet?" he asked. "Remember I am an English Fool, not a French one."

"Fools are fools in any tongue, friend Patenson," said Wyatt. "In plain English—if it be safe to use plain English any more in England —you look like the Jack of Diamonds on the new deck Monseigneur the French Ambassador presented to Henry last Twelfth Night revels. Does he not, watch?"

One of the watch looked up from his cards.

"Very like the Knave of Diamonds, my Lord," he said indifferently.

"My old master, Lord Chancellor More," said Patenson, "did not care for cards. Nor for chess, either."

Wyatt laughed bitterly.

"Master More was out of fashion in every possible way!" he said. "But the King himself no longer loves the King's game. There are too many Knights and Bishops on the board, and but one Queen to a King. Besides, it is easier to pack a deck or cog a pair of dice than rig a chequered board. And Henry loves to win. Well, who has won today's grim game? It is dealt out to its final hand now. But who has won? Queen Anne took in her last trump when greathearted More went to the scaffold. The hounds have belled, the noble unicorn is bayed, the quarry has gone quiet to his rest. But who has won the game?"

364

"You were at Tower Hill this morning?" asked Patenson.

"I was there," said Wyatt. "I did not play. Poets do not play. I watched the great ones play, instead. Who has won the game? The King? I do not think so. The Queen? I poured scented water from a silver ewer over her white hands on Whitsunday's Coronation morning. The hot scent and reek of blood is on them now. It ill becomes her long white hands. No, I do not think Queen Anne has won the game. Who then? Master Secretary Cromwell?"

"God damn his soul!" said Patenson.

"You waste good breath, friend Harry," said Wyatt sardonically. "Master Secretary Cromwell has taken care of that little matter himself, without assistance from anyone else unless it be the Prince of Darkness. But I cannot tell if even Cromwell has won the game, because I cannot tell the stakes he plays for. He is too passionless for me. He plays neither for love nor lust, not for drink, not for sport. He plays for power, it is true. But he cannot eat power. He is a new man, I think. If so, God deliver our old world from his new century! But maybe no one wins. Maybe we all lose. Old England loses of a surety."

Henry Patenson was not the man to exorcise grief by metaphysical speculation.

"But Master More loses most!" he said, a sob in his voice. "My old master was a fool! Why, what ailed him that he would not swear? Why did he stick to swear? I swore the Oath myself."

"I am a species of poet, friend Patenson," said Wyatt, compassion in his voice. "So I think I know why your master forebore to swear. Your master was a true man. That, in the world's light scales, means he was a fool in earnest who could play out to its bitter end the chapfallen jest a Fool by profession might nimbly and safely toss across a banquet board into the teeth of a King. Truth is a mighty chancy commodity to hawk about a court. It fetches too high a price by the span of one's head. I am no hero like your master, friend Patenson. But neither am I fool or knave. So tomorrow I go back to Kent and there set down this verse in my new satire:

> *"Nor I am not where Christ is given in prey*
> *For money, poison and treason at Rome,*
> *A common practice used night and day:*
> *But here I am in Kent and Christendom*
> *Among the Muses where I read and rhyme;*
> *Where if thou list, my Patenson, to come,*
> *Thou shalt be judge how I do spend my time."*

An oar squealed in its thole pin. A chain clinked against an iron ring. The watch sprang to attention. My Lord of Canterbury's barge was docking at the landing stairs. When Wyatt heard the guards' salute, he plucked his mantle across his face.

"Good even, friend Patenson," he said hurriedly. "This night of all nights we twain make perilous acquaintance. But I will expect you by my fire down in Kent."

Wyatt rounded Greenwich gate just as Archbishop Cranmer reached the head of the water stairs at the break in the parapet.

"Take the barge back to Hanworth," he instructed the boatmen.

My Lord of Canterbury, looking more like a liquid-eyed deer than ever in his full ecclesiastical regalia, was just back from an audience with the Queen at Hanworth. But, good-natured as always, he yet had time to speak not unkindly to a Fool. One might not be able to find it in one's heart to admire my Lord of Canterbury. It was hard not to like him. Nevertheless Henry Patenson succeeded in this latter task.

"What! Master Patenson!" said Cranmer. "Not afraid of the night ague that creeps up from the fens so far down river as Greenwich that you sit here thus like a salamander on a wall? What do you do in your pied raiment away from your master's house? Never tired of playing the Fool even on holiday, eh, Master Patenson?"

The forked legs executed a caracole to land on one knee at the ornate hem of Cranmer's robe.

"Aye, my Lord of Canterbury," said their owner. "It is in truth a holiday, this eve of the feast of St. Thomas. But never pause to ask whose or why. Misprision of treason has been declared for less. That is why I wear my motley, for that the calendar is altered. They are shifting the Feast of Fools from April First to today, to honor the new Prince, the King of Fools. The King of Fools is dead! Long live the King! You are a churchman, my Lord of Canterbury, and must know of such matters. May he not one day come to be the patron saint of fools?"

Henry Patenson began to laugh eerily to himself in the gathering dusk.

"I say no more," he said, looking up from his kneeling posture into Cranmer's uneasy face. "I say no more where more is not required, since, in our new English fashion of seemly abstinence, more is become unwelcome except in the unimportant matter of a plurality of wives. But there—'ware the eel-pie, lest it be compounded of a paste of serpents! More shall go down the road More went."

A shadow seemed to pass across the dusk's old-gold. Cranmer shivered on a sudden. He thrust a hurried gold piece into the capering fellow's hand, plucked a furred gown tighter across his throat despite the warmth of the summer evening, and continued on up the landing stairs to Greenwich gate, cursing himself for an utter fool for dallying in talk anywhere so close to the execution. He had forgotten whose man this unchancy creature once had been.

One of the men-at-arms threw down his cards, and walked over to speak to Patenson. He was the same one who had replied to Wyatt's question about the Jack of Diamonds. But he was no longer indifferent in his manner.

"Well thrust," he said, leaning on the river wall. "Well thrust, friend Patenson. I like not the dirty business much myself, nor such scarlet popinjays as that one, either. My Lord of Canterbury struts higher nowadays than peacock Argus or his good peahen goddess, Juno, used to back on Master More's green terrace at Chelsea."

At that Patenson recognized the fellow for one of the serving men who used to hand round the wine when Erasmus or Colet or even the King came to dine.

"I thought I knew you," he said, putting out his hand. "You are John the serving man who passed around the wine in the days when **Sir Thomas was Chancellor.**"

"I saw our old Chancellor this morning," said the bearded guard, "on his way to ripen on the medlar tree. He carried himself like a man who cared not over much for the good things he was leaving behind; for the ale in casks in Chelsea. For that best of wines he always kept by his own golden salver and did not have served even to his best-loved guests, well though he feasted them otherwise."

Patenson laughed in shrill mockery. He took Cranmer's gold piece from his pouch, and, with contemptuous deftness, sent it spinning to the halberdier who just as deftly caught it in mid-flight.

"There, sirrah watchman!" he mocked him. "Take my Lord of Canterbury's coin and quaff the health of the great toper you mourn for. It is not a great deal, I know, but, without spending a groat of it, you may buy hogsheads of the precious wine-draughts Master More used to drain apart from the rest of us in his high hall. You have jackdaw eyes for some things, John Lackwit. For bottle tops and what is under a wench's placket. But your eyes were yet not sharp enough to spy out the clear water our old master, the Chancellor, poured out from his private decanter. For his own foolish reasons he drank no wine. But he was no grinning death's head at the feast nor canting Lenten clerk to spoil merry sport for others. He kept his own secret counsel and grew mellower with each toast than if he had sipped choice Malmsey instead of cold water. Even so today did he wish the Headsman and the officers that they would all meet together, he and they, right merry in Heaven."

The man-at-arms stood still a moment.

"Then he was a bigger fool than I bargained for," he said a trifle huskily. "But I like such fools, even if there be no profit in them."

He spun the coin high in the air and caught it as it fell again.

"This is one coin," he said, before going back to his fellows who never left off slapping down their cards upon the paving stones, "that goes not wholly to the pothouse and the brothel. I shall take half of your guerdon to wash the bad taste from my mouth of this morning's evil work. The other half shall go for a goodly waxen taper to burn for our old master's soul."

The Jester leaned back upon the parapet and stretched his supple arms against the greening sky. But the negligent pose soon turned to wary attention as a black-clad personage, in close-fitting jerkin and sable fleshings, a black mask hiding his face, rounded the corner, matching Henry Patenson's gay Jack of Diamonds with his own grim Jack of Spades, except for the sinister difference that one of the little pages who followed him carried a great ax instead of an heraldic sword, while the other bore a silk camlet gown ominously spattered with dark stains about the collar. Master Patenson recognized the garment as More's, a last gift from the learned Italian mercer, Signior Bonvisi. But it did not take any such contributory detail as this for a Londoner bred and born to know the King's headsman. The Fool made a mock obeisance.

"Master Wyatt's deck of cards," he muttered to himself, "continues to be dealt out, I see. Now we have the Jack of Spades."

Then, louder:

"Greetings, Messire Headsman! I see your knave carries my late master's cote. Well, Master More has no further use for it, though they say it is cold where he has gone, and the garment is warmly lined with silk and vair. Your kind leech's ministrations have removed him forever from any reason to fret over a cold in the head—or a quinsy in the throat, either."

An executioner's walk in life does not well equip its holder for bandying jokes. Moreover, the man in black had encountered Master Patenson before and knew the household to which he had once belonged. And, after the events of the morning, he felt kindly disposed to anything or anyone pertaining to the man whose head he had that day parted from his body. He tapped the garment.

"This is a headsman's perquisite, friend Fool," he reprimanded gently. "Like the vails good Master More used generously to bestow on you at Christmastide. A comely present it is, too, and has an angel of gold in the pocket. I am told my Lord Lieutenant did protest, saying that I was but a javel that did not need so rich a cote, but Master More would have it so. He did not esteem me so great a javel, but that he would needs kiss me on the scaffold. And he did jest, too, at the moment of death, requiring me to be courteous to his beard, for that it, at least, had done no harm, asking the Sheriff's officer to see him safely up the shaky stairs, but adding that, as for his coming down, he could shift for himself."

"Aye," said Patenson slowly, "he could jest right well. I am but his pupil there. But he did not use to have a beard. I saw Meg Roper cry out at the shaggy length of it. He was a fool. He would keep three things whole: the Church, the King's marriage, the peace of Christendom. And he could not even keep his body whole, but that you must needs lop head from trunk. What think you of him for a great fool, Master Headsman?"

"Nay, Master Patenson," said the executioner, beckoning to his pages, "he was an honest and a gentle man."

The dusk turned from honey to dove; the river from silver to rubbed steel. Three ruffling horsemen went spurring by in the argent armor the arrogant retainers of the Howards had begun to affect. Two white barges passed, swan like in the half light, full of masked revelers for the King's fête in the gardens of Greenwich, pleasure craft from Richmond saluting pleasure craft from York House. Mistress More, tall, hard-favored, wrapped in a cloak, made her slow way by the parapet. Flat-headed, never beautiful even in a youth that had never bloomed, grief had not softened the deep lines about her mouth. Henry Patenson had always cared for his former mistress more than most. Now sorrow made him almost loving toward her—though one could never rid oneself of some meed of exasperation in Mistress Alice's angular presence.

"Good even, Mistress Alice," he said low, not to startle her.

There was no need for the precaution. Nothing, short of the clap of doom, could startle Mistress More this night. She stared at him for a long moment, cold and unseeing. Finally half perception dawned in her red-lidded eyes.

"It grows late, Fool," she said harshly. "Why are you not home and withindoors at this hour? Your master, soft-hearted fool though he is, will be right angry."

Henry Patenson grew unreasonably angry himself.

"Old basilisk!" he said to himself. "She wanders. She is back in

370

Chelsea, and yon cold corpse swinging in the moonlight yet keeps the Great Seal of England."

"In good time, in good time, Mistress," he said aloud, placatingly. "The Lord Mayor feasts late this evening. I am not required till midnight. He does not keep the seemly hours we were used to back in Chelsea under yourself and good Master More."

The gentle reminder of whose Fool he now was brought her to herself. She laid a hand clumsily on his garish knees, tears starting from the dull eyes so like the flat eyes of an Indian.

"Yes," she said, the harsh voice creaking like an old inn sign in the wind, "yes. I was forgetting. You were there this morning. You weep for him, too."

"I weep for him, Mistress," said Henry Patenson, his voice expressionless that he might keep back a storm of tears.

"Then," Mistress Alice cried out, beating her hands together in anger and shame as well as grief, "you weep for a fool! Why need he have died? It was very folly. But he was ever a fool, ever sitting still by the fire, and making goslings in the ashes as children do. 'What the good year, Master More,' I told him in the Tower, 'I marvel that you, that have been always hitherto taken for so wise a man, will now so play the fool to lie here in this close filthy prison, and be content thus to be shut up amongst mice and rats, when you might be abroad at your liberty, and with the favor and good will both of the King and of his Council, if you would but do as all the Bishops and best learned of this realm have done. And seeing you have at Chelsea a right fair house, your library, your books, your gallery, your garden, your orchard, and all other necessaries so handsome about you, where you might, in the company of me your wife, your children, and household, be merry, I muse what a God's name you mean still thus fondly to tarry.' And what answered the dear fool to me, sirrah Fool? Only: 'Is not this house, Mistress Alice, as nigh Heaven as mine own?' And to what end, Master Patenson? Are not these the words of a fool?"

"Even so, Mistress," said Henry Patenson, sighing. "Of a very great fool. And to no end that you or I can see. But he is gone now to his

proper house where all good fools go at the last, and that is—
Heaven."

The film of noncomprehension came down over her eyes again.
She stared at him a space, then gathered up her skirts, grumbling, and
walked off, talking to herself.

"Tilly vally, man," she said, *"Bone deus,* but you are as arrant a
fool as your master."

Patenson's long vigil was almost over now. It was hard on ten
o'clock. A burst of music, carried on the wind, brought to his ears the
merrymaking of the King and his guests in Greenwich gardens. He
hoped the masquers would stay out of his way when the time came
for him to do what must be done. Even as the clock chimed forth the
hour, Will Roper came out of the shadows of a waterfront building,
shivering a bit, for the night mists had begun to gather damp on the
stones, and the business he and Patenson had in hand was not a
pretty one.

"Friend Roper?" asked Patenson, uncertain at first.

"The same," said Roper, gesturing to the moon white over London
Bridge. "A pretty day. And a prettier night, with the heads outlined
dark against the moon on London Bridge. What say you? Is the boat
and pole and lanthorn ready?"

Patenson jerked thumb over shoulder in the direction of the river
stairs.

"They will be at eleven, friend Roper," he said.

The other brushed one hand across his eyes in a quick distracted
motion.

"By God!" he said in a sudden fury. "We do what we must! My
father shall not be utterly cheated! He told me often, walking by
Thameside, conversing with Dom Erasmus and myself, unfolding his
inner heart to me in his study, that, upon condition three things were
well established in Christendom, he would as lief be put in a sack and
here presently be cast into the Thames."

"I know, I know," said Patenson wearily. "I can tick them off on
these three poor fingers. First, an universal peace. Second, a perfect
uniformity of religion. Third, a good conclusion of the King's marriage.

Thameside, Evening, July 6, 1535

We march against the French again today. Spain will be hot at our throats tomorrow. There is a heretic dog baying his own Gospel atop every midden in Europe. The King has got his trull by law, much pleasure may he find of her. And our own sweet sovereign, Catherine, may go whistle for her name and fame. Well, friend Roper, I think we can spare your father his sack, at least, if our luck holds and the moon is down within the hour. Consecrated ground is sweeter bread to the lips of a dead man than summer air to lover's mouth. And the Book says naught against such merciful theft as you and I intend. Besides, we but anticipate the executioner. Bishop Fisher is dead no longer than a fortnight. Today they kicked his head into the river to make room for Master More's. Our signal is still a whistle?"

"This," said Roper.

He whistled once and went off again into the shadows. Patenson hunched his shoulders once more against the parapet. He snapped his fingers to ward off the growing chill and, for the same practical purpose, executed a little dance all alone in the moonlight, with only his grotesquely elongated shadow to accompany him. For the watch, too, after the last barge of masquers was received, had gathered up its halberds and gone off. After the uncanny *pas à seul* was finished, in order to make his last hour of waiting more tolerable he began to sing, low, a little song. A woman came into the shadow of the water stairs. The velvet vizard she wore was white; and, in the white light of the moon, it almost seemed as if she had no face.

> *"Hey nonny no!*
> *Men are fools that wish to die!*
> *Is it not fine to dance and sing*
> *When the bells of death do ring?*
> *Is it not fine to swim in wine,*
> *And turn upon the toe,*
> *When the winds blow and the seas flow?*
> *Hey nonny no!"*

"I should know that song," spoke a soft voice from the shadows. "*Jesu!*" said Patenson, terrified.

Then he recovered himself.

"I should know that voice," he said cautiously, feeling his way, playing for time.

And, indeed, he did know the voice, though, for the life of him, he could not yet set a name to it. Even in his nervousness the thought came to him that, if one had a fancy for such things, here was the sort of voice a man would sell a crown for. Or, maybe, more than a crown. Maybe a soul. Gingerly he tried this tack.

"It is a lovely voice," he said, still groping. "It is a voice a man would sell a crown for."

"Take care, sirrah Fool!" said the faceless voice peremptorily.

Jesu! Patenson swore to himself again. He had gone too far this time. One should keep one's blabbing mouth shut tight within the purlieus of Greenwich Palace. But audacity might yet retrieve what audacity seemed to have lost.

"I have it!" he said, snapping his fingers. "It is King Henry's song. Master More would have me sing it for him evenings when he walked with the King on the palace leads and talked with him of the stars."

He fell to one knee, and kissed her skirt.

"My Lady Queen!" he said.

Anne Boleyn, the white velvet vizard across the strange green eyes and pointed face, stepped forth into the starlight. She came late to the revels from Hanworth; and by land, not water. By land, one saw not London Bridge.

"I remember you," she said. "You were his Fool. I saw you ride a hobbyhorse one day. But have no fear. I strike not at Fools. Fools cannot harm me."

Henry Patenson gave an antic caper as if he were back on his hobbyhorse again in the Westminster antechamber of my Lord Chancellor More's state office.

"Only one fool can harm you, my Lady Queen," he said.

And then, though he could have bitten his tongue out after:

"Yourself!"

"Take care, sirrah Fool!" said the Queen imperiously. "Even a Fool's long license hath a limit; and I have small stomach for jesting tonight.

374

But there is one thing I would know, and it may be you can tell me. Why did your master hate me?"

"He did not hate you, my Lady Queen," said the Jester simply. "He said he wished you only well. He said he was vastly sorry for you."

"Oh," said Anne Boleyn; and no more.

The soft voice was quite uncertain now. Then, after a long pause:

"That I find hard to believe. But if what you say is true, then he must needs have been a very great fool indeed. For I hated him in life and do hate him more in death."

And, with a rustle of brocaded silk, the Queen had passed on to the midsummer revels on the green lawns of Greenwich Palace; and with her the ranked guardsmen who, while she spoke to Patenson, had hung back five pikes' length. After they were gone, a lamplighter lit a cresset where the parapet wall made an angle. It occured to Patenson that, under the circumstances, it might advantage him to take his stand a rood further down the river, and come back to the water stairs only when he heard Roper's whistle. While he was still debating with himself the relative advantages and disadvantages of this move, there came one more interruption. Another masked reveler in yellow velvet, heavily built, spade-bearded, walked into the light of the cresset flare.

Friend Wyatt, thought Patenson to himself, while he measured the King from a distance, was a fortune teller. He would play cards with him no more. For, like most fortune tellers, he had marked this night's deck. First, a pair of Jacks: one red; one black. Then a Queen. It was only fitting for a King to follow suit now—especially such a King after such a Queen.

"Good even, Sire," he said aloud, and with a certain degree of familiarity; for he had known him of old in Chelsea.

The King started. As usual at this hour, he was half gone in drink. Who was this slim fellow in flame color? Was he a ghost? Did ghosts wear red for Purgatory? Henry shivered a little, and brushed a hand across his eyes. There were too many ghosts about him now. The Duke of Buckingham. Sebastian Newdigate. The Carthusians. My Lord of Rochester. This ghost's old master. For he recognized him now. It was a humble and a witty ghost. It did not write against

375

heretics. It did not correspond with the Pope. Charles the Emperor did not care a jackstraw for it, dead or alive.

When the King spoke, there was some measure of affection in the drink-blurred voice.

"Which are you, Master Patenson," he asked, "alive or dead? Quick or a ghost? I have not seen you these twelve months and more. Is your crackbrain as nimble as of old? Come, crack me a jest for old times' sake !"

The Fool scratched a supplicating palm.

"A noble jest, Sire?" he asked. "Alas, I have no noble, and without a noble my poor-bred wits are but lame. I can render nothing to my noble Caesar, without one of my Caesar's nobles."

Smiling a little, the King tossed him a coin. Patenson caught it and scrutinized it closely.

"Perpend," he said, considering. "A goodly piece. Whose superscription is here? A man died today—a very fool, your Grace—for that he could not answer this simple catechism. Was he not a fool?"

A faroff cry of *Eastward ho!* drifted faintly up the river. The Jester cocked his head; then cupped one ear to listen.

"Were he not a fool," he said, when the cry was not repeated, "he might be rowing home from Lambeth now. He had a manor on this very river. A pleasant manor, too. But he was a fool, Sire. A fool beyond even a fool's redemption. Of all the fantastic, cracked, fiery elements that go to make up the *genus, fool,* this man of whom I speak was the quintessence. He was a fool of fools, my Lord King. You spoke?"

Henry shook his head. Slowly the clock bell tolled out the hour of eleven. Patenson nodded at every stroke of the clapper. He did not venture to speak again till the final echoes had died away in the quiet dark. Then he looked over at Henry.

"A very fool, my Lord King," he said slowly. "Fool—rule. Rule—fool. The very word tolls like a knell."

He held up the noble the King had flung him.

"*H-e-n-r-i-c-u-s,*" he spelled out, his voice breaking. "*R-e-x. Henricus Rex.* Henry the King. See, it is easy. I spell it out at once. Yet he who taught me the few letters I know—enough to decipher coins and tavern reckonings—could not con it. Was he not a fool? I weep for a fool. He was a fool and I weep for him. I weep for all fools."

The pathetically thin crimson shoulders began to shake. The King put out a staying hand.

"Would you weep for me?" he asked; and perhaps the husky voice under the black domino was not husked only with drink now.

Patenson looked up through his tear-stained fingers.

"For you, Sire?" he asked, wondering. "You are a wise man, my Lord King. I jest for you. I weep for fools."

"Then weep for me," said Henry roughly.

And the King, too, was gone in his turn.

Henry Patenson did not stir for quite a while. The tide began to suck about the stairs as it went out. Thunder muttered off in the distance. Lightening flickered on the horizon. The moon had gone down now. The sky was starless, as the black clouds moved across the heavens. A low whistle sounded a little upstream in the direction of London Bridge. Patenson listened carefully. After an interval, the whistle was repeated. It was the signal. He walked slowly down the landing stairs to the waiting boat, even as a fine rain began to fall.

The rain fell in gray sheets on the Channel; on the ships riding at anchor in the roadsteads after their eastward crossing from the New Found Land. It fell in the North on Kimbolton where Queen Catherine slept her uneasy sleep. It fell on Bruges where the Emperor lay that night. It fell on Rome where now lived my Lord Cardinal Pole. It fell on Basle where, in the house of Jerome Froben, Desiderius Erasmus worked over his commentary on the fourteenth Psalm.

On the wings of the wind flew the news. To Kimbolton where, the black cancer stone that was to kill her already twined about her heart, Catherine wrote the Farnese Pope that he should bear the realm of England especially in mind, that he should remember in his prayers the King, her lord and husband—there spoke the Spanish woman in whose high Castilian tongue there is no word for *apology,* but many for *prayer* and *love* and *lordship*—and her daughter. "For Your Holiness knows, and all Christendom knows, what things are done here, what great offense is given to God, what scandal to the world.

If a remedy be not applied shortly, there will be no end to ruined souls and martyred saints."

My Lord Cardinal Pole, sitting in Rome, thought on the Greek actor who said of those that did Socrates to death: *Ye have put to death him who was the noblest of all the Greeks.* And, setting pen to paper, my Lord Cardinal Pole addressed these ringing words to the City of London: *Ye have put to death him who was the noblest of all the English.* John Rivius, Lutheran of Altendorf, put down in his *Meditation on Conscience* this judgment on his great opponent: *Thou losest this mortal life but gainest that which is true and never-ending. Thou leavest the society of men but enterest the company of the angels and saints.*

They were afraid, at first, to tell Erasmus who already languished, *debilitor usque ad mortem*—sick unto death—with his last illness. But the young Dutchman, Lambert Coomans, who nursed him in Froben's house, insisted that the sick man know. The old scholar sadly did what he had to do, even as, in their different fashion, Henry Patenson and William Roper had done what they found necessary. He celebrated the fame of his beloved *Morus* in one last letter that ended: "The French will assist a Frenchman, the Germans a German, the Scottish a Scot. But he was a friend to all, whether Irish, French, German or Scottish. His goodness of heart endeared him so much to all that they grieve for his death, as they would for a father or a brother. I myself have seen many shed tears who had never seen More nor had any intercourse with him. And even as I write these lines, in spite of my efforts tears rise unbidden to my eyes. The sword that beheaded More wounded many noble hearts."

But all this came later. That same night, while Patenson and Roper, their mission at an end, sculled back to Chelsea in the rain, the Lady Anne danced at Greenwich, and Philippe de Chabot, Admiral of France and François' new Ambassador to the English Court, looked on the spectacle with enigmatic eyes. Afterward when, her own galliard over, the Queen sat next to this honored guest on a crimson dais, they watched together as Henry led a masked partner through the dreamy mazes of a pavane. Suddenly the Frenchman felt her stiffen at his side. Then she burst into peal after peal of hysterical laughter. He spoke to her. She laughed the shriller. Offended, the French Lord rose to his feet.

"Do you mock me, Madame?" he demanded, while the high-pitched *glissandi* of laughter continued to peal out till tears ran down the Queen's powdered cheeks.

Monsieur de Castillon, who had been conversing with Monsieur de Marillac, touched the Admiral's arm and whispered a few words in his ear. Then the Admiral understood.

Henry, unmasked and unsmiling, stood in front of them on the dancing floor, staring balefully at the Lady Anne. The unmasked partner on his arm, in the masquerade costume of a Queen, was Mistress Seymour. She smiled at Anne Boleyn.

CHAPTER XXIII

PORTENT IN THE SKIES

THE story was not ended. No story is ever ended. The timeless lustra whirled about the radiant heart of faëry, spun within the center petals of the *gran fior's* yellow rose, turned, annihilating time and space, inside the blazing core of the terrible crystal that is the eternal here and now. In time a cold wind blew off the ocean up the long river, over Tower Bridge, over Windsor where, in Saint George's Chapel, Henry slept his four hundred years' sleep beside Jane Seymour, over the Abbey, into the aisles of the great new Minster where tall candles flickered in the draft before the Chapel of Saint Thomas More, through the secular branches of the Chancellor's mulberry tree at 28 Beaufort Street, Chelsea, London S. W. 3, where the Sisters of the Congregation of *Adoration Réparatrice* kept their perpetual vigil in public reparation for a murder long ago.

The plane of history tilted as time shifted on its axis. The wind blew colder. The brave new world, which for centuries had been moving steadily away from the anarchy of Ur-chaos into the ordered Kingdom of reason, now, like some battle charger gone suddenly mad, leaped precipitately back into the iron age of mythos. On the rim of outer space great presences gathered. The dragon's teeth were sowed again by Mars and Thor. Helmeted women on flying horses, huge mailed warriors loomed through the dark. Three gray shapes spun in the gloom; spun and measured and clipped with shears. Wolf Fenris opened his shadow-maw, gaping horribly. The Midgard snake unslacked its hold about earth's middle; and, as it did, the great adversary, whom Dante saw breast-high in the girding ice, groaned and sat up. A fat man in a Marshal's uniform, with face and eyes startlingly like those of Thomas Cromwell, rode the middle air and, on a sudden, gave orders that death and fire rain over London. The world's ax-age and sword-age, the wind-age and wolf-age of the earth returned, while the cosmocrats of the dark aeon held their conclave. Sirens skirled in the great City. From Richmond to Chelsea the Thames ran red like blood, reflecting the inferno of the heavens. A direct hit demolished Chelsea Old Church, all but the More tomb. The Moor's head and the unicorns stood out the sharper for the crimson glare.

Later spring and, for a time, peace came back to Chelsea; and rosemary ran riot in the ruins. The Chapel at the Beaufort Convent had gone up in flames, but the mulberry tree bloomed once again in what had been my Lord Chancellor More's garden by the river. It was the only living witness of those faroff times when the King's great matter had convulsed the world. It kept its own green counsel but, like the Talking Oak of Dodona, it had tales to tell to those who would pause to listen—those like the invalid Sister whose duty it was to await the right time for culling the leaves and then, a latter-day Sibyl, to pluck and press them on a card for whosoever might wish to keep the great Chancellor in memory. Like the More family in the lean days after Sir Thomas had resigned the Chancellorship, all England—and most of the world, besides—went, first, on Lincoln's Inn fare, and then, by hungry degrees, descended to New Inn fare and Oxford fare. The wolf-age hardened, the wind-age blew colder. In the black-seared cellar holes and pitted bomb-craters the hart's-tongue fern lapped like green fire over the ground: the male fern whose seed begets invisibility; the sword fern and shield fern that bring invulnerability; good talismans all for the ax-age of the world. Perhaps, after his and their long sleep, the fays returned from Avalon to Arthur's island. The silver river, which is time, flowed on. The bees stored their golden honey of achievement. The herb sacred to remembrance grew fragrant through the long days and nights.